Mystra

Crystalphoenix

Crystal phoenix

Copyright © 2016 Crystalphoenix

All rights reserved.

ISBN: 1535317558
ISBN-13: 9781535317559

DEDICATION

To Andre Norton who taught me how to dream.

CONTENTS

	Acknowledgments	i
1	Prologue	Pg# 1
2	Chapter One	Pg # 3
3	Chapter Two	Pg # 28
4	Chapter Three	Pg # 43
5	Chapter Four	Pg # 61
6	Chapter Five	Pg # 78
7	Chapter Six	Pg # 90
8	Chapter Seven	Pg # 100
9	Chapter Eight	Pg # 117
10	Chapter Nine	Pg # 141
11	Chapter Ten	Pg # 161
12	Chapter Eleven	Pg # 172
13	Chapter Twelve	Pg # 191
14	Chapter Thirteen	Pg # 206
15	Chapter Fourteen	Pg # 218
16	Chapter Fifteen	Pg # 236
17	Chapter Sixteen	Pg # 260
18	Chapter Seventeen	Pg # 288
19	Epilogue	Pg # 301

ACKNOWLEDGMENTS

Thank you to all the wonderful folks who gave me the encouragement and the occasional kick to the rear that made this novel possible. My story sounding board Sheila whom I could never have made it without, Sadie for the steadfast encouragement to go for my dreams, my cousin Renee who always believes in me even if I don't, and my grammar guru Mary. Thanks guys, this one's for you.

PROLOGUE

The planet Mystra ...a world as beautiful as she was mysterious. Pulses of multicolored lightning flashed through the dense white clouds that shrouded the planet's surface, hiding her secrets from prying eyes. Once sister world to a multitude of planets, she is now alone. Surrounded by the debris of what at one time were viable worlds, she is the last vestige of life in an otherwise barren system. In solitude, she waits for those who would come to unlock her mysteries...those with the skills and courage to breach the flashing clouds surrounding her and reach the surface below.

With a rippling of space, the sleek golden starship dropped out of hyperspace and settled into orbit around the jeweled planet. At long last her wait was over.

CHAPTER ONE

2605 Day 232

The exploration vessel Ourora smoothly exited hyperspace and settled into orbit around the nearby planet. The dark haired young man sitting trance-like in the pilot's seat, hands resting on the two glowing plates set in the console before him, stirred and opened his eyes. It was a perfect run.

Breaking his mind-link with the starship, he stood and stretched. The Ourora was shaping up to be a sweet ship. Once the strangeness of joining his mind to the ship's instruments and controls had worn off, he had found piloting by thought as natural as breathing. This was not really surprising, considering that his people had built the vessel. In fact, it was on this very ship that he had been found adrift in space as a child, the last survivor of his race, of his entire planetary system.

2590 Day 143

Jake Blackthorn watched as the image of a golden starship grew on his ship's monitors. The Wanderer had been returning to Earth after a profitable trading run when they had stumbled upon the derelict. The ship's golden skin and graceful lines were like nothing he had ever seen.

"She's beautiful, but where did she come from? That's no Alliance ship."

Jake had been so engrossed in studying the alien vessel that he had not heard anyone approach. Turning, he found Dr. Nicole Wright standing at his side. "I have no idea Nikki but I intend to find out."

"Uh oh, you have that explorer look." She teased feeling the excitement radiating from him.

"Once an explorer always an explorer. Take us in Pete," he instructed the pilot. "I want a good look at this lady. Any energy or life sign readings?"

"It's hard to get a fix, some kind of energy dampener," came the reply from the science station. "It's scrambling our sensors."

"Captain," Pete called, "you'd better see this."

Returning his attention to the view screen, Jake stared as the Wanderer approached the far side of the derelict ship. A sick feeling began in the pit of his stomach as he saw the gaping hole ripped into the golden metal of the ship.

"No survivors then." Jake said sadly, "all right let's get a tractor beam on her…"

"Captain, I think I'm getting a life sign reading."

Jake turned to the science station. "What do you mean you think you're getting a reading?"

"Well, it's faint and it keeps drifting in and out. The dampener field is playing hell with the sensors, but there is something over there."

After a heated debate, which Jake naturally won, he and Dr. Wright boarded the damaged ship. As they explored the craft Jake felt his excitement grow, much of the vessel's interior appeared to be intact. The bridge, engine room, and cargo holds seemed untouched. It was only as they explored the damaged area of the ship that his excitement waned. As they entered what appeared to be crew quarters Jake froze, nausea rising in his throat. "Oh, my God, they're children." Jake barely heard Nikki's anguished whisper. He was staring at the rows of bunks crammed into the room. The ship's passenger and crew cabins were filled with children, children of diverse races, some of which he had never seen before. They were all dead. Their lifeless bodies still strapped to their bunks.

"They never had a chance." He whispered. "Let's get the hell out of here."

"Wait," Nikki grabbed his arm and pointed to the scanner she held clutched in her hand. "I'm getting that phantom signal again."

"Can you get a fix?"

"Yes! One deck down and to the rear."

Following the faint signal, they made their way to the rear of the ship. Rounding a corner, they froze. Standing in what appeared to be a galley, surrounded by a golden glow, was a raven haired, golden eyed boy about ten years old.

"Hello," Jake spoke softly and held out his hands in what he hoped was a friendly gesture. "We're here to help."

The boy studied the two space-suited figures intently, but made no move. Encouraged, Jake slowly approached the still youth. Suddenly, the glow surrounding the boy intensified and a strong forced hurled him back.

"Please," Nikki begged. "We only want to help you. You're all alone now. Let us help. We mean you no harm."

"Nikki, we have to go," Jake whispered. "I think I cracked something, my suit's losing air. I can't stay much longer."

"We can't just leave him."

Keen golden eyes seemed to bore into Nikki's soul

as the boy studied her intently. She almost gasped in relief when he turned to scrutinize Jake in turn. Whatever he saw must have reassured him. Indicating that they should follow, he led them into the next compartment. Nestled in the chamber was a large golden sphere. Jake and Nikki watched as the boy placed his hand against the side of the globe. A portal suddenly appeared. Motioning for them to follow, he entered the sphere. Once inside, the portal closed, leaving no sign it had ever existed. Gazing around in amazement, Jake turned to find the boy, minus the golden glow, sitting on a plush looking couch against the far wall watching them curiously.

"A life pod. Jake, I read a breathable atmosphere, constant temperature... the works. This is how he survived."

"Yeah, but that doesn't explain how he can walk around out there with no suit, and what about that glow?"

"That doesn't matter now, the main thing is getting him, and us, back to the ship."

A sound of rustling caused them both to turn. The boy was standing a few feet away holding a silvery suit in one hand and a metallic capsule in the other. Seeing he had the adults' attention, he offered the suit to Jake.

Taking the offered garment, Jake examined the delicate material. "I think it's a spacesuit."

"You're right, "Nikki examined the now open storage cabinet, "there's a whole rack of them in here, but they're all for adults. What do we do about him?"

"The capsule must be some kind of carrier. We put him in there and carry him across."

With the boy's help, Jake removed his damaged suit and donned the alien garment. The suit molded itself to his body and Jake marveled at the freedom that it gave him. Excitement stirred in him, what other marvels did this ship and its lone occupant hold?

After checking to make sure Jake's suit was working properly, the boy opened the life support capsule and stepped inside. Once more he studied the two adults, then calmly closed the carrier, entrusting himself to the strangers' care.

Returning to the Wanderer without incident, Jake ordered the derelict ship taken in tow and set course for his most secure research center. This was too important a find; he was taking no chances. Leaving the boy in the doctor's capable hands, he wasted no time in staking his claim to the alien derelict.

Jake Blackthorn was a powerful man and he now used that power. By pulling a few strings and cashing in a few favors, he obtained exclusive salvage rights to the alien vessel. The bodies of the deceased children would be turned over to the authorities, but no mention was made of the boy. Satisfied that he had taken every precaution to protect his find, Jake headed for sickbay. He couldn't say what had made him keep the boy's existence a secret from the authorities, but his gut told him the kid was special. There was no way he was going to let some government social worker get their hands on him. Besides the kid had trusted him, Jake shivered as he remembered the boy's golden eyes staring into his, searching his soul. The child was as unique as his craft. Jake usually had little use for children, but there was something about this one that stirred all his protective instincts. The kid was his, by God, and nobody was taking him away.

Six months later, Jake was ready to consign both the ship and its golden-eyed master into the fiery depths of the nearest sun. After six months of intensive study, the starship was still an enigma. Even his best experts could not fathom how the strange vessel operated. There were no noticeable controls, just panels of colored crystals set into the consoles. The engines consisted of smooth sided boxes and crystal globes. No dials, switches, or knobs were to be seen. There was no sign of power, though they knew that it existed. Jake fumed; all that power, all that technology just out of reach, it was enough to drive an entrepreneur mad.

The boy was proving to be as impenetrable as his vessel. The shock of the accident had severely damaged the kid's memory, erasing any knowledge of what had happened to him or his ship. Quiet and reserved, he cooperated fully with the scientific team examining him but volunteered nothing. Except for a few unknown factors in his DNA and body chemistry, he was remarkably similar to humans. Yet, it did not take the team studying him long to realize that he was not your typical ten- year old boy. His golden eyes held wisdom beyond his years; and he always seemed to know what was wanted of him, even before he was shown or asked. He proved to be extremely bright and learned at an amazing rate. In a very short time, he mastered enough Galactic-Standard to communicate. Yet, nothing they tried could unlock the memories buried deep in the boy's mind. It was as if every thought concerning his home world or his flight to this system had been locked away behind an impenetrable barrier. He was a blank slate, which could soak up knowledge, but offered none in return.

Jake was not prepared to give up his discovery without a fight. Every day, their guest was becoming more relaxed and comfortable with his new home. With time, Jake hoped that his memory would start to return. It was another month before the first breakthrough occurred. Since he could not remember his name, the young castaway had been christened "Kid" by the researchers studying him. For seven months, the boy answered to the name "Kid", so Jake was surprised when the youth fixed him with a golden eyed stare and said, "My name is Jasen, not Kid." After that, snatches of memory began to return.

On a hunch, Jake decided to see what would happen if Jasen was reunited with his starship. Maybe the sight of the vessel and the familiar surroundings would jog the boy's memory. At least, he might be able to show them how the ship operated.

It was soon obvious that returning to the ship was a shock for the youth. He wandered through the vessel as if in a daze. With each section of the ship revealed and explored, his face grew paler. By the time they reached the bridge, Jake was afraid the boy was going to collapse. On one side of the bridge was a large console inset with a panel composed of some type of blue crystal. Jasen went to the console, placed his hands palm down on the crystal, and closed his eyes. The panel immediately began to glow and flash. After a few minutes, the glowing stopped and Jasen opened his eyes. Removing his hands from the console, he began to tremble uncontrollably and then to cry. Rushing to him, Jake held the sobbing child as delayed trauma finally hit.

Viewing the information contained in the ship's library computer, as the console turned out to be, and reliving past events through the psychic traces left in the ship, had broken through the mind block the boy had erected. Later, when he had calmed down and been reassured that he was safe among friends, he freely answered Jake's questions. The ship was totally thought controlled. It had been built by a race of telepaths, from a planet in the Gamma3 planetary system. It was a type of ark, a last ditch effort to save a remnant of the people of that system. Creatures of fire and light had appeared out of nowhere and attacked their worlds. The attacks had been quick, unexpected, and vicious. Caught off guard, most planets stood no chance against the invaders. Jasen's world was the oldest and most advanced of the system. They were able to hold out long enough to launch three ships before being destroyed by the attackers. Only Jasen's ship had made it out of the system, but not without taking damage. An energy blast had hit the ship severely, damaging its shields and compromising a large section of the hull. The ship's crew had been working to repair the damaged section when they had been caught in an unexpected meteor storm, most likely debris from the destroyed worlds. The ship's compromised shielding had been unable to stop one of the huge projectiles from striking the damaged hull and ripping it open. The two adults on board had been caught in the impact zone and killed. Jasen had been attending to some minor repairs on the side of the ship farthest from the rupture. His telekinetic abilities had allowed him to protect himself long enough to reach the safety of an escape pod. The others on board had not been so gifted.

The Gamma3 system was an old system with a high level of technology. They were not novices at space travel or exploration and had even visited the Alliance worlds to observe. That they could be wiped out so quickly and completely boded ill for the Planetary Alliance. After hearing the news Jasen brought, Jake became obsessed with the attackers. Who were they? Why did they attack? Had other systems fallen? He devoted a good part of his empire to finding out the answers. Jake soon lost his heart to the courageous child. He was determined to protect the boy, and the unusual gifts he had begun to display once freed from the mind block his fear had created. In time, Jake adopted him, named him his heir, and helped train him to use his gifts and hide them from the outside world.

Adapting to his new home proved difficult for Jasen. His planetary system had been on the opposite side of the galaxy from Alliance controlled space. The people of his world had enjoyed strong, friendly ties with the other sentient races of the nearby systems. They had been respected and honored for their technology and for their roles as peacemakers and diplomats. Things were far different in this new land. The Alliance worlds had an inbred, almost manic, fear and hatred of telepaths. Jake had tried to explain it to him once.

Many generations ago the Alliance worlds had been invaded by a race called the Kryllidar. The Kryllidar were a militant, barbaric insect-like race that possessed a high level of technical skill and little regard for other sentient life forms. They were a race that lived to conquer and enslave the populations of other worlds. The Kryllidar loved order and insured that the worlds they conquered adhered to their concept of obedience. Using drugs and machines, they subverted the minds and wills of those they invaded, turning them into perfect drones fit to serve the elite Kryllidar race.

The Kryllidar invaders swept across the galaxy like a plague, leaving worlds of mind-controlled zombies in their wake. Almost half the galaxy had fallen before the Alliance armada had been able to rally. Joined by ships from the outer fringes, they had been able to turn and repel the attackers. Once freed from the invaders' mind-controlling apparatus, the enraged Alliance inhabitants had hunted down and exterminated every Kryllidar they could find, then followed up with an all-out attack on the Kryllidar home world. The Kryllidar race was totally wiped out, along with a number of neighboring planets that possessed similar life forms. The drugs and machines used to enslave the conquered worlds were rounded up and destroyed. The Alliance vowed never again to allow their people to be controlled in such a manner. A deep phobia of mind-control in any form sprung up among the sentient races within the Alliance systems, which was carefully passed down and instilled in each succeeding generation. From this phobia, a dread of telepaths emerged, which grew in strength with each retelling of the past atrocities. Telepaths were viewed as the ultimate masters of mind-control. Machines could be broken, drugs could be neutralized, but the only way to stop a telepath was to kill him. Also, unlike the Kryllidar, a telepath could blend in with the populace of a given world. They could lurk unknown and undetected among the citizens of the Alliance. One could never be sure if his thoughts were his own or being manipulated by another.

Soon the slogan, "The only good telepath is a dead one," became common. It was into this climate of hate that the young Jasen had been thrown. He was the last surviving telepath in the galaxy. He lived in constant fear of exposure and death. He was looked upon as a monster, a demon; he was fair game for all. No one would hesitate to destroy him if he were discovered.

There were few people in his life that he dared trust implicitly. Fortunately for the young telepath, it was Jake who discovered him. Jake was a shelter of love in an otherwise dark and hate filled universe. The explorer did not share the rest of the Alliance's loathing and terror of telepaths. He had been born in a remote sector far from the alien invasion. When that cluster's sun went nova, Jake had brought his thriving corporation to the Alliance worlds. Most of those on Jake's personal staff were refugees from his home system. Like Jake, they viewed Jasen as different but not horrible. He was a bright and charming boy and they soon grew to love and admire him as Jake did. They vowed to protect the vulnerable youth and his secret. Jake raised the boy as a son and taught him how to survive in his new home.

2605 Day 232

With a shake of his head, Jasen shook off the thoughts of the past. He was no longer a frightened boy of ten, but a man of twenty-five and he had work to do. Jake was dead and it was up to him to finish what his adopted father had begun. He gave the instruments another quick metal scan to assure that everything was as it should be then left the bridge and headed for the ship's lounge. Hawk. He wished his friend had not insisted on coming, but nothing he had said had dented Hawk's resolve to accompany him.

2605 Day 111

Jasen had been working on the Ourora's data banks, when a wave of dizziness dropped him to his knees. Pain knifed through his temples, then he was falling. When the vertigo passed, he found himself on the deck of a starship, but unlike the Ourora's golden decks, this ship was gunmetal gray.

"What have we got?"

Lifting his head, Jasen glanced around the busy control room and spotted a familiar figure standing near the science console. Oh no, Jake.

"The readings are all over the map, sir." The science officer handed Jake a printout. *"I detect at least two separate energy layers with strong turbulence in the secondary layer."* He checked his readouts. *"Looks like it would be a bumpy ride down."*

"What about the planet itself?"

"There's no way of telling. The energy fields are causing too much interference. It could be a Garden of Eden or a barren rock."

"What about the energy layers, are they dangerous?"

"Nothing is showing up on the scanners, but," he shook his head and gave a frustrated sigh, *"with the amount of interference I can't be absolutely sure that we're not missing something."*

"What about a probe?"

"We used the last one navigating that debris field two days ago. All we have left is the emergency message drone."

Jake stared at the image on the view screen. *"What are you hiding?"* He muttered. They had searched three star systems, and found only rubble until now. Why was this world the only one to survive? Jake knew in his soul that this planet held the key that he had been searching for, he could not just walk away. He turned to the communications officer. *"I want all data from the Empress's databanks transferred to the message drone. Link in a live feed and continue to transfer everything we get. At the first sign of possible trouble, launch the drone."*

"Aye sir."

"Pete, take us into the outer layer. We'll take this one step at a time."

As the Empress glided toward the planet, Jasen prayed to be anywhere else, but the cosmic forces that had brought him here turned a deaf ear to his pleas. He could only crouch on the cold deck and watch as the ghastly drama played itself out.

The Empress shuddered as it entered the energy barrier surrounding the planet, but there was no other outward sign.

"Status?"

"All systems green, Captain."

Jake felt some of the tension leave his body at the familiar words. *"Full scans, let's see if we can't get this lady to give up some of her secrets."*

With a lighter heart the crew set to work.

An hour later, a nervous call from the science station interrupted Jake's study of the latest data feed. *"Sir, I think we may have a problem."*

"What is it?"

"I'm losing contact with the sensors, it's like they're suddenly not there."

"What?" Jake stared at the readouts. *"How is that possible?"*

"That's not all, we're getting reports of equipment failure throughout the ship."

Before Jake could comment, an emergency siren cut the air.

"Captain, this is engineering; we're losing containment on the power core...it's..., it's disintegrating."

"Launch the emergency message drone. All hands abandon ship."

"Sir, the life pods are disintegrating. There are hull breaches on decks five and twelve...oh my God."

Jake turned to see the science officer staring at the far corner of the bridge. Following his gaze, Jake gasped. The metal walls of the bridge were rippling and as he watched, what was once impervious metal flaked to dust, then vanished in a puff of light.

All through the ship sounds of panicky crewmen mixed with the sounds of dying metal. Glancing at the beautiful but deadly world Jake whispered, "I'm sorry, Jasen." Then the Empress vanished in an explosion of light.

"NO!" With a jolt, Jasen found himself crouched on the Ourora's golden decks. Hunching over, he sobbed out his loss. Shock and grief collided with the exhaustion left by the vision, plunging him into darkness.

When he awoke much later, one fact stood out in his mind, Jake was dead, along with the entire crew of the Empress. He had felt them die, there would be no survivors found. Pulling himself together, he made his way back to his quarters. Once within the safety of his rooms, he put in a call to the corporate office. When the calm face of Mathew Chambers, Director of Operations for Blackthorn Industries and Jake's right hand man, appeared on the screen Jasen gathered his strength and delivered the news.

"Matt, it's Jasen, Jake's dead." Emotion tightened his throat. "They're all dead."

"What...how...Jase are you sure?" At the younger man's nod, he slumped back in shock. "What happened?"

"The planet they were exploring... the energy fields were dangerous. The ship exploded."

"What do you want me to do?"

"They managed to launch a message drone before they …before the ship exploded. We need to retrieve it."

Chambers turned to a console and entered a command. "We have a courier ship in the quadrant, it should be able to reach the Empress's last known coordinates and return here in five days."

"Good, they're to fetch the drone only, under no circumstances are they to approach the planet."

"Understood." Chambers, like most of Jake's personal staff, was well acquainted with Jasen's unusual gifts. If he said Jake and the others were dead, then they were dead. If he said the planet was deadly, then it was. He would make very sure the crew of the courier ship understood and followed their orders. "I'll dispatch the ship immediately." He paused uncertain of his next words. "Jase, are you ok?"

"No," Pain and fatigue were reflected in the golden eyes. "But I will be, thanks Matt."

"If you need anything…."

"I'll call. Let me know when they return with the drone."

A week later, the courier ship returned with the emergency message drone and the news of Jake's death. The following days passed in a blur for Jasen, as he assumed the reins of Blackthorn Industries and arranged a memorial service for Jake and the Empress's valiant crew.

A month following Jake's funeral, armed with every shred of information that he and Jake had amassed on the enemy, along with the information contained in the emergency message drone, Jasen started making his plans. When the plans were complete, he went searching for Hawk.

He found Hawk just where he expected, in the

engineering lab puttering with a piece of bright golden metal. Hawk was of the Filidae race and Jasen's closest friend. He was tall and slender with a mane of snow white hair and silvery blue eyes. The eyes' pupils were slit, hinting that there was some feline DNA hidden somewhere in the Filidae evolutionary tree. Usually he moved with an unconscious fluid grace that Jasen envied. Today however, he was hunched over a workbench; the elegant planes of his face pulled into a frown of concentration as he muttered to himself in his native tongue.

Jasen had known Hawk for a long time. When Blackthorn Industries had started exploiting the technology found in the alien vessel, they had gone to the Filidae for help. As Jasen's mind healed he was able to unlock the secrets of the golden starship. Unfortunately, those secrets were not so easy to share. How could you use a technology that was controlled exclusively by the power of the mind? The ability to sense and control psychic energy was a lost art in the Alliance. Anyone with the necessary skills had been killed or fled the system during the telepathic purge following the Kryllidar War.

Jasen's people were magi. They had visited the earth once, long ago. It was their exploits that gave rise to the myths and legends of magicians and magical feats. In truth, what those ancient humans saw as magic was actually science, although a science different from that of the Alliance. The magi learned the key to harnessing the energy that resides in all things and controlling it with their will. Their science was based on collecting, storing and programming this energy to carry out assigned tasks. If Jake was going to adapt the alien technology for Alliance use, it was going to take some out of the box thinking.

Another trait the Filidae shared with those ancient feline ancestors was an innate curiosity about... well everything. The Filidae were brilliant scientists who loved nothing more than unraveling a new puzzle. They were the perfect partners in testing and developing the discoveries found aboard Jasen's ship…discoveries such as the power crystals, which fueled the ship's drive. The crystals stored vast amounts of energy. Devising a way for a non-telepath to access and direct that energy was a puzzle that could take decades to unravel. They had already come up with a way to grow and charge the crystals. Cut off from the strong psychic energy fields of their home world, the crystals needed a planet with an abundance of life to grow. The Filidae had a strong affinity for the natural world and their planet was teeming with life both plant and animal. Jasen still had to program the crystals, but the vibrant life energy of the Filidae world and its strong ley lines insured that the Ourora would have a steady supply of replacement power crystals.

Recently, Jasen had given Hawk a sample of the golden metal used to construct the Ourora with a challenge "to see what he could make of it". He had been trying to uncover its secrets ever since. So far, only Jasen had been able to do anything with the metal, and he wouldn't say how. It had become a game to see if his friend could guess the answer. Jasen couldn't help but smile when he saw the look of fierce concentration on Hawk's face.

Silently, he walked up behind the engrossed scientist and peered over his shoulder. "Well, have you solved the mysteries of the universe yet?"

"What?" startled Hawk dropped the lump of metal he had been studying and spun around in his seat. Seeing his friend's amusement, he grinned. "Where did you learn to be so sneaky all of a sudden? You scared me out of a hundred years' growth?"

Jasen laughed, "I've been taking lessons from you. Besides you were so lost in thought, you wouldn't have noticed if the whole building had collapsed on your head. What have you discovered?"

Picking up the metal lump, Hawk gazed at it thoughtfully before answering. "This is the strangest stuff I've ever seen. I've tried drills, acids, heat, cold; even radiation and I've barely been able to dent it. I give up. What is this stuff?"

Studying his friend closely, Hawk's tone grew serious, "Are you all right? You've been cooped up in your office so long I was beginning to worry."

"I'm fine. I'm just tired. I've been trying to figure out what happened to the Empress and to see if there is a way around it. Hawk, I'm going to finish Jake's mission. And no, I haven't lost my mind. I think I've found a way; it's risky, but I think I have a chance of succeeding."

"We have a chance of succeeding. You are not going anywhere without me. Don't even think of trying to talk me out of it."

With a sigh, Jasen turned toward the door, "Let's go to my office, we can discuss it there." Picking up the lump of metal, Hawk rose and followed Jasen from the room.

Later, comfortably seated in Jasen's office, the lump of metal resting on the desktop between them and steaming cups of coffee in their hands, Jasen began to bring Hawk up to date.

"Some of this you already know and some of it is new information. Ever since Jake found me, he has been trying to learn all he can about the creatures that destroyed my home system. The Ourora's memory banks held everything that my people knew about the invaders, plus this."

Jasen touched a button on the side of the desk and a viewer rose from one corner of the smooth desktop. "This tape was recorded by the Ourora's scanners as she fled my home world."

On the screen a golden starship lifted from the planet's landing field. As the ship rose from the planet's surface, a ball of red-gold light streaked toward the fleeing ship. Jasen touched the screen and magnified the image. The ball resolved itself into a creature resembling a huge bird of prey with a golden head and wings of flame. As the Firehawk, as Jake had named the creatures, flew near the escaping ship, one of its wings brushed against the ship's side. Where the wing touched, metal shimmered, vanishing in a flash of light, which was absorbed by the Firehawk's body. In a few seconds, no sign of the ship remained.

On the planet's surface the grisly scene was being replayed. A horde of flaming Firehawks flew across the planet, beams of crimson energy streaming from their bodies. Wherever energy beams or flaming wings touched, matter disintegrated instantly, converted into energy which the Firehawks absorbed.

"Energy weapons appear to be useless. They only seem to strengthen the creatures or else have no effect at all. They feed on energy."

"Then how can they be stopped? What chance have we against an enemy who can transmute matter to energy?"

"A slim chance. There is one kind of energy that seems to have an effect on the creatures. Telekinetics were common on my world, but telekinetics who could manifest their energy as solid fields of force were rare. There were a few such adepts in the capitol when the Firehawks attacked. Pooling their talents, they erected a force shield around the spaceport. That's how we managed to launch the three ships we did. For some reason, the Firehawks would not cross the shield. It wasn't that they were afraid or hurt by it, more like they noticed a barrier and flew around it. So far we have not been able to duplicate the energy pattern; we'll keep trying, but the chances for success are slight."

"Our best chance seems to lie here." Jasen altered the viewer's screen until an image of a milky white planet streaked with flashes of colors appeared on the screen.

"Using the coordinates in the ship's computer, Jake placed my home world to be on the far side of the galaxy. He sent an exploration team to investigate. Every planet in the system was the same, either totally disintegrated or reduced to rubble. The destruction extended to my system and two others, then stopped. No sign was seen of the creatures, but some of the stars in the farthest system showed erratic energy patterns. I have a hunch they are still around, maybe resting somewhere after their feeding spree. How long they may stay there, no one knows. But one thing I do know, if the creatures start moving again, more systems will die. We must find some way to defend ourselves."

"The exploration team did discover one interesting anomaly. Every planet in the creatures' path had been razed except one." Jasen pointed to the planet displayed on the viewer. "This world was untouched. It seems to be in the center of the affected territory. It could be the creatures' planet of origin or not; but either way, it has escaped unscathed. Our best chance of surviving is to find out how."

"Easier said, than done my friend." Hawk gazed at the planet displayed on the screen. Something was familiar about it, something he should know. Suddenly he had it. "Isn't that the planet Jake was investigating when his ship exploded? How are we going to get through the energy field which destroyed the Empress?"

"What do you mean, we? I'm going alone. It's too risky to chance anyone else. Besides, I need you here; someone has to carry on in case I fail. That's why I'm telling you all this. You have to stay."

"Wrong. I'm going. If you think I'm going to stay

here while you risk your neck to save the universe you're crazy. Besides, you're going to need help. You can't do everything alone, Jase."

Jasen studied his friend intently, weighing his words. He was deadly serious. His mind was made up. Jasen was not leaving without him. He knew he could force Hawk to stay. A quick mental probe and Hawk would forget all about accompanying him. But he couldn't, he wouldn't do that. The first thing a telepath learned was to respect the rights and privacy of others. This primary law was deeply ingrained in Jasen. Besides, Hawk was his friend and deep down he knew he was right. He couldn't do this alone.

Exasperated, Jasen raised his hands in a sign of surrender. "All right. If you want to be stupid, far be it for me to stop you. Just don't blame me if you change your mind later."

Hawk gave his friend a wry smile. "Why, thank you very much for the vote of confidence. I promise to take full responsibility for my stupidity. Now, what's your plan?"

Taking a large manila folder from a desk drawer, Jasen removed a report and handed it to Hawk. "This is a transcript of the information Jake sent just before the Empress exploded. The vessel was destroyed because she was made of metal. The atmosphere of the planet is ringed with an unstable energy vortex which breaks down the molecular structure of metal. We have one chance of getting through; it all depends on whether we can get the Ourora space ready in time."

Hawk scanned the report in his hands and tried to absorb its implications. The Empress was destroyed because it was metal. The message drone had barely made it out of the atmosphere without disintegrating. Yet, Jasen was going to take the Ourora into the same energy stream. What chance did the Ourora have, that's assuming they could repair her and Jasen could fly her?

Looking up, Hawk noticed the lump of golden metal resting on the desktop and froze. Picking it up, he stared at Jasen in wonder. "It's not metal is it?"

"No, it's not. My home world had little in the way of natural resources. Wood, metals and water were in short supply. What it did have was crystals and a strong psychic field. All the crystals on the planet respond to psychic energy. That is actually bark. The crystal forest was one of our most prized possessions. The trees' outer bark produced a crystalline substance that absorbed psychic energy, as well as sunlight, to help fuel photosynthesis and protect against insects. Every year, the trees shed their outer bark as well as their crystal leaves. We used the leaves as data crystals and the bark as a building material."

"Wow, no wonder it's a company secret. A pseudo-metal that can be grown, is harder than the best-known alloys, yet is light and compact. An endless supply of cheap, quality metal-like material, you'll not only corner the energy market, but the metal market as well." The implications were staggering. First, however, they had to deal with the Firehawks.

"OK, so the Ourora is made of crystalline pseudo-metal and should be able to pass through the field. But Jase, the Ourora is far from space ready, and there is no pilot, even if we could repair her. Besides, I've tried working this stuff; it's next to impossible. There's no way we can mold enough of it to patch the Ourora's hull."

With a sly smile, Jasen reached out and took the lump from Hawk's hand, "Oh, I wouldn't be so sure of that." Pulling three small crystals from his pocket, he placed them in his hand next to the golden lump. Closing his eyes, he directed his thoughts at both crystals and bark. The lump and crystals began to shimmer then glowed softly. When the glow died, Jasen held a golden disc threaded through with delicate lines of crystal. Reaching across the desk, Jasen pealed back the corner of Hawk's shirt and placed the disk against his left shoulder. The disc gave a brief flash of light and then vanished. Hawk looked at his shoulder in disbelief. A tattoo of gold and crystal lines in the shape of an eight rayed star blended seamlessly with his skin.

"OK, is this your way of telling me you have a thing for guys with ink? And how is this going to help us fix the ship?" Hawk kept running his fingers over the new tattoo. The symbol was slightly cool but he could detect no edges or seams. The design was now a part of his skin.

"Even after it is shed, the bark retains a psychic charge indefinitely. The substance is psycho-sensitive. It shapes itself to the thoughts of its user. Every ship carries a store of bark to use for repairs or to shape into useful tools. If the adults onboard the Ourora had not been killed when the ship was damaged, they would have used the bark in storage to repair the weakened hull. During the accident, I was trapped for a time, cut off from both the hold and the rupture. There was no one else on board who was telepathic, most were refugees from other destroyed planets; without a telepath to use the bark and order repairs, they died."

Shaking off the somber thoughts, Jasen nodded at the tattoo. "That's where this comes in. If you are going to come with me, I don't want you stranded in the middle of nowhere if something happens to me. The Ourora is totally thought controlled, a non-telepath can't even get a cup of coffee from the galley. I've modified this to be a psychic amplifier and keyed the crystal to your thought pattern. As long as the tattoo is intact, it will amplify and focus your thoughts into a beam the ship's systems can pick up. The ship is keyed to my thought pattern. It will respond to no one else. I've entered a code into the crystals which will give you access to all ship's functions. It will accept your commands as if they were mine. Oh, and don't worry, no one else will be able to pick up your thoughts. The ship operates on a special wavelength; you won't be blasting your thoughts into my head every time you order coffee. I thought of just making you a bracelet but this way is much safer. No chance of you losing or misplacing this, and anyone seeing the tattoo will have no way of knowing what it really is or what it can do. So you like? I can change the design if you want."

"No, it's perfect." Hawk gave his friend a suspicious look, "You had this planned. You knew that I would be coming with you."

"Actually, I had hoped to talk you out of coming; but, knowing how stubborn you are, I wasn't sure I'd succeed. I had a sneaking suspicion you might not let me off world without you. I've been working on a way to allow others access to the Ourora. I thought I'd best be prepared."

"As for piloting, the Ourora's data banks contain all the knowledge of my home world including plans for a teaching device. A few sessions and I'll be a master pilot. So what do you think? Still want to come?"

In answer, Hawk jumped from his chair and headed for the door. Pausing in the doorway, he turned, cocked his head to one side, and raised an imperious eyebrow at Jasen. "Well, what are you waiting for? We have a starship to repair and a universe to save. Let's get with it."

Shaking his head, Jasen rose and followed the enthusiastic Filidae from the room. Well, one thing was for sure, with his friend's quicksilver personality, the trip would be anything but dull.

True to his words, repairing the Ourora had gone smoothly. Under Jasen's mental control, the ship had turned itself from a derelict into a first class starship. Building the telepathic teacher proved to be a little more complicated; but when it was finished, it worked even better than Jasen had hoped. Along with knowledge, the teacher transmitted experience and instinct as well. After three sessions, Jasen was a veteran space pilot and competent to handle the Ourora under any circumstances.

Unfortunately, the teacher only worked on Jasen; a flaw Jasen was determined to remedy when he had time. Since he couldn't teach Hawk to pilot the ship, he settled for loading a series of programs into the ship's autopilot and keying them to Hawk's tattoo. If something should happen to him, at least Hawk would have a chance of returning home.

Three months later, they were ready to go. Leaving Blackthorn Industries in Matt's capable and trustworthy hands, the two set out on their mission. Now they were here and the real work was about to begin.

2605 Day 232

Jasen entered the lounge just as Hawk removed a second cup of coffee from the ship's food dispenser. Handing Jasen a cup, he raised his in salute. "Welcome to planet XK7, the garden spot of the universe." Walking to the far wall, Hawk placed his right hand on the smooth metal surface and willed a viewing port into existence. Immediately, the metal surface of the wall shimmered and a transparent plate appeared in the ship's side. Beyond the plate, the jewel-like planet gleamed in the darkness of space. "It's hard to believe something so beautiful could be so deadly. What's our next move?"

"Looks all too often are deceptive." Tearing his gaze from the lovely view, Jasen walked across the room and dropped into one of the chairs set around the table bolted to the floor in the center of the room. Setting his cup on the table, Jasen closed his eyes and rubbed his temples. Piloting took a lot of concentration and always left him with a headache. Besides which, he was tired. He and Hawk had both been working nonstop for the past forty-eight hours. They had gone over every inch of the ship and checked every piece of equipment and instrument on board. He didn't want any surprises when they began their descent.

"First, I think we can both use some sleep. I'll set the ship to running scans of the planet and the surrounding systems. I want to verify the Empress's data before I try entering the energy field. I've placed the ship on full alert; the computer will wake us if there is the slightest change in the planet or the energy patterns of the nearby systems."

"Sounds good to me. Do we have any probes on board? I don't remember seeing any. It would be a good idea to see how our crystal pseudo-metal reacts with the field, just in case."

"There are none on board, but we can easily construct one. I'd like to have all the information we can before attempting a landing. I'll see what the computer can come up with, then I'm for bed. See you in the morning."

Rising from his chair, Jasen headed for the bridge to start the computer on the task of constructing the probes. Hawk gazed at the planet once more, then ordered the ship to erase the viewing panel and headed for his cabin. Tomorrow should prove to be an interesting day.

CHAPTER TWO

2065 Day 234
Kingdom of Aquilla, planet Mystra

King Arcus sat in his study, located high atop the castle's main tower, and stared at the scroll lying on the desk before him. The execution order waited ominously, needing only his signature to turn it into law. The early morning sunlight streamed through the window cut into the chamber wall behind the desk, turning his auburn hair into a flaming halo. The golden rays fell on the parchment before him, highlighting the words written there in warm pools of light.

...will be put to death on her twenty first birthday.

With a curse, he flung the scroll to the floor and rose to pace before the open window. His green eyes flashed with anger. He couldn't do it! He couldn't sign that accursed order! He couldn't sentence her to death! It wasn't fair! Stopping before the window, King Arcus gazed at the land spread out before him. As far as the eye could see in any direction, he ruled. He was king of the largest and most prosperous kingdom on Mystra. He controlled the lives of thousands of people. In all things, his word was absolute law...in all things but this. No king could revoke a rule of the first ones; not if he valued the lives of his subjects. The ancients had not issued many decrees, but those they did leave behind were not to be ignored.

When colonists first settled Mystra, she was a paradise world. A temperate climate, lush vegetation, coupled with abundant wildlife made her ideal for colonization. But Mystra possessed a secret. The energy fields in and around the planet were unique and inimical to technology. The effects of these fields were not apparent at first. The colony ships landed and the settlers began to build their new world. Then, strange accidents began to happen. Generators used to power the camps exploded. Radio waves became beams of force which blew apart buildings. Soon, even the simplest machines failed to work properly. One never knew what the results would be when a machine was activated.

Then other accidents began to happen. Buildings collapsed or eroded away. Only those made of metal were affected. It was not long before the scientists confirmed the theory. Mystra did not tolerate metal of any kind. Wood, glass, and ceramics were fine. But anything made of metal either deteriorated or was warped by the planetary energy field, causing machinery containing metal components to behave erratically with often disastrous results. Since all Alliance technology depended on some metal components, the colonists made a decree. Anything containing metal was to be banned from the planet.

They loaded all machines and anything containing metal onto the colony ships and sent them on a one-way trip into the nearest sun. They turned their backs on technology and adopted a new way of life. All that is, except for a small group of scientists. These men had been outlawed from their home world for conducting experiments considered too dangerous by the Scientific Review Committee of that world. Before the authorities could seize their laboratory, they had fled off world taking their precious equipment with them.

Those who settled on Mystra were a mixed lot. The Kryllidar War had left many worlds ravaged, forcing the survivors to search for new lands. Some were the last remnants of old civilizations which had fallen to ruin. Others were species whose unique differences or abilities had caused them to be pursued and hunted. While some just wanted to escape their overcrowded home worlds or thirsted for adventure. What they all had in common was the desire for a new start. It had been easy for the scientists to change their names and forge papers that would allow them to join the expedition. They had smuggled their equipment on board with them and were ready to pick up where they had left off. They could not accept the ban on technology and refused to give up their work. They moved their equipment into caves deep underground, trusting that the thick layers of rock would protect them from the planet's unique energy. They continued their experiments in secret. Their dream was to open a portal to other dimensions; and nothing would stop them from realizing that dream. One night they attempted The Great Experiment. The resulting cataclysm almost destroyed the entire planet. A new Mystra was born that night. Fierce storms ravaged the land, earthquakes shook the earth and sea; mountains were leveled and new ones born. Volcanoes came into existence, continents shattered and, high up in the outer atmosphere, the curtain of lights was born, a barrier of death cutting the planet off from the rest of the universe.

For the colonists not killed in the initial upheaval, life became a struggle for survival. The survivors were reduced to hiding in caves and foraging for food. Battling the savage elements, they clung to life. Then, the elementals appeared. An alteration in the genetic structure of certain women gave rise to individuals who could interact with the forces of nature and bend those forces to their wills. As the number of elementals increased, the tide began to turn in the colonists' battle to survive. Pooling their powers, they began to redirect the violent forces of nature. With the elementals monitoring and channeling the planetary forces, the settlers began the long fight back from near extinction.

During the turbulent years before the elementals, the colonists had been scattered across the planet. Now a feudal type society made up of many sects and kingdoms grew up. But, in every kingdom and population, one thing was constant—elementals were highly valued and revered; for without them life could not continue. As much as they were revered, they were also feared. Such unchecked power was frightening. The political influence wielded by the women was almost as great as the natural forces they controlled. A kingdom or group at odds with the elementals could not long survive.

Then, the change occurred. Suddenly, some elementals started to go mad. Their powers ran out of control, destroying themselves and everything around them. Mystra's second great crisis had begun. In time, a solution was found. The forces wielded by the elementals destabilized their biochemistry, destroying them at a cellular level. The very trait which allowed them to become Mystra's saviors, was now causing them to be her destroyers. Elementals were all women from an ancient Druidic line, direct descendants of an alien race of magi who had visited the earth long ago and mixed with the native population. A weaker version of the gene that allowed those ancient mages to wield the power of creation had until now lay dormant in their descendants. Upon activation, it gave them the ability to manipulate vast power.

When the elementals first appeared, little attention had been paid to the males of the species. Like the women, the men also carried the gene. In the male line, rather than allowing the bearer to wield the forces of nature, the gene bestowed more spiritual gifts. When the colonists lost their technology, they also lost access to the ships' databases. Since most knowledge was stored in electronic format, they now had no way to retrieve the knowledge stored by the ships' computers. Men with the alien gene were gifted with the ability to travel to the spiritual realms. One of those realms was the great library which stored the sum of human knowledge and experience, including the written word. While in a trance, the traveler could access the stored knowledge; and using automatic writing, record it back on the physical plane. If more technical skills were needed, such as the ability to build a boat without the use of metal parts, the departed spirits of ancient craftsmen were more than willing to teach an apt pupil. The ability to connect with the unseen world brought its own dangers, as it was too easy for the dreamers to abandon this reality and become trapped in the world of their visions. But nature had a solution to both dilemmas. When an elemental's gene activated, it triggered the dormant gene of her male complement. The two halves were drawn to each other. Guided by visions, the male made his way to his bondmate's side. Once together, the two joined on a spiritual level. This binding brought control to the elemental and stabilized her biochemistry, while giving the male an anchor in this reality. No matter how deep the trance, an elemental could always reach her bondmate, or kiosan, and guide him home. Together, elemental and kiosan protected the colonists, gave them the necessary skills to survive and insured that they retained the knowledge of the past; even if they were no longer able to use much of it in this new world.

An elemental's power came fully online at midnight on her twenty first birthday. Up until then, she had been using only a fraction of her full potential. Unbonded, she could not control the sudden increase in power. If the bond was not in place before the critical hour, the elemental would not survive.

As well as stabilizing an elemental's system, the kiosan was also responsible for ensuring that his mate did not misuse her abilities. At the time of bonding, he was entrusted with a shutdown command buried deep in the elemental's genetic code. Using the command, he could neutralize his mate's powers temporarily. It took an exceptional man to bond with an elemental. The shutdown order gave him the ability to access her powers temporarily, but it was up to him to enforce the command. He had to be able to overcome any opposition she threw at him, and hold firm. An elemental could not use her powers directly against her bondmate, but she could resist his command. If a man wavered or was unsure, he could easily be consumed by the powers she wielded.

With each generation, more elementals of exceptional strength were born. Elementals who could control more than one element were rare in the ancients' time. With each generation, the number of those possessing mastery over multiple forces increased. Elementals who could control all four elements with equal strength were still a rarity, and thankfully so. The more powerful the elemental, the stronger the bondmate needed to be to match her. There was only one kiosan match for each elemental and their bond was for life. If an elemental's kiosan was not found, for whatever reason, the elemental did not survive. Only twice, in the following generations, had an elemental failed to find an appropriate mate before her powers matured. The results of the destruction unleashed before death claimed them were stilled remembered. The ruling council had passed a decree and made sure that it was passed down to each generation.

Any elemental not bonded by midnight on her twenty first birthday must be put to death for the good of herself and Mystra.

That decree had stood for centuries; and, no matter the pain, it had to be upheld. King Arcus turned from the window and searched the floor for the scroll he had flung away only moments before. Locating it in the far corner of the room, he picked it up and returned to his desk. Sitting down, he unrolled the parchment and read it one last time.

By order of the King, in accordance with the law of the ancients: Unless a suitable bondmate can be located by midnight tomorrow, Tivonna, daughter of King Arcus of Aquilla, will be put to death on her twenty first birthday.

Taking a deep breath, King Arcus reached for a quill and dipped it into the ink well on the desk. He was a King first, a father second. His people depended on him; he couldn't risk their lives, not even for his own daughter. With tears streaming down his face, he signed and sealed the execution order.

An hour later, King Arcus left his study and handed the scroll to the guard captain waiting outside the door. Dismissing the guard, he headed down the corridor toward his chambers. His wife would need to be told.

As the king entered his chambers, the Lady Sivena looked up from the needlework she had been stitching. The light from the window beside her accented her beauty. Her long golden hair was caught back from her forehead by a wooden circlet and she was dressed in a velvet gown of sapphire blue the exact shade of her eyes. Those eyes studied her husband closely as he entered the room. He looked tired, like a man who had been wrestling with his own personal demons and lost. His auburn hair was disheveled, and there was no sparkle in the emerald eyes. The fate of their daughter had been decided, and she could see what it had cost him to make that decision. Restraining her grief, she marshaled her strength. He needed her support and comfort now; there would be time for tears later.

"It is done?"

Nodding his head, Arcus walked across the room and stood looking out the chamber window, unable to face his wife's reproach. With the catch of unshed tears in his voice, he answered, "If she is not bonded by midnight tomorrow, our daughter will be executed. I'm sorry."

Rising from her chair, Sivena walked over and stood silently behind her husband. She could feel his pain. He loved their daughter dearly, as did she. Gently, she slipped her arms around his waist and rested her cheek against his broad back, offering what comfort she could.

"You had no choice. Tivonna is the strongest elemental to be born in many generations. If she loses control of her powers, she could destroy the entire city. Already she is stronger than many mature adepts. When her powers mature, she will be formidable. You just can't take the chance. You are a king. The safety and prosperity of your people come first, no matter what the personal sacrifice."

"This sacrifice is too great! If only there were some other way. If I could send her away or lock her away somewhere 'til we knew for sure. Maybe the ancients were wrong; maybe things have changed. Maybe the madness no longer comes."

"No, my husband. Take my word for it; things haven't changed. We elementals are still cursed by the change. And where would you send her that she couldn't endanger others; what prison could hold her once the madness struck? Believe me, I have experienced a touch of that madness. As the fatal hour draws closer the darkness grows stronger. You saved me from that horror. I remember the feel of your spirit wrapping around mine, bringing order and calm. But the brief glimpse I had was enough. I would spare Tivonna that trial. If she is not bonded, then death will come anyway. This way is less painful, and she will harm no one else with her madness."

Sighing, Arcus turned and faced his wife. Taking her in

his arms, he held her tightly, taking comfort from her nearness and her love. How could she forgive him? How could she still love him? "I remember the fear that gripped my heart. The fear that I would not be able to reach you in time. I just wish we could do something. I feel so helpless. I have sent ships to the far corners of the planet searching for a suitable mate, and found none. No one seeks her. On this entire world, there is no man with the necessary gene able to match her power. My visions have been quiet. If there is a way to avoid this, I have not seen it."

"There is nothing we can do except spare our daughter a painful death. If we love her, we must do this for her. And you must do this for our people. You are king. You must do what is necessary for your subjects."

Taking a deep breath, Arcus let it out slowly. She was right. He had no time for self-pity or grief. He was king and he had duties. "I must go, as you say, I am the king. I can fall apart in here; but out there, I must be the perfect monarch."

Releasing her from his embrace, he turned and slowly walked across the room. Reaching the door, he paused with one hand on the doorknob and looked back at Sivena, still standing near the window. "We'll go on because we must. But I don't think I'll ever know joy again. Will you tell her?"

Not trusting herself to speak, Sivena nodded her head in agreement. As the door closed behind her husband, Sivena sank to the floor and allowed the tears she had been hiding to fall freely. Yes, they would go on, they were monarchs trained to live for the good of their people no matter the cost. But, like her husband, she too would never be the same. Tomorrow, her daughter would die, and there was nothing she could do to stop it. Outside, gray storm clouds gathered in response to Sivena's despair, and the earth groaned in sympathy to her pain. Gently, the rain began to fall, an accompaniment to her tears.

The Lady Tivonna was much like her father. As well as possessing the auburn hair and emerald eyes of the king, she also possessed his stubbornness and strength of will. Picking up a spare blanket, she shoved it into the open pack resting on her bed. Earlier today, her mother had brought the news of her impending execution. The news had not been unexpected. Tivonna was well versed in the lore of the first ones. Past history was a hobby of hers. Her father had no choice but to order her death. But that didn't mean she was going to meekly submit herself for execution. Death might claim her, but not without a fight. Tivonna was not a fool. She knew her potential and what that potential could do if uncontrolled. She also knew that the ancients did not leave decrees without good cause. The madness was real. But, was bonding the only answer? Maybe she wouldn't go mad, maybe she would be able to control the increase in her abilities. She meant to try. Besides, she knew her parents loved her dearly. She knew the pain ordering her death had caused them. She was determined to spare them the pain of actually putting her to death. If she were to die, it would not be at her parents' hands. She could do that much for them at least. Nor would she willingly endanger others. The ancients were seldom wrong and she suspected that they were not wrong now. She would go to the ruins in the mountains on the other side of the Painted Forest. There were no people there and she would be far enough away that any forces she unleashed in her madness would not harm others.

Having made her decision, Tivonna set about collecting the supplies she would need. She was wilderness trained like all royal heirs, and would have little trouble living off the land. She exchanged her court gown for a forest green tunic of soft suede with matching pants and boots. Gathering her long auburn hair into a tight braid, she tied it securely with a strip of green leather. Rummaging through her closet, she pulled out a black hooded cloak and added it to her supplies. That should do it. She glanced around the room one last time. No, she hadn't forgotten anything. If all went well, she should be back here in a few days. If not, well at least she would have spared her parents the guilt of her death. Collecting her gear, Tivonna left her chambers and headed for the stairs leading to the servants' quarters. It was midnight and the area was empty; everyone was sleeping. Passing through the living area, she made for the servants' entrance located in the rear of the castle. Checking to make sure she was unobserved, she crept out the door and headed for the stables.

Dodging the guards was easy; she had been doing it since she was a child. When she was little and couldn't sleep, she would creep out of her chambers and hurry to the stables where Jonas would always welcome her. Jonas was her father's master trainer, but he was also her friend and confidant. It was Jonas who had taught her to ride, to pull a bow, and to survive in the wilderness. He had always welcomed her late night excursions, and would let her pet his precious chargers or tell her wondrous stories of the races and places of Mystra. When her plans were ready, she had gone to Jonas for help. The mountains were far away. If she was going to make it there by midnight tomorrow, she would need transportation and no animal ever left the stable without Jonas's knowledge.

When Tivonna reached the stables, Jonas was waiting for her, as she knew he would be. He was tall and lean with the look and bearing of a soldier. His short brown hair was tinged at the temples with gray and his clear gray eyes missed nothing. Jonas had changed little over the years she had known him. Beside him, stood three mounts saddled and carrying packs. Stopping before the animals, Tivonna looked at Jonas in surprise.

"What's all this? I had intended to take only Midnight?"

Jonas looked down in embarrassment, "Take them, my

lady. I have a hunch you'll be needing these extra mounts and supplies."

Jonas was descended from the Eurodians, a race hunted and persecuted for their ability to foresee the future. The surviving members of the race had fled to Mystra. After the cataclysm, most of the races on Mystra became intermixed. There were no true Eurodians anymore, but traces of their ability could still be found in their descendants. If Jonas said she would need the extra supplies and mounts, so be it.

"Thank you. How will you explain their absence? I don't want you to be in any trouble."

"Don't worry about me. I've known your father a long time; no harm will come to me. He'll probably be relieved. Now, you'd best hurry, you have a long way to go and little time."

Tivonna handed him her pack to be secured with the other supplies and turned to the large black stallion waiting serenely beside the other two mounts. As she approached, he dipped his head in greeting. The horn on his forehead shimmered with a soft golden light. Her people had brought the almost extinct unicorn with them when they settled on Mystra. They were the perfect transport in this no technology world. They were intelligent, loyal, swift and of course beautiful. Midnight was her own personal mount; she had raised him from a colt. It was nice to know that she would not be alone in her exile. The other two mounts were both exceptional animals. Jonas had picked only the best for her. Both were a sparkling white, one with a horn that glowed with an inner silver light, while the other gleamed with a burnished gold. Mounting quickly, she secured the lead ropes of the other two mounts to her saddle and turned to face her friend.

"I don't know how to thank you. You are the best friend I've ever had."

"Just come back safely. That's all I ask. Now go, you

haven't time to waste."

With a wave, Tivonna turned Midnight and headed for the trail to the Painted Forest. Skirting the city which sprawled beyond the castle's boundaries, she kept to the little used trails. It would not do to be seen. Midnight was restless from being cooped up in the stables and wanted to run. Giving him his head, she was soon flying down one of the secret trails, which wended through the great forest. At this pace, she would reach her goal in record time.

The Painted Forest lived up to its name. It was one of the rare wonders of Mystra. The trees of the forest were not green like the other plants on Mystra, but instead displayed a kaleidoscope of colors. Entering the cool shelter of the forest, Tivonna traveled the winding trail until she reached a tree whose trunk was crimson shot through with bands of gold and silver and whose leaves were a riot of crimson, silver and gold. This was the King Tree, halfway point between the castle and the ruins. Stopping beneath the tree, Tivonna set up a temporary camp. It was just past daybreak. She was making good time. She would eat and rest a few moments before going on. After freeing the animals to graze, they would not stray far and Midnight would return to her call, Tivonna prepared a light breakfast. Then, rolling up in her blanket, she lay down at the foot of the great tree and drifted off to sleep.

After what seemed to be only a few minutes, Tivonna was jerked awake by something cold and wet being pressed to her cheek. She opened her eyes to see Midnight standing over her; it was he who had awakened her. Shaking his head and tossing back his long dark mane, he turned and went to join the other animals waiting quietly by the trail. Judging by the sun's position, she had been asleep for a few hours. Thankfully, Midnight had woken her. She was tired enough to have slept the day away, and she still had a long way to go. Rising from her place beneath the tree, Tivonna quickly broke camp and prepared to travel. She was halfway through the forest; and the mountain ruins were a good half-day journey beyond the Painted Forest. It was time to be going. In moments, she was astride Midnight and heading for the mountains.

Tivonna was almost to the forest edge when a strange feeling began to come over her. She felt fevered and light headed. She was just passing the Sea Tree, a tree whose colors mirrored those of the ocean, when she was struck by a wave of dizziness and plunged from the saddle. Too dizzy to rise, she lay huddled on the ground, her body racked with alternating waves of fever and chills. It was too soon! The change had come half a day early! Tivonna sobbed in despair. She was too close to the castle. If she could not control what was about to happen to her, she would destroy not only this beautiful forest but those she loved as well.

It was becoming harder to think. Her awareness began to expand. Suddenly, she could sense the entire planet. Earth, air, fire, and water, all called to her. She was power; nothing was beyond her. No! That way led to madness! She must not lose control! Tivonna's world faded to be replaced with a vortex of swirling colors. Red, blue, green and yellow, they dominated her awareness. Her body burned as forces of tremendous power rose and clashed within her. She could not contain all that power; her body was disintegrating under the stress. It was only a matter of time before her mind broke under the strain. The four opposing forces racked her body with waves of pain, consuming her from within. After what seemed like hours but was in reality only minutes, Tivonna could hold out no longer. With a mental scream, she fell forward into a bottomless black pit, oblivious to the forces tearing apart the fabric of her being. As the blackness closed in, her mind cleared for a moment. She had lost. Without her will to check them, the forces would run out of control. Striking at everything around her, they would leave destruction in their wake. She had been a fool; the ancients were right. She should have died. Now it was too late. Then, the blackness descended, and she knew no more.

How long she lingered in the void between life and death she didn't know; but suddenly, Tivonna became aware of a calm, soothing presence within her mind calling her up out of the darkness. The presence was gentle but strong. It cooled her fevered body and brought order to the forces clashing within her. Where chaos had reigned only moments before, now four bands of color flowed serenely. The bands of her power waited quietly for her commands, now completely under her control. As she returned to awareness, she felt the presence retreat from her mind. Yet, even after she knew he had gone, a trace of his essence remained. Taking comfort from this, she began to slide into an exhausted sleep. She had so many questions. Who was the man who had rescued her? How she knew that the presence was a man she did not know, but she was certain that was the case. Where had he come from? How had he saved her? Was she now bonded to this strange man? She was too tired to search for answers now. She had survived the change. Her parents were safe. Everything else could wait.

CHAPTER THREE

2605 Day 233

Dawn was just breaking over the kingdom of Aquilla, when high above the planet's atmosphere in the cold void of space the Ourora's timekeeper chimed a wakeup call. In his cabin, Hawk stretched and climbed from his bunk. He hadn't realized how tired he had been. Stumbling across the room, he activated the cabin's refresher and stood letting the warm cleansing mist soak life back into his sleep stiffened muscles. Exiting the unit, he quickly donned a clean gray flight suit. Now, he felt ready for anything. Whistling a merry tune, he left his cabin and headed for the lounge to meet Jasen. The sensor and probe data should be in by now. If all went well, they would soon be making their descent to the planet.

Hawk entered the lounge to find Jasen seated at the table pouring over a data-pad. Grabbing a cup of coffee, he joined him.

"Morning. Anything interesting?"

Looking up, Jasen fixed his friend with a feigned look of disgust. "Well, the dead have decided to return to life."

Hawk threw up his hands, "OK. So, I'm not a morning person. Sue me. Filidae are nocturnal you know."

Laughing, Jasen showed Hawk the report he had been reading. "Here, take a look at this. It's the weirdest thing I've ever seen. No wonder the Empress was destroyed. Jake had no idea what he was flying into until he was actually inside the planet's atmosphere."

Scanning the data before him, Hawk gave a low whistle and looked up at Jasen in amazement. "This is incredible…an energy barrier that doesn't register from the outside, but which sensors can scan once inside. If it hadn't been for the Empress's data, we would never have suspected anything was amiss."

"Correct. Even more interesting, it appears that there are actually two fields. There is a second layer of energy nestled inside the larger outer zone."

Scrolling down, Hawk continued to study the data. "So it's the outer field that destroys metal. The inner field hardly registers. Any clue as to what it is? Anything we should worry about?"

Shaking his head, Jasen rose and walked over to the food dispenser and refilled his coffee cup. Turning, he leaned against the cabin wall and sighed. "Aside from readings of high turbulence, we know very little. The best we can do is keep the ship's shielding at full strength, and take our chances. As long as the field doesn't overload the shields, we should be able to make it through. It's a chance we have to take."

"Sounds fun. So when do we start?"

"No time like the present. I've picked us a landing spot on the planet's largest landmass. Most of the continents are fractured. Whatever happened here, the planet took a beating." Stowing their cups and making sure all furnishings were safely secured, the two headed for the bridge. Entering the flight deck, Jasen immediately went to his station and began checking the ship's systems. Once they began their descent, there would be no room for malfunctions.

Taking his seat next to the pilot's station, Hawk tucked the data-pad away and strapped in. As always, seeing Jasen at the helm of the huge starship awoke a longing in him. What must it be like to see space unfettered by the metal shell of a spaceship?

"Hey, wake up over there." Jasen's words formed directly in Hawk's mind, jarring him from his musings. *"I'm going to establish a link so that you'll be able to see what's happening. I don't know what we'll run into down there, but two heads are better than one. Besides, I can't have you getting bored and running around while I'm trying to land this thing."*

As Jasen formed the mind-link, Hawk suddenly felt himself thrown forward into space. He was no longer on board the ship; he was the ship. The sensors were his eyes and ears. He was drifting naked and alone in the blackness of space. He was falling, falling…

Suddenly, Hawk's world righted itself. He was still conscious of the space around him, but now he felt anchored. He could feel the ship pulsing around him, but he was also aware of his own identity.

The data from the ship's sensors flowed slowly through his mind and a strong warm presence enfolded him. Hawk relaxed. He was tuned to the ship but no longer fused with it. He was Hawk again.

"Sorry. That's a little too much to take in all at once. How's this?"

Hawk gave a sigh of relief, *"Thanks, much better. Now, what?"*

In answer, the world around him changed and he was looking down on the northern pole of the planet. Hawk gasped. It was beautiful. Unfiltered by viewing screens and portholes, the planet gleamed like a pearl and the stars shone like diamonds. Hawk felt as if he could reach out and pluck them from their velvet nests. In all his years of space travel, he had never experienced the beauty and mystery of space as he did now. This was just a fraction of what Jasen must be sensing, but to Hawk it was a priceless gift.

"Well, shall we take a closer look at our jeweled lady?"

Hawk chuckled. He wasn't the only one captivated by the mysterious planet. *"We can't very well sit up here forever. Whenever you're ready, maestro."*

"Then hold on to your seat. I'm taking us down."

Obeying Jasen's will, the ship glided downward toward the planet's surface. It slid smoothly into the upper atmosphere and passed through the planet's first energy ring unscathed, the metal dissolving barrier having no effect on the crystal vessel. Continuing downward, the ship approached the second barrier of strange energy. As the ship penetrated the second zone of energy, they were hit by a wave of turbulence. Violent forces battered the Ourora from all sides. It took all of Jasen's borrowed skill to keep control of the wildly rocking vessel.

Halfway through the layer, the turbulence eased. Jasen drew a deep breath in relief, which quickly turned to a gasp of horror. A bizarre, constantly changing landscape now replaced the familiar stars. They floated in a place filled with creatures and things that could not exist in their reality. Alien thoughts and sensations impossible for the human or Filidae mind to comprehend beat against Jasen's mental shields. Tightening the mental defenses around his and Hawk's minds, he shut sensory input down to a minimum. The inhuman images continued to beat against his shields. He didn't know how long he would be able to withstand the onslaught but what he did know was that their unshielded minds would not survive contact with the alien environment for long.

Just when he was sure that he had reached the end of his strength, they broke through the field into the clear morning air of the planet. Quickly, Jasen slowed their descent and sent the vessel toward the southern mountains. They should be far enough away from people to be unobserved, yet close enough to establish contact with the inhabitants when they were ready.

Gliding down through the blue sky, Jasen set the starship down in a secluded valley. Shutting down the engines, he slumped back into his flight chair and dissolved his mental links with the Ourora and Hawk. They were down.

Freed from Jasen's mind-lock, Hawk stirred and opened his eyes. That was some ride. Jasen had shielded him from most of the distortions, but what had gotten through was enough. Jasen! If it was this bad for him, it must have been much worse for the telepath. Unstrapping himself, Hawk rose and staggered over to the pilot's chair. Jasen was slumped in his seat, his face pale. Hawk grabbed both shoulders and shook him.

"Jase! Are you all right? Talk to me!"

With a groan, Jasen opened his eyes. Seeing his partner's worried face, he gave a weak smile. "You wouldn't happen to have a giant aspirin handy would you?"

With a sigh of relief, Hawk stood and looked down at his friend, "What you need is a good cup of stimi tea."

"I'd rather die. I hate stimi tea."

With a chuckle, Hawk walked over to the bridge's dispenser and ordered two cups of the herbal stimulant. Taking the steaming cups back to the pilot's station, he handed one to Jasen. "No arguments. Drink your medicine like a good boy."

Obediently, Jasen took the cup and drank. However, he couldn't suppress the grimace of distaste which came to his face. The tea had a bite, but it worked. Already he could feel the energy creeping back into his body. Straightening in his chair, Jasen studied Hawk. He wasn't the only one looking a little pale. "And how are you? Any aftereffects?"

"Well, it's not an experience I relish repeating, but I'm

fine. You shielded me from the worst of it. Thanks."

"Anytime. Let's see how the Ourora made out." Running a quick scan of the ship's functions, Jasen looked up in satisfaction. "All systems online and in the green. And I intend to see that she stays that way. I've set the null field to maximum deflection; it should neutralize any energy not compatible with the Ourora's operating systems. About the only thing that can get through is gravity and thought."

"Won't that be a power drain?"

Jasen nodded, "Yes, but this planet has too many surprises for my taste. I don't want to come back and find the ship's systems have been eroded by some strange energy source. At least this way, we should find things like we leave them. Getting stranded here is not in my game plan."

"Mine either! How long do we have before we must up ship?"

"I packed a dozen power crystals. We could stay here for years and still have enough power to return home. But I don't want to be here any longer than we have to. The Firehawks could leave these systems at any time. It's a race between them and us."

"So how do we precede? I doubt this planet has a large scientific community dying to give us answers."

"No, but they may have records. We know this planet was settled by people from hi tech worlds. Something must have happened, and it may have something to do with the energy fields. Anyway, it's a start."

"So our first move is to establish contact with the natives. Dangerous. The Ourora may be the only ship to ever make it through the barrier. I have a hunch that your crystal technology may just work on this world. Your people's science is based on the principles of crystalline structures, light waves and psychic energy, not electricity, and there is no metal in sight. If the inhabitants find out you possess such technology, you may never leave this world."

"We'll just have to be careful. We'll scout the area before revealing ourselves. The translator implants will allow us to speak and understand the language and I'll be alert for any hostile thoughts. The first thing we need is clothes. These flight suits are a dead giveaway."

"Where do we start looking?"

Jasen touched a crystal and a large viewing panel appeared on the wall before them. The screen showed an aerial view of the surrounding terrain. Starting with their present position, Jasen traced their route. "At the edge of the mountain range is a forest, at least I think it's a forest. I've never seen one quiet that color before. Beyond the forest is a large settlement; we should be able to gather some information there. We can camp in the forest until we decide how to proceed."

"Sounds good. Let's go pack. It's been a while since I've been camping."

Leaving the bridge, the two headed for their cabins to gather the gear they would need. An hour later they were ready to go. Exiting the ship, Jasen secured the airlock and made sure the null field was operating correctly. Hawk could be right, this strange planet might not be able to harm the starship, but he was not taking any chances. Assured that everything was in order; the two started toward the trail cut into the side of the hills surrounding their valley. Once through the gap they would be a day's journey from the forest.

Walking in the cool crisp air, Hawk felt light and free. His people lived close to nature, working in harmony with the land and its creatures. He had been cooped up in the cities of Terra far too long. He welcomed the warm sun on his face and the light breeze, which stirred his long white hair. Plant and animal life was plentiful. Jasen too was enjoying being out in the open. Sending his mind outward, he scanned the surrounding area for any signs of danger. His mind touched only animal thoughts. Some were content, lazing in the sun. Others throbbed with the thrill of the hunt or fled in blind panic. All was as it should be.

As the light began to wane, the two friends made camp on the bank of a sparkling stream. After a leisurely meal, Jasen spread his bedroll and stretched out. The soft roar of the water as it rushed over rocks was soothing. He had intended to rest only for a moment but was soon fast asleep.

Jasen awoke the next morning to the smell of fresh coffee. Opening his eyes, he was surprised that he had slept so long. Sitting up, he spotted Hawk by the campfire. Hawk grinned wickedly when he saw Jasen was up. "Well, well! Look who finally decided to get up. I thought you were going to take root and grow. You'd make a lovely tree."

Picking up a twig, Jasen threw it at his grinning friend. "OK, OK! So I'm a sluggard. Your bad habits are finally rubbing off on me. Hey, is that breakfast? I'm starved."

Hawk laughed and filled a plate with food. Soon, they were both consuming a hearty meal. As they ate, Hawk covertly studied his friend. Jasen looked better. He had been close to exhaustion last night, though he would never have admitted it. Stimi tea couldn't take the place of rest. The tea could only give you access to your remaining reserves of strength. When those reserves ran out, the body demanded sleep. Last night's rest seemed to have returned much of Jasen's energy.

Finishing their breakfast, they broke camp and resumed their journey.

They made good time and were discussing the best place to stop for a break when they came upon the ruins. Topping a steep rise, they paused and gazed at the scene displayed before them. Below was what must once have been a fertile and prosperous valley. Now it held only death. The ground was blackened, and huge craters and trenches dotted the landscape. In places, the soil had been fused solid. In the center of this desolation, were the remains of what looked to be a large castle. The castle was now reduced to rubble.

Hawk studied the scene before them in amazement. "What could have caused such destruction? It looks like nature had a war."

"I have no idea. Whatever happened, it looks safe enough now. We have to go through here to reach the forest."

Descending the hillside, they stepped onto the valley floor. Up close, the destruction was even worse. They had to tread carefully. Reaching out with his senses, Jasen tapped the energy of the earth, building a mental model of the surrounding land. The ground was crisscrossed with deep chasms and the powdery soil was like glass. In places, the soil was only a hard crust over a deep pit. He mapped a safe route across the treacherous terrain, then carefully started forward. After what seemed an eternity, they reached the castle. Here, the ground seemed more solid. They decided to stop for a moment. It was almost noon; they could use a break.

Crawling up onto a fallen block that had once been part of the castle's outer wall, Jasen opened his pack and took out two ration bars. Tossing one to Hawk, he opened the other and took a bite of the energy rich bar. Gazing at the terrain they had just crossed, Jasen shook his head in wonder. They had been lucky so far. Aside from a few near misses, they had made the trip without incident. Turning his head, Jasen scanned the area they still had to cross. On the other side of the valley was the forest. If all went well, they should reach it before nightfall.

"Hey Jase! Come take a look at this!" Looking around, Jasen spotted Hawk poking through the castle ruins. Leave it to the curious Filidae to go exploring. Rising, he went to see what his partner had uncovered. Near the center of the ruins was a room, which still remained somewhat intact. It was almost as if the forces unleashed had gone outward away from the area, leaving it virtually untouched. Hawk was on the far side of the room sorting through a pile of books.

"Look at these. Some were made by machines while others are hand crafted." He was holding two large volumes a look of excitement causing his eyes to sparkle. One appeared to be a sort of history book. The vinyl covering and crisp white pages showed that it was the product of advanced technology. The other book was a type of journal. Its worn leather cover and yellowing pages bespoke of great age and a culture where modern preserving techniques were unknown. Without thinking, Jasen took the journal from Hawk's hand. Instantly, images and feelings from the past slammed into his mind. One of Jasen's talents was the gift of psychometry. He could relive or experience past events through the psychic traces left on an object. Usually, he was very careful when handling strange artifacts. He did so only with his mental shields at full strength. This time he had been careless. As the psychic emanations swept over him, he was thrown back in time...

He was a woman...a woman of power. She was sitting at a desk writing in the journal. It was almost time. Fear gripped her heart. She didn't know if she would be able to control what was about to happen. She had been unable to find a suitable complement for her powers. Now it was too late. Suddenly, her body was engulfed by pain. Power grew within her. She was ultimate power; she was a god. Staggering up from her chair, she stood in the center of the room and screamed. She could not contain the power. It flooded her being. The forces hungered to be free. They fought for release. She couldn't withstand the strain any longer. Waves of raw power exploded from her body in all directions. The streams of energy rippled outward. They struck the castle's walls, shattering them to dust. Earthquakes shook the surrounding area, cutting deep chasms in the earth. Lava pushed its way up from deep in the planet's core, forming craters. Liquid death poured from the craters and, from their centers, clouds of ash spewed out. Violent winds swept across the valley, and fires raged out of control, consuming everything in their path. Huge lightning bolts struck the ground, fusing the soil into sheets of glass. As the destruction ranged across the valley, her mind began to darken. The pain began to fade, replaced by a growing numbness. She was sinking into a pit of cold blackness....

Suddenly, Jasen was snapped back to the present by a savage blow to his wrist. The journal dropped from his numbed hand. Blinking in surprise, he found himself sitting on the ground, his back propped against a stone block. Hawk was kneeling next to him holding the journal. A look of relief passed across his face when he saw that Jasen was once again in the present. "I would think that you'd know better by now. One day you are going to pull a stunt like that and there's not going to be anyone around to help you. Want to tell me about it?"

"All right. I was careless. The psychic impressions were too strong. The owner of the journal was the one who caused all this." Jasen replied, indicating the destruction around them.

He paused to rub the wrist Hawk had struck, causing him to drop the book. It was starting to throb. He would have a nasty bruise tomorrow. It was no more than he deserved. Hawk was right; this could have been bad. He had been reliving the woman's death. If the Filidae hadn't severed the contact, he might have died with her. Banishing the thoughts, he turned to his friend and held out his injured wrist. "Thanks for breaking the link, but couldn't you have been a little less zealous. I'll never use this again."

"Ha! It serves you right for nearly scaring me to death. You were muttering about power and growing numb. I was afraid you were a goner." Pointing to the devastation around them, Hawk asked, "What happened here Jase? Did one person really cause all this?"

"I'm afraid so. It was a woman. I could feel her fear. She was about to inherit great power, but she was scared she wouldn't be able to control it. She was right. The power killed her, but not before running amok and causing all this."

Rising to his feet, Jasen began to strap on his pack. "Come on. We had better get going. I want to be out of here before dark."

Glancing at the ravaged valley, Hawk agreed. He didn't want to stay here one minute longer than necessary. Grabbing his pack, he started walking in the direction of the forest. But, he had forgotten one very important thing. The craters. He had gone only a few feet beyond the castle ruins when the ground beneath his feet gave a loud crack, and he plunged downward into a huge black hole.

The crater was wide with smooth sides. They gleamed as if made of polished glass. There was nothing to grab hold of to stop his rapid descent. He glanced downward and gasped. The shaft was deep, but far below a number of sharp spires grew from the smooth walls. They crisscrossed the crater, pointing upward like huge crystal teeth. If he didn't stop his fall before he reached them, he was a dead man.

Hawk was sure that he was going to die when suddenly he was jerked to a halt. His pack strap had snagged on a lone spike sprouting from the crater wall not more than twenty feet from the circle of death. It was the only one in sight. He had been lucky! He had one chance, but he had to make it fast. The lifesaving spear was already being to crack under the strain of his weight. He concentrated and a sphere of white light surrounded his body. A few seconds later, the light vanished; revealing a large white hawk with silvery blue eyes, a golden brand gleaming on its breast. No sign remained of the Filidae except for the empty pack swinging from the crystal spine. Extending its wings, the bird launched itself into the air. With a rapid beat of wings, it flew upward toward the top of the crater, leaving the deadly spires far below. Bursting from the pit, the beautiful white hawk dipped and soared in the clear air before spiraling down to land near Jasen. A brief flash of white and Hawk, complete with clothes, stood where the bird had been only moments before.

Jasen pulled back from the crater's edge and offered up a prayer of thanksgiving. He had lost sight of Hawk as he had plunged downward into the black pit. He had been sure that he was doomed. If he had not been able to shift forms in time, he would have died. As always, Jasen marveled at his friend's shape changing talent. It both mystified and intrigued him. Most Filidae could assume another form, but only one. Hawk was a rarity; he was not limited in the number of shapes he could take. He could become any living creature he had actually seen in real life. Pictures wouldn't do; he had to be close enough to the creature to feel its auric field in order to copy its form. Having this strange gift was part of what made them friends. Hawk was the first person, aside from Jake, not to fear Jasen's abilities. He accepted Jasen for who he was, not what he could do. It didn't matter that others looked upon Jasen as strange or someone to be feared. Being an oddity was old hat to Hawk, and he had taught Jasen that being different was not always bad.

The Filidae walked up beside Jasen and looked down into the pit that had almost been his tomb. After a moment, he looked back up. "That was too close. Sorry about the pack." Glancing back at the crater, he shuddered. "I don't ever want to see another hole in the ground for as long as I live. Let's get out of this death trap."

Jasen shared his friend's sentiments. "I can't say I'll miss this place. But this time, we take no chances. We could have lost a lot more than a pack. No one goes anywhere without checking the ground first, remember?"

"I do now!" With a flourish of his hand, Hawk waved Jasen in the direction of the forest. "After you. You lead the way and I'll stick to you like glue. Consider me your shadow."

Giving his companion a disgusted look, Jasen moved away from the crater and began the long trek to the nearby hills. Scanning the ground for traps, he slowly guided them across the remaining distance to the valley's edge. A quick climb later, and they were standing on top of the hillside gazing at the brightly colored forest spread out before them.

Hawk stared at the natural wonder with a look of reverent awe on his face. "It's beautiful. I have never seen anything like it before."

"Nor I. Come on; if we hurry we can be under the cover of the trees before nightfall."

The two friends made camp just as the sun lowered, casting the forest into twilight. They awoke the next morning to the sounds of bird song. After a quick breakfast, they broke camp and resumed their hike through the dense woods.

Seen in the bright light of day, the forest was even more stunning. Studying the riot of color around them, Jasen once again marveled at the wonder of nature. "I can't believe these trees are natural. Some of the colors..." Jasen's words died as a sharp pain knifed through his brain. Clutching his head with both hands, he fell to his knees blind to everything but the agony. As the burning in his mind receded momentarily, he was able to think clearly. There was something familiar about this pain. He had felt it before. The ruins! The mysterious lady that had destroyed the valley! One like her was near, and in pain. A new wave of agony washed through his body making further thought impossible.

"Jase! Can you hear me! What's wrong?"

Hawk's urgent words penetrated the haze of pain. Jasen

forced his eyes open. Hawk knelt beside him, supporting him with one arm. Jasen fought the pain knifing through his mind. He had to make his friend understand before it was too late. Finally, the pain faded enough that he could speak. Through clenched teeth, Jasen forced out his message.

"Must...get to her. Woman of...power. Losing...control. Have to...reach her in time."

"Woman? What are you talking about?" Hawk was puzzled at the strange words. What woman and what was that about losing control? Suddenly, a wild thought struck him. It couldn't be! "Jase, what woman...a woman like the one that destroyed the valley? There's one like her nearby and she's losing control?"

Jasen nodded, "Must reach her...not much time. I can...stop her. Help me... get to her!"

Hawk was stunned. The idea of the vast destruction he had seen in the valley being loosed here sickened him. How could Jasen stop it? Hawk trusted his friend. If Jasen said he needed to reach the woman, then Hawk would see that he got there. Without another word, he placed his shoulder beneath Jasen's arm and levered him to his feet. Encircling his waist with his free arm, he steadied the reeling telepath.

"Which way?" He asked quietly.

Jasen pointed to the trail cut through the heart of the great forest.

"There," he gasped.

Hawk helped Jasen walk the twisting trail cut through the woods. As they penetrated deeper into the trees, Jasen began to recover somewhat. The pain eased and he no longer had to lean on Hawk to walk. However, now he moved like a man entranced. He seemed to be following some inner summons that Hawk couldn't hear or feel. The Filidae didn't like this one bit.

Turning a sharp bend in the trail, Hawk froze. Before

them stood a tree of turquoise accented with pigments of blue, sliver and white. Beneath the tree lay a young woman. Her body convulsed and her face was etched with pain. He started toward her, only to be blown back as a sudden gust of wind swept him off his feet. Moments later, a fiery circle leaped into existence surrounding the prone figure. Black clouds gathered and lightning flashed through the air, narrowly missing him. Underneath him, the ground trembled. Climbing to his feet, Hawk gazed at Jasen in question. How were they going to help her if she wouldn't let them near her?

Jasen laid a hand on his friend's shoulder. "Wait here. This is my task." Stepping forward, Jasen began walking toward the circle of flame. Lightning flashed toward him to be met and deflected by a shimmer of gold. He had activated his telekinetic shield. Reaching out with his mind, Jasen parted the fire and stepped through the deadly ring. Kneeling beside the troubled young woman, he placed his left hand on her forehead and closed his eyes. Gathering his power, he projected himself into her mind.

He was in a world of chaos. Her mind was a maelstrom of colors. Red, yellow, green and blue swirled and clashed. Somehow, Jasen knew that this was wrong. The colors should not be mixed. Searching the mindscape, Jasen sought for a sign of the woman's mental essence.

There! Huddled on the edge of a black pool lay a faint glow of silver. Bringing the spark to him, Jasen encased it behind his mental shields to protect it from the violent forces ripping through the expanse around him. Now assured that what was left of the woman's personality was safe, he turned his attention to the whirling forces. He had to separate the colors and keep them apart. Reaching out with mental hands, he gathered a strand of yellow energy and pulled it to him. Grasping other strands of yellow, he began to braid them into a cord of pure color. When all the yellow strands had been tamed, he caught another color and repeated the process. Using all his strength of will, Jasen wove the chaotic colors of power into bands of controlled energy. When he finished, four cords of color flowed serenely across the mindscape. All was calm. The wild forces had been harnessed. His first task was complete.

Scanning the terrain around him, he searched for clues as to what he must do next. Except for the four bands of power, the only other noticeable feature was the dark pool in the center of the mindscape. Of course! Grabbing the colored cables, he placed one end of each band into the black void. The cords glowed and hummed, filling the pool with power. Gently, Jasen drew the silver spark out from behind his shields. Feeding it his strength, he called to the mind hidden deep within the faintly glowing mote. After what seemed an eternity, he felt a faint pulse from the spark.

She still lived! He had feared her mind had been shattered beyond repair. He felt the mental presence quiver to life. Carefully, he pushed the slowing, pulsing dot into the heart of the pool. Instantly, the spark began to grow larger and the glow intensified. The bands of power hummed and throbbed, keeping time with the pulsating ball of light. The silver radiance began to spread, until it filled the entire pool with brilliance.

A wave of dizziness hit Jasen. He was at the end of his strength. With a last act of will, he severed the contact and flung himself back into his own mind. He caught a last glimpse of the sparkling light as it flooded the mindscape with pools of silver shot through with red, blue, green and yellow.

Awakening, Jasen looked up and smiled at the worried Hawk. Then, giving in to his body's demands, he relaxed and sank into the soft welcoming darkness.

Hawk caught his friend as he slumped forward, unconscious. Gently, he laid the telepath on the ground and checked for signs of life. Jasen was breathing regularly and his pulse was steady, if somewhat weak. Shock and exhaustion, Hawk decided. With rest he should be all right. Leaving Jasen for the moment, he bent and examined the girl. She too seemed to be stable. Glancing from one unconscious figure to the other, Hawk gave a wry smile. It looked like he was elected guardian. He would make them comfortable and keep watch until they awakened.

Whatever Jasen had done seemed to have worked. As soon as he had touched the girl, the wild elements had subsided. Fire and wind had both vanished. Hawk had watched Jasen's Herculean battle for the woman's mind. He hadn't known what his friend was doing, but the struggle and effort were obvious. But Jasen had been victorious. They were safe. There was now no danger of this beautiful forest becoming another valley of death and sorrow.

His thoughts were broken as a twig snapped. Sharp senses alerted him to the presence of animals nearby. Turning, he spotted the unicorns as they stepped from the brush. They were magnificent. They were also carrying packs. He had need of what those packs contained. Cautiously, he approached the animals. The leader, a huge black, snorted and tossed his head in warning.

Hawk smiled. Stopping, he held out his right hand palm up and began speaking to the beast in his native tongue. The Filidae had a natural way with wild things. At the sound of the alien speech, the animals froze, ears straining forward. After a few moments, the black unicorn walked over to him and pressed its nose into his outstretched palm. Accepted. Stripping the packs from the now docile steeds, he set them free to graze and began making camp. In no time, he had a cheery fire going and his patients snuggled in blankets lying next to it. Making himself comfortable, he prepared to wait.

CHAPTER FOUR

Tivonna awoke to the quiet sounds of the forest. The morning sun filtered down through the leaves of the enchanted woods, caressing her with golden light. The warm rays felt good on her face; there was a definite chill in the air today, a storm was coming. As she stirred, memories flooded her mind. She was in the Painted Forest. The change had come early. She had been dying, then someone had saved her.

Glancing at her right arm, Tivonna gazed at the intricate tattoo that flowed from the back of her hand along her forearm before ending just shy of her elbow. The elaborate Celtic knot pattern was the symbol of her house. Its delicate swirls depicted her lineage, and the accomplishments of her house. She had traced the indigo lines many times in her life, finding strength and comfort in this reminder of her roots. Today, however, instead of the familiar display of dark blue lines, the design blazed with color. Lines of red, blue, green and yellow twisted and flowed to form the familiar marking. What had once been a symbol of her house, now served a new purpose. Long ago, those of her race had discovered that the dye used to make the house markings reacted with the power of an elemental upon maturation. The number and strength of the colors reflected the abilities of the newly awakened elemental. Tivonna stared at the four colors comprising the tattoo, no one color held dominance. Not only did she have all four abilities; but she also possessed them in equal strength. The change was complete, and she was now marked with the symbol of her power. It hadn't been a dream; she was a level four elemental. How had she survived? Coming to full wakefulness, Tivonna sat up and looked around her. She was lying in a clearing near the Sea Tree. Gazing across the clearing, she spotted a lone figure standing on the other side.

Hawk was standing near the edge of the trail grooming the black unicorn. Once the big black had accepted him, they had become fast friends. He had already tended to the other two mounts and was now currying the stallion. Suddenly, his sharp hearing detected the rustling of cloth. Turning, he saw the woman sitting up and staring at him. Putting the comb away, he slowly walked back to the fire. The woman's bright green eyes followed his every move. He had to be very careful; he didn't know who this strange lady was, but he had a good idea of what she could do if riled. Stopping beside the fire, he dropped into a cross-legged position on the ground. Reaching for the coffee pot warming in the blaze, he filled a cup with the steaming brew. Putting on his most charming manner, he smiled and offered the cup to the woman.

"Hello. Feeling better? Would you like something to drink?"

Tivonna studied the stranger with avid curiosity. She had never seen anyone like him. She knew most of the races of Mystra, and nowhere among the many diverse peoples of the planet was there anyone like him. Also, he had been petting Midnight. Unicorns were intensely loyal; they did not tolerate just anyone touching them. Midnight was especially selective; only she and Jonas could freely handle the black. Yet somehow, this stranger had gained the stallion's trust. Was he the one who had saved her? She did not fear him; somehow she knew that he meant her no harm. His smile was infectious; she couldn't help but like him. Yet, she felt no recognition within her; he couldn't be her bondmate. But; if not him, then who?

Cautiously, she gave him a shy smile and accepted the cup from him.

"Thank you. I am Tivonna. Are you my kiosan?"

Tivonna had thought the words in the language of Aquilla, but they had come out in what one part of her mind recognized as Galactic Standard. Where had she learned these words?

Hawk too was surprised. The woman's accent was different, but the words were clear if somewhat puzzling. "I beg your pardon? I'm Hawk. And I'm not exactly sure what a kiosan is."

"Then, who saved me?" Now it was Tivonna who was confused.

"Oh, you mean Jasen." Hawk said, pointing to the still sleeping figure lying on the far side of the fire.

Tivonna had been so preoccupied with the stranger that she had not noticed the other man. Rising from her bed, she walked over and knelt beside the prone figure. Instantly, her heart leaped; he was the one. The man was tossing fitfully in his sleep, his black hair damp with sweat. There were dark circles under his eyes, and his face was ashen; the battle to save her had been costly. Reaching out, Tivonna tentatively placed her hand on his forehead. He was burning up! She looked up at the white haired stranger in alarm, "He is ill!"

"What!" Instantly, Hawk was beside Jasen. How had he gotten sick so fast? The telepath was in bad shape; the exertions of the past few days had taken their toll. He had caught a chill in the night and was now gravely ill. His breathing was labored and his pulse was weak; fever racked his body. Hawk had to get him medical aid immediately. Looking up at the worried girl, he tried to gauge her character. Could he trust her? He would need her help to care for Jasen. "It's serious. I must get him to a doctor."

"We must take him to the castle. There are healers there; I know that they can help him. He mustn't die!" Tivonna was adamant; her bondmate must live!

"I have medicine back at our home; I must get him there. I'll need to borrow your mounts." Hawk had to get Jasen away from the girl and back to the Ourora as quickly as possible. In his fevered state, Jasen's shields were weak. It was only a matter of time before he lost the ability to protect his mind from the thoughts of others. A castle was the last place he should be.

Tivonna studied the Filidae closely. He cared deeply for the one called Jasen; maybe he knew best. "How far is your home?" she asked.

"In the mountains beyond the ruins." Hawk answered her vaguely. He couldn't reveal the Ourora to anyone.

The young woman shook her auburn head. "No, it is too far. You must come to the castle with me." As Hawk opened his mouth to protest, she raised a hand pleadingly and continued. "Please, there is a large storm forming. We must be under cover before it arrives. The mountain ruins are too treacherous to cross with an injured man, especially at night." Holding up her right arm, she displayed the elemental's sign for Hawk to see. "Believe me, what I say is true. The castle is his only hope."

Hawk sighed and nodded his head, "I do believe you; but the castle is dangerous for him. There are things about him you don't know."

"He is my kiosan. I would do nothing to harm him and no one else would dare. He will be safe at the castle. My father is the king; he will see that he has the best of care."

Hawk had no doubt that she was sincere. Yet, her

words disturbed him. "That's the second time you've used that word. Just what do you mean, he's your kiosan?"

Tivonna stared at him in amazement. How could he not know what a kiosan was? Everyone on Mystra knew about elementals and their bondmates. Where had he been hiding? Suddenly, a wild thought struck her. No, it wasn't possible; no off-worlder could land on Mystra! Or could they? There had been no one on the planet to bond with her, yet she lived. Dreading the answers, she asked the baffled stranger, "Who are you? Where do you come from...you are not from Mystra, are you?"

The moment of truth had come. Hawk had no choice but to trust her; Jasen's life depended on her help. Choosing his words carefully, he tried to explain. "No, Jasen and I are visitors to your world. You call it Mystra?"

Tivonna was stunned. No ship could penetrate the curtain of lights; it was impossible. As the thoughts crossed her mind Jasen stirred and murmured fitfully, "ship...penetrate...curtain of lights...impossible."

Tivonna's eyes widened in fear. Rising, she backed away from the muttering figure. He had known her thoughts! Monster! Demon! The man tossing deliriously by the fire echoed her thoughts and fears.

Instantly, Hawk was on his feet and advancing on the frightened woman, his silvery-blue eyes flashing in anger. Heedless of the danger, he grabbed her and gave a sharp shake. "Stop it! You'll kill him! You must get control of yourself. He can't protect himself."

His words penetrated Tivonna's fears and deep inside her instinct stirred; she was endangering her bondmate. Looking up at Hawk, she tried to control her fears. "I do not wish to be afraid; I can't help it."

"It's OK; I understand. Most races have been taught to fear telepaths. They view them as some kind of monsters who will force them to do things against their wills and plunder their deepest secrets. But, it's not true; Jasen isn't like that! He's not trying to read your mind; you're screaming your thoughts at him. With the fever, his shields are weak, he can't protect himself."

With Hawk's words, Tivonna realized what she was doing. She had let childhood stories cloud her thinking. This man was her kiosan; he could not be the monster she had been imagining. The change had left her emotionally unstable; it would pass. For now, she must master her fears. He needed her help, and she would not fail him.

"I'm sorry. Please forgive me; I know I am being foolish. He is my kiosan; he could not be evil. Now I see why you did not wish to go to the castle. But please, you must trust me; I would not, could not harm him; he's too important to me. There is not time to explain everything to you now. We must leave at once if we are going to reach the castle before the storm. I promise, I will do all I can to guard your secrets."

Hawk had little choice; without help, Jasen would die. He would have to trust the girl; he just hoped it wasn't a mistake. Nodding his acceptance, they quickly broke camp. Gathering limbs, leather thongs and a spare blanket, Hawk quickly constructed a travois and fastened it to one of the spare mounts. Then wrapping Jasen snugly in a warm blanket, he tied the ill man securely to the mobile stretcher. The telepath had grown quiet; Hawk feared he had slipped into a coma. They had to hurry! Mounting the second white unicorn, he secured the lead lines from Jasen's animal to his saddle. He had found a long black cloak in the spare packs. Donning the garment, he pulled the hood up to conceal his exotic features, and followed Tivonna toward the castle. Hawk's mood was bleak; he had a bad feeling about this.

King Arcus paced the floor of his study. What's taking them so long? It was now long past midnight and, for the hundredth time, he cursed his errant daughter. Oh,

Tivonna had been very clever. Leaving messages for her parents and instructing the servants not to disturb her. She would spend her remaining time visiting with friends in the nearby village. After saying her goodbyes, she requested solitude to prepare herself for her coming death. They had honored her wishes until noon. Sivena had gone to check on her just before the midday meal, desiring to spend some time with her daughter. Instead, she discovered Tivonna was missing.

The following hours had been chaos. A quick search had revealed no sign of the missing girl; now midnight was almost upon them. In desperation, he had sent word to the Elemental High Council requesting their aid. The council had immediately dispatched a number of its strongest members to Aquilla. If they could reach the castle in time, they might be able to deflect some of the coming destruction.

They had arrived only moments before midnight. All had waited as the dreaded hour had come and gone. Nothing happened! The council members and Sivena had immediately closeted themselves away to discuss the ramifications of this momentous event and to decide what to do about Tivonna. Arcus had been left to pace and wait. But what was taking them so long? Surely, they had reached a decision by now?

The king's musings were interrupted as the chamber door opened to admit Sivena. Rushing over to her, he took her hands in his and searched her face for any sign of distress. She didn't look upset; maybe the news was not as bad as he feared. "They have decided?" he asked tentatively.

Giving her worried husband a reassuring smile, Sivena nodded. "They have rescinded the death order. She is to be found and brought before the council. This is an unprecedented occurrence. We must know what has happened."

Arcus felt the tension drain from his body as relief swept over him. The death order was canceled! "Then, you think she still lives?" He couldn't believe it was possible.

Sivena's smile grew brighter. "Oh yes, if she had gone mad, we would definitely have known. Arcus, I cannot believe it; it's a miracle."

Holding his wife tightly, Arcus agreed. It was a miracle. He didn't want to think about what this odd occurrence might mean to Mystra. Right now, he was just thankful that his daughter lived. Breaking off his embrace, he gave his wife a kiss and headed for the door. "I'll cancel the death warrant and send out search parties. Don't worry; we'll find her." Then he was out the door and gone.

Sivena watched her husband leave and smiled. The grief had vanished; he was like a man reborn. Soon her family would be together again; but for now, she had work to do. Exiting the room, she returned to her chambers where the other elementals waited.

Hawk and Tivonna were just passing the King Tree when the soldiers appeared. Spotting the armored figures, Hawk prepared to flee; but Tivonna quickly reached out and laid a restraining hand on his reins. "Wait, they are my father's men." The soldiers drew nearer and surrounded the trio; flight was out of the question now. Pulling his hood lower over his face, Hawk waited.

"My lady," The guard commander dipped his head in a sign of respect. "We have been sent by your father, the king; he requires an audience with you." Turning, he stared at Hawk, curiously trying to penetrate the concealing cloak. "And who might your companions be?"

"They are my friends. The one who is ill is my kiosan; we must get him to a healer immediately. You may escort us to the castle; I'll see my father when he has been cared for."

Tivonna's tone and manner left little room for arguments or questions. She was a royal princess and, by her words, a fully bonded elemental as well. The commander had no wish to incur her wrath with prying. He would take them to King Arcus; the king could decide what to do after that. With the soldiers surrounding them on all sides, Tivonna and Hawk began the long ride back to the castle.

As they rode, Hawk studied his escorts. They seemed to be good soldiers who wanted no part of this duty, but were just following orders. They were careful to keep their distance and none approached Hawk or Jasen, except to offer food and water during rest stops. It was obvious no one wanted to risk angering the elemental. This gave Hawk hope; maybe Tivonna could get them safely hidden away in the castle without anyone guessing that they were really from off planet. He would just have to wait and see. Thankfully, Jasen was still quiet. While the coma worried him, it was also a blessing. The guards had no idea that a telepath was in their midst.

It was beginning to grow dark when the company finally reached the castle. Halting in the courtyard, they waited while the commander reported to his superior. There was a brief discussion, then he returned. He did not look happy. Turning to Tivonna, he reluctantly broke the news. "I have orders to take you immediately to your father. Your friends are to be held in the dungeon until the king decides their fate. I'm sorry."

At those words, Hawk tensed, then relaxed as he felt the sword point pricking his back. Glancing around, he saw that a circle of obsidian blades surrounded him. The soldiers had all drawn their swords; fighting was not the answer. He would give Tivonna time to work things out; then, if necessary, he would act. His abilities were still secret; he would keep it that way. When the time came, he would have little trouble escaping the castle's cells.

Tivonna was livid! Turning on the guard, she vented her outrage. "How dare you! These are my friends! You will not throw them in a dungeon! I will not stand for it!" In the distance, thunder began to rumble and a slight wind blew through the clearing. The commander swallowed hard; this was not going well. Helplessly, he glanced at Hawk, and paled when he saw the swords pointed at the stranger. Instantly, he looked away; but it was too late. Tivonna's attention had been focused on her companion and what was happening to him; her temper flared anew.

"Leave...Him...Alone!" Lightning split the sky in punctuation to her words, causing the guards to flinch.

Seeing what was about to happen, Hawk intervened. Speaking perfectly in the language of Aquilla, he addressed the angry elemental. "Tivonna, you must control your temper. This is not helping Jasen. Do as they say; this is not their fault. I'll look after Jasen; you talk with your father."

Hawk's soothing words pierced Tivonna's anger. Jasen was still lying on the litter; fighting would not heal him. She nodded, "So be it. But," she turned to the frightened guard commander, "I hold you personally responsible for them. If anything, anything at all happens to them, even a bruise; I'll make you wish you had never been born. Do I make myself clear, commander?"

"Yes, my lady, I'll see to them myself. No one else will be allowed near them; they will receive the best of care." The guard was much relieved. He owed the stranger a big debt; this could have turned ugly.

"See that you keep your word." Walking over to Hawk, Tivonna glared at the guards around him and they hastily put away their weapons. In a softer tone, she addressed him in Galactic Standard. "I will be as quick as I can; my father should be reasonable. I'll come for you personally. Go with no one else."

The Filidae nodded and asked in the same language.

"And if they prove uncooperative?"

Tivonna's eyes narrowed, "Then they will regret their decision!"

Hawk smiled and patted her shoulder. Then, switching to the language of Aquilla, he spoke loud enough for the guards to hear. "Just don't level the castle; we'll be in it too." He chuckled as the guards paled and looked uneasily at the elemental. Good, let them be nervous; it served them right.

Tivonna smiled wickedly and whispered, "You have a vicious streak in you, sir."

Hawk echoed her smile. "I know." Then, in a more serious tone he continued, "Now off you go and be quick. Jasen doesn't have much time."

Tivonna nodded. Her new friend's ploy had worked. She was still angry, but now her anger was controlled. That made her all the more dangerous. The guard commander delivered her to his superior and returned to escort Hawk and Jasen to their cells. He was determined that nothing would be allowed to happen to the two visitors.

Tivonna nodded to the Captain of the Guard. "You may take me to my father now."

The captain bowed low and waved her toward the West Tower. "This way my lady, the king will see you in the Main Audience Hall."

Puzzled, Tivonna followed the guard to the appropriate chamber. Why would her father wish to see her in the Audience Hall? He usually met with her in his private study. Oh well, she would know soon enough; they were here. The captain opened the door to the chamber and waved her in. Obediently, Tivonna entered the room.

As she stepped into the chamber, a flood of elemental forces struck at her from all sides. The waves of pure power overwhelmed her and sent her reeling into the chamber wall. What was happening? Instinctively, the powers deep within her stirred. Rushing outward, they met and blocked the strands of energy threatening to engulf her body. As her own strength grew, the attacking beams of force began to weaken. With an act of will, Tivonna deflected the oncoming energy, hurling it back to its source. Abruptly, the attack ceased.

When the forces died, she looked around the chamber; her father was nowhere in sight. Instead, five members of the Elemental High Council were lying in a semi-circle on the floor before her. They were the ones who had launched the attack.

"Why?" She demanded of the stunned adepts. "Where is my father and why did you attack me? I am no threat to you!"

Firice, the oldest of the council members, slowly rose to her feet. She was pale and shaky; having her own powers thrown back in her face was a new and unwelcome experience. "We are sorry. You are an unknown, possibly dangerous. We had no way to know your state of mind; we thought it best not to take any chances. Once you were subdued and there was no chance of your powers running out of control, there would be time to discuss your change. We are very interested in learning what happened to you."

The woman was scared; she feared they had made a grave mistake. Their attack had failed to neutralize the young woman and had instead succeeded only in alienating her. It was obvious that she was in full control of her abilities, and they were formidable. She had defeated some of the council's best. They would be at her mercy if she chose to retaliate. Also, her father, King Arcus, would not like what had happened here; neither, for that matter, would the rest of the High Council. Tivonna had no reason now to trust them. They may have lost the council the services of this unique young woman, as well as the friendship and patronage of the powerful King of Aquilla. Why had she listened to Tyr? She should have known better!

The rest of the council members managed to struggle to

their feet. Tyr rose gracefully and swept her long black hair back over her shoulders. Her pale ivory features betrayed nothing of what she was thinking. She stood still, inscrutable as a porcelain statuette, and studied the auburn haired woman before her with calm black eyes. The rumors were true; Tivonna was indeed powerful. She had defeated them all and she hadn't even been trying! The Duke of Cenchrea would be greatly interested in what had transpired here. The duke had plans for Mystra and the beautiful elemental might be of use to him. Tyr would contact Gaius. He and his spy network would keep a close eye on Tivonna and her mysterious companions. They too might prove valuable to the duke.

Tyr's thoughts were interrupted as King Arcus stormed into the room followed by an equally outraged Sivena.

"What is going on here?" The king demanded. "Why was Tivonna brought here instead of to me as I instructed?"

"Your Majesty please, we just wished to question her about the change. We must know how she survived; we meant no harm." Firice tried to ease the tension building in the room; things were getting out of hand.

Before the king could speak, Tivonna intervened. She had had enough of this farce. "I have nothing to say to you; not now or ever. I will have nothing to do with you or a council who attacks first and asks for explanations later. If that is your idea of requesting information, then you will get no answers from me. I have broken no law. I was bonded before midnight of my twenty-first year; you have no authority over me. I wish you to leave this castle, immediately. I have no desire to see any of you ever again."

"What do you mean attacked?" Arcus was becoming angrier by the minute. Glancing at his wife he asked, "Did you know what was planned here?"

Shaking her head, Sivena answered, "No, if I had known I would have stopped them." She stared at the members of the council in disbelief. "How could you? My daughter came here peacefully; there was no danger. Why would you do such a thing? Be sure that I will be filing a full complaint with the High Council against your behavior here tonight. I suggest you return to them and explain yourselves."

"I will not have anyone usurping my authority in my own castle. You have offended both my wife and my daughter; you are no longer welcome here. You will leave here at once!"

The adepts bowed low to the angry royals and, glancing nervously at Tivonna, hastily left the room before the angry king changed his mind and locked them in the dungeon.

"Bunch of idiots!" The outraged monarch muttered. He glared at the backs of the departing council members. "Attack a man's daughter in her own home. Countermand a king's orders in his own castle. Who do they think they are anyway?"

Tivonna watched her father angrily pace around the room muttering under his breath and broke out laughing. "Oh father, how I've missed you!" Running to her startled parent, she threw her arms around his neck and gave him a tight hug. "And you mother." Turning, she embraced the queen as well. It was good to be home but she could rejoice later; there was something important she must do now.

"Father, I am sorry for the trouble I caused. It really was for the best. I don't have time to tell you everything now. The Captain of the Guard had my kiosan and his companion thrown into the dungeon. My bondmate is very ill. I must get him help immediately."

"What! Who ordered him thrown in the dungeon? I issued no such order!" The irate king glanced at the door through which the council members had departed only moments before. He had a nasty suspicion who had been responsible; but he could take care of that later, first things first.

"Explanations can wait; I'm just glad you're home safe and I want to make sure that you stay that way. Go see to your young man; we'll talk later."

Giving her parents a grateful smile, Tivonna ran from the room. Grabbing a passing servant, she ordered the East Tower Suite prepared. That part of the castle was nearly empty, there would be no prying eyes to uncover the two's secrets or bustling crowds to disturb the sick telepath. Her first priority was to get Hawk and Jasen safely hidden away; then she would decide what to tell her parents.

The king watched bemused as his daughter fled the room. It certainly was turning out to be a strange day. His thoughts were interrupted by a soft chuckle from his wife.

Sivena shook her fair head and smiled at her husband. "Well, no one can accuse us of leading a dull life. I've had enough excitement to last me a lifetime."

Arcus walked over and embraced his wife. "We have been lucky, my wife; far luckier than I would have dared hope. Today could have turned out very differently. How much trouble are we in with the council?"

Sivena laughed. "Not very much. They need my powers and your patronage. They can't afford to stay at odds with us. I'll send a letter to the council head tomorrow. A few explanations and apologies on both sides and things will be fine. What are we going to do about Tivonna and this mysterious bondmate of hers?"

"We wait and try to be patient. When she is ready, she will tell us what happened; for now, it is enough that she is home and safe."

"Speaking of safe, I have one more task to perform or none of us will be safe."

"The storm? It's near?"

"Very near. The forces are almost assembled. I must go divert them or we will face major trouble. Want to come watch?"

"Of course, I love to watch you work."

Arm in arm, the king and queen left the chamber and headed for the walkway running along the top of the central tower. From here, Sivena would be able to channel the storm's intensity into less destructive avenues. Pausing in the entryway leading onto the balcony, Arcus watched as his wife walked out onto the platform to face the storm.

Sivena could feel the forces of the gathering storm tingling through the air. The storm was big and violent. She thought of asking Tivonna for aid but then decided against it. Tivonna had more important worries and she should be able to manage this on her own. Lifting her hands toward the malevolent clouds above, Sivena reached out and grasped the airy forces and bent them to her will. She channeled the more violent, destructive elements to the South, out over the nearby ocean where they could spend their savage fury on the unrelenting sea. Snagging a few of the tiny harmless rain clouds, buried in the center of the storm, she pushed them eastward where their gentle rains would nourish the settlement's growing crops. When all was as she wished, she lowered her hands and turned to face her husband. "It is done."

Arcus watched his wife as she joined herself to the savage elements of the storm. She was beautiful. The wind lifted her long golden tresses and blew them wildly about her head. Sparks leaped from her fingertips and arched between her palms. She looked like a pagan goddess, a sprite of the air, at one with the storm. When she had finished, Arcus stepped forward and wrapped her in a tight embrace. "You are the most beautiful woman I have ever seen. How is it that I have such a wondrous creature for a wife?"

"Didn't you once tell me you were born under a lucky star? It must be true." Placing a kiss on his cheek, she stepped back. "Shall we retire, my husband? I for one have had more than enough activity for one day."

"And I." The two weary monarchs, arms intertwined,

left the balcony and headed for their chambers. Behind them, the night sky was quiet and a soft breeze blew through the treetops.

CHAPTER FIVE

Hawk, carrying the unconscious Jasen, had quietly followed the guards to a cell in the castle's dungeon. He had refused the commander's offer to help carry the ailing telepath. He liked the commander. Once out of sight of his superior, Tychicus, as he was called, had done everything in his power to make the cell habitable. Placing them in the driest and warmest cell available, the soldier had provided him with blankets and all the cold water he needed to care for Jasen. They had to try and keep his fever down.

He was busy changing the compress on Jasen's forehead when the cell door banged open. It was Tivonna. From the look of happiness on her face, the meeting with her father must have gone well.

Tivonna's smile died as she saw the worried look on Hawk's face.

"Is he worse?" She hastily dropped to her knees beside Jasen's cot and reached out a tentative hand to check his temperature.

Replacing the old compress with a fresh one, Hawk nodded. "I'm afraid so. I can no longer get him to take water. He won't last long without liquids. We have to do something!"

Tivonna stood. "The first thing is to get him out of here. Come, I have arranged rooms for you in an isolated part of the castle."

Making sure that his cloak still concealed his appearance, Hawk lifted Jasen and followed Tivonna out of the cell and down a narrow corridor leading to the East Tower. Shortly, Jasen was snugly ensconced in the center of a large warm bed.

Hawk studied his friend's pale face and labored breathing, then worriedly began pacing the room. He had to do something, but what?

"Should I send for the healers?" Tivonna was sitting beside Jasen's bed watching the frantically pacing Filidae with concern.

Hawk shook his head.

"Perhaps they can help. They are the best in my father's kingdom."

"No. That wouldn't be a very good idea. We have no way to get their medicines down him even if they would work on his metabolism. They would probably do more harm than good. If he were conscious, he could tell us what was wrong and what medicines would work on him. As it is, we would be taking a very big risk. I don't want to do that unless there is no other hope. There's got to be another way!"

As he paced the room, his eyes fell on the backpack sitting in the far corner of the room and a wild idea struck him. Jasen had talked of packing a medi-comp. They had debated on whether it would be safe to use on the planet. If Jasen had brought it...

Hawk rushed across the room and tore open the knapsack. No, this wasn't Jasen's but his! Somehow the packs had become switched. He had been wearing Jasen's, not his own, when he had fallen into the crater at the ruins. If Jasen had brought the device, it would be in that pack.

Hawk had last seen the backpack dangling from the crystal spine in the pit. If it was still there...It was worth a try; he would go for the pack. If the medi-comp wasn't in the other backpack he would try for the Ourora. It was Jasen's best chance.

Turning from his place beside the pack, Hawk studied the worried girl. How to break the news?

"Tivonna, Jasen has one chance. We brought medicine with us from our home world. I must get it for him; I need you to stay with him and keep him safe. I'll get the medicine and return as quickly as I can. If all goes well, I should be back in a few hours."

"But how? Your home is too far away. How can you make it there and back so quickly?"

Hawk took a deep breath. "Tivonna, do you trust me?"

"Yes."

"Then I'm going to tell you a secret. Jasen is not the only one with unusual abilities."

Instantly, a bright light flashed and a large snowy owl flew to the chamber window. It landed on the sill and watched the woman with silvery-blue eyes. Stunned, Tivonna rose from her chair by the bed and walked across the room to the casement. Opening the window, she watched the beautiful bird take flight, heading for the distant mountain ruins.

Hawk was a Wer. Tivonna shook her head, who would have thought? Was there no end to the surprises her new friends possessed? The owl should be able to reach the mountains and return quickly. They had a chance. Tivonna returned to her place by the bed. Replacing the now warm compress on Jasen's forehead with a new one, she prepared to wait and pray. As she watched the man on the bed before her, Tivonna felt a strange longing. She wanted to know this mysterious person who had risked so much to save her. Even pale and fevered, she found him compellingly attractive. She didn't even know the color of his eyes. He must be a special person to have such a loyal friend as Hawk. She hoped she would have the opportunity to find out.

Hawk flew as swiftly as he could toward the mountain valley. He picked up a strong tail wind, which he suspected was due to Tivonna and reached the ruins in record time. Circling the area, he searched the terrain for any sign of the giant crater. Spying the huge pit, he spiraled downward into the gaping black hole. The pack must be here! He really didn't have the time to return to the Ourora; Jasen was failing fast. At last, he saw the familiar crystal spine and, yes, swinging from the spear was the backpack.

Lighting on the rocky projection, he tore open the knapsack and searched inside. Yes, good old Jasen, he should have been a Boy Scout. The medi-comp was there near the top of the pack. Hopping onto the box-like instrument, the bird grasped the device's carrying handle in both talons. Now, if only it wasn't too heavy! With a strong beat of its wings, the owl took flight carrying the medi-comp tightly in is clawed grip. The bird flew rapidly toward the castle aided by a friendly wind, which pushed him along increasing his speed. He had to make it in time!

Castle Aquilla was old. Hundreds of generations of monarchs had lived and died inside its walls. The castle was honeycombed with secret passages and spy holes left over from past ages. Many of the passages had been sealed over or forgotten, and few remembered they even existed. Gaius was one of the few who knew that the passages existed and how to operate the hidden entrances.

When Tyr had asked him to spy on the princess and her companions, Gaius had thought little about it. Royalty was always spying on each other and it was a good way to make some easy money. He had thought it was just another boring job. Now he was not so sure. The princess had closeted herself away in the East Tower and no one was allowed to enter. Even the king and queen stayed away. And where was the second visitor? He was not in the room and no one had seen him leave the tower. There was something strange going on and he was determined to find out what.

The East Tower suite had once been the guest quarters for visiting royalty. The ceiling of the chambers had been lowered to form a loft type space above the room, where spies could lay and watch the occupants of the suite. Gaius was snugly tucked away in the spy hole watching the princess care for the sick stranger, when a large white owl clutching a golden object in its talons streaked through the chamber's open window. Landing in the middle of the room, the bird vanished in a flash of light, and an exotic white-haired stranger stood holding a rectangular box in his hands. This just might prove interesting.

As the white bird flew in through the window, Tivonna rose from her place beside Jasen's bed and moved to the center of the room to meet it. She waited impatiently as the beautiful owl spiraled to a landing in front of her. "Did you get the medicine?"

Transforming from bird to man, Hawk held up the medi-comp for her to see. "Got it!" Stepping past the stunned girl, he walked to the bed. "How's Jase? Any change?"

Receiving no answer, he turned from the bed and looked back at Tivonna. She was standing frozen in the center of the room staring at the golden box in his hands.

Technology! Tivonna could not believe what she was seeing. Was he out of his mind? He would destroy them all! Getting hold of herself, she walked over to stand beside the puzzled Filidae. He was an off worlder; she had to make him understand the danger.

"Hawk, I know you care for Jasen very much but you can't use that. Technology is forbidden on Mystra. If you activate that machine, you will destroy us all. I can't let you do that; I will stop you if I must."

Understanding dawned; of course, she feared technology and rightfully so. He had to be very careful, she was quite capable of carrying out her threats. She would not hesitate to attack him if he tried to use the medi-comp. He had to convince her it was safe.

"Tivonna, it's all right. I know about machines and how they react on Mystra, but this one is different. The technology of Jasen's planet contains no metal. It won't react like the others. We just landed an entire starship in the mountains, and nothing happened. I would never do anything to harm you or your world. You have to trust me. This box is Jasen's only chance; you must let me help him."

Tivonna stared at him, fear warring with hope, then slowly nodded her head in assent. Hawk had trusted her, now it was her turn. Please, God, let him be right.

Immediately, Hawk turned to the bed and placed the medi-comp on Jasen's chest. The instrument was another scientific wonder from Jasen's people. Made of the golden pseudo-metal, it was featureless except for one round crystal set in its center. Once activated, the instrument scanned the patient's body and diagnosed the illness or injury. Then, it synthesized the proper medications and injected them automatically, as needed. It was like having a doctor and laboratory in a box. Hawk pressed the crystal, Jasen had assured him no other action was needed, and prayed. Immediately, a soft hum filled the room and the box began to glow.

"You are sure that it can help him?" Tivonna watched the softly glowing device with awe. It was the first machine she had ever seen.

Before Hawk could answer, the humming stopped and the golden glow expanded to encompass the still figure lying on the bed. Alarmed, Hawk reached for his friend only to be stopped by the now impenetrable force field. Beyond the curtain of light, the medi-comp began a strange metamorphosis. The surface of the box seemed to melt and, as Hawk and Tivonna watched in alarm, golden tentacles began to erupt from the device. They could only watch in horror as the golden appendages attached themselves to Jasen's body. Hawk shuddered; they seemed to be burrowing into his skin. Tivonna gasped as one of the tentacles came to rest on Jasen's face, completely covering his nose and mouth. "Hawk, we have to do something. It will kill him."

Hawk struggled to calm his thoughts. Jasen told him the box was a healing device. He had no reason to think it was a lie. "I don't think it's meant to hurt him. I think it's trying to save him."

As if in answer to Hawk's words, there was a soft chiming and words began to form on the force shield. Taking a step closer, he scanned the information written in Galactic Standard displayed there. As he read, he felt the tension ease from his body. Jasen had been right; the box was a healing device and it was busy trying to save the telepath's life. Finishing the message, he watched as the words faded from view as mysteriously as they had appeared. Turning, he found a worried Tivonna watching him expectantly.

"It's OK. The force shield is to protect the patient while he's helpless. The tentacles allow the medi-comp to monitor his condition and provide the treatment and support he needs. Everything is going to be fine; we were in time, but it was close. The stress and strain of the past few days threw his body chemistry out of balance. The medi-comp is injecting him with the necessary electrolytes and compounds to stabilize his metabolism. Unfortunately, he also has a bad case of pneumonia. But we kept his temperature down, and he is not dehydrated. As soon as his body chemistry is stabilized, the medi-comp will start antibiotics; it's also giving him oxygen. Barring complications, he should be fine in a few days. Now, all we have to do is keep him warm and quiet. Our doctor-in-a-box will do the rest." He pointed toward the glowing shield. "The device will disengage when treatment is complete. I know it looks ghastly, but he's in good hands."

"But, how can a golden box do all of that?"

Hawk shook his head. "I'm not sure. Jasen's race has a strange affinity with what he calls the energy of creation. They can program the energy to take the form they need. It's all too close to magic for me."

"Magic, the ancients spoke of beings that came from the stars and could mold the universal force, what they called the fifth element or spirit. It is believed that individuals with psychic gifts and the ability to wield elemental energy are from their blood lines. I never dreamed I'd meet one."

"Well, if what he believes is true; he is the last of his kind."

"All the more reason to keep him safe."

Gaius quietly withdrew from the spy hole. This was quite a scoop; the duke would pay well for this information. Technology that worked on Mystra! The man who controlled such technology would be ruler of the entire planet. He would be a god. Yes, the duke would give a lot to know about this. Slipping from the tower, he prepared to travel. This was too good to wait; he had to reach Tyr immediately.

Unaware of the spy in their midst, Tivonna and Hawk sat beside Jasen's bed and watched as the medi-comp gave its life-giving treatment. Spying a bowl of fruit and a plate of cheese on the table by the bed, Hawk made himself comfortable and began to eat; flying was hard work. Looking at Tivonna, he smiled.

"Thank you."

"For what?" The girl turned startled green eyes on the Filidae.

"For trusting me. You have every reason to fear machines. It took a lot of courage to let me use that."

"I am just glad that he will live. If he dies, so do I."

"What! What are you talking about?"

"He is my kiosan."

"I think it's about time you told me about this kiosan business. What is Jasen to you and you to him?"

Collecting her thoughts, Tivonna tried to explain. "An elemental cannot control her power without help. When her power matures, what we call the change, she must be bonded to an appropriate mate. One who can help her tame her powers and establish her control. If not, she goes mad and her power goes wild, then she dies. You have seen the ruins."

Hawk nodded.

"That was the result of an unbonded elemental's death. The same would have happened to me if Jasen had not come. But more happens during bonding than just taming the elemental's abilities. My race is the result of breeding between my human ancestors and alien visitors to our world. We carry a gene from those alien visitors that was activated by the forces unleashed during the cataclysm. The gene allows me to access vast amounts of energy. But, that energy is too much for a human body to contain on its own. The forces over time break down my cellular structure, eroding my control and eventually killing me. Bonding to someone with the gene that is complementary to me in power prevents the breakdown."

"Wow, that's…just wow."

Tivonna nodded. "There is one thing else. A kiosan is also entrusted with the ability to neutralize his elemental's powers, at least temporarily. If she starts to misuse them, he can stop her; he is the only one who can."

"It's sort of like a safety switch to control all that power."

"Yes. Once bonded, an elemental cannot live apart

from her kiosan, her chosen, as you would call him. If he dies, she dies. If he leaves her for more than three months, she will become ill, then die. The working theory is that male and female each received only half of the genetic information to safely channel power. During bonding, they share the information from their respective genes, creating a stable whole. So you see, Jasen is very important to me; I could never harm him. My instinct is to protect him at all cost."

"I see. What does this mean to Jasen? Are you lifemates? Married?"

"No, most elementals marry their kiosan, but it's not a rule. I only have to stay near him. Everything else is up to the individuals. I know that Jasen is different. In fact, I'm amazed that I'm still alive. I have never heard of anyone that could stabilize an elemental once the change had begun. In fact, I've never known of anyone, not of my race, being able to bond at all." She held up her right arm. "Yet according to this tattoo, I am not only bonded and in full control of my abilities but I have all four gifts, each equal in strength. I don't wish to cause him hardship. But I can't undo what has happened."

Hawk gave Tivonna a reassuring smile. "Don't worry. Jasen is a reasonable fellow. We'll work it out somehow. Why don't you try to get some rest? I'll take the first watch."

"Sleep sounds good." Tivonna rose and walked to the door leading to the hallway, and the second set of chambers beyond. Stopping in the doorway, she watched the Filidae sitting quietly by the bedside. She realized she had grown fond of this strange being. He made her feel that everything would turn out alright. She trusted him and was glad he was her friend. Exiting the room, Tivonna prepared to get some much needed rest.

Hawk sat thinking about his conversation with Tivonna. He had no doubt that Tivonna believed what she said to be true. But Hawk didn't buy it. If Jasen was the only man on the planet that could match the elemental, he bet that Tivonna was bonded closer to the telepath than she knew. He wouldn't be surprised if the girl found herself in love with Jasen. And what of Jasen? Hawk knew a little about his people. Telepaths married those who were their mental complement. He knew that Jasen despaired of ever finding a suitable mate since he was the only living telepath left. What if this strange girl turned out to be Jasen's match too? How deep had the mind-link gone? Things could get pretty interesting in the coming weeks. Hawk couldn't help but smile. He couldn't wait to see the expression on Jasen's face when he found out that he had inherited the auburn haired, green-eyed elemental for life.

During the following days, Tivonna and Hawk took turns keeping watch on the telepath. Three days after Hawk returned with the medi-comp, Jasen's condition began to improve. A day later and the machine ended its treatment.

As it became obvious that her bondmate was going to live, Tivonna left the room long enough to visit with her parents. The king and queen had been extremely patient. They had not pressed her for an explanation but instead had offered her every assistance. She and Hawk both agreed that it was time they knew the truth about their otherworldly guests. After much debate, the two decided to take the monarchs fully into their confidence, withholding only the knowledge of Jasen's telepathic abilities. Tivonna was overjoyed; she disliked keeping secrets from her parents.

One evening while Tivonna was visiting with her family, Hawk sat dozing in a chair beside Jasen's bed. He was jerked awake by a soft moan coming from the bed. Leaning over, he smiled as Jasen opened his eyes.

Groggily, Jasen looked up at Hawk and muttered, "You look horrible. You should be getting more sleep." The words trailed off as the telepath drifted off into a natural healing sleep.

Bemused, Hawk reached over and laid a hand on Jasen's forehead. It was cool; the fever had broken and the coma ended. Jasen was on the road to recovery. Now, if only he could find a way to tell him about Tivonna. Oh well, that could wait till later. He was too tired to figure it out now. Jasen was going to be just fine, that was all that mattered. Everything else would sort itself out given time. Rising, Hawk headed for his own chambers and bed.

CHAPTER SIX

Jasen slowly swam upward through the layers of darkness enshrouding him toward the light above. Coming to full wakefulness, he blinked and gazed in confusion at his strange surroundings. Where was he? How had he come to this place? And why did he feel so weak? The last thing he remembered clearly was sighting the brightly colored forest. What had happened?

Jasen studied the room carefully. It reminded him of pictures depicting Terra's Middle Ages he had seen in books. There was a cheery fire crackling in a huge stone fireplace to his right and, beyond the foot of the bed on the far wall, golden sunlight streamed through a high window. There were doors on either side of the room, possibly leading to other chambers. To his left, placed in the wall against which his bed rested, was a third door leading probably to an outside corridor. Bright tapestries decorated the walls and the desk, tables and chairs dotted around the room were skillfully crafted of richly polished wood.

Jasen's musings were broken as a sound came from the door beside his bed. Turning his head, he watched as the door opened and an auburn-haired woman carrying a large tray entered the room. The tray held a teapot, cups and a covered bowl. Placing the tray on the bedside table, the young woman turned to him and smiled.

"Good morning. I'm glad to see you're finally awake. You had us worried. Do you think you could eat something? I brought some broth and tea."

"Who are you? Where am I?" Jasen was even more confused. The girl spoke Galactic Standard. Where had she learned it?

"I am Tivonna. You are in my father's castle in the kingdom of Aquilla, on the planet Mystra. Your friend Hawk and I brought you here. You have been very sick. Now you must try and eat. It's the only way to regain your strength. Hawk can explain everything to you later."

Placing her arm behind Jasen's back, Tivonna raised him up and rearranged the pillows behind him so that he could sit up. Then, she began feeding him the broth. She refused to answer any questions or to let him see Hawk until he had finished the broth.

Looking at the man before her, Tivonna's heart beat wildly. His eyes were the color of burnished gold. They seemed to look into her very soul and weigh what was hidden there. Suddenly, she felt shy. For some reason, it was very important that he think well of her. At that instant, Tivonna knew that she loved this strange man. She was bonded far closer than she had ever suspected. No matter who or what he may be, she was his for life; no other would do for her.

Tivonna felt the waves of confusion coming from him. It was the same emotion she had sensed when he first discovered his surroundings; that was how she had known he was awake. How she knew these things she did not know, but it seemed perfectly natural for her to do so. Yet would Jasen accept her as a mate? He might not return her love. She would have to go slow and give him time to accept her. That he would eventually be her husband, she did not doubt. Her task was to get him to recognize it too.

Jasen studied the vision before him and struggled with memory. He should know her, but the memory stayed tantalizingly just out of reach. He felt a wave of acceptance and, was that affection, coming from the woman? He should not be able to feel the girl's emotions so strongly. He was weak, true, but his shields were firm enough that he should be able to block stray emotions. Why was she different? And why did he feel so attracted to her? Who was this mysterious woman and how were they connected? Thinking was too great an effort; he was too tired to deal with this now.

Jasen had eaten only half the broth, when he had to stop. Even the simple act of swallowing, took more energy than he could spare.

"That's OK. It's a start. What you need now is rest. Sleep is the best healer." Tivonna set the bowl aside and rearranged the bedding to make Jasen as comfortable as she could.

"Where is Hawk? I must talk to him." Jasen needed answers. From what the girl had said, Hawk was safe and had the run of the castle. He had to find out what was going on.

"Not another word. You can barely keep your eyes open. Go to sleep. I will tell Hawk that you were awake. You can see him after you rest. All you have to know now is that you are safe. Concentrate on getting well."

Jasen started to protest when a wave of lethargy engulfed him and he drifted off to sleep. Tivonna stood smiling at her oblivious bondmate. She had a feeling that disagreements in the future would be much harder to win. He did not seem the type to let others order him around. Leaning over, she gave the sleeping man a light kiss on the forehead. "Sleep well, my love." Picking up the tray, Tivonna quietly left the room. She would dispose of the tray and then go searching for Hawk. He would be glad to hear of his friend's recovery.

When next he awoke, Jasen looked up into the smiling face of Hawk.

"Well, Sleeping Beauty awakes. How are you feeling?"

"Better." Propping himself up in bed, Jasen studied the Filidae with interest. Hawk was dressed all in leather. Tunic, pants and boots were all made of soft high quality leather dyed a deep sapphire blue. A short blue cape and a hunting cap, complete with feather, finished the outfit. Shaking his head, Jasen indicated his friend's new regalia. "What's all this? Going to a costume party? I can't decide if you're supposed to be Puss N' Boots or Robin Hood?"

"You can't expect me to run around in off world clothing can you? When in Rome you know. Just wait 'til you see yours."

"Why do I get the feeling I've just woke up in Wonderland? Well, it's obvious you've been getting along with the natives. What's going on? What happened?"

"What do you remember?"

"Not much, I remember climbing the hillside and sighting this beautiful wildly colored forest. Then things get hazy."

Hawk sighed. "I see. Things got a little complicated after that." Choosing his words carefully, Hawk filled Jasen in on what had been taking place while the telepath had been unconscious.

At the end of Hawk's tale, Jasen sat stunned staring at him in disbelief. "I've got a what! I can't believe this!"

"Sorry, old boy, but it's true. When you run around saving powerful elementals from madness, you have to take the consequences. It's not really so bad. All you have to do is let her tag along with us. We could use someone with a firsthand knowledge of the planet."

"Are you sure that's all there is to it. She just has to stay near me, nothing more. There's not something you're forgetting to tell me is there?"

"Positive. All you have to do is make sure she doesn't wreck the planet. Outside of that, you're a free man."

"What about when we leave this world? What happens then?"

"Well, I'm not quite sure. We'll just have to wait and see."

"All right. I don't like it, but there's not a whole lot I can do about it now. We'll deal with it when we have to. The important thing now is the Firehawks. What have you been able to find out about the energy fields?"

Hawk gave an inward sigh of relief. Jasen had taken the news better than he had hoped. At least he was prepared to tolerate Tivonna near him. Nature would take care of the rest. "Not much. The king and queen have been very helpful. The city has an extensive library and Tivonna is well versed in historical lore. When you're up to it, we can start a search of the records. To be honest, I've been too worried about you to think of the Firehawks."

"I'm sorry to have put you through so much trouble. Now that I'm fully awake, I can speed up the healing process. I'll be good as new in a few days. Meanwhile, you can start gathering records for us to study. We don't have any time to waste."

Hawk gave a mock bow. "Yes master, I'll begin at once. Your wish is my command, master."

Jasen laughed. "The day you bow to anyone's will, hell will definitely have frozen over. Now get out of here, you scamp, and let me rest. I have to get well in a hurry. Someone has to save Mystra from you."

Chuckling, Hawk left the room. It was good to have Jasen back. He had sorely missed his friend. With Jasen awake and joking the future didn't look so bleak.

Over the next few days, Jasen's strength slowly returned. Four days after his talk with Hawk, he was able to stand and walk around the room. Two days later Tivonna entered the sitting room of Jasen's suite and dropped a number of old records on the table. Hearing no sound from the bedroom, she walked over, opened the connecting door and froze.

Jasen, seated in a lotus position, was hovering a few inches above the floor in the center of the room. His eyes were closed and he was breathing slowly. Sensing the girl's presence, he stirred and opened his eyes.

Lowering himself to the ground, he stood up and eyed the girl warily. This was usually when the fear and hate began. "I'm sorry if I frightened you. I was just taking an internal inventory. Making sure everything is in order."

Tivonna shook her head and met the telepath's eyes. "I wasn't frightened, just startled. It's not every day that I find a flying man in the bedroom. Jasen, I know about your abilities. I admit I was scared of you at first, but you are my kiosan. I know that you are a good man; you would never intentionally hurt others. I trust you completely. You have no need to hide who you are from me, not now or ever."

Jasen studied Tivonna closely. There was no fear or revulsion in her. She showed none of the usual reactions he had come to expect from people when they learned of his powers. Slowly he relaxed, she accepted him. It didn't matter that he was different. She trusted him and cared for him. She saw past the powers, to the man behind them.

"Thank you." It was a simple statement but it carried a world of meaning.

"You're welcome."

Suddenly the bond between them sprang fully to life. For an instant they were one soul. They had no need for words. Each saw and knew the other completely. There was no shame or fear, only acceptance.

Realizing what was happening, Jasen wrenched his mind from Tivonna's and severed the link. They stood staring at each other in stunned silence as their minds adjusted to what had just taken place.

Finally, Jasen rallied himself. "I'm sorry. I..."

Shaking her head, Tivonna reached out and gently pressed the fingers of one hand to his lips. "No, no apologies, I have no regrets. We have been joined since that night in the forest. It has just taken us this long to realize it."

"But Tivonna, this is impossible. It can never work. We are from two different worlds."

"It doesn't matter. You are my bondmate. Where you go, I go. I am yours, now and forever. I can wait. In time, you will see that my words are true." Turning, she walked back into the sitting room. They had taken the first step. She knew now that he loved her as well. But he would need time to admit it to himself. Others had hurt him; he would not trust his heart easily. But that was fine; he was hers, she could afford to wait. Now she must ease the tension between them, give him room. "I believe we have some records to study. Are you coming?"

Totally bewildered at the strange turn of events, Jasen followed her into the room. She was an exceptional woman. Where their futures led he still wasn't sure, but they were irrevocably joined. There was no escaping that. Truthfully, he wasn't entirely sure he wanted to escape. But why couldn't she see that a relationship between them was impossible? The universe could be a cold place for one who was different. How could he ask her to give up her life here and face a future of fear and secrecy? If they exterminated telepaths on sight, what would they do to an elemental? He would have to monitor the link carefully from now on. It was a subtle bond that was easy for him to forget. This trip to Mystra was turning out to be much more than he had bargained for.

Three hours later, Hawk entered the sitting room and paused, studying the scene before him. Seated at the table, raven and auburn heads pressed close together, Jasen and Tivonna were poring over an old weathered book. There was an air of camaraderie about the two. Something had happened and Hawk was dying to know what.

"Well, what do we have here?"

The two jumped, startled. They had been so engrossed in the book that they failed to hear the Filidae approach.

"Hawk, we've found the diary of the leader of the original colonist. He chronicles the trip and initial settling of Mystra. This could be the clue we're looking for." Jasen was ecstatic.

"It also tells of the great cataclysm and how Mystra was almost destroyed. Jasen thinks that was when the curtain of lights came into existence." Tivonna's green eyes sparkled with excitement.

"Great. So fill me in."

Before Jasen could speak, Tivonna intervened. "It is almost time for the evening meal. My parents have requested that you both dine with us in the Great Hall. Why don't we discuss this afterwards? It will save having to repeat everything twice. That is, if you are planning to tell my parents.

Smiling, Jasen reached over and gently squeezed Tivonna's hand. "I think that's a fine idea. The king and queen may have knowledge we can use. Besides, I can't just kidnap you without telling them. Hawk will just have to suffer till then. However, there is just one problem; I can't appear before your people in off-world clothing."

"That is no problem at all; just check your wardrobe. You'll find everything you need. I took the liberty of having some things made for you when we were outfitting Hawk. I think you will find them a perfect fit."

Rising, Tivonna walked toward the chamber door. "Now, I'll leave you gentlemen to get ready. A servant will come to escort you to the Hall. I will see you at dinner." With that, she was out the door and gone, leaving the two friends alone.

"Well? Are you going to tell me?" Hawk propped himself on the edge of the table and regarded his friend with interest. Something had definitely taken place and he was not letting Jasen out of this room until he spilled it.

Seeing the resolve in Hawk's eyes, Jasen sighed. He might as well get it over with. The Filidae was tenacious; he wouldn't give up until his curiosity was satisfied. "I don't know quite how to explain this. It seems that Tivonna and I are bonded in more ways than one. When I was in her mind, I established a link between us. Hawk, she says that she's in love with me."

"I see, and what about you? How do you feel?"

"I don't know. It's impossible. It can't possibly work. She could never be happy with me." Jasen rose and began pacing agitatedly around the room.

Hawk smiled to himself. It was as he suspected; Jasen loved the girl but he couldn't accept the fact that she loved him as well. All the women in Jasen's life had met him with fear and loathing once they had seen his abilities. Jasen could not accept that Tivonna was different. Oh, Tivonna had powers of her own, but it wasn't the same. The abilities of other races were guardedly accepted and sometimes even respected in the galaxy...all that is except for telepaths. Hawk remembered the one planet of telepaths that had been discovered. The planet had been blown to dust rather than risk the possibility of its people learning space flight and contaminating the galaxy. Jasen couldn't allow himself to hope; the pain of disappointment would be too great. Tivonna had her work cut out for her, but Hawk had great faith in the elemental; in time, Jasen would see the truth.

"Why don't you give it a chance? She may just surprise you. Come on, let's check out your wardrobe. We don't want to be late to our first royal banquet."

Entering the bathing chamber, Hawk opened the huge wardrobe built into one wall, and gave a low whistle. Tivonna had not been idle. Inside the closet, hung a number of beautifully made garments. Reaching in, Hawk pulled out one, which caught his eye. The silk-like material of the tunic was black edged with an intricate pattern of gold and silver threads. The matching pants and boots were unadorned.

"How about this one. You'll take all the palace ladies by storm."

"And what, pray tell, are you wearing?"

"Oh, you're not the only one who's been given new threads. Wait and see." With a cheery wave, Hawk left the room and headed for his own chambers across the hall.

Jasen watched his friend with resignation. Hawk would never change and that was fine with him. At least life with the Filidae was never boring. Dismissing his friend from his thoughts, Jasen set about getting ready for dinner. Hawk was right in one respect; it wouldn't do to keep the king and queen waiting.

CHAPTER SEVEN

An hour later Jasen and Hawk followed a servant to the main dining hall. True to his word, Hawk was immaculate in a tunic made of the same exquisite fabric as Jasen's but in a spectacular shade of green. The tunic was the color of a Terran rain forest as seen through a veil of moonlight. A mesh of silver threads accented the gleaming fabric. The silvery-green suited the Filidae well. Like Jasen's, his pants and boots were an unadorned black. They looked like visiting royalty instead of two space travelers.

They followed the servant down the twisting, turning corridors until he paused outside of two large ornately carved wooden doors. A footman in bright livery opened the doors and ushered them into the Great Hall.

Entering the room, Jasen paused and gazed in fascination at the panorama before him. The Great Hall certainly lived up to its name. It was a huge cavern with a high vaulted ceiling. One could house an army within its walls and have plenty of room to spare. Four wide stone fireplaces, two per side, warmed the chill from the chamber. Everywhere lavish, brightly colored tapestries decorated the walls, and hundreds of candelabras lit the vast expanse of stone.

Two columns of long, heavy wooden tables ran the length of the room. At the far end of the chamber, sitting on a slightly raised platform, was the king's personal table. Strolling minstrels, jugglers, and dancers wandered among the tables, providing entertainment, and everywhere servants scurried about carrying heaping trenchers of food and jugs of wine.

Seated at the head table was a tall, broad shouldered man decked out in royal burgundy and wearing a golden circlet on his forehead. His resemblance to Tivonna left little doubt that this was her father, the king. Beside him, sat a beautiful blonde-haired woman regally dressed in a gown of pale pink. She also wore a golden circlet of rank on her forehead. This must be Tivonna's mother, the queen. On the right hand side of the table, seated nearest the king, sat Tivonna wearing a gown of molten copper and a silver circlet of rank. Two place settings had been laid out on the left hand side of the table. It looked like they were to dine with royalty this night; a privilege few commoners were ever allowed.

The other tables in the hall were crowded with flashily dressed nobility. The nobles sat according to rank. Those occupying the tables nearest the monarchs were dukes and earls. The middle tables were reserved for barons and lesser nobles. In the far rear of the room, sat the soldiers and men at arms. Jasen and Hawk followed the servant down the length of the room to the king's private table. As they passed the citizens of Aquilla, the curious nobles carefully scrutinized them. Reaching the head table, they bowed formally to the royal family and took their places. They were just in time; the meal was about to begin.

As Jasen and Hawk entered the Hall, King Arcus studied Jasen curiously. He knew little about this man except that Jasen had saved his daughter's life and was not from Mystra. When the king met Hawk, he was impressed by the

Filidae's wit, intelligence, and character. He was curious to see what type of man Jasen was that he could win the loyalty and devotion of one such as Hawk as well as the heart of his fiery daughter.

As King Arcus watched Jasen, the first thing that struck him was the air of authority surrounding him. His bearing was that of a royal prince or king. It was not something learned or copied from others, but was a natural, integral part of the man. Jasen was a born leader. Here was one used to giving commands and having those commands obeyed. He was not a stranger to power or responsibility.

As the meal progressed, the force of the man's personality struck Arcus. It was magnetic. Servants and nobles alike seemed to be drawn to him. He treated each with respect and dignity. The calm golden eyes met his without flinching or reservation. They seemed to look deep inside and weigh what was hidden there. Arcus found himself wanting this soft-spoken young man to think well of him; it was an odd sensation.

The king decided that he liked this enigmatic stranger. He was controlled and reserved, true, but to Arcus' surprise he was not cold. There was warmth that belied his calm, cool exterior and a sense of humor too. Jasen proved well able to hold his own against Hawk's quick wit. There was a keen mind and a strong will behind those piercing eyes. This man was no fool and would not easily be taken in or fooled by others. Jasen could be an invaluable ally or a deadly enemy. He could see how such a man could win his daughter's heart. Arcus was determined to keep on Jasen's good side. He would not relish having him as a foe. Yes, he was pleased; Tivonna had done well.

Breaking off his contemplations, the king turned his attention to the conversations in progress. Jasen was deep in a discussion with Sivena concerning the royal banner displayed on the wall behind their table. The crest of Aquilla was a rearing winged horse. The banner was a swirl of muted shades of color, radiating from a central point outward to the edges of the banner. The colors seemed to mirror the spectrum from the reds and yellows going through the blues, greens and violets. Surprisingly, the colors were not garish but soft, one blending into the next like a circular rainbow. Imposed on the field of colors was a rearing white winged horse. The horse's wings were fully extended and tipped with silver, his hooves were done in the same bright silver shade.

"Your Royal Standard is beautiful, a true work of art. Whoever wove it was a gifted craftsman. I have never seen such fabrics and colors as you have here, especially the metallic shades. How do you get gold and silver without metal?"

Sivena gave a bright smile. "I wish we could take all the credit, but the fact is that most of the colors and textures of our cloth are due entirely to the plant from which we gather the fibers. In truth, dyeing is an unknown art in Aquilla."

"What? I'm afraid I don't understand." Jasen gazed at the uniquely colored clothing around him. Hawk's silvery-blue was impressive but Tivonna's copper was even more spectacular. Upon closer inspection, it proved to be shot through with flashes of green. The cloth itself rivaled the finest silk; it could not have just grown that way.

Seeing his bafflement, Tivonna laughed and explained. "It's true, Jase. The thread we use to make our fabrics comes from the Mirror plant. It is one of the true wonders of Mystra. We discovered that the plant produced pods containing thousands of silk-like fibers, which could be spun into thread. The cloth is more rugged and easier to care for than silk, but just as lovely and soft. Even more amazing, we discovered that governing the type of soil in which the plant grew could control the color of the threads produced by a given plant. In truth, the fibers would mirror the minerals or organic matter in the soil. Since an earth elemental can control the soil, it proved easy to tailor the plant's growing environment to make the colors desired. The copper from flower petals with a smattering of emeralds for my dress and jade mixed with silver bark for Hawk's fabric. Our circlets are actually wood painted with pigments made from colored bark mixed with diamonds for shimmer."

"Wow!" Hawk exclaimed. "With a racket like that, you could corner the off-world clothing market. No one would be able to top you. Think of it, custom grown fabric in the finest material both rugged and beautiful."

"Get a hold of yourself, my friend. First things first, we deal with the present problem, then you can become a fashion tycoon." Jasen looked at the king and queen and shook his head. "You'll have to forgive him. He gets carried away when you mix money and shiny objects together."

Everyone broke into laughter as Hawk looked indignantly at his partner. They had grown fond of the whimsical Filidae during the past few weeks and were pleased to see someone finally get the better of the quick-witted visitor.

Arcus smiled at his two entertaining guests, "Well, I can't think of when I've enjoyed a meal as much, but speaking of present problems, I think it's time for us to retire somewhere quiet and discuss yours." Thus saying, the king rose and led the party to his private sitting room.

As the group left the Great Hall, Jasen and Tivonna walked close together. "I had a wonderful evening. Your people are very warm and charming."

Tivonna looked at Jasen and smiled. She had been pleased and amazed at his manners and decorum throughout the evening. No one would ever guess that he was not royally born. She gave a soft laugh. "I do not think Aquilla will ever be the same. Between Hawk's wit and your charm all the ladies of the kingdom will be pining away for you."

"There is only one lady in Aquilla that I am interested in. You look lovely tonight." Jasen's golden eyes seemed to smolder as he gazed at her. Tivonna's pulse raced and it suddenly became hard to breathe. The bond between them hummed to life, filling her with an unexpected warmth and tenderness. Could he finally be willing to acknowledge his feelings for her? Her question was destined to go unanswered. The moment was lost as they arrived at the king's suite.

Entering the room, they made themselves comfortable around the table located in the center of the room. This might take a while. At first, the five sat staring at each other wondering where to begin. Finally, Jasen took the initiative.

"I want to thank you again for all that you've done for us. Not everyone would have been so quick to open their home to two strangers. I owe you my life."

"No, it is I and Aquilla who owe you for saving my daughter and my kingdom." Arcus gazed fondly at his daughter. He owed this man a great deal indeed. "I know very little about why or how you came to Mystra. How can I aid you?"

"It's a long story." Collecting his thoughts, Jasen filled them in on his and Hawk's mission. "So you see it is vital that we find out how your world survived. It may be the only hope for the rest of the galaxy." Jasen concluded his recitation. "Do you know anything that might help us?"

Arcus was silent for a few moments, then answered, "I'm not sure how much help I can be. My people have been away from the stars for a very long time. Fortunately, my ancestors were scholars. They tried to preserve every scrap of knowledge they could, even though much of it could no longer be used on Mystra. Have you searched the old records?"

"Yes, I'm convinced that the Firehawks' aversion to your world has something to do with the energy fields surrounding the planet. Do you know exactly when and how they were formed?"

"Mystra has always possessed strange energy patterns. They are the reason that technology was outlawed. No machine containing metal can function on Mystra and no ship can land on the planet." Arcus looked intently at Jasen. "At least, no ship ever has until now."

"Then how were you able to land?" Hawk tried to steer the king's attention away from the subject of spaceships. He didn't want Arcus to take too strong an interest in Jasen's technology. He might decide to keep them here. "Why didn't the field destroy the colony ships as well?"

"That particular field didn't exist then. The energy distortions were only on the surface. The curtain of lights was unknown on Mystra until after the Great Cataclysm. Then, everything changed."

"Yes, what about the cataclysm? The diary we found said that a group of scientists tried an unlawful experiment that went awry. Do you know what they were trying to do and where their lab was located?" This was the information Jasen sought. If he could find the lab, he might find a clue to the energy barrier's secret.

"Rumor was that they were trying to open some kind of doorway to other worlds. They were supposed to have been located somewhere in the far North." Tivonna glanced at her father for confirmation. "I don't think anyone really knows for sure."

Arcus nodded. "She is correct. The exact location of the laboratory has been lost for centuries. The only one who might know is the Duke of Cenchrea, and I would not advise asking him."

"Any particular reason why, or are you just at odds?" Hawk asked.

"I'm afraid the only thing that interests the duke is power and machines. He is obsessed with technology and making it work on Mystra. It would not be wise for him to learn about you. He would do anything to possess your knowledge and technology…anything."

"And what about you King Arcus? What would you do to obtain such technology?"

The calm, soft-spoken words struck Arcus like a blow. He met the cool, golden eyes and sighed deeply. "I can't deny that I've been tempted. You hold a secret that could change the face of this planet. But I don't think you are the type of man who could be coerced into doing anything against his will. Frankly, I would rather have a willing partner that I can trust than a reluctant slave."

Jasen smiled and gave the king a nod in salute. "I'm glad you feel that way. I too prefer to make friends instead of enemies. There will be plenty of time to discuss technology after we have settled the matter of the Firehawks. Agreed?"

Arcus returned Jasen's smile. He had to give the young man credit; he certainly had guts. "Agreed."

"Well, now that you have settled that, what are your plans, Jasen and how can we assist you?" Sivena had listened to the ongoing discussions in silence. She liked and approved of her daughter's bondmate, but she feared the task he had undertaken. She knew that Jasen would not be swerved from his goal, and was determined to do all that she could to help assure the trio's success and safety. There was no doubt in Sivena's mind that Tivonna would accompany Jasen and Hawk on their quest.

Jasen shrugged and leaned back in his seat. "Our only choice is to go north. I believe the key to this whole mess is locked away in that secret laboratory if it still exists. We'll travel north and see what we can find out. Maybe someone we talk to will know its location. It's a long shot, but it's the best option we have at the moment."

"It will not be an easy trip. Aquilla is in the extreme south. You'll have to cross hundreds of miles and almost every type of terrain to reach the northern settlements. Not to mention having to pass through the territories of a number of the kingdom's more belligerent inhabitants. Let me see...I think I have a map here somewhere."

Arcus rose from his seat and walked over to a large chest set against the wall near the door they had entered. Opening the chest, he rummaged inside seeking a current map. As the king searched the chest, Jasen relaxed. He had been unsure how the monarchs would take his tale. He was relieved that Arcus believed him and was willing to help. He and Hawk would have had a tough time navigating the kingdom on their own. They needed the supplies and information the king could give them.

Suddenly, Jasen stiffened. Being a telepath, he was always in danger of exposure. Discovery meant death. It had become a habit of his to periodically scan his surroundings for danger. He did so almost subconsciously. Now, however, every sense was alert. His mind had swept the room and registered an unknown intruder; they were being observed.

Carefully probing the room, Jasen soon pinpointed the presence he had sensed. High up above the ceiling in the far back corner of the chamber was a spy. How long had they been observed? What had the man learned? And more importantly, was this the first time they had been spied upon?

Jasen was in a dilemma. He couldn't let the man escape. The question was, could he risk exposing himself to Arcus and Sivena? His options were limited. He could contact Hawk and send him after the man, but that would be risky. There were a number of entrances to the spy hole. The man could be gone before the Filidae reached him. Besides which, Hawk suddenly leaving the room would alert the spy to trouble, as well as arousing the others' curiosity. They could not take a chance of letting the man escape, not without learning what he had seen and heard in the castle.

There was only one thing to do. Jasen cringed at the thought. He would have to bring the man down and question him under truth lock. This could be dangerous. He was unsure of how the king and queen would react to learning about him; he and Hawk might be forced to run from the castle. And what about Tivonna? She had accepted that he was a telepath, but actually forcing his will on another was quite a different matter than just reading thoughts; she too might turn on them.

Jasen gave an inward sigh. There was no other way. Quickly, he sent a mental warning to Hawk. *"Get ready. We have an intruder. I'm going to bring him down. This could get messy."*

Hawk glanced worriedly at Jasen, and gave a slight nod. He would back any play Jasen made.

Rising from his chair, Jasen fixed his gaze on the far left corner of the ceiling.

"Come Here." Uttering the words of command, Jasen reached out with his mind and took control of the man's nervous system and will. Hidden away in the loft, Gaius jerked as if electrocuted and slowly lowered the trap door into the chamber below. Throwing down the knotted rope he used as a ladder, he carefully climbed down into the king's sitting room. Still entranced, he walked over and stood before Jasen.

"What the..." King Arcus watched dumbfounded as Jasen stood and spoke to the empty air. He was even more astonished as he watched Gaius, a kitchen servant, leave his hiding place and move to stand before Jasen.

"What's going on here?" The king walked over and confronted Gaius. "What were you doing up there? Who do you work for? Why are you spying on me?"

Gaius stood mutely staring straight ahead. He did not move, utter a sound, or acknowledge his ruler's presence in anyway.

"He can't answer you." Jasen steeled himself; things were about to get messy. "I have him in a mindlock. I can compel him to answer truthfully, but you must ask your questions slowly, one at a time."

Arcus was stunned by this strange turn of events. His mind tried to cope with what he was seeing and hearing. "What do you mean mindlock? Who...what are you?"

Tivonna stepped forward and faced her father. Lifting her head, she gazed directly into his eyes. "He is a telepath and my bondmate!"

She turned to Jasen. "Find out what he knows; we can't afford to have anyone learning about you and Hawk."

Surprised, Jasen nodded. She was actually defending him! But just how far would her trust go? What if he had to mind-wipe the spy, would she be so quick to defend him then? Jasen feared not. Ignoring the waves of fear and distrust coming from the monarchs, Jasen faced Gaius. Under his careful probing, the spy soon divulged all he had seen and heard.

"Well, what do we do now?" Hawk gazed at the people gathered around Gaius. "Anyone have any bright ideas how we get out of this one?"

Jasen shook his head. "I'm afraid the damage is done. The duke knows about us, but he doesn't know why we are here or where we are going. At least, we can keep that much a secret." Glancing over at Arcus, he continued, "Your Majesty the way I see it we have two choices. You can kill Gaius but, in doing so, you alert the duke to the fact that we are on to him. Also, there is no guarantee that he won't send another spy to take Gaius's place." Jasen hesitated. He did not want to say what he knew he must.

"And the second option?" The king had regained some of his composure, but was still wary of this strange, fearsome, young man.

"To rearrange his memories. I can make him forget what he has learned here tonight. He will also cease to spy upon you. If the duke asks, Gaius will tell him there is nothing new to report. It will buy us time."

Arcus, Sivena and even Tivonna stared at Jasen in

horror. All the childhood tales and horror stories were coming true before their very eyes. This man stole the will of others and twisted their minds and memories to suit his pleasure. What kind of a monster was he?

Jasen blocked the waves of horror, outrage, and distrust slamming into his mind; he had a job to do. He led Gaius to the table and bade him sit; no one moved to stop him. Dropping to his knees beside the still figure, Jasen reached out and placed a hand on either side of the spy's head. Fighting his own revulsion as well as that of the others in the room, Jasen steeled himself and plunged into Gaius's mind.

Contrary to popular belief, delving into another's mind was not something a telepath particularly enjoyed. All of Gaius's greed, fear, and unscrupulous desires beat against Jasen's mind during those first few moments of contact. It was like wallowing in mire.

Quieting the terrified mind around him, Jasen sought for the cord of memory he needed. Locating the thoughts in question, he slowly began to unravel the threads. When Gaius's mind had been wiped clean of all memory of this night, Jasen painstakingly began to weave a new thread of thought to replace the old. When he had finished, Gaius remembered nothing of the conversations he had overheard, but instead remembered a quiet evening at home.

Leaving the memory cords, Jasen delved deep into the subconscious. Seizing the center of will, he set a deep compulsion. Gaius would never again spy on Aquilla's rulers. Also, if questioned by his employer, he would act as if he had been spying as ordered but had nothing new to report.

Withdrawing slightly from Gaius's mind, Jasen surveyed his work. He hated this; the violation of another's mind was loathsome to him. It went against the deepest code of his race; but sometimes there was no other choice. At least this way, Gaius would live. Planting one last set of instructions, which would take Gaius from the chamber to his home, Jasen gently withdrew from the spy's mind.

Opening his eyes, Jasen stood and faced the others in the room. A second later, Gaius opened his eyes, rose and left the room to return home. He would remember nothing out of the ordinary.

The emotions in the room were electric. Arcus and Sivena fairly screamed horror and loathing. Tivonna's emotions were more controlled, but her face was pale. Only Hawk was calm though alert for any sign of danger. Jasen sighed deeply. He couldn't deal with this now. The intense emotions were threatening to overwhelm his shields. He would give them time to calm down before trying to reason with them. Meanwhile, he would prepare for the worst. The king could easily order his death or at the very least exile him from Aquilla. Without a word Jasen turned and left the room, leaving emotional chaos in his wake.

Tivonna watched Jasen exit the room in stunned silence. She could not believe what she had just witnessed. Everything she had ever heard about mind-robbers was true. She had been horrified, but then reason asserted itself over blind emotion. This was not some unknown soul-stealing monster. This was Jasen, her bondmate. She knew him and knew the self-loathing and pain this had caused him. In his concentration, he had forgotten to shield himself from her. She had felt his struggle and his resignation to do what was necessary no matter the personal cost. Tivonna loved him all the more at that moment. He had risked everything for their sake. She was determined to see that the price was not too high.

"I want that monster out of here!" King Arcus was beside himself with fear and anger.

Hawk's eyes blazed, but before he could move, Tivonna stood before her father, green eyes flashing with her wrath.

"How dare you? He is the same man now as he was ten minutes ago. Would you have rather he let the spy escape, or maybe you would rather have killed him. Do you really want his blood on your hands or to live in fear of spies? Jasen did what he had to. Don't think that it was easy for him. He hated what he had to do. Controlling another's mind is repugnant to him, it violates everything he stands for."

"Then, how could he do it? If this task was so distasteful, how could he have gone through with it?"

"How could you order your own daughter's death?"

Tivonna's soft-spoken words hit Arcus with the force of a slap jarring him to his senses. His anger died; he was acting like a fool. Jasen had done nothing to harm him or his family, yet he was treating him like some kind of demon. Tivonna was right. The telepath had done something he detested because he had had to. Nothing he had seen of Jasen led him to think that the visitor was anything less than a man of honor. What right did he have to judge him, especially based only on old wives' tales and myths? All right, so Jasen was a telepath and that was frightening. But he was also the man bonded to his daughter. Arcus had seen nothing to make him doubt Jasen's integrity. Just the opposite was true.

"I'm sorry, daughter. It was just so unexpected. You're right, I have no right to judge him." The king looked at Hawk. "I am truly sorry, Hawk. I know that you would not be friends with someone who was unworthy of your trust. I guess I let my fears rule my thinking. I can't say that I feel completely at ease having a telepath around. I will, however, try to judge him by his actions and character, not by old prejudices and fears. You are both welcome to stay in the castle and we will offer any help we can to aid you in your mission."

"Yes, I too am sorry. I know my daughter would not be bonded to a man who was unworthy of her. I guess the shock of seeing our worst fears come to life caused us to forget. How can we make amends?" Sivena echoed her husband's words. She too was ashamed of the way they had treated Jasen. She hoped Hawk could convince him of their sincerity. The telepath still made her nervous, but she knew he was not the monster she had feared.

"I'll come with you Hawk." Tivonna wanted desperately to talk to Jasen. Had he picked up her initial fear? What must he think of her? He had looked so dejected when he had left.

"No, I'd best go alone. I doubt Jasen will be in the mood for visitors just yet. I'll let you know what happens."

Thus saying, Hawk exited the room and went in search of his distraught friend. Hawk had felt some of the tension in the room. It must have been awful for the telepath. He just hoped he could talk his friend into giving the monarchs and Tivonna another chance. Jasen could be extremely stubborn when he chose. Hawk's first problem was to locate him. Where would he go? Glancing around, his gaze fell on a narrow stairway leading upwards. Of course, Jasen would want to get as far away from people as possible. Making his decision, he began the long climb to the top of the tower. Reaching the summit, Hawk walked out onto the narrow balcony encircling the top of the tower. As he had expected, there was Jasen. The telepath stood on the far end of the platform leaning against the retaining wall running along the edge of the balcony. He appeared to be lost in thought, oblivious to the majestic view spread out before him.

"Well what's the verdict, execution or exile?" Jasen spoke without turning around, keeping his back to his approaching friend.

Hawk did not need to see Jasen's face to know the pain he was going through. It was evident in his voice, which was flat and lifeless. He had feared as much. Jasen had walled himself away. He would not be won over easily. It would be hard for him to trust the nobles again.

"Oh, it's nothing like that. We are free to go or stay as we wish. The king and queen wish me to extend their apologies for their less than gracious reactions. Jase, it's not you they fear. Like everyone else in this particular universe, they have an inbred fear of telepaths. It was like seeing the boogieman come to life. They realize now that you are the same man you always were and it is unfair to judge you by their prejudices. It is not easy for them, but they are willing to try."

The raven head nodded slowly and some of the tension left Jasen's body. But he still would not turn and face Hawk. "What about Tivonna?"

The question was asked so softly, that only the Filidae's keen hearing allowed him to catch it. "What about her?"

Jasen turned and faced his friend. "Hawk, she despises me. I expected it from the others, but I thought, hoped, that she was different. I felt her fear and loathing. She thinks I'm some kind of monster. How can I be around her everyday knowing that if it wasn't for the fact that she'd die, she too would happily kill me?"

This was bad! Jasen had felt Tivonna's initial fear, but had failed to register her change of feelings and acceptance. "Jase, she doesn't hate you. She loves you. You should have seen her stand up to her parents. She made them see how foolish they were. Believe me, she cares deeply for you and this episode hasn't changed that, except to draw her even closer to you. Don't shut her out."

The look in Jasen's eyes was answer enough. "Nice try, but there's no way I'm going to believe that!"

Hawk sighed. "Look, give it time. For now, we are free and safe. The king and queen are trying to accept you for who you are instead of giving in to groundless fears, and Tivonna is firmly in your corner even though you won't believe it. Take it one step at a time. Arcus has offered us help and anything we need for our mission. Let's take advantage of his generosity and get on with the mission. OK?"

Jasen laughed and the tension drained from his body. Looking at the serious expression on Hawk's face he couldn't help but smile, it was so unlike his happy-go-lucky companion. "So when did you suddenly become wise and responsible?"

"Oh, I have my moments. But you'd better get yourself together quickly. I can't take too much of this intense seriousness. I have this wild urge to go do something outrageous."

"Then, I'd best stop giving in to my self-pity and rescue this poor world from you. Come on my friend, let's turn in. Tomorrow, we make our plans. Oh, and by the way, thanks."

"Anytime partner, anytime."

Side by side the two left the balcony and headed for their chambers.

CHAPTER EIGHT

The huge black dragon beat his mighty wings, banked sharply and glided toward the green oasis nestled at the foot of the eastern mountains. This was the Kingdom of Cenchrea, home of Duke Malycon. Spiraling downward, it headed for the castle's highest tower.

Malycon, Duke of Cenchrea, watched the dragon approach. He was thrilled as always at the sight of the giant reptile and with the knowledge that he, of all Mystra's inhabitants, could demand obedience from the mighty creatures. There was no love between the dragons and the duke. They served him because they must. It was a point of honor for them.

Dragons possessed no elementals among their kind and rarely associated with the other races on Mystra. They made their homes in caves high in the mountains to the west. Unaware of the danger, they had built their hatchery above a major fault line in the earth. Malycon used the dragon's mistake and ignorance of the outside world to his advantage. He allowed Tyr to aid the dragons and, in exchange, the dragons provided him with rapid transportation and communication across Mystra. Dragons were extremely swift. His spies' reports were in his hands hours after they were written. It was an invaluable service, which he was not about to lose.

Malycon had a dream to rule Mystra and turn her into a technological paradise. Keeping tabs on the various kingdoms and societies across the planet was important to his goal of ultimate rule. It was an advantage few knew he possessed. So far he had been able to keep the truth from the dragons. The Elemental High Council was pledged to provide assistance to any community in need of an elemental's help. They evaluated the needs of a community and dispatched an elemental with the appropriate powers to rectify the problem. Fortunately for Malycon, the council cared little for the politics of the ungifted. They existed to train and monitor elementals, nothing more. Since an elemental rarely left their assigned sector, the council depended on reports from their agents to keep tabs on the land and to assign assistance when needed. This isolation among the elementals played nicely into his plans.

He had purposefully kept the knowledge of the council's existence and purpose from the dragons. All message drops took place at night in remote areas where encounters with other lifeforms would be limited. A careful planting of stories and rumors led the dragons to believe that they were hated and feared by the other citizens of Mystra. They had no choice but to form an alliance with him. Without Tyr's help, their eggs would be destroyed. To survive, they must serve him, but it was an uneasy partnership. The dragons would serve him until he made a mistake, then they would destroy him. The duke gave a sardonic smile. Fortunately, he did not make mistakes.

The king dragon came to rest on the edge of the balcony wall and primly folded his immense leathery wings. Fixing Malycon with one enormous eye, he nodded his head. "Greetings human. What is it you wish of me?" The dragon's voice was gravelly and rumbled up from deep in his broad chest.

"I have need of your help, Lord Dragon. My spies have located a visitor to the Kingdom of Aquilla…a very talented and intriguing visitor; but my spies seem to have lost him. I want him; find him and bring him to me."

"That is not part of our agreement. I provide you with dragonlings to transport your men and messages. I did not agree to kidnap unsuspecting beings for your amusement. I have little interest in the affairs of humans. What is in it for me?"

Malycon fumed. The wily lizard never did anything for free, and bullying and force were out of the question. It was going to cost him a great deal to secure the dragon's aid, but if the creature delivered, it would be worth it. "Very well. Bring me the human known as Jasen and your debt to me is paid in full. Tyr will still be available to assist you whenever she is needed, but you need serve me no longer."

The dragon studied Malycon with interest. This human must be valuable indeed for the duke to make such an offer. Oh well, that was no concern of his. He had little patience for the antics of humans. This was a chance for his people to be free. "Very well. Describe this human and how I will find him. I will bring him to you."

"He is tall with black hair and eyes of gold. He will be traveling with two companions. One is unique; a man with long white hair and silvery-blue eyes slit like a cat's. His movements are graceful and swift. He is unlike any being you have ever seen. Beware, the white haired stranger is a shapeshifter. The other companion is a woman with auburn hair and green eyes. She possesses the elemental's mark on her right arm, four colored. Also be wary of her."

"And what of the companions? Do you wish them as well?"

"They are of no importance, just bring me the dark haired stranger."

"I will send out searchers immediately. Your quarry will not elude us for long. I will bring you the human then our alliance is ended." With that, the dragon unfurled his wings and took flight. Soon he was a distant speck in the sky.

Malycon turned and left the balcony heading for his private sanctum. He hated losing the services of the dragons, but somethings couldn't be helped. If what he knew of the stranger was true, it would be worth the price. Entering his private chamber, he secured the door and seated himself at the desk in the far corner of the room. Picking up the letter lying on the desk, he read it through again for the hundredth time. Gaius was one of his most valuable and trustworthy spies. If what he reported was true, his dreams were about to become reality. A technology that worked on Mystra!

The duke threw the letter down in disgust. Rising from his desk, he began to pace nervously around the room. Gaius had sent that letter weeks ago...since then nothing. Oh, he continued to make his scheduled reports; but so far he had not been able to uncover anything new about the strangers. Could they have caught on to him? The king was trusting and unimaginative. He would never suspect that Malycon had been spying on him in his own castle. Could the strangers somehow have uncovered the truth? It made no difference. Gaius was reliable and he trusted his initial report. The dragons would find the visitors, and then he would get his answers.

Malycon stopped pacing and gazed about the room. It was his personal laboratory. Here, he concocted drugs and potions, which assured him the loyalty and obedience of his people. His troops were the best and fiercest on Mystra. They knew no fear and would obey to the death. Soon, he would rule Mystra as he ruled Cenchrea. In the very near future, this laboratory would turn out machines which would make him ruler of the world. Yes, his bargain with the dragons had been worth it. In time, he would again control the proud, independent creatures, as well as the fiery, beautiful daughter of King Arcus. She would regret spurning his love. He would have made her Queen of Mystra; now he would make her his slave.

Smiling to himself and humming a tune, the duke left the room to continue his duties. Yes, it wouldn't be long now. His dream was about to be fulfilled. A new Mystra was dawning, a Mystra where he ruled and others obeyed. He could hardly wait. As Malycon gloated, dozens of dragons took to the skies. The hunt was on.

Turning in her saddle, Tivonna gazed one final time at the walls of Castle Aquilla. Swallowing the lump that had suddenly appeared in her throat, she turned back around. That was the past. Searching the trail before her, she fixed her eyes on Jasen. He was her future now; where he went, she would follow.

Thoughts of Jasen brought with them a new source of pain. Things were different between them now. Oh, he was polite, even friendly, but the camaraderie, the closeness they had shared, was gone. Even the bond was closed to her. No trace of his feelings reached her. It was as if he had erected an impenetrable wall around his heart, shutting her out.

"Hey Red! Snap out of it. This is an adventure not a funeral march." The Filidae's words snapped her out of her reverie. She had not heard him ride up beside her.

"Red? My name is Tivonna." Tivonna entered good-naturedly into Hawk's teasing. He had become a good and trusted friend. She had a great need for friends just now.

"And a right pretty name it is too; but a bit long for adventuring. Why, by the time I yell, 'Tivonna, look out!' a whole mountain range could fall on your head. Much better to just say, 'Red, duck!'"

Tivonna could keep a straight face no longer. Clutching

her sides, she burst out laughing. "Oh, Hawk! What am I going to do with you? Don't you take anything seriously?"

"Between you and Jasen, there's more than enough seriousness in this group, thank you. Besides, can I help it if I'm charming and witty?"

"And modest."

"That too. It's good to see you smile. You've been awfully gloomy lately."

"I know. I'm sorry. It's just that I have not had much to smile about."

"You regret leaving home?"

"No, I will miss my parents, but you and Jasen are my family now."

"So, it's Jasen then."

Tivonna sighed and nodded, "I just can't seem to reach him anymore Hawk. For a while, I really thought we were becoming close; that I was getting through to him. Now..." Tivonna shrugged. "I don't know what to do."

Hawk reached out and patted her shoulder. "I know it's tough, but don't give up. Even Jasen can't fight nature forever. He was hurt, Red. You did get through more than any woman ever has. You touched a part of him he never knew existed and feared never could. He started to hope, then that hope was snatched away. Oh, I know." Hawk held up a hand to forestall Tivonna's angry denial. "I know you don't hate or despise him. But, Jasen believes you do. You have to prove him wrong, and believe me it won't be easy. He has all his defenses raised against you. You're just going to have to get out your hammer and chisel and start whacking at that wall of his. It's going to take time and effort. Are you game?"

Tivonna's eyes were shining. "So you think that deep down he still loves me? He's just afraid of rejection?"

"Count on it."

"Then sir, just watch me whack away. Whenever he turns around, I'm going to be there, loving him, and nothing is going to shake me this time."

"Good girl, Red, and if you need any help, I'll be happy to sit on him while you pound away."

"Hawk, you're a rogue."

The Filidae flashed her his radiant smile, which had broken hearts across the galaxy. "Yes, but I'm a lovable rogue." Suddenly turning serious, he looked her straight in the eyes. "Remember, Red, I'm on your side. If you need me, I'll be there. Jasen needs you as much as you need him, only he just doesn't realize it yet. Jase is my dearest friend, my brother, but it wasn't always so. It wasn't easy for me to gain his trust. He's hard to win over, but believe me, he's well worth the fight."

"I'll remember and thanks."

With a cheery wave, Hawk spurred his steed forward to catch up with Jasen. Watching the two riding side by side, Tivonna felt a pang of jealousy at their easy, relaxed relationship. She quickly squelched the unkind thought. Jasen trusted Hawk. One day, she vowed, he would trust her as well and she would never again violate that trust.

Tivonna lifted her auburn head. So, it was a fight then. Well, she was her father's daughter. She could wage war with the best of them. Let Jasen beware; he was hers and she would never surrender him to another, not even himself. Her mind made up, Tivonna galloped forward to join the other two. She might as well start now.

Watching the girl riding beside him, Jasen could hardly believe his eyes. She appeared completely relaxed. She laughed and joked with Hawk, and even dragged him, in spite of his intentions otherwise, into her and the Filidae's antics. It was almost as if the night in King Arcus's chamber had never occurred. She did not shy away or try to avoid his gaze. If he had not known otherwise, Jasen would have thought that she trusted him completely. Only he knew the truth. He had felt her terror, her horror, at what he had done and had seen the loathing in her eyes. No, he must not forget that. It would be all too easy to allow himself to care for this lovely, spirited creature. That would be a fatal mistake. He would have to be very careful not to let himself be swayed. She was open and friendly now, but he had to keep his guard up. When she remembered what he was, the loathing would return. Jasen knew he could not face that rejection a second time. It was better not to risk being hurt than to experience such pain again.

Hawk watched Tivonna as she began the process of piercing Jasen's armor and smiled. He had to give the girl credit; she was a trooper. Good, she would need all her strength for the task ahead. Poor Jasen, he needed Tivonna, but was too blind to see it. Love was blocked by pain and fear. Whether or not Tivonna's love could pierce Jasen's protective wall, Hawk didn't know, but he would do everything in his power to help. Maybe the two could use some time alone together. When they stopped to make camp, he would try to find some way to leave the two alone for a while. Nature would have to do the rest.

As they rode through the fields and dells which lay between the castle and the forest, Jasen could not help but notice how happy the people were and how much they loved their princess. Aquilla was indeed a prosperous kingdom. The forest was a good half day's journey from the castle. Night was just beginning to fall when the trio arrived at the edge of the Painted Forest. Deciding to wait for daylight before penetrating the dense woods, the three set up camp for the night. The first rays of dawn found them preparing to enter the forest. Once inside the woods, they quickly located the winding trail which would lead them to the northern most border of the Painted Forest and the territories beyond.

The three rode along in companionable silence, gazing in awed appreciation at the wondrous beauty of nature surrounding them. Mystra was indeed a lovely world. Jasen remembered little about being in the forest before. He was amazed at the variety and combinations of colors displayed by the enormous trees. It was the most breathtaking ride he had ever taken. Every bend in the trail uncovered a new and previously unseen wonder to amaze and delight the eye.

Riding in this fairy tale forest, some of his stress began to ease. Ever since uncovering and dealing with the spy, he had lived under a subtle but draining tension. True to Hawk's words, the king and queen had done everything they could to assist them in preparing for their journey. They had provided mounts, supplies, and native clothing for the two off-worlders. The monarchs had been gracious and hospitable to them in every way. They had even gone so far as to provide money for the journey. Yet, underneath their polite exterior, Jasen sensed wariness. He made the rulers uncomfortable. They were unsure of how to treat him and were cautious not to offend him. Jasen appreciated their efforts. They were trying hard not to let their fears rule them, but deep down he still made them nervous.

It was a relief to finally be away from people. Jasen had not been aware of the tension he had been under until it lifted. He suddenly felt light and carefree. The cool, crisp air was invigorating. It was as if he had been liberated from a heavy burden. Unconsciously, he began to hum a merry tune. A moment later Hawk joined him and the two began to amuse Tivonna with a series of lively songs from a hundred worlds. Soon, Tivonna began to pick up the words to some of the simpler ballads and joined in the fun. The three rode along the brightly colored trail singing and laughing in the brisk morning air. The easy camaraderie continued throughout the coming days as the trio made their way through the Painted Forest.

On the first day of their second week of journeying, the trio came upon a small clearing. Nearby a bright, bubbly stream flowed serenely through the trees. The water cascaded over a small waterfall and formed a still quiet pool before trickling over a large sunken tree and continuing on its way.

Jasen called a halt. "It's getting late. This looks like a good place to make camp."

Dismounting, the three began to set up camp. In no time, they had a cheery fire going and sleeping mats arranged around it. Hawk looked up from straightening the last blanket on his bedroll and glanced toward the stream. "Say, I wonder how cold that water is. I'd love a swim. How about it?"

Tivonna turned from the fire where she was preparing the evening meal. She had grown tired of bland trail rations and had gathered roots and herbs along the trail. Tonight, she had volunteered to make something special for their evening meal. "I'd love a swim. If the stream is too cold, I can always heat it. Why don't you and Jasen go check the water, while I finish up here? I'll put the stew where it will stay warm and join you shortly."

Jasen finished tending to the mounts and joined the others at the fire. Grabbing their cloaks, the two men made their way to the nearby brook. Reaching the stream, Hawk pulled off his boots and stuck one toe into the pool. He quickly drew it out with a startled yelp. "Yow! That's freezing. We definitely wait for Tivonna."

Suddenly, Jasen and Hawk stiffened and gasped. In the center of the pool, a long flume of water began to rise from the still surface of the basin. The two men watched in amazement, which quickly turned to alarm and outrage, as the watery column bent toward them and dumped a stream of freezing water on their unsuspecting heads.

Shivering and half drowned, they turned to find a giggling Tivonna standing behind them. Tivonna tried to control her laughter; but seeing them standing there like two drowned rats, she couldn't help herself. "You should see the looks on your faces."

Between chattering teeth, Hawk growled at the gleeful elemental. "You wouldn't think it so funny if it had happened to you. I'm freezing!"

Jasen stared silently at Tivonna, a small smile curving the corner of his mouth. Tivonna had a brief instant to register alarm as an invisible force suddenly seized her and, her arms pinned tightly to her sides, swept her off her feet. In a flash, she found herself hanging two feet above the freezing pool unable to move or summon her powers.

"Well, what do you think we should do with our merry little prankster? Maybe a taste of her own medicine?" At Jasen's words, Tivonna plunged toward the water then halted only inches before hitting."

"No way, I think she owes us a drying out and a nice warm swim. After all, people who play practical jokes and then allow themselves to get caught deserve a stiff fine."

Hawk and Jasen were both grinning at her now. They were not really mad. They were treating her as one of them. Here was another chance for her to show Jasen that she trusted him and did not fear him. She had no doubt that it was his power, which held her so securely. He had momentarily forgotten to hide his gifts from her, and was reacting naturally by turning her joke back on her.

"I see I still have a great deal to learn about practical jokes. If you two are quite finished, I think it's time to get on with our swim or we will miss the chance. If you would like to swim in warm water instead of ice, I suggest you let me down and I will think about it."

Jasen's smile grew wider. He gently drew her toward shore, and set her down on the bank beside them. "Apology accepted. Now about that swim?"

True to her promise, Tivonna heated the pool, turning it into a luxuriating spa. Diving in clothes and all, the three frolicked and swam in the relaxing waters. Finally, much cleaner and refreshed, the three left the pool, hunger winning out over fun. With a wave of her hand, Tivonna drew the water from their hair and clothing leaving them completely dry.

"Say, you're pretty handy to have around. Now how's your cooking? I'm starved!"

Jasen shook his head and glanced at his friend. "Her cooking can't be worse than yours." Turning to Tivonna, he extended his arm. "May I escort you to camp, my lady? I'm looking forward to sampling your excellent cuisine."

Taking Jasen's arm, Tivonna joined in his light mood. "I would be honored, sir. But what about your companion?"

"Let him get his own date."

Arm in arm, Jasen and Tivonna walked back to camp leaving Hawk to follow. "It's not fair, you always get the girl." Watching the couple before him, Hawk smiled. This was more like the old Jasen he knew and loved, and Tivonna was fitting in nicely. Her reaction tonight was perfect. Jasen had treated her like a friend, and she had responded to his teasing with a brand of humor all her own. Yes, it was turning out to be a lovely night.

Jasen banked up the campfire and glanced over at the two sleeping figures rolled up in blankets nearby. He couldn't remember when he had enjoyed a more relaxing evening. Tivonna had turned out to be a pretty fair cook, and they had enjoyed a sumptuous meal. Hawk and Tivonna had decided to turn in early; but Jasen found it hard to sleep.

He felt so light and carefree. The last time he had been this relaxed was when he had visited Hawk's world. The two had hiked deep into the lush forest of the Filidae home world far away from civilization. It had been one of the best weeks of his life. Far from the thoughts of others, he had been able to let down his guard. This night had been much like then.

Jasen was amazed that he felt this easy with Tivonna.

He wasn't really sure when he had stopped regarding her as an enemy. She now seemed a natural part of the group. He ached to take her in his arms and declare his love for her, but he still couldn't bring himself to believe that they could have a life together. A life of fear and secrecy was not something he wished for the beautiful elemental.

Looking upward, Jasen studied the night sky. It was unlike anything he had ever seen. Flashes of bright colors shot through the inky black expanse. Stars glimmered faintly in the blackness beyond Mystra's skies as if shrouded from view by a silvery mist. Mystra was a world of surprises and she hid her secrets well. Glancing over at Tivonna, Jasen sighed. Some surprises were more unexpected than others.

Studying the sleeping girl, Jasen felt a stab of tenderness for this amazing person. Lying there with the fire sending highlights of gold and red through her auburn hair, it was hard to believe that this lovely woman could literally level mountains, or that she would choose to love him and share his life of danger and exile. Jasen shook his head in resignation. His life always seemed to be out of his control. Why should he be surprised that fate had thrown him another curve? Jasen looked over at Hawk. He remembered another who had decided to love him in spite of himself.

Jasen sighed. Tivonna was turning out to be full of surprises. Over the past few days, she had slowly chipped away at his belief that she hated and feared him. She took every opportunity to prove otherwise, like tonight. He still couldn't believe that he had pulled such a stunt, or that she had responded favorably. It had never even occurred to him that she might fear his powers. He had just responded naturally to her teasing. The elemental had demonstrated her love for him in a thousand ways during their time together. The mental link they shared had grown stronger, as well revealing the truth of her feelings for him. So why was he so afraid to admit that he loved her too? He still couldn't make himself believe that she wouldn't vanish one day as all the others had in the past. He knew he was being unreasonable and that Tivonna accepted him as Hawk did, but he still felt it would be unfair to tie her down to him. She would have to give up her whole world to face a universe that would only be too glad to kill them given half a chance. She was better off on Mystra, no matter how much he wished otherwise. They would find a way around this kiosan business. Then, she would be free to live the life to which she was born. She deserved better than to be exiled on a strange world with a man hunted and loathed by the rest of the galaxy. Jasen gave up trying to sort out his conflicting emotions. Rising from his seat beside the fire, he stretched and headed for his own blankets. Tomorrow would be another demanding day. If he didn't get some sleep he wouldn't be any good to anyone. A few moments later he was fast asleep.

Jasen came awake to the sounds of birds and animals moving cheerfully through the forest around him. Turning his head, he saw a smiling Tivonna coming toward him bearing a steaming cup of fresh brewed coffee. "Good morning. I thought you might need this."

"Thanks." Bracing himself on one elbow, Jasen accepted the cup. Taking a careful sip of the hot liquid, he gazed around the clearing. The animals were all loaded and, except for his blankets and the cooking gear, everything was ready to go. Hawk and Tivonna had been busy. The Filidae was nowhere in sight. "I see you and Hawk have everything under control. By the way, where is Hawk?"

Tivonna shrugged. "He said something about stretching his wings and seeing what lay ahead. He turned into a bird and flew down the trail."

"What!" Jasen sat up in alarm. "You let him go off alone!"

"I did not let him do anything. Relax, there is no danger in the forest."

"You don't know Hawk. If there is a way to get into trouble, he'll find it. He attracts disaster."

Seeing Tivonna's worried expression Jasen relented. "Don't worry. It's not your fault. Hawk can be impulsive sometimes. You're probably right anyway. He should be safe enough within the forest. I'll just check on him to be sure."

Closing his eyes, Jasen formed a mental image of the white hawk and sent his mind outward along the trail it had taken. After a few moments, his mental probe encountered his friend's thoughts.

"And just what do you think you're doing?"

Hawk jerked as Jasen's thoughts flowed into his mind, then sighed. He had thought to give Jasen and Tivonna some time alone together, but it seemed his plan had backfired. He should have known Jasen would be concerned that he had gone off alone in strange territory.

"Oh, just having a look around. Getting some fresh air and exercise."

Jasen's mental chuckle sounded in Hawk's mind. *"Yeah, you really need the exercise and the forest air is real stuffy."* He had no illusions as to what his friend was up to. *"You make a lousy Cupid. Well, as long as you're out there, what's the terrain like?"*

"Why not have a look for yourself?"

At Hawk's invitation, Jasen linked his eyes to those of the hawk. There was a moment of vertigo as he adjusted to the new perspective, then his sight cleared. He had forgotten what it felt like to fly. In their youth, he and Hawk had often practiced this maneuver. By linking with the Filidae while he was in animal form, Jasen had experienced what it was like to be many types of creatures. But of all the experiences, flying had been his favorite. Using the bird's keen eyesight, he scanned the ground below.

Hawk's flight had taken him out of the Painted Forest and over a vast grassy plain.

"How near is the plain?"

"Very near. We camped just inside the edge of the forest."

"Any sign of life or water?"

Before Hawk could answer, a lance of pain shot through his right side where the wing joined the body. With a cry of anguish, the hawk plummeted to the ground to lay stunned and unmoving. As awareness faded from his mind, he seemed to hear the roar of distant hooves, then blackness took him.

Back in camp, Jasen slowly became aware of someone speaking to him. Swimming up through the blanket of fog, which seemed to be wrapped around his mind, he stirred and opened his eyes. Tivonna was shaking him by the shoulders and calling his name. It was her voice he had heard.

"Jasen?" Seeing sanity return to his eyes, Tivonna released him and sat back down beside him. "What happened? You were quiet, then you screamed. After that, I couldn't wake you. I was so worried."

Shakily, Jasen lifted a hand to his aching head. He had been talking to Hawk, then pain. "Something happened to Hawk! We have to get to him!"

Jasen quickly climbed to his feet then swayed as a wave of dizziness swept over him.

"Easy, you cannot help Hawk until you help yourself." Tivonna reached out and steadied the reeling telepath. "Where is he?"

Recovering, Jasen filled Tivonna in on what had happened. "He is somewhere on the plain north of here. I don't know what struck him or how badly he's hurt. The sudden pain severed the link."

Climbing aboard Midnight, Tivonna looked at Jasen, a

worried expression marring her face. "I have an idea what could have happened, and it's not good. We have to hurry."

Turning Midnight onto the trail, Tivonna sped toward the plain with Jasen close behind her. As they broke from the cover of the trees, Jasen began receiving faint thoughts from Hawk. Using them as a beacon, he guided them to the wounded Filidae. After what seemed an eternity, they spotted the white hawk lying on the ground with an arrow sprouting from its right side. They weren't the only ones to spot the downed bird. In the distance, a group of large creatures were bearing down on the wounded hawk. Spurring his mount forward, Jasen reached Hawk and dismounted just as the first of the creatures arrived on the scene. Placing himself between the wounded bird and the newcomers, Jasen studied the apparition before him.

The being was huge. From the waist down, it resembled a large roan colored stallion but above the waist the creature resembled a human man. The skin was tanned a light golden brown by the sun, and his hair was the color of sun-ripened wheat. Bright blue eyes looked out from a handsome face. The face and torso of an Adonis on an equine body…Jasen had heard of such creatures in myth and legends. The creature before him was a Centaur, and if everything legend claimed was true they could be deadly. As he studied the Centaur, Jasen gently probed his mind. It was as he feared; the being before him was quick tempered, rowdy and violent. He would not easily give up something he considered his, but he was also a being of honor. He would not break his word once given. The Centaur had one weakness; he was vain. He was the greatest marksman in his clan and took great pride in his skill. Jasen could use that pride against him.

"Ho, human. I am Chauras, master warrior and hunter. You stand between me and what is mine. Be gone or face the consequences."

"I salute you Chauras, mighty hunter, but you are mistaken. What you claim as yours is rightfully mine."

"What; a petty human would dispute with me? I will crush you like the insect you are!" The Centaur moved forward, only to be stopped as a huge lightning bolt struck the earth between his two front hooves. All eyes turned to Tivonna. She stood behind and to the right of Jasen. The Centaurs had been concentrating so hard on Jasen, they had not seen her approach. They certainly noticed her now.

"I am Tivonna. He is my kiosan. Touch him and you die."

Seeing her standing there, power leaping and crackling between her outstretched palms, no one doubted that she was capable of carrying out her threat. Chauras studied the two humans. No one with any sense would harm an elemental's kiosan. Especially an elemental as powerful as this one appeared to be. Yet, he could not let the man have his prize. He would lose face before the tribe.

Following the Centaur's thoughts, Jasen offered him a way out.

"Chauras, no one needs to get hurt. The hawk you felled is not an ordinary bird. He is a shapeshifter and our friend."

"So? What I bring down is mine. Either food for the pot or a slave for the clan, it makes no difference."

Jasen scanned the being's mind. Chauras was implacable. His code of honor would not let him give up the bird. Surrendering his catch to a weaker foe would discredit him before the others. Time was running out. Hawk's thoughts had faded to a faint whisper. If something weren't done soon, they would lose him. He had one chance.

Quickly Jasen sent a message to Tivonna. *"I have a plan but it's a long shot. Stand by and be ready to back my play."*

Tivonna stiffened slightly as Jasen's words formed in her mind. She slowly moved to stand beside Hawk and faced the Centaurs. Glancing at Jasen, she gave a faint nod. She was ready for whatever came.

Jasen looked at Chauras. "Well, I have no desire to see Tivonna destroy all of you, so I'll tell you what. We'll have a contest. Whoever can hit the farthest target wins the bird. What do you say, think you can outshoot me?"

The Centaurs pranced and howled with laughter. Outshoot a human?

Following Jasen's lead, Tivonna cut through the Centaurs' merriment. "Perhaps the mighty Chauras is afraid to shoot against a mere human."

Chauras's laughter died at the words. Sobering, he turned to Jasen. "Come, little man and I will show you what archery is all about; then I will claim my prize and the two of you as well."

Quickly, the Centaurs produced a bow for Jasen and fashioned a target from hide. The bow was strong and it took all of his strength, plus a little applied telekinesis, to string it. The Centaurs murmured when they saw the strung bow. It belonged to one of their strongest. Few hunters in the tribe could pull it. Chauras stepped forward and positioned himself on the firing line. "We will shoot for both distance and accuracy."

As Chauras readied to shoot, Jasen studied his opponent. The Centaur's upper body was well muscled and his bow seemed to be even heavier than the one he had been given. In a fair contest, Jasen knew he would stand little chance of beating the Centaur. But, then, who said he was going to shoot fair? Jasen glanced over at Tivonna. She stood tensely watching the two young warriors position the make-shift target in the proper spot. Jasen had to admire her; she had handled herself beautifully. She had no idea what he was up to, but had backed him unquestioningly.

Jasen's thoughts were interrupted as the two young warriors galloped back to join the others. They had finished securing the target some 200 yards away, and the contest was about to begin. Sighting carefully, Chauras pulled back the bowstring to full extension and let fly. The arrow left the string with a loud twang and flew unerringly to the target. Bull's-eye. The Centaurs cheered. The smiling Chauras turned to Jasen. "Ready to admit defeat little man?"

Returning the smile, Jasen took his place on the firing line. Reaching out with his mind, he grasped the bow and arrow firmly with his power. Probing the target and flight path of the arrow, he calculated the force and angle he would need to equal Chauras's shot. Using his telekinetic abilities, Jasen bent the huge bow and shot. The arrow streaked from the bow and flew as if by magic to bury itself in the target next to Chauras's shaft. The two arrows were so close the fletching on their shafts interlocked. The Centaurs stared at him in stunned silence. Then, everyone started talking at once. It was impossible. No human could shoot so well.

Chauras was livid; no puny human could equal him! He ordered the target moved back and again shot. Once more Jasen matched his shot. Three, four times Chauras had the target moved and each time Jasen echoed his shot. Finally, in desperation Chauras ordered the target moved back to 1000 yards. There was a murmur among the Centaurs that such a shot was unheard of. Chauras readied himself, shot and missed the arrow, falling just short of the target.

Silently all eyes fixed upon Jasen as he prepared to shoot. This was the moment of truth. If he could make this shot, he would win and Chauras would be honor bound to hand Hawk over to him. With a silent prayer Jasen shot. Aided and controlled by the power of Jasen's mind, the arrow flew swift and sure to bury itself deep in the center of the target. Jasen turned to face Chauras. "I believe the bird is mine."

Tivonna tensed. This was it. Either Chauras would

honor his word and give them Hawk or he would attack. She was ready to back Jasen either way.

Chauras stood staring at the puny human who had bested him. The emotions mirrored on his face ran the gamut from anger and humiliation through fear to humor. Jasen waited to see which emotion would win. Finally, Chauras threw back his head and laughed. "You win human. I don't know how you bested me, but I honor my word. The bird is yours; none of my people will bother you."

Jasen dipped his head in salute. "You are as wise as you are mighty, great Chauras. I thank you." Turning, he handed the bow to a young warrior standing next to him. "Please return this to its rightful owner with my compliments. It is an exceptional weapon."

Leaving the still stunned Centaurs, Jasen made his way to where a nervous Tivonna stood guard over the injured hawk. Giving Tivonna a reassuring smile, Jasen dropped to his knees beside his friend. Cradling the wounded bird with both hands, Jasen carefully probed for any sign of life. The hawk stilled lived, but not for long. The arrow had penetrated deep into the bird's small body causing severe damage. Unless Hawk returned to his own form, he would die. Shock and pain had shaken the Filidae's hold on the bird spirit within the form he wore. He was unable to regain mastery of the body he now inhabited and change. Jasen would have to help him reestablish control and shift shapes before it was too late.

Looking up at the worried elemental, Jasen explained the problem. "Hawk's trapped in this form. I have to go in and try to help him change. Keep an eye on our new friends for me. Once I make the mind-link, you probably won't be able to reach me. If there's trouble, do what you think best."

Tivonna gave a nervous nod and looked over to where the Centaurs stood watching them. She did not like having both Jasen and Hawk helpless, but there was little choice. There was no way to judge how Chauras would react to Jasen's work. Right now, the telepath needed her support, not more worries. It would take all of his concentration to help Hawk. She would guard them both. If the Centaurs decided to make trouble, well, she could handle that as well. She gave Jasen a reassuring smile. "You take care of Hawk. Leave our new friends to me."

Returning her smile, Jasen prepared himself for the task ahead. Trusting Tivonna to handle any trouble, he cleared his mind of all distractions. Gathering his strength, he reached out and joined with the bird's mind.

Immediately, he was assailed with fear, panic and waves of pain. It was worse than he had thought. The animal spirit of the bird form reigned supreme. There was no sign of Hawk's presence. Calming the frightened mind around him, Jasen began searching for any sign of his companion. Reaching out with all his senses and power, he called to his friend's spirit. Finally, after what seemed like hours, he detected a faint pulse of awareness. Locking onto the faint trace, he followed it to its source. Pushed far back into the bird's mind was Hawk. He was lying huddled on the ground. His mental image pulsed from Filidae to bird form. He was trying to regain control of his shape, but the bird's terrified primitive instincts were too strong for him to control in his wounded state.

Grasping the struggling mind, Jasen supported it with his own. Adding his strength to Hawk's, Jasen fought to subdue the wild spirit running amok through his friend's mind. Finally, the mental image of Hawk stabilized and grew clearer and the Filidae form gained dominance.

"Jasen? Is that you?" Hawk's thoughts, weak but clear, flowed through Jasen's mind.

"I'm here. Everything is fine. Hawk, you must change forms. You must resume your natural shape now."

"Can't. Can't focus."

Jasen had been afraid of this. The shock and the fall had left Hawk too stunned to concentrate clearly. He probably had a concussion as well. *"It's OK. I'll help you."*

Deepening the mind-link, Jasen integrated himself fully into his friend's mind. He had to make this fast or risk being permanently bound in Hawk's mind. Sensing the mind and body around him, Jasen located the proper commands and thought patterns to trigger a transformation. Fixing Hawk's Filidae form clearly in his mind's eye, he triggered the proper responses.

The mental landscape around him tilted and blurred then steadied. There was a subtle difference to the mind around him. The terror and panic were gone, now only the pain and a great weariness remained. They had done it. The bird essence was gone; only the Filidae remained. Feeding Hawk his strength, Jasen slowed the flow of blood from the arrow wound in his right shoulder. Soothing the frayed and stressed nervous system, he attempted to lessen the shock gripping mind and body. Finally, he sent his friend into a deep, healing sleep. Surveying his handiwork, Jasen sighed. Hawk was stable for now; it was time to go. He was profoundly weary. The battle for the Filidae's mind and life had taken more energy than he could spare. He had to get back to Tivonna. There was no telling how the Centaurs had taken this episode. Separating his mind from Hawk's, he severed the mind-link.

Opening his eyes, Jasen gazed at his friend sleeping peacefully in his arms and smiled up at the worried Tivonna. "He's going to be all right."

"But are you?" Tivonna frowned at the sound of Jasen's voice; it was dangerously weak. Seeing the puzzled, dazed expression in his eyes at her words, Tivonna sighed and turned to Chauras. "He's exhausted. We'd better get them both to bed. Is the tent ready?"

"Aye, will he let us aid him?" Chauras studied the telepath intently. He was everything Tivonna had claimed and more.

Tivonna saw the awed expression on the Centaur's face and laughed. "He's so far gone he probably will not even notice." Turning, she motioned to a young warrior standing nearby, then turned back to Jasen. "Jasen, you must let us have Hawk now. We must treat his wound; give him to me." At her signal, the warrior carefully lifted the sleeping Filidae from Jasen's arms.

Jasen watched bemusedly as Hawk was carried away. He was so tired. What was he supposed to do now? He couldn't seem to remember. Suddenly, the choice was taken from him as Chauras swept him up in his powerful arms. Chuckling, the huge Centaur carried him as he would a child toward the large tent set up nearby on the plain. "Sleep now my friend; all is well. There will be time for explanations later." Nestled securely in the Centaur's strong arms, his head resting against the broad chest, Jasen's exhausted mind and body finally won out and he drifted off into a deep healing sleep.

CHAPTER NINE

Slowly, Jasen made the transition from sleep to wakefulness. Blinking open his eyes, he gazed in surprise at his strange surroundings. He was in a huge tent lying on a grass mat padded with furs and hand woven blankets; more of the brightly colored blankets covered him. His body felt sluggish as if he had slept a long time. Jasen frowned. How had he come to this place and, more importantly, just where was he? He vividly remembered encountering the Centaurs and the battle for Hawk's life. Everything else was cloudy. He had a vague recollection of being carried by Chauras and had the Centaur called him friend? He wasn't quite sure what was truth and what was dream.

Glancing around the room he spotted Hawk. His friend, still asleep, was lying on a bed similar to his on the far side of the tent. A white bandage was wrapped around Hawk's head and more strips of white cloth securely bound his right shoulder and chest. It looked as if someone had rendered medical assistance to the wounded shapeshifter.

Jasen's thoughts were interrupted by the sound of hooves outside. The tent flap was pulled aside and Chauras entered, carrying a large coffee pot and a stone mug. He smiled when he saw that Jasen was awake. The large Centaur walked over and knelt beside the bed.

"Good morning, or rather good afternoon. How do you feel?" Pouring a cup full of coffee Chauras set the pot aside and offered the cup to Jasen. "Here, your lady said that you are partial to this brew. I believe you call it coffee. She said you do not fully awaken without it."

"Yes, thank you." Pushing himself into a sitting position Jasen accepted the cup. Taking a sip, he studied the Centaur. He could detect nothing false about the creature. His sudden friendliness was not an act. Jasen was puzzled. What could have happened to so change the Centaur's attitude toward him?

Chauras watched the stranger with amusement. Jasen was clearly confused by his change of attitude, and could find no plausible reason. It amused the Centaur to be one up on the extraordinary man before him. Chauras's amusement changed to concern as he remembered his discussion with Tivonna. From all that the elemental had told him of Jasen, he could well understand the telepath's misgivings. He had taken a big risk to save his friend. He had expected Chauras and the other Centaurs to react with fear and loathing. Their sudden friendship must be hard for the man to understand. Chauras was amazed that sentient beings could so mistreat one of the Wise Ones. Well, he would suffer no such indignation here.

Jasen finished his coffee and placed the cup on the ground beside the bed. Fixing the Centaur with calm golden eyes, he asked the question upper most in his mind. "Why?"

Chauras met his gaze. He understood exactly what Jasen was asking. "Because, you are one of the Wise Ones."

"I don't understand. Who are the Wise Ones, and what makes you think that I am one of them?"

"I had better start at the beginning." Chauras made

himself comfortable. This could take a while. "When you first came here, I saw you as just another human; an extraordinary one, true, but still just a human. When you went to care for your friend, I watched you."

Jasen stiffened. "And what did you see?"

Chauras smiled. "I saw a legend come to life." Seeing Jasen's puzzled expression, he continued. "Oh, I admit when I first saw what you were doing I was frightened, but then I remembered the old stories and I knew what you were. I confronted your lady. She was very stubborn and refused to answer my questions at first, but after hearing the story of the Wise Ones, she gave me the information I sought. I know that you are a telepath and that you are not from this world. I also know that you are the last of your kind, and that fills me with great sadness."

"Why? Telepaths are not well loved. Most people would be glad that we are gone. You do not hate or fear me, why?"

"Because I know who you are. Long ago, my people lived on a world in the Gamma3 star system. We had no technology even then. One day our planet's orbit became unstable. As our planet drifted out of its natural orbit, destruction ranged across our world. It would soon destroy itself and us. Then the Wise Ones came in their golden ships. They came to help. They had much learning and a technology beyond our greatest imagining. They also possessed tremendous powers, powers of the mind. They used those powers to save my people. Many of the Wise Ones died transferring their vital energy to the sick and injured. When I saw you giving your life to your friend, I remembered the legend. Then, I knew how you had beaten me. It was impossible for a human, but not for someone possessing the mind powers of the Wise Ones." Chauras leaned forward eagerly. "Are you truly of the Wise Ones?"

Jasen stared at the Centaur stunned. He had read the historical records of how his people had saved the

Centaurs, but no one had ever dreamed that the Centaurs would remember that time or that they would revere the race that had saved them. In a hushed voice, he answered the expectant Centaur. "Yes, Chauras, I am of that race or rather was. My world no longer exists and, as far as I know, no other survived its destruction."

Chauras nodded his head, sadness mirrored on his face. "Your lady told me of the destruction of your world and of your quest. It makes it all the more vital that I and my people aid you now."

"Chauras, I thank you for your help but you don't owe me anything."

"Nay! From long ago, the legend has been carefully preserved and handed down to each generation, along with a charge to be ready to aid any of the Wise Ones we may meet. You are the last. It is my duty, my privilege, to help you in any way I can."

Jasen lowered his head, touched by the Centaur's words. It had been a long time since his race had been met with respect, instead of contempt. "Thank you."

Chauras studied the man closely. Jasen possessed all that was good and noble in his people. That anyone would throw away such a one as this filled the Centaur with anger. He could not lessen the burden of life in a cruel galaxy, but he could offer sanctuary. Choosing his words carefully he made his offer. "The galaxy beyond Mystra's barrier is dangerous for one of your kind. They would destroy you if they knew what you are. I cannot change how the universe views telepaths, but I can offer you the friendship of my people. Know that you always have a place here with us. Anytime you want or need a safe haven you will be welcomed. You are clan brother, now and forever."

Jasen shook his head in wonder. This day was turning out to be filled with wonders. He didn't know how to answer the Centaur. "Chauras, I don't know what to say. Thank you, I am honored. I will try to never betray your trust or to bring dishonor on the clan."

The huge Centaur smiled. He was right. This one was worthy to be made a part of the clan. "It is little enough to repay you for the lives of my kind. Now, how about some food? I promised your lady I would see you well fed and cared for. She has gone to divert an earthquake nearby. I do not want her to return and find you neglected. I, for one, do not wish to face her wrath."

Jasen laughed. "Then let's by all means eat. I would hate to see such a fate befall your kind and generous people."

Laughing, the two left the tent and headed for the cook fire. Chauras watched the man who he now called friend and shook his head in amazement. Fate had indeed been kind. After generations of waiting, the Wise Ones walked among them again. At long last, honor could be satisfied and the debt repaid, at least in part. He could not wait to introduce Jasen to the tribal council. Chauras's name would go down in legend.

Tivonna searched the ground around her for signs of weakness; a large quake was building. The shockwave would travel north toward the Centaurs' main camp and wreck untold damage on the nomadic tribe, unless she could divert its force away from the area. Vaguely, she wondered why the elemental assigned to this quadrant had not already taken care of the problem. Oh well, she would worry about her missing sister later. For now, she would deal with the situation herself.

As Tivonna's senses probed the earth, her mind turned to the unusual events of the past day. Jasen and Hawk were both out of danger, and the Centaurs had accepted them as friends. Tivonna laughed; if anyone had told her that she would one day be staying in a Centaur camp as an honored guest, she would have thought them crazy; but here she was helping protect the Centaurs' home.

She sighed. It was all because of Jasen. Her love for the mysterious star traveler grew stronger with each facet of his character she uncovered. She had been astonished to learn of his people's unselfish aid of the Centaurs. Yet, when she thought about it, things were not as farfetched as they sounded. Ever since she had met the telepath, he had been engaged in helping others, often to his own detriment. First, herself, then Gaius, and now Hawk. Each time, he had risked himself to aid another. His mission to Mystra was another example. He came here to help save a galaxy, not for any personal gain. She would have to watch him in the future. His compassionate, self-sacrificing reverence for life could get him killed if he wasn't careful. She would have to help protect him from himself.

As Tivonna reviewed the past, she felt a thrill of joy. Jasen had trusted her and had turned to her for help. He had spoken to her, mind to mind. The sensation had been strange but not unpleasant. It gave her hope. She was certain he did not take such liberties with just anyone, maybe with Hawk, but not with others. That he had accepted her and confided in her filled Tivonna with an inexplicable excitement. His wall was weakening. Oh, when he thought about it, he maintained his distance; but when a crisis had come, he had instinctively reached out to her. He was more hers than he knew. Hawk had been right; it was only a matter of time.

Tivonna's thoughts were diverted by a tingling sensation along her body. Her senses had finally located what she sought. A faint fault ran west away from the main fault line. By diverting the stresses along this secondary crack, she could relieve the underground pressure without endangering the Centaurs. Joining herself to the earth beneath her, Tivonna reached out and tapped into the underground forces. Molding the earth to her will, she closed off the fault line leading to the Centaurs' camp and opened a path to the secondary crack, leading away from the inhabited areas of the plain.

Tivonna savored the power coursing through her veins. She delighted in the feel of the earth sliding and moving in obedience to her will. This was the danger of the elemental. The siren song of power urged her to surrender herself to the elemental forces swirling around her and become one with the power she wielded. She would not answer that call. Another stronger power sang in her mind, the power of her kiosan. She could not leave him.

When all was as she wished it, Tivonna withdrew from the earth. The new fault line was now firmly established and the old one filled in completely. The Centaurs would never have to fear another earthquake again. With a smile of satisfaction, Tivonna and her escort headed back to camp where Jasen would be waiting for her.

Hawk groaned and struggled to open his eyes. He had been having the weirdest dream. Prizing his eyes open, he scanned his surroundings. Maybe, it hadn't been a dream after all. He was in a tent and, from the bandages around his chest, he must have been hurt. He didn't remember coming here or being wounded. What had happened, and where were Jasen and Tivonna? The confused Filidae continued his study of the room, and froze as his gaze fell on the large, fearsome looking creature standing at the entrance to the tent. Hearing Hawk's movements, the creature turned and walked toward the bed.

Seeing that the visitor was awake and lucid, the Centaur smiled. "Welcome back to the world of the living. How do you feel?"

Hawk stared at the mythological being before him. "Are you real or have I lost it totally?"

The Centaur laughed. "No friend, I am quite real. I see that you are truly back with us. I will summon the Wise One. He has been most anxious about you."

The large creature turned and left the tent, leaving a

puzzled and slightly bemused Hawk behind. Centaurs? And who was the Wise One? What had been happening? He felt like he was suddenly in another dimension.

Hawk's thoughts were interrupted as the tent flap was lifted and Jasen entered. Hawk was stunned. There were dark circles under the telepath's eyes. What could have happened to leave Jasen in such a state? He had a sneaking suspicion that his friend's condition was somehow tied to him and his wound. It would be just like the telepath to endanger his own life to save a friend.

Jasen smiled and sat down on the edge of Hawk's bed. "Well, well, you finally decided to join us. Have a good nap?"

"Oh, just lovely, but it looks like you're the one who needs a nap. You look horrible."

"Why, thank you so much for the compliment." The amusement left Jasen's eyes and he studied his friend closely. "Are you sure you're all right? You gave us quite a scare."

"Everything seems to be in working order. Jase, what happened? Where are we and how in the world did you find Centaurs of all things?"

Jasen sighed. "It's a long story."

"I don't seem to be going anywhere."

Jasen laughed and shook his head. It was good to have Hawk back. There had been a time when he had feared he would never again be the victim of his friend's quick wit; but that time was now over. Hawk was going to be just fine. Taking a deep breath, he brought the Filidae up to date.

"Whew! And I missed all that?"

"Well, people who go flying off into strange territory and then fail to pay attention to their surroundings usually get to miss the fun."

"OK, OK, so next time I'll be more careful and less impulsive."

"Hah, that'll be the day. Now, think you can eat something? Chauras has been a most gracious host."

At Hawk's nod, Jasen rose and went to the tent opening. Lifting the flap, he turned and grinned at his bedridden friend. "Don't go away now. I'll be back in a moment."

Hawk scowled; he hated being helpless. "Yeah, I'll try not to run any foot races until you get back."

Chuckling, Jasen left the tent. Hawk lay staring at the exit through which his friend had left. There was more to this story than Jasen was telling. Such as how hard the battle for Hawk's mind had been. Losing control of a form was a danger every shapeshifter faced. The primitive instincts and emotions of a wild animal were hard to control. Having to confront those forces without the aid of the shapeshifter, was no small task. No wonder Jasen looked so tired. For the millionth time, Hawk thanked the Creator for such a friend.

Moments later, Jasen entered the tent, followed by a young warrior carrying a large blanket. Jasen smiled wickedly at him. "We decided that some fresh air would do you good." Before Hawk realized what was happening, the young warrior advanced and scooped him up in the warm blanket.

"Put me down! I can walk, thank you, it's my shoulder that's hurt not my legs!" Having to be carried through the camp was humiliating.

"Now Hawk, people who go around getting themselves shot have to suffer the consequences. So, be a good boy, and behave yourself." Holding open the tent flap, Jasen grinned as the warrior carried the irate Filidae from the tent. It wouldn't hurt Hawk to suffer a little embarrassment. It served him right for nearly scaring Jasen to death.

Seeing his friend's amusement, Hawk relented. The truth was that he still felt weak and unsteady. Besides, it was good to hear Jasen laugh. Hawk wasn't the only one who had had a close call. He could suffer the indignation for such a worthy cause. He just hoped Tivonna didn't see or he would never live this down.

The young Centaur deposited his burden in a nest of warm furs beside the campfire. The Centaurs had constructed ingenious chairs for their non-equine guests from packs and furs. They could lean back comfortably and still remain upright. Settling into his chair, Hawk watched the activity going on around him.

Jasen sank into a seat on Hawk's right and pulled a brightly colored blanket around his shoulders to ward off the night chill. A large roan colored Centaur knelt to Hawk's left and offered him a bowl of stew. He gratefully accepted the bowl. Suddenly, he was ravenous and the stew smelled wonderful.

Chauras watched his guest with something akin to wonder. He had heard of the Filidae, but had never before seen one of the mysterious race. None of their race had come to Mystra; still the stories of their accomplishments were well known even on this no tech world. The Filidae were a legend throughout the universe. Most of the technological wonders of the day were due to them. Without them, many races of the Alliance would have perished and few, if any, would have reached the stars. They were very much like the Wise Ones. It was no wonder that Jasen and the Filidae were friends. Chauras shuddered. To think that he had almost killed this one, he put the grim thought behind him. That was the past, he must concentrate on the future. It was a time of change for Mystra. A Filidae and a Wise One walked her land and he, Chauras, was a part of it. He glanced at Hawk. His first task however was to make amends for his earlier folly.

"I am glad you are recovering. I am Chauras. I fear I am the cause of your injuries. I am sorry. I did not know you were something other than you appeared."

Hawk looked up at the Centaur and smiled. "Forget it. I should have been more cautious, as I keep getting reminded. You are just fortunate that Jasen came along when he did. Filidae are very unappetizing. Too tough, I would have made a lousy stew. This however is delicious."

Chauras laughed. "We are indeed fortunate."

Placing his empty bowl on the ground beside him, Hawk surveyed the camp. "By the way where is Tivonna? She didn't get tired of you and run off did she?"

Jasen chuckled. "What and leave such splendid company? No she is dealing with the small problem of an earthquake. It seems while we were napping she decided to do some work."

"Well, someone has to work. You two certainly don't."

Startled, the men watched as Tivonna walked toward them. She had silently approached the camp and had stood quietly listening to the ongoing discussion. Smiling at their startled faces, she stepped forward into the light of the fire.

Jasen's eyes twinkled with amusement. She was getting as bad as Hawk. "Welcome home. Come join us. I'll even share my blanket."

Tivonna circled the fire, walked over and sat down near Jasen. Pulling her into his arms, Jasen snuggled the blanket securely around them both. Tivonna smiled to herself. Being an elemental she was immune to both heat and cold. But sitting here leaning comfortably against Jasen's chest with his arms around her and his chin resting on her auburn hair, she wasn't about to spoil this moment by telling him. Instead, she gloried in the feel of being held safely in his arms. He had missed her.

Holding Tivonna close, Jasen felt contented, and his tensed muscles unwound a little. Hawk had been right; he was still tired but he just couldn't seem to sleep anymore, too many thoughts kept running through his mind. There was so much to do, and little time. As Jasen sat with Tivonna cuddled near, a lassitude began to steal over him and the problems of the galaxy didn't seem to weigh as heavily as before.

Hawk watched the two, elemental and telepath, and smiled. Yes, Jasen's wall was definitely cracking. His friend had been under a tremendous strain ever since reaching Mystra. Part of that strain was due to his resisting his feelings for Tivonna. Over the past few days, she had managed to convince Jasen that she did not fear his powers or hate him. Still, the telepath would still not admit his love for her. His mind told him that loving him was wrong for the elemental, while his heart yearned for her. From the looks of things Jasen's heart was finally winning out over his head. A little privacy might just finish the job. Hawk hoped so; he didn't know how much longer his friend could survive his inner battle.

Hawk turned and addressed Chauras. "Thank you for the meal, but I seem to be weaker than I thought. Could you help me back to bed?"

Glancing at the oblivious couple, the Centaur smiled. "It would be my pleasure to assist you." Scooping his guest up in his arms, the Centaur carried Hawk back to his tent, leaving Jasen and Tivonna alone by the fire.

The couple sat together in companionable silence for many minutes, staring into the dying fire. Neither wanted to be the first to shatter this rare moment. Finally, Tivonna turned in Jasen's arms so that she could see his face. He looked tired but the wary, watchful look was not in his eyes. For one of the few times since she had known him, Jasen was unguarded. Tentatively, she reached up and brushed her fingertips along his cheek. "Are you sure you are all right?"

Jasen smiled at the worried expression on the beautiful face turned trustingly up to his. The green eyes were full of concern. "I'm fine. There's nothing wrong that another good night's sleep won't cure. I had to transfer a great deal of energy to Hawk to stabilize his system and speed up the healing process. Sleep will restore my reserves, honest."

"I believe you. But if sleep is what you need, why are

you awake?"

Jasen chuckled. "I wish I knew. I just can't seem to let go. Any suggestions?"

Tivonna's eyes sparkled. "Maybe." Leaving Jasen's embrace, she tugged at his arms until he vacated the chair. Settling into the abandoned seat, she patted the ground next to her. "Lie down here and put your head in my lap." Seeing the surprised and doubtful expression on Jasen's face, she laughed. "Come on. I don't bite. Trust me."

Shrugging, Jasen complied.

"Turn on your side." As Jasen obeyed, Tivonna began to gently massage his neck, back and shoulders. She had often watched her mother do this for her father when he had had an especially trying day and couldn't sleep. After a few minutes, Tivonna felt the muscles beneath her hands relax. She was sure that Jasen had fallen asleep, when he spoke.

"Tivonna, have you ever thought about marriage?"

Tivonna quickly suppressed her surprise. Could he finally be ready to express his feelings for her? She chose her answer carefully. "Yes, I have often dreamed of one day finding a man I could love and respect and who would return my feelings. Why do you ask?"

Jasen turned over and gazed up into Tivonna's emerald eyes. She was stunned by the expression on his face, and the feelings mirrored in his golden eyes. There was so much pain and love in those eyes.

"I don't want to stand in the way of your happiness. I have nothing to offer you except a life of uncertainty."

Tivonna shook her auburn head. "Oh, Jasen, do you not realize that my happiness comes from being with you? Nothing else matters. And as for finding another, it is impossible even if I wanted to; which I do not."

"I don't understand. What do you mean impossible?"

"An elemental cannot choose who she marries, any more than she can choose where she lives. Jasen, my soul has picked you; no other is possible or desirable for me. No man may touch an elemental except her kiosan; it is death to any other."

Jasen was stunned. "But..."

Tivonna pressed her fingers to his lips stopping his words. "I want you to listen carefully. This is not a burden or a curse. There is no one else I desire. I love you, not because you are my kiosan but because you are you. Is that clear? I put no ties on you. You are free to follow your heart. Whatever you decide, my heart is yours now and always, and nothing you say or do will ever change that. I am in love with you, Jasen Blackthorn. No other will do for me."

In stunned wonder, Jasen reached up and brushed the tears from Tivonna's cheeks. She meant it, all of it. She truly loved him. Sitting up, Jasen gathered her carefully into his arms as if afraid to break the spell and find out that it was all a dream. The warmth of the body held snuggly in his arms proved that this was no dream. She was real as was her love. Jasen leaned forward and gently kissed her. Leaning back, he met her bright green eyes and smiled. "And I love you. I know it's crazy. I know I shouldn't but I don't care. I can't fight it anymore. I want you with me always. I am sorry for the way I've been treating you. I just couldn't believe that you could love me. Then, I saw Hawk lying there near death and I finally realized what was truly important. The future doesn't matter; none of us may live past today. I don't want to waste the gift of your love by fearing things that may never come to pass. Besides, you've seen me at my worst and are still here. If I haven't sent you fleeing in terror by now, I doubt that I will. I still don't think it's fair to you, but then I'm selfish. I don't want to lose you. Tivonna, when this mess is over, if we survive, I would like you to be my wife. Think it over carefully, it would mean leaving this world and all you know to brave the dangers beyond Mystra's skies."

Gazing at the man before her so strong yet so vulnerable Tivonna's heart soared with joy, at last. Throwing her arms around him she gasped out her reply. "Oh, Jasen, there is nothing to think about. I would go anywhere to be with you. I will be glad to be your wife. No more talk about it not being fair to me. You are everything I need or want."

Jasen ended the embrace and held up a hand to still her excitement. "Before you make up your mind, there is something you must know. When telepaths marry, they are joined by more than words. They are bonded in mind, as well as body. You have felt our link. What we share now can be broken without undue consequences for either of us, but a marriage bond is for life. It can be broken only by death. Could you bear having me permanently in your head?"

Tivonna met Jasen's eyes calmly. How could a smart man be so stupid? "I know you. I don't fear the bond. The only thing I fear is losing you. Now, what are you really afraid of?" She held up her right hand and fire raced along her arm, wreathing her elemental tattoo in golden flames. "I am not a weak maid who needs protecting from the things in the dark. You are not here to protect me, but to protect others from me. We are soul bonded, there is no stronger link. We are already joined until death do us part. If you have some dark secret you are afraid the bonding will reveal, you might as well tell me now for I will always be at your side."

Jasen searched her face intently and opened his receptors to her thoughts and feelings. She meant it. She would gladly face anything to be with him. Jasen was filled with awe. He did not deserve such a woman. With a sigh, he prepared to reveal his greatest fear.

Sensing the import of what he was about to say, Tivonna extinguished the flames and gave him her undivided attention.

"I have very little memory of my world. I've read the ship's records, but I have little firsthand knowledge of where I come from. I was young when Jake found me, but even with a damaged memory I had full control of my telepathy and telekinesis. Sensing and manipulating energy is instinctive. I obviously received extensive training at an early age, but I can't remember the lessons. It's like there's a barrier in my mind. Something or someone blocked much of my power when I was very young. I have to wonder, why? Was I such a dangerous child that they felt the need to hobble me? If so, what might I do if the barrier fails? I could kill you or Hawk. If you are linked fully to me, I could destroy your mind."

"Do you remember anything of your family?"

"Snatches, I think they loved me, but I also made them uneasy."

Tivonna nodded. "Jase, would you give a baby an unsecured weapon and hope that he doesn't injure himself or another? No, you keep the weapons secured and out of the hands of the young or untrained. It's much the same with power. If you developed strong gifts early, the adults in your life would try to protect you and themselves by binding your gifts until you were old enough to use them safely. I doubt the barrier was meant to stay in place this long. But, you had to flee your world and with no other telepaths around there was no one to remove it. The fact that you are afraid of what your power can do tells me that you are not the type to misuse it. I've touched your soul. You have nothing to fear. If the barrier falls, you will be ready for whatever happens. Now, if I go power crazy and run amok, you must promise to stop me and I'll do the same for you. Deal?"

Jasen shook his head in amazement. "You are truly a wonder."

"And don't you forget it, mister." Tivonna fixed her future mate with a stern gaze. "We will survive this quest and then we will be married. Though I have to warn you, I am very jealous. You are mine and I do not share."

"I consider myself warned."

Lighter in spirit than he had been in a long time, Jasen rose and pulled Tivonna to her feet. "Now, I think it is time to rest. I believe I can finally sleep."

Arm in arm, the couple walked to their tent. Jasen laughed. "I can't wait to see Hawk's face when we tell him."

"Better wait until he recovers. I would hate to have him die of shock." Tivonna continued in a more serious tone. "He cares deeply for you. He will be pleased."

"I know. I don't know how I rated the good fortune to have the two of you. It is more than I ever dreamed possible."

"Hawk and I are equally fortunate to have you. Now, not another word: sleep!" Entering the tent, Tivonna pushed Jasen toward his bed. "I do not want to hear another word until morning. That is an order."

Giving a mock salute, Jasen obediently headed for his sleeping mat. Lying back on the thick furs, he opened the bond linking him to Tivonna and sent his love and joy winging through the darkness into her mind. As sleep stole over him, he felt Tivonna's own feelings echo back along the link. With a smile of contentment, Jasen finally let his weary body slide into sleep.

Across the room, Tivonna smiled as she felt Jasen relax into slumber. She savored the bond between them. She was still amazed that he had actually feared that he would hurt her with his power. Everything she had seen and felt until now proved the exact opposite. Jasen would never do anything to harm her or cause her discomfort. It was not in his nature. She smiled. At long last, he had finally admitted that he loved her. More than that, he had actually asked her to marry him. Clutching the warmth of Jasen's presence to her, Tivonna slipped into a gentle sleep.

Jasen awoke the next morning to find both Tivonna and Hawk already up and about. He quickly rose and went in search of the missing twosome. The night's sleep had fully restored his energy and he felt ready for anything. He found Hawk and Tivonna with Chauras, eating breakfast by the cook fire. "Good morning, is there anything left for me or did you three finish it all off?"

Watching Jasen approach, Hawk grinned and held up a bowl. "Oh, we saved you a little. I know how grumpy you get if you're not fed."

While Jasen ate his breakfast, Hawk studied his friend closely. Jasen looked good; the night's rest had refreshed him but it was more than that. He looked as if a great weight had been lifted from his shoulders. Hawk glanced over at Tivonna. Yes, she looked different too, like the proverbial cat that swallowed the canary. What had happened last night?

While Hawk was pondering the sudden change in Jasen and Tivonna, Chauras carefully examined his three guests. Hawk was almost well. Jasen's healing touch had intensified and speeded up the healing process, to the point that now only a stiff shoulder remained to trouble the Filidae. He was fit to travel and both Tivonna and Jasen appeared to be rested. It was time to discuss the future. "Well, since you three appear to be fully recovered from your ordeal, my people and I will be returning to our main camp today. You are welcome to travel with us if you wish. The plains can be dangerous to those unfamiliar with them. You will have a place in our village for as long as you care to stay."

Jasen considered the Centaur's offer. Since he and Hawk knew little about the local terrain, native guides could be useful. Also, someone in Chauras's village might know where the laboratory was located. Chauras had mentioned a shaman who kept the tribe's records. It wouldn't hurt to check. "Thank you, we are headed north anyway. It'd be a pleasure to have company. Besides, I would like a chance to speak to your shaman. He might have information which will aid us in our search."

"Excellent, I will see that your mounts are readied."

While Chauras left to supervise the breaking of camp, Hawk turned to face Jasen and Tivonna. "OK, who's going to tell me?"

"Tell you what?" Jasen gave him a puzzled expression. "I don't know what you're talking about."

Tivonna smothered a giggle. If she didn't know better, she would have sworn Jasen was totally baffled. Hawk, on the other hand, was not buying it for a second.

Hawk folded his arms across his chest and looked from Tivonna to Jasen. "It won't work. I know something happened last night. It's written all over you two and I'm not letting either of you alone until you tell me, so give."

Unable to hold his pose any longer Jasen broke into a wide grin. "OK, you win." Reaching over, he grasped Tivonna's hand. "Hawk, last night I asked Tivonna to marry me and she said yes. Want to be best man?"

"Do I want to be best man? Just you try and stop me! Jase, this is terrific!" Hawk fairly bounced with excitement. "This is great! It's about time you came to your senses, though why Tivonna would have you I can't imagine. When's the wedding?"

"Whoa boy, take it easy." Jasen chuckled. It had been a long time since he had seen his heart brother this enthusiastic about anything. "The wedding is on hold until after this mission is over. Unfortunately, we just can't spare the time a full joining would take. Besides, I would like Tivonna's parents to be present. After all, I can't very well steal her away off planet without letting them know what's happened."

"Well, at least you won't be able to complain that you had a boring engagement. It's not every couple who gets to save the universe while planning their nuptials."

"I don't think boredom is something any of us have to worry about for a long, long time. Mystra seems determined to keep throwing us one surprise after another. Speaking of which, it's about time to see what she has in store for us next. Let's pack! I'd hate to keep our guides waiting."

Hawk glanced at the huge Centaurs busily dismantling the camp around them. "Good idea, the last person I want to have mad at me is a Centaur."

Tivonna rose gracefully to her feet. "Why Hawk, they are really very sweet, just stay out of bow range."

"Yeah right."

Chuckling, the three friends headed for their tent to collect their packs. Tivonna and Jasen may have resolved their differences, but the Firehawks remained.

CHAPTER TEN

King Arcus stood staring out his study window as the last glimmer of sunlight faded from the evening sky. It had been over a month since Tivonna and her two off-world allies had left Castle Aquilla to embark on their dangerous quest. He had heard nothing from them since. She was out there somewhere tonight. Was she safe or had some disaster already befallen the valiant trio? Arcus sighed and began to pace before the open window. It was maddening; this waiting and not knowing what was happening was driving him insane. He should never have let Tivonna go off alone like that. Arcus gave a wry chuckle. As if he could have stopped her from going. Tivonna was not a child. She was a grown woman, and an elemental at that. She was far from helpless nor was she alone. Both Jasen and Hawk were with her and they would do everything in their power to ensure his daughter's safety. He was just being a foolish, overprotective father again.

Arcus stopped pacing and gazed once more out into the night. Much had happened since the three adventurers had left for the northern wilds. Jasen had proved correct; executing Gaius would have been disastrous. Using the information gleaned from Gaius's mind, the secret passages and spy holes had been located and sealed. Arcus had ordered Gaius watched and had discovered a vast spy network existed within his kingdom. It seemed that Gaius was the chief contact for all the duke's spies within Aquilla. If Gaius had died, the duke would have been alerted and the spy network would have replaced him, with Arcus none the wiser. Instead, now the king knew his enemies and could use the duke's own men against him. By feeding Malycon false information, Arcus could ensure that Aquilla's true secrets remained hidden. Yes, better a known enemy, then an unknown one.

The king shook his head. He had been a fool. Aquilla had been at peace for generations and he had grown complacent, forgetting the stories of Mystra's bloody history. Then, faction had vied with faction for possession of land and for control of the vital elementals. There had been those obsessed with controlling all the elementals, and thus becoming rulers of Mystra. He had been foolish to think that type of greed and lust for power was no longer a threat. Malycon was a dangerous and ruthless man. He was determined to rule Mystra, and would do anything to obtain his goal. Arcus had ignored him far too long. If not for Jasen's intervention, he might never have realized Malycon's true danger until it was too late. He owed the telepath much.

Arcus gave a deep sigh. He had not shown his appreciation very well and was ashamed of his previous behavior. He was not a child to be spooked by old tales. He had always prided himself on being fair and open-minded. Yet, when he had discovered Jasen was a telepath, he had discarded everything he knew of the man and condemned him as evil. When reason had returned, he realized how foolish his actions had been. Telepathy was a gift just like the gifts possessed by the elementals. Having power or talents did not automatically make a person any better or worse than any other. It was how a person exercised their abilities that governed the type of being they were. It was a matter of character. From all that he had heard of Jasen, as well as his own personal observations, the telepath was a man of impeccable character and having telepathic gifts did not change that. And what of Tivonna? She could never love a man who was unworthy of her. Jasen had done only what was necessary and had taken no pleasure or pride in his ability to manipulate others. He had conducted himself with both integrity and honor while within Aquilla's borders.

How could he have so quickly forgotten the lessons of the past? Mystra had been settled by races persecuted and hounded by others, as well as races near extinction due to past mistakes. All had come to Mystra for a second chance. They had sought a world where all could live freely without the hatreds and prejudices of their home worlds. He now saw that not all old fears and hatreds had been left behind. Arcus's own world had nearly destroyed itself with racial wars. He had read the accounts of those dark times, and had vowed that such things would never happen in his kingdom. Yet, he himself had come close to doing the very thing that he abhorred. He had been ready to condemn Jasen because of what he was, with little regard to the man himself. Well, no more, Aquilla was a free kingdom. Anyone could live within her borders as long as they kept the law and gave fealty to her king. From now on, telepaths and all other races of beings were welcome in Aquilla. The next time Jasen visited Castle Aquilla he would receive a far different reception. The young starfarer would always have a place in Aquilla, a safe haven where his welcome was always assured.

Arcus smiled to himself; besides, it was only fitting that a prince be comfortable in his own kingdom. If he knew that daughter of his, she would not let a catch like Jasen get away. Oh, it would not be an easy task. Jasen would not soon forget what had happened here; but given time, he was sure that Tivonna could win the young man over. Then, there was nature. Nothing could keep an elemental and her kiosan apart for long, no matter how stubborn the parties involved. Yes, it was only a matter of time before Aquilla had a Crown Prince, and that suited the king just fine. Now, that he no longer looked through the eyes of prejudice and hate, Arcus saw that Jasen was a fine young man and a perfect match for Tivonna. Once they reconciled their differences and put past mistakes and hurts behind them, they would be very happy together. There was one thing Arcus knew for certain, their lives would never be mundane. Being married to an elemental was quite a challenge, and he suspected that being married to a telepath, a star roving one at that; would be equally exciting, not to mention dangerous. Arcus just hoped they lived through their present ordeal to enjoy a future together.

Well, worrying about what he could not change would not help anyone. He had great confidence in the three young adventurers. They would succeed. He would see his daughter again and he would have his chance to rectify things with Jasen. The king turned away from the window and headed for the study door. It was almost the dinner hour and Sivena would be waiting for him. All they could do now was wait.

Malycon, Duke of Cenchrea, was in a foul mood. Servants and subjects treaded warily, hoping to escape their ruler's notice. The people of Cenchrea feared the duke's dark moods, for no one knew when or how he would react when the cold rage seized him. In the past, men, women, and children had perished to appease the duke's anger. They had been the lucky ones. Others not so fortunate had served as subjects for his fiendish experiments.

Jacob had been Malycon's personal servant for many years, and had come to recognize the signs of the duke's displeasure. Malycon sat at his desk staring broodingly at the stack of reports lying before him. His dark features were pulled into a fierce scowl, and he toyed absently with the dagger he kept on the desk as a paperweight. Suddenly, he leaped to his feet, jabbed the dagger into the polished desktop, and flung the reports to the floor.

Clutching his cleaning cloth to his chest, Jacob froze, not daring to make a sound and risk drawing Malycon's attention to himself. He studied his master intently. The duke's face was flushed with anger and his body was rigid with barely controlled fury. Malycon stared at the dagger quivering in the desktop, and some of the tension slowly left his body. Taking his eyes from the dagger, he glanced up at Jacob.

"Bring me Tyr." The duke's voice was cold and flat, a sign of anger the servant recognized only too well. Quickly, Jacob scurried from the room to obey, thankful to be away from his irate lord.

With a muttered oath, Malycon began to pace restlessly. Nothing! It had been weeks and still the stranger eluded him. His spies could find out nothing. According to their reports, all was well. Yet, he knew that all was not well. He could feel it. Somehow, the off-worlders had managed to outwit his spies. They were loose on Mystra somewhere and he was determined to find them.

The duke's mental tirade was interrupted by a soft knock on the study door. Seating himself at the desk, Malycon reached into a drawer and removed a small packet containing a light green powder and placed it on the desktop before him. Then, leaning back in his chair, he addressed his caller. "Come."

In response to his invitation, the door opened and Tyr glided into the room. Malycon's dark mood lightened at the sight of the beautiful elemental. Of all the people in Cenchrea, she alone did not fear him. She served him because she must. If given the opportunity, she would cheerfully squash him like a bug without a second thought. The duke smiled to himself. It was a chance she would never have. He owned and controlled her, despite her power. He alone of all the inhabitants of Mystra had found a way to bind the powerful elementals to his will; it was a victory he relished.

"You wished to see me?"

As always, Tyr's tone was calm and composed. Malycon couldn't help a momentary twinge of irritation. The delicate ivory features were as inscrutable as ever. The black eyes met his unflinchingly. No sign betrayed her thoughts or feelings. In all the years Tyr had served him, Malycon had never once been able to ruffle her calm, cool demeanor. It was a minor source of annoyance to him. He might have her obedience but he had not broken the proud woman before him. Never mind, as long as she obeyed. He did not care what she felt about him.

"What news have you of our rogue elemental? Have you located her yet?"

"I have little to report. There has been one unscheduled use of elemental power in the Great Plains to the South, but the incident was not long enough for me to obtain a precise reading. It felt like Tivonna. She possesses the necessary power for such a working and, as far as I know, the Centaurs have no elementals of their own, nor have they requested aid from the council. However, I cannot be sure."

"So the Centaurs have chosen to defy me. They harbor an unknown elemental in their midst and did not inform me. How inconsiderate of them, such impudence. We will have to teach them a lesson, won't we my dear?"

Tyr suppressed a shudder. When that mocking tone entered the duke's voice, there was danger. She had long suspected that Malycon was mad. He was unpredictable and could change moods in an instant. She didn't like the sound of this present line of thought.

"A lesson, my lord?"

Malycon gazed at the lovely elemental, his black eyes glittering. "I want the strangers. I have given strict orders for all my subjects to search for them, and to bring them to me immediately if found. The Centaurs have disobeyed me. Instead of delivering them to me, they have chosen to conceal them from me and aid their escape. They will pay for their defiance. I will not tolerate disobedience! Yes, a storm I think, that should do nicely."

"Storm, my lord?" Icy fear gripped Tyr's heart, but she showed no outward sign of her panic. Surely, he couldn't mean what she thought he meant. It was inconceivable.

"Yes, My Dear. I want you to create a storm and send it to the Centaur camp. If Tivonna is in the vicinity, she will use her powers to neutralize the storm and save her friends. When she does, you will be able to detect her use of power and discover her exact location. Correct? If she is no longer nearby, well, then the Centaurs will pay the price for their folly."

"No, I can't." Tyr's pale face drained of all color at the duke's words. "What you ask is forbidden. No elemental may use her powers in such a manner. It is unthinkable. I won't do it!"

Malycon leaned forward and picked up the packet of greenish powder lying on the desktop and tossed it to the stunned woman standing before him. "Oh, I think you will." His voice suddenly hardened. "You will do as you are told or your kiosan will suffer the consequences. Never forget that you are mine. I own you. You will do precisely what I tell you to do when I tell you to do it. Understand?"

Staring at the tiny packet she held, Tyr slumped in defeat. Malycon's foul concoction was all that stood between her kiosan and a painful death. Like all the times before, she had no choice but to obey the duke's commands. There was no point in pretending otherwise. As long as Malycon controlled her kiosan, she was his to command.

"I will do as you command, but be warned. Storms possess a life of their own. Once I harness the forces and push them toward the Plains, I will not be able to control what happens. What reaches the Centaur camp may be far different than what I unleash here. Tivonna may be unable to stop it. You could be risking the lives of those you wish to find."

"Enough!" The duke slammed his fist onto the desktop and fixed Tyr with his cold black eyes. "You will send the storm and you will control it. You know the penalty for failure. When Tivonna deflects your sending, you will pinpoint her exact whereabouts, and I will send the dragons to fetch our prey. Now go. You have work to do."

Tyr bowed her head in defeat. "Yes, my lord. It will be as you command."

Malycon smiled as the stunned elemental turned and silently left the room, the packet of green powder clutched tightly in her hand. She would obey. She really had no other choice. Yes, things were looking up. He was still annoyed with the dragons. The wily Dragon Lord had claimed that no adult dragons could leave the mountains for the present, since it was the time of mating. Oh, he still had the young and immature dragons to serve him; but, their flying skills were limited to short distances and well established flight patterns; they were useless for extensive searches. Malycon suspected that the sly old lizard was playing some game of his own. Maybe he hoped to find a way to use the strangers against the duke. Well, it was no longer important. The dragons may have failed him, but Tyr would not. She knew the consequences too well to defy him. She would locate Tivonna, and then he would force the dragon king to fetch them. Best of all, since the dragons had not fulfilled their part of the bargain by locating the travelers, his deal with the Dragon King would be forfeited, and the dragons would be forced to continue serving him. By this time tomorrow, the strangers would be in his possession and both the dragons and Arcus's fiery-haired daughter would be enslaved to him forever. Yes, life was indeed good.

The rest of the day was a nightmare for Tyr. She spent her time walking and thinking as she waited for nightfall and the task she must perform. She was too stunned by what had occurred to pay much attention to anything else. What the duke asked of her violated everything the elementals stood for. Had she really sunk so low that she would even consider carrying out his insane plan? She had never claimed to be a saint. She was ambitious and had a love for power and the finer things in life, but she had never betrayed her duty as an elemental, until now.

As darkness fell, Tyr headed for her rooms at the top of the castle's southern tower. Entering her chambers, Tyr walked over and gazed at the man sprawled across the bed. Her face softened at the sight of the slumbering figure. Bryon, her kiosan, was captain of the duke's elite guard. He had been pulling double duty for the past two days, and now slept the sleep of exhaustion. Lying there, his curly brown hair tousled and his clear gray eyes closed in sleep, he did not look like the strong valiant warrior he was; instead he looked vulnerable and defenseless. Tyr reached out and ran a finger along one stubbled cheek. He was her life and she would do anything for him. Bryon knew nothing of the price she paid daily to keep him safe. The duke's vile potion was odorless and tasteless. It had no effect on the body as long as the subject received a small dose of it daily. However, should one fail to receive their prescribed portion, excruciating pain followed quickly by death resulted. Only Malycon knew the powder's secrets and he guarded them well. Thus, she served him, and her bondmate lived oblivious to his danger and her battle to keep him alive.

Leaning down, Tyr placed a kiss on her beloved's forehead and smoothed back his sleep-rumpled hair. "Sleep well my love."

Silently, she left the bed and headed for the balcony. If all went well, Bryon would never know of this night's work or what it cost her. The night sky was clear, the sparkles of color darting across the black expanse were breathtaking, but Tyr was in no mood to enjoy their loveliness. Walking to the edge of the balcony, Tyr raised her hands toward the night sky. Reaching out with her power, she began to gather the elemental forces she would need. One by one she bound the glimmering strands of energy to her will and forged them into a swirling cone of concentrated power. When she had gathered all the energy she needed, Tyr carefully began to shape the vortex of power into the pattern she desired. Under the direction of her will, the cone of power began to assume the essence of a thunderstorm. To the south, thunder began to rumble and shafts of lightning arched across the sky, illuminating the horizon with brilliant flashes of light. When all was as she desired, Tyr pushed the building forces of the storm toward the Plains and the Centaur camp. Releasing her creation, the weary elemental sank to her knees and buried her face in her hands. Sobs racked her body and tears streamed down her cheeks. It was done. The storm was now out of her control. There was no telling what it would be when it finally reached its destination. Tivonna was powerful, but even she had limits. The forces of Mystra were not so bound. If the young elemental failed to stop the storm, it would destroy the Centaurs. Was living really worth this price? Tyr didn't know. It was too late now anyway; what was done was done. She could not stop or undo the forces she had set into motion. It was now up to Tivonna and whatever powers of fate guided the universe. She just hoped the young, untried elemental was up to the task, for both their sakes.

Following Tyr's commands, the budding storm system drifted toward the southern plains. However, things were not destined to go as the elemental had hoped. Weather on Mystra was a chancy thing at best, and the reaches between the northern mountains and the southern plains were notorious for their unpredictable weather fronts. This night was no exception. As the storm front drifted toward the plains, it entered an area rife with unstable elemental energy fields. The storm cloud became a focus for the randomly flowing currents of power. Absorbing the energy around it, the storm began to grow in size and intensity. As the raw elemental forces poured into the heart of the storm, it began to undergo a deadly metamorphosis. What had started out as a simple thunderstorm, now became a destructive force of nature the likes of which had not been seen on Mystra since the days of the Great Cataclysm. In those days, giant storms had raced across the planet's surface, annihilating everything in their paths. They had caused havoc and destruction at every turn, until the elementals had arisen to combat and tame their wild energies. Now, such a storm, this time forged by an elemental's own hand, was loose on Mystra again ready to spread its devastation across the face of the unsuspecting world. Far to the south, directly in the storm's path, the Centaurs slept peacefully, unaware of the harbinger of death soon to be visited upon their unprotected camp.

CHAPTER ELEVEN

Straightening in his saddle, Jasen tried to ease his cramping muscles. Unlike Centaurs, humans were not created to spend almost three days continuously in the saddle. Chauras's estimation of a day's ride back to the Centaur main camp had turned out to be overly optimistic. They were now into their third day of straight travel. The party had stopped only briefly during the trek to allow the non-Centaurs to tend to their needs. Much more of this and he would become a Centaur himself permanently glued to his saddle.

Turning his head, Jasen located Tivonna and Hawk riding slightly behind him. They looked as weary as he felt. The three of them were riding in the middle of the Centaur band. Chauras was taking no chances of anything happening to his prizes before he had a chance to present them to the Centaur's tribal elders. Jasen's attention was suddenly pulled to the front by a sharp piercing whistle.

"What's up?" Turning his head to the left, Jasen saw that Hawk had ridden up beside him. Giving his friend a reassuring smile, Jasen directed his attention to the front of the party where Chauras was slowly walking toward a small band of Centaurs that had suddenly appeared on the plains before them.

"I'd say we've been spotted. Looks like we're getting close."

"Thank goodness." Tivonna sighed from Jasen's right. "I was beginning to fear I would be stuck in Midnight's saddle forever."

Hawk chuckled. "You're not the only one. I may never walk again. Filidae were not meant to ride like Centaurs. What do you think Jase? Are our observers friendly?"

A furrow creased Jasen's brow as he concentrated on the unknown band. "They're a hunting party. The main settlement is about a half days ride ahead, sorry. They appear to know Chauras and are not alarmed; however, they also haven't spotted us yet either."

"Oh, great. We're just going to waltz right into the midst of a Centaur camp unannounced and uninvited and say 'Hi, we were in the neighborhood and thought we'd drop in for a visit.' Then they are going to have us for lunch."

"Now Hawk, we have been invited. Chauras promised us safe escort, or don't you trust our newfound friends?"

"Him, I trust. It's the other couple of thousand or so camped ahead who don't know we're friends that I have doubts about. And unless I miss my guess, Chauras isn't so sure about them either. Why else insist we ride in the center of the group, huh?"

Tivonna looked from Jasen to Hawk. "Are we really in danger? I thought Chauras was our friend. Does he now mean us harm?"

Jasen glanced over at the puzzled girl and shook his dark head. "No, Chauras is our friend, but the Centaurs in that camp are unknown to us. Hawk is right. We must be prepared for trouble. Once Chauras explains our presence, I'm sure everything will be fine. But, there is always the chance of something happening before Chauras has a chance to plead our case. We had best be on our guard."

"I have a feeling Chauras shares our misgivings." Hawk pointed to the large Centaur making his way through the party toward them. "Here he comes now. Looks like the meeting's over."

Chauras ambled up to the trio with a worried looked on his face. "We are near the camp my friends, but I fear all is not well. It seems the duke has been searching for you. He has demanded that you be brought to him at all cost. That band was but one of many who have been sent out with orders to look for you. Fortunately, they did not spot you way back here. The duke especially wants you Jasen. It may not be safe for you to enter the camp. There are many who fear and serve Malycon. They may try to take you."

Jasen reached out and grasped the Centaur's shoulder. "It's all right Chauras. We knew that the duke would be after us eventually. I don't see your people as the type to serve a cruel tyrant like him. I think we'll take our chances with you. After all, we are not exactly helpless now are we?"

Chauras studied the three smiling figures before him and laughed. Helpless? Hardly. Woe unto the duke or anyone else who tried to cross swords with these three. Maybe, they would provide the spark that his people needed to rebel against the evil Duke of Cenchrea. He hoped so. Centaurs were meant to run free, unshackled by the likes of Malycon.

"Very well, my friends. We go together then. But take care, the duke is dangerous and the people's fear runs deep."

"We'll be careful. Now, let's find this camp of yours. I, for one, have done enough riding for a lifetime. However, this time we ride together."

Kicking his mount, Jasen followed closely by Hawk, and Tivonna rode to the head of the party. Shaking his head at such foolhardy souls, Chauras joined his young friends.

Together, they headed for the Centaur's main camp and whatever dangers awaited them there.

Topping a low rise, Jasen gained his first sight of the Centaurs' home. On the horizon, a number of rocky spires seemed to spring from the flat grassland. The huge stone monoliths gleamed in the sunlight, giant guardians of earth marking the entrance to the Centaurs' lair. The Centaurs had chosen to make their permanent dwellings near the edge of the Great Plains where the grasslands suddenly gave way to rugged hills and mountains. They were a nomadic people who roamed the vast prairie during the warm season, and returned to the warm caves and crystal streams hidden within Mystra's mysterious rocky peaks in the cold, stormy months of winter.

As they traveled through the treacherous peaks, Jasen wondered how the duke had managed to force the proud, spirited Centaurs to do his bidding. These rocky spires and mountains were riddled with caves and crevasses. An unsuspecting traveler could get lost in here forever. If the Centaurs chose to withdraw to these hills, no one would be able to root them out. How could the duke threaten such a people?

Just after mid-day, they passed through a narrow gap into a small, secluded valley. Stopping his mount at the top of the pass, Jasen gave a low whistle. Who would have believed? A Garden of Eden tucked away amid the unyielding, barren stone of the surrounding peaks. It was lovely with lush vegetation, crystal streams, and sparkling waterfalls; the Centaurs had truly found a treasure. Jasen's stunned amazement was broken by a chuckle from his left.

"Quite a surprise after all that rock, isn't it?" Chauras laughed noting the stunned looks on his friends' faces. "What do you think of our winter retreat?"

"It's beautiful. I've never seen anything like it." Jasen broke off his enraptured study of the valley and turned to face the Centaur. "How is all this possible?"

Chauras shrugged. "Few know; an accident of nature perhaps. Hot springs, underground lava, plus just the right air currents all come together to make this place. The forces of nature are held in a delicate balanced here. One change, one element out of balance, and all this would be lost. Come, we must go."

Nodding agreement, Jasen urged his mount forward and followed Chauras down the narrow trail leading into the secret valley. The Centaurs' home was as vulnerable as it was beautiful. One wave of an elemental's hand, could see it all crash into ruin. Jasen had heard nothing of the Centaurs' having an elemental amongst them. That would make them easy prey to anyone having access to elemental powers. He would talk to Tivonna. Surely something could be done to secure the valley and keep it safe from elemental attack. Threatening to destroy the Centaurs' home unless they served him seemed like just the kind of thing the duke would do. From all that Jasen had learned of Malycon, he was ruthless and utterly without conscience. He would have no compunction about destroying the valley if the Centaurs failed to please him. Yes, that would explain why such a proud and valiant people served a man who they despised.

The Centaur camp was located near the center of the valley. Sharp-eyed sentries guarded the trails leading through the giant trees surrounding the village. Evidently, Chauras was highly regarded by the Centaurs. The sentries studied them closely, but upon recognizing their escort, made no effort to stop them from entering the camp.

The village was similar to those of most other nomadic tribes. Tent dwellings dotted the clearing and cook fires threw smoke into the afternoon sky in preparation for the evening meal. Around the camp, Centaurs were busy cooking, weaving, caring for the young, repairing weapons, or competing in games of skill. Children galloped and scampered everywhere playing and laughing as the young of every species do. It was a scene of domestic peace and normalcy; that peace was shattered as Chauras and his party entered the village. The silence was oppressive, as all activity ceased and every eye turned to stare at the strangers, but especially at Jasen. Waves of fear battered at Jasen's mind, causing him to reel in the saddle. Slamming his mental shields shut tight, Jasen open his eyes to find Hawk holding him upright and Tivonna studying him with worried eyes.

As he straightened in the saddle, Hawk released his hold on Jasen's arm and turned his attention to their surroundings. "Looks like trouble."

Following Hawk's gaze, Jasen had to agree. The Centaurs had gathered in a crowd around their party and a large male Centaur was arguing with Chauras. It didn't look good.

"You dare to bring him here! Are you mad? You know Malycon's orders." The Centaur was furious.

"What do I care for Malycon or his orders?" Chauras scoffed. "I have found one of the Wise Ones. Would you have me abandon him to such as the Duke of Cenchrea?"

Jasen cracked his shields and scanned the crowd. Not good, but not all bad either, the Centaurs were frightened of the duke and what he could do to their world but they were also intrigued and excited by the prospect of meeting one of the legendary Wise Ones. Chauras had not exaggerated when he claimed that the Centaurs revered the race that had saved them. But was their gratitude greater than their fear?

Chauras raked the Centaurs with a gaze rife with scorn and contempt. "What has become of our honor? We are pledged to render aid to any Wise One we meet. Have we become such cowards, that we would now break our oaths?"

"You lie Chauras! The Wise Ones are a myth. You endanger us for nothing. Malycon wants this one, and he shall have him!"

With a rumble of agreement, the Centaurs moved toward Jasen determined to take him by force if necessary.

Chauras' party prepared to defend their charges, when suddenly a golden barrier of light sprang into being separating the two groups. Behind Jasen, Tivonna raised her hands and twin bolts of pure lightning sprang from the center of her palms arched over the barrier, and struck the ground directly between the lead warrior's front hooves. Silence descended upon the clearing as the Centaurs stared in shock and confusion at the beings before them.

As the panic and bloodlust died, Jasen lowered the shield barrier. Riding up to the warrior who had led the attack, he studied him with calm golden eyes. "Things are not always as they seem, and myths are often based in fact. Chauras speaks the truth, Fireheart. You would be wise to listen to him."

Transfixed by the stranger's eerie golden gaze, fear and awe gripped Fireheart's being. Here was power. He had been a fool to attack this one. His mind in turmoil, he spoke the first thoughts that came into his head. "How...how... do you know my name?"

Jasen smiled and shrugged. "I'm a Wise One. I know many things. Now, suppose we start over all right?"

Jasen's manner was contagious. He no longer appeared so terrifying, but was no less commanding. In fact, Fireheart felt himself drawn to this enigmatic traveler. Timidly, he returned Jasen's smile. "Well, you know my name, may I know yours?"

"I am Jasen. This is Tivonna, daughter of King Arcus of Aquilla. As you may have noticed, she is an elemental. This is Hawk."

"Welcome to our village, young ones." All eyes turned toward the large tent in the center of the village. Standing before the tent was a Centaur wearing a brightly colored ornate vest and headdress. Slowly, the Centaur left his place before the tent and made his way toward Chauras's group. The crowd parted before him, allowing him to reach the combatants unhindered.

Jasen studied the being as he approached. This Centaur was old but far from decrepit. His hair and body were silvered with age, but the gray eyes were clear and bright and filled with wisdom. Power and authority radiated from his presence. This must be the tribal shaman. Now they would learn their fate.

"I am sorry for your rude welcome. Youth is often reckless and many times ignorant as well. I am Shamar; I have long awaited your coming. You need have no fear. You are welcome here. Please be my guest, I feel we have much to discuss."

"We'd be honored." Jasen was intrigued by the shaman's words. How had he known of their coming? And more importantly, what did it mean to the Centaur?

A few moments later, Chauras, Jasen, Tivonna and Hawk were comfortably ensconced in Shamar's tent. Lying back on a pile of soft cushions and sipping his cup of tea, Jasen studied their host. Shamar radiated excitement as if he had finally received something he had long desired. Well, it was as good a time as any to try and find out what he knew.

"Shamar, you said earlier that you had been waiting for me to come. I'm afraid I don't understand."

Seeing Jasen's puzzlement, the old shaman smiled. "I'm not surprised. The pawns of fate rarely know what game it is they play. I will try to explain. As Chauras has told you, when your race saved us from extinction, we swore a Great Oath that we would never forget the sacrifices your people made to aid us and that we would always be alert, ready to aid you if you should ever have need of us. After we made the oath we were given a gift. The shaman of our tribes began to have visions. They showed us growing in wisdom and finding a new home where we could run free and prosper. Then we saw a darkness coming upon us, shackling us and stealing our spirit. We no longer ran free but were bound to another's will. When all appeared lost, the visions changed again. This time they showed deliverance. The Avatar of the Wise Ones would arise again and come to break the chains of darkness. He would come seeking aid against an even greater darkness, but his coming would set us free. You Jasen are the promised deliverer."

Jasen stared incredulously at the Centaur. Clairvoyance was not unknown among his people but, that the Centaurs had been waiting all these centuries for his coming, was unbelievable.

"Shamar, I do not doubt your power. I'm just wondering, how can you be sure that I'm the one you seek? I was separated from my people when I was ten. There is so much about them and myself I don't know. I don't see how I can help you. I am not a deliverer."

"Oh, but you are young one. Tell me how much do you remember of your people? Did you ever wonder why you were different?"

"What do you mean different?"

"How many of your people were dark of hair with golden eyes?"

For the second time in as many minutes, Jasen sat stunned by the shaman's words. "I ... I'm not sure. My memories of the past are hazy, incomplete. I remember little of my home world or its people. I mainly remember isolation and lessons, endless studies and lessons. I saw few people outside of my teachers but, now that you mention it, most of them were fair."

The old shaman nodded. "Exactly. The Wise Ones were a race of fair-haired, fair-skinned people. But when a crisis threatened, one would be born with hair the color of the night and possessing the golden eyes of power. Throughout your people's long history, whenever they were threatened, a leader would arise to combat the evil and protect the people. Their raven hair and eyes of gold always marked them. You, Jasen, are such a one."

Jasen's pale skin had grown even paler as he listened to the old Centaur's words. It was crazy, but it also made a strange kind of sense. He had never given much thought to why as a child his gifts were so much stronger than his teachers, or why he could do things they couldn't. He never questioned the isolation and endless studies and practices, now it all fit. But things were different now; he was no longer among his people and his training was incomplete.

Jasen shook his head. "Shamar, even if what you say is true, I don't see where it makes a whole lot of difference. My training was never finished. I'm afraid I'm a flawed avatar. I will help you in any way I can, but I may not be able to accomplish what you hope."

The shaman smiled at the young man before him. Oh, child, if you only knew, you are far greater than you ever dreamed. "Do not worry. Follow your destiny and do what seems best to you. All will come to pass as it should. Now, how can I aid you?"

Grateful for the change of subject, Jasen told Shamar of their mission on Mystra. When the tale was finished, the old Centaur studied his young guest with troubled eyes. "Your task is indeed grave. The place you seek is known to me but beware, to reach your goal you must first pass through the territories of the Wer folk and the Mermen.

"But, they are friendly. Why would that be a problem?" Tivonna had studied Mystra's inhabitants thoroughly. Both the Wer and the Mer were allies of Aquilla.

"Things have changed, daughter of Arcus. Except for your father's kingdom, all now serve the Duke of Cenchrea. You will find no friends here in the North."

"But...how...why? I can't believe it. The Wer and Mermen hate Malycon, why would they serve him?"

"Ah, child, they, like us, have little choice. Your father's kingdom is rife with elementals. We of the North possess few, and those that once lived here are now either dead or bound to Malycon's service. We serve him or perish."

"No!" Tivonna face mirrored her horror. "No elemental would do such a thing. To abuse our power so, it's unthinkable."

Shamar reached out and gently laid a hand on the stunned girl's shoulder. "I'm afraid it is true. Malycon has found a way to bind the elementals to his will. Many of them are dead now. Those that remain are firmly in the Duke's power. We either serve him or he will destroy us."

"Then, we must leave at once." Jasen's calm voice broke through Tivonna's shock. All eyes turned to face the telepath. "You are at risk as long as I am here. For some reason, Malycon wants me. If you refuse to turn me over to him, you risk attack. We must leave."

The shaman's answer was destined to never come. Suddenly, the ground beneath them shook with such force that the cups flew from their hands and they were tossed helplessly across the tent floor. As the tremor died, Jasen opened his mind and probed the valley. What he saw drained all color from his already pale face. Quickly, he turned to Tivonna. "It's a storm. Lightning is striking the surrounding mountains and more tremors are on their way. So far the main force of the system hasn't entered the valley, but it's coming this way fast. Can it be stopped?"

Righting herself, Tivonna extended her senses and searched the surrounding area for elemental activity. What she felt filled her with dread. Facing the others, she spoke quickly. "I need to get to high ground. This is no ordinary storm. I ... I may not be able to stop it."

"You will do your best. That is all we can ask of you." The old Centaur was calm. They had lived in fear of just such a thing. Now, that the disaster had finally come, it no longer had the power to terrorize him. These young ones would help all they could. It was now in the hands of the

Creator.

Suddenly, Jasen turned to the shaman, a strange expression on his face. His gaze was vacant, almost entranced, as if he looked at something not visible to others. "You must get your people out of the valley. Malycon has sent the storm to kill you and to locate us. It has been aimed directly at the heart of your camp. You might have a chance if you can get out of the valley in time."

Hawk studied his friend intently. Jasen's voice was soft with a dream-like quality he had never heard. He appeared lost in some inner world of his own. Hesitantly, Hawk reached out and gently shook his shoulder. "Jasen how do you know about the storm. Jase, are you with us?"

"What?" Jasen blinked as if awakening from a long sleep.

"I said how do you know that the Centaurs will be safe if they can get out of the valley?"

Jasen shrugged. "I just know. Come on, we have to hurry. That storm will be here within the hour. We have to find a way to delay it."

Shamar had already left to begin carrying out Jasen's orders, and Tivonna and Chauras were bringing their mounts to the front of the tent. Leaping into their saddles, they raced for the mountains at the valley's edge. If Tivonna could get up high enough, she might be able to turn the storm. After what seemed like forever, they reached the narrow trail that lead to a small plateau high upon the mountainside. Following Chauras, they made the rugged climb in record time. Soon they were standing on a flat mesa overlooking the prairie to the North of the hidden valley. There, on the horizon, wreaking havoc on the vast grassland and closer mountain peaks, was a huge dark swirling cloud.

Sighting the storm, Tivonna motioned for them to stop. "This is as far as you go. I must make the climb from here alone."

Dismounting, she followed the steep trail farther up the mountain. At last, she reached the narrow plateau that marked the top of the peak. Steeling herself, she turned northward to face the approaching storm. Reaching out with all her senses, she studied the phenomena approaching her. As her awareness brushed the edge of the cloud, a wave of raw energy slammed into her. By the Creator, what was this thing? Tivonna's stomach knotted in horror and she almost forgot to breathe. This was like no storm that she had ever encountered. It was a monster, nature gone wild. But not just nature; there was a familiar feel to some of the forces swirling within the monstrosity she called a storm. This was elemental work. How could an elemental so pervert her powers as to spawn such a horror as this? Time for that later; her task now was to stop it. Even as the thought formed, she knew that she was no match for the airborne demon before her. Just as her spirits began to sink, a soft, warm presence flooded Tivonna's mind reassuring and strengthening her.

"All you have to do is delay it. We have to buy Shamar time to evacuate the valley. You can do it. I know you. You have the power. Don't be afraid, just give it your best shot. I love you. I'll be with you every step of the way"

Jasen's calm, soothing thoughts stilled her fears. She was an elemental. This was her task. She might fail, but it wouldn't be because she didn't try. Raising both hands, Tivonna reached out for the nightmare creation before her. Extending her senses to their limits, she probed for the heart of the cloud. The only way to banish a storm was to unravel the strands of force that composed its central pattern, or heart. Carefully, Tivonna searched for the core and encountered chaos. There was no pattern, only a tangled mass of brightly glowing lines of power! Even as she watched, more and more bands of energy were added to the tangle as the storm sucked in forces from the surrounding air. It was still growing! Gathering all her power, Tivonna reached for the raging heart of the storm. Pitting her will against this thing of nature gone mad, she tried to unravel the forces swirling madly in the cloud's heart. Tried and failed! She could touch the center, feel its lines of force, but she could not prize them loose from the tangled mass that had once been the thunderstorm's central pattern. She could halt the storm, but she could not banish it. She simply wasn't strong enough to tame the wild power pulsing through the swirling vortex at the heart of the cloud. She had failed. She could delay the storm, but not for long. Already, she was weakening. Power was draining from her at an alarming rate, and still the storm raged. As she weakened it grew stronger. They were lost; when her power was spent the valley would die.

Jasen, Hawk and Chauras watched as Tivonna pitted her will against the tremendous power of the storm. Holding their collective breaths, they watched the titanic struggle.

"It's stopped moving." Chauras pointed to the dark menacing cloud. "The lightning no longer strikes the ground and the shocks have stilled."

"She has stopped it but for how long? It doesn't appear to be weakening at all." Hawk's voice was full of concern as he watched the valiant struggle taking place above them. "She can't keep that up forever. Isn't there something we can do to help her?"

Jasen had kept a light mind-link with Tivonna and now read her despair and fatigue. He watched the Herculean battle in puzzlement. Something wasn't right. The storm was powerful, true, but Tivonna was a fourth level elemental. Jasen, of all people, knew the amount of power she wielded. His memories of taming her wild powers were still hazy, but he sensed that she was using only a fraction of her total power. Gently, he reached out and joined his mind more firmly to hers. Being careful not to break her concentration, Jasen probed deeply into her mind. Finally, he located what he sought.

The mindscape shimmered and resolved itself into a barren plain across which ran four brightly pulsing bands of color. Or, at least three of the bands pulsed brightly. The fourth was a dim yellow which grew dimmer as he watched. Studying the bands, Jasen understood. An elemental could only work with one element at a time. She could not cross power streams. There had to be a way. If Tivonna could tap into the earth, she could use the power of the planet itself to fight the storm. But how? Suddenly, knowledge came to Jasen. Just as he knew that the storm had been sent to destroy the Centaurs, he now knew what he must do. They had one slim chance. He would try to use his own mind to bridge the separated bands of power. He had harnessed Tivonna's powers once, could he do it again? There was only one way to find out. After all, he really hadn't anything to lose. If they failed, the valley and the Centaurs died; he had to try. Trusting to instinct and his new sense of rightness, Jasen reached out for the glowing stands of energy. Grasping the shining cables of pure power, he melded them together into a single crystal filament of energy pulsing with red, blue, green and yellow. Using every ounce of his will and mental powers, he meshed the streams of raw power into one. Meshed them and screamed, fire poured through his mind and raced along his nerves as the power of a planet coursed through his brain. Coursed through him and into Tivonna filling her with power. He dimly felt Tivonna's shock at the sudden influx of energy, then power raced through the crystal line of force as Tivonna pulled energy from the earth and the fire at the planet's heart, and channeled it into the raging storm. Jasen's world became a red sea of agony. Fighting the pain and willing himself to stay conscious, he grimly held the melded forces together, praying Tivonna succeeded. After an Eternity the flow of energy slowed. Mustering the last of his fading strength, Jasen carefully released the bands of power back to their natural states, then blackness took him.

Tivonna struggled to hold the storm in check. Just

when she was sure her strength was spent, energy coursed through her body. It was heady. Suddenly, she could sense the whole planet. She could feel the earth beneath her feet strong, steady and charged with power. And deep beneath the earth, fiery lava pulsed with energy, and everywhere water gurgled and roared with elemental force. How this was possible she didn't know, but it was a miracle she could not ignore. Reaching out, she tapped into the energy of the world around her. Pulling power from earth, fire and water, she channeled her new found strength into the heart of the raging storm. Backed by the limitless power of the other elements, she seized the swirling vortex of chaotic energy at the storms center and bent it to her will. Strand by strand, she unraveled the bands of force making up the heart of the cloud, and released them back into the natural energy flow of the planet. When she was finished, the sky was calm and no sign remained of the storm cloud. Cherishing her new gifts, Tivonna turned her attention to repairing the damage left by the unnatural storm. Huge craters dotted the grassy plain and several new fault lines had arisen as a result of the lightning blasts. Drawing from fire, water and air, Tivonna molded the earth to her will, sealing the faults and craters. When she was done, no sign remained to betray how close they had all come to destruction. Then, as suddenly as it had come, the energy vanished. Tivonna staggered as her senses narrowed from sensing all four elements to just one. Yet, even though the power was gone, an echo of it lingered. She could still sense the earth, fire, air and water around her and she was not as drained as she should be. Even now, she could feel her energy regenerating. The rate was not fast but it was steady. What had happened to her?

Suddenly, Tivonna became aware of another change. This one filled her with fear. The slender link she had with Jasen was gone. Stilling her panic, she raced down the trail leading to the lower plateau. Of course, Jasen, somehow he had given her access to all her power at once, something no elemental had ever done, but then no elemental had ever been bonded to a telepath before either.

Fearing the worst, Tivonna raced to where she had left the others. What she saw caused her throat to tighten and a hard, cold knot suddenly materialized in the pit of her stomach. Hawk and Chauras were kneeling beside a still, prone figure. Jasen lay on the rocky ground pale as death. He wasn't breathing! Hawk was frantically working to revive his unconscious friend.

Seeing Jasen's pale, worn face jarred Tivonna from her shock. Running forward, she dropped to her knees beside her bondmate. Up close, Jasen looked even worse. He appeared to be drained of all life. But, what had happened? Suddenly she knew. Bridging her powers must have taken every ounce of strength Jasen had. He had sacrificed his energy, his very life force, to funnel to her the power she had needed to combat the storm. He had saved nothing for himself. Chauras had said that many of Jasen's people had died using up their vital life energy to aid others. If Jasen was going to survive, he must replace some of his depleted strength. Since he was presently unable to do so, she would have to do it for him.

Stilling her fears, Tivonna reached deep inside herself. In her mind's eye, she saw the center of her power. There, glowing brightly, were the cords that symbolized her mastery over the elements. But something had changed; before there had been four separate cords, now, however, tiny lines of force crisscrossed the power streams. Tiny channels through which energy could flow from one band of power to another wove themselves among the cords of her power. Even now, energy was flowing from the red, green, and blue into the yellow, replenishing its spent energy. It wasn't the same as when Jasen had acted as the bridge, but it would suffice. Reaching deeper, Tivonna searched for any sign of the link Jasen had established between them. Every elemental was taught how to find and manipulate the mental bands that represented her powers, but never before had Tivonna used her weak mental skills in such a manner. Desperately, she called to that part of herself that was her soul mate. There! Far back in the corner of her mind was a gossamer thin strand. It was so fragile looking that Tivonna feared to touch it for fear it would snap. If she was going to save Jasen, she had to risk contact. Now, which energy source? Earth. The power of earth was warm and steady, just what Jasen's ravaged system needed. Sinking her senses deep into the earth beneath her, Tivonna pulled its serene strength into herself. Then, hesitantly, she reached out and gently brushed the delicate filament that linked her to Jasen. Slowly, she fed power along the fragile thread. As the energy flowed into the link, it began to glow faintly. As the bond strengthened, Tivonna increased the flow of power. How long she kept up that steady flow of energy she couldn't say, but finally she felt a resistance along the bond. Immediately, she stopped the energy flow.

Opening her eyes, Tivonna looked at Jasen and sighed in relief. He was breathing! He was still pale and his breathing shallow but he was alive. Looking up, she found Hawk watching her intently.

"Thank you. I'm not exactly sure what you did but thank you."

Tivonna turned to him, tears streaming down her face. "Oh, Hawk, he was dying. He used up all his energy so that I could fight the storm. He had none left for living. I was so afraid I wouldn't be able to help him. I tried to do what he did but...Hawk is he going to be all right?"

Taking the distraught girl in his arms, Hawk offered her a shoulder and let her cry out her fear and anxiety. It had been close, and Jasen still wasn't out of the woods yet.

"It's going to be OK. Jase is a fighter. All he needed was a little boost." Looking over the girl's head, Hawk caught Chauras's eye. The big Centaur had not spoken since Jasen's collapse, but his worry and concern were written plainly on his face. "We'd best get these two back to camp. We'll sort everything out later."

Nodding, Chauras bent forward and scooped up the unconscious telepath in his well-muscled arms. Cradling him like a child, the big Centaur set off down the mountainside. Helping Tivonna to mount, Hawk grasped the reins of Jasen's mount and headed down the steep trail. They were safe for now, but not for long. There was no way that Malycon's elementals could fail to sense that working of power. It was no telling what the duke would throw at them next. Hawk glanced at the exhausted girl beside him, and then looked ahead to where Chauras carried the unconscious Jasen. He just hoped they were ready in time.

CHAPTER TWELVE

"You lost them! Incompetent fools! You had them in the palm of your hand!" Malycon slammed his clenched fist onto the desktop in outrage and frustration, then glared up at the silent guardsman standing stiffly before him. "People do not disappear into thin air. I want them found."

"I'm sorry, my lord. We searched the entire valley. Nothing, there was not a living soul in sight. We also searched the surrounding prairie, but there was no sign of the Centaurs or the strangers." Byron stood rigidly at attention before the duke's desk. Ignoring Malycon's outburst, his face held expressionless, he calmly continued with his report on the failed excursion into the Centaur Valley. "Those mountains are honeycombed with caves and underground tunnels. Some of the passages reach as far as the Wer Forest. They could be anywhere by now, and the dragons are useless for working underground. We searched as long as we could, but the dragons were becoming restless, so we returned."

The duke sat silently studying his head guardsman. Byron would not lie to him. If he said the valley was uninhabited, then it was so. While the valiant warrior was not overly fond of him, Byron was a man of honor. He had sworn loyalty and would die rather than betray that oath. So his prey had eluded him again. Well, it would not be for long.

"They must be headed this way. If they had returned to Aquilla, you would have spotted them."

"Yes, my lord. The grasslands were empty and they hadn't the time to reach the Painted Forest before we arrived. If they had headed south, we would have found them."

"So that leaves these underground passages of yours."

"They must have taken shelter underground. The Centaurs are not stupid. They must have known you'd send dragon soldiers. Underground is the one place where dragons can't follow. They're too big and most of those passages are tight even for a man."

"Well, they can't stay hidden forever. I want patrol sweeps between here and the mountains. Eventually, they have to enter Wer or Mer territory. When they do, we'll be waiting."

"Begging your pardon, my lord, but if they seek refuge in the Wer Forest, we won't be able to spot them from the air. Those trees are huge and the foliage is too thick even for dragon eyes to pierce."

"The Wer know better than to cross me. If the strangers enter their territory, they will deliver them to me. Anyway, sooner or later, they will be forced to leave the forest. Once out from under the shelter of the trees, they will be easy targets for your dragon warriors. Soon the strangers will be mine. You have done well, Byron. See to the patrols. You may go."

Bowing gracefully, Byron turned and left the duke's study. Strange things were happening in Cenchrea and across Mystra. First the dragons were becoming uncooperative. He was sure that they knew more about the mountain passages than they were telling. And, was it that they couldn't enter the tunnels or wouldn't? And what of the Centaurs? They had obviously defied Malycon to help the strangers, even knowing that he possessed the means to destroy their home and would not hesitate to use it. Who were these mysterious strangers, and what magic did they hold that the duke would risk all to possess it? He had become like a man obsessed. These were indeed strange and unsettling times. And the most unsettling of the many thoughts running through the warrior's mind was: If the Centaurs could turn against Malycon, why not the Wer or others?

Time held little meaning for Jasen. He was enshrouded in a world of mists and chaos; dreams and visions swirled around him. He reached out to grasp them, only to have them melt into wisps of color. Other dreams sprang up one after another to replace the vanquished ones in a jumbled series of tangled images and feelings. How long he drifted in this other realm of color and images he didn't know. His world was narrowed to chaos and pain. His every nerve flamed with agony and each new vision sent shafts of new torment along his frayed nerves. Then, suddenly, the images faded to be replaced by a cool, numbing darkness. He drifted aimlessly in this tranquil sea of nothingness. Finally, the pain began to fade and with its passing, awareness returned to Jasen's mind. With an effort of will, he fought his way free of the soothing blackness back into the world of light. Giving a low moan, Jasen opened his eyes and saw green. Everything was green. As the fog slowly cleared from his mind, he realized that he was in a forest. Unlike the Painted Forest, the trees in these woods were all a vibrant green.

Looking around, Jasen discovered that he was lying snuggled in blankets on a thick bed of soft green boughs. A lean-to type structure, fashioned from the same green limbs that comprised his bed, loomed over his head. Where was he? What had happened? Jasen's thoughts were interrupted by the sounds of someone approaching. Seconds later, Hawk poked his head under the canopy of limbs. A smile lit his face when he saw that Jasen was awake and that there was sanity in his eyes. Sitting down next to Jasen's bed, he reached out and placed a hand on his friend's forehead.

"The fever's gone. How do you feel?"

Jasen gave Hawk a tired smile. "I'm not really sure. I feel like I've been turned inside out, but everything seems to be working. Where are we? What happened?"

"After that fool stunt you pulled, you're lucky you can feel anything at all. As for where we are this is the edge of the Wer Forest. And before you ask, you've been out for almost five days." Hawk's voice took on a serious note. "You really outdid yourself this time. If it hadn't been for Tivonna feeding you energy, you would have died. You were too drained to even breathe, and afterwards, your shields were practically gone. We had to risk moving you or have you go insane. As it was, we've been taking turns watching you and trying to guard our thoughts. Between shock, fever, and hallucinations, we weren't sure what you might do." The Filidae shook his head. "During one particularly bad episode you hoisted Chauras clear off the ground. He was quite a sight dangling there in midair, all four legs churning madly. Fortunately, the effort drained you before you could toss him against a tree. Unfortunately, it set off another spell of fever. You make a terrible patient."

"My pardon, it seems I'm beginning to make this a habit." Jasen felt the fear and pain behind Hawk's light words. He had gravely worried his friend. Suddenly, something his friend had said registered on his tired brain. "Chauras? Hawk, what in blazes has been going on? What about Malycon? Are the Centaurs safe?"

Hawk chuckled. "Never mind. All you need to know is

that everyone is safe for now. Go to sleep. You are still far too spent. Tomorrow, I promise to give you a thorough briefing. A lot has happened since you decided to take your little nap."

Jasen started to protest, when a sudden wave of fatigue closed in on him. Against his will, his eyes closed and he was soon lost in sleep. Hawk let out a huge sigh of relief. Thoughts of the past few days made him shudder, but thankfully, the worst appeared to be over. Silently, he left the sleeping figure and headed to the campsite nearby. There were others who needed to hear this news.

Jasen awoke from a long refreshing sleep to the feel of cold steel caressing the pulse point at his throat. Not daring to move, he carefully opened his eyes and glanced up at the silent figure kneeling beside him. The dagger never moved from its place against his throat nor was there any sign of alarm at his awakening in the amber eyes that watched him steadily. The figure before him was impressive. There was a wild alien light in the stranger's eyes that reminded Jasen of a predator who had just cornered its prey. They were dangerous eyes and not quite human. He would have to be careful. His captor obviously considered him dangerous. One wrong move and the dagger would rip the life from him.

Jasen lay quietly under the stranger's scrutiny and studied him in turn. The man's shoulder length hair was a silvery gray, yet his well-muscled physique showed him to be in his prime. He was dressed all in dark brown leathers, except for a vest made from the pelt of a wolf whose fur was the same silvery gray as his hair. After a few moments during which each took the others measure, his captor spoke.

"We have your friends. Try anything and they die."

Receiving Jasen's careful nod of understanding, the man slowly removed the dagger from Jasen's throat. Then, in one smooth, lithe movement he ducked from under the canopy of limbs and rose gracefully to his feet. Returning the dagger to its sheath, he motioned for Jasen to rise.

Obediently, the telepath slowly rose from his pallet and exited the shelter to stand beside his silent captor. The effort of standing after being prone so long caused a wave of vertigo to wash over him, but it quickly passed. He was still weak but he did have some reserves, and he could feel his strength slowly returning. If it came to a fight, he wouldn't be entirely helpless but for now he must conserve his energy. The first order of business was to find the others; he could make no move until he was sure that they were safe.

Jasen's captor waited patiently, while the telepath regained his equilibrium. Seeing his prisoner recovered, he motioned for him to walk. For the first time, Jasen noticed the clearing beyond his shelter and his stomach tightened with anxiety and all thoughts of making a move against his jailer fled from his mind. The clearing was swarming with warriors and, far to one side, tightly bound and kneeling within a ring of armed guards were Tivonna, Hawk and Chauras.

Tivonna's eyes brightened as she spotted Jasen unharmed and once more among the living. Instinctively, she struggled to rise and go to him, only to be roughly caught and dragged back by her Wer guards before she had taken but a step. The bruising grip on her arms served to remind her that she was a prisoner and not free to roam. She stood passively within the guard's hold and looked longingly toward her bondmate. Inside, her heart was singing. Jasen was well again, all would be well.

Across the clearing, Jasen saw Tivonna jerked back and held tightly by one of the warriors guarding her. Even after halting her coming to him, the guard continued to restrain the elemental and, from the look on Tivonna's face, his grip was anything but gentle. Seeing his mate's pain, Jasen's temper finally snapped. Ever since landing on Mystra they had been beseeched by one set of troubles after another. They had been delayed and hindered in their search at every turn. Well, he for one had had enough. Oblivious to the danger, Jasen stalked across the clearing toward the Wer holding Tivonna captive. He moved so quickly he was standing before the young warrior before his silver-haired guard could make a move to stop him.

"Take your hands off her. Now!" Jasen's voice was soft and low. Hearing the gently uttered words, Hawk broke into a cold sweat and icy shivers raced down his spine. He knew that tone; it meant death. He had only heard it once before. It meant Jasen was furious and out of control.

Even as Hawk watched, a faint golden glow began forming around the telepath, pulsing ominously. All the pent up stresses of the past weeks were rising to the surface and looking for a place to explode. If the young Wer wasn't very, very careful, he would soon be wishing he had never been born, and not one soul in the camp would be able to save him. Hawk had no illusions to just how dangerous Jasen could be. Even in his weakened state, the telepath was capable of leveling the camp. Usually, Jasen kept his powers and emotions on a tight rein but, from the look of things, that rein had snapped and what little control he still possessed was shaky at best. That soft, calm tone was a warning. One wrong move from their erstwhile captors and all hell was going to break loose. With a warning sign to Chauras, Hawk prepared to hunt for cover. Since subtlety and diplomacy didn't appear to be Wer traits, he had a feeling he might soon be needing it.

Looking up, the young warrior flinched as he stared into a pair of blazing golden eyes. With a cry, he jerked his hands from Tivonna's arms and took an unconscious step backwards. There was death in those eyes.

Ignoring the terrified Wer, Jasen turned toward his bound friends. The glow around him increased and three flashes of gold shot from the swirling energy cloud and sped toward the captives. Watching the globe of golden energy speed toward him, Hawk tensed in alarm then relaxed as he saw Jasen's intent. Nearing the bound Filidae, the globe resolved itself into a blade of pure telekinetic energy. Three flashes of gold and three sets of bonds fluttered to the ground neatly severed by Jasen's finely focused force blades.

Keeping her hands behind her to hide the bruises left from the Wer's callous grip, Tivonna slowly moved away from her former guard to stand quietly beside Hawk and Chauras who had regained their feet and now watched the Wer carefully. While Hawk and Chauras watched their enemies, Tivonna watched Jasen. She could hardly credit that this was the same man who had lain sick and near death only a few hours ago. The power radiating from him was incredible. His psychic aura was almost tangible. She could feel him struggling to regain control of his turbulent emotions. The golden curtain of energy surrounding him brightened and dimmed in response to his battle for control. So far, Jasen had managed to retain control of his powers, but that control was tenuous at best and could slip at any minute. The golden wall of pulsating energy swirling around him strained to break his hold and run rampant. He was barely succeeding in holding it in check. She had to do something and fast.

Silver, leader of the Wolf Clan of the Wer, stared at his former captives and tasted fear. He had badly underestimated his enemy. He had been warned that this man was dangerous. Malycon was obsessed with finding him. Watching the strangers, he had assumed that the dark haired human was too ill to be a threat. That assumption had been wrong. This one was anything but helpless.

A cold shiver ran down the warrior's spine. If the dark one was this powerful ill, what would he be capable of when well? Silver feared that he had made a great mistake in antagonizing these visitors to Wer Forest. It was Wer law that all outsiders entering the forest must be brought before the leaders of the Wer Clans for judgment. Those who found favor with the rulers were given permission to travel through the forest, while those judged as unfit were escorted out of Wer territory. Silver and his band had approached the strangers' camp with this purpose in mind, when he had realized that these were the ones Malycon was searching for. Malycon's orders were clear. Anyone spotting these travelers was to capture them and bring them to the duke immediately. Seeing that one of the strangers was ill and that the rest of the party was worn out from caring for him, the warrior had decided to attack the camp. If they could gain possession of the dark haired stranger, he might offer them a means of striking out against Malycon. The Wer held no love for the evil duke, and the visitors might just prove to be the weapon they needed to break his hold on them. They would have no better opportunity than this to capture them.

As expected, the strangers were exhausted and clearly not expecting trouble. The Wer attack took them completely by surprise. The warriors had seized the camp and bound the travelers before they had been able to react. Everything had gone well until now. Who would have guessed? The man must be the elemental's kiosan, judging by his sudden violent reaction to seeing her detained. Who could have known that an elemental would be traveling with the party and that the man they sought was bound to her? Now, not only were they faced with this dark haired demon, but the elemental was unbound and free to use her own abilities which she would do if her kiosan were threatened. What a mess.

Silver watched the glowing figure before him with something akin to awe. What an ally he would have made. No wonder Malycon was so desperate to find him. With this one's aid, they could destroy Malycon's hold on them forever, but that chance was now lost to them. By antagonizing the strangers, they had lost any hope of obtaining a weapon against the duke. They would be lucky to escape with their lives. But what could he do? How could he salvage the situation?

Before Silver could formulate a plan, the beautiful elemental took matters from his hands. Stepping forward, she slowly walked to her mate's side. Ignoring the power tingling in the air around her, Tivonna carefully reached out and laid her hand on his rigid shoulder.

"Jasen? Jasen!" After several tries, Tivonna's words finally penetrated Jasen's anger. With an effort he reined in his temper and lowered his eyes to meet those of the woman standing tensely at his side.

Tivonna sighed in relief. At least he was paying attention to her, now if only she could make him understand. "Jasen, it's all right. We are free and unharmed; there is no danger."

Jasen's gaze locked with Tivonna's as he struggled to master his seething emotions. One thought burned in his mind, if he destroyed the camp his friends would die as well. Silently, he fought for mastery. It had never been this difficult before. His powers had been changing since coming to Mystra. Talents he had not known he possessed were awakening, and abilities he already had were growing stronger. His anger had broken through the last barriers blocking his powers, and their hidden strength had come crashing into his unprepared mind. His anger fled, replaced by a desperate battle to tame his wild talents. It was a fight Jasen wasn't sure that he could win, but he had no choice. If he lost control, his powers would destroy them all. Friend and foe alike would die. He had to win.

The silence was oppressive as all waited to see what their fate would be. Then, as suddenly as it had come, between one heartbeat and the next, the power was gone. Sighs of relief echoed around the clearing as Jasen turned and looked at Silver.

"If this is how you always greet your guests, I'm not surprised you have so few callers. Why did you attack us?"

Silver lifted his eyes to meet the golden ones now calmly regarding him, and knew that they were not safe yet. Those golden eyes were still charged with power, but now that power was tightly leashed. Somehow, that was even more frightening than the unbridled fury of a few moments ago. Studying the man before him, Silver knew that only the truth would satisfy him. Steeling himself, he tried to explain.

"It was my duty to try and capture you. Malycon, the Duke of Cenchrea, has ordered that you and your party be taken on sight and delivered to him unharmed. The Wer are oath bound to Malycon and honor demanded that I try and fulfill his orders." Silver gave a wry smile. "Unfortunately, I seem to have underestimated you. Rumor has it that your party is highly dangerous; it appears that the rumors are true."

A slight smile tugged at the corner of Jasen's lips. "True indeed. The question is what do we do now? You must realize that you have no hope of taking us by force now and, while I have no objections to meeting your leaders, I have no desire to become Malycon or anyone else's prisoner."

Silver nodded in understanding. "It would be foolish to even think of attacking you. With you so miraculously recovered and the elemental free, it would be suicide; besides which, I fear what evil Malycon could do with you as allies. But, my wishes are unimportant. I am a warrior of the Wer and as such I must uphold the honor of my clan. I must attempt to bring you in even if it means my death."

"You hold no love for Malycon, yet you serve him, why?" Tivonna asked.

"Love him, no." Silver snorted, shaking his head in

disgust. "I and every other Wer hate him."

"Yet, your people swore loyalty to him." Chauras stated.

"Not by choice, Centaur. Many moons ago, the elementals guarding Wer Forest disappeared. Then, Malycon came with his soldiers. We fought him of course, but then the dragons came and the fires began. We had no choice but to surrender. We Wer are bound to the forest, without it we would die. With the elementals refusing aid and the dragons able to strike at will, there was little we could do. We swore allegiance to Malycon."

"An oath taken under coercion isn't binding." Hawk interjected. "You don't owe him anything."

"The word of a Wer is inviolate. It matters not why it was given."

Jasen sighed. It didn't take his newly heightened senses to see that Silver meant what he said. The warrior was a valiant and honorable man. He would keep his word no matter the cost. There must be some way around this. He saw one slim chance. "Does your oath call for turning us over to Malycon personally, or will presenting us to your clan elders suffice?"

Silver pondered the question a long while then answered. "No, if you accompany me to our camp and present yourself to the elders for judgment, honor will be satisfied. But I do not see how that will help you. They will just order you turned over to Malycon."

"Never mind. I propose a truce. We will willingly accompany you to your camp. In exchange, you agree to make no move against us until after we have spoken to your clan leaders. Agreed?"

Silver stared in disbelief at the man before him. "I do not understand. The elders will turn you over to Malycon. Why would you risk such a fate by accompanying us?"

Hawk gave the puzzled Wer a dazzling smile. "Why not? What's life without a little risk?" The Filidae's mood quickly sobered. "Besides, it buys us time. Give us enough time and we may be able to figure a way out of this mess. At the very least we all get to live a little longer." He gave an elegant shrug. "Anyway, what do you have to lose?"

Silver shook his head. Never had he met such as these. "As you say, I have little to lose. Very well, you have your truce. I am Silver, leader of this pack. You have my word that no action will be taken against you until after you speak with the Elders. The rest is up to them."

"Good enough. I am Jasen. These are my companions Tivonna, Hawk and Chauras. We are in your hands. What's our next move?"

"Gather your things. Tonight is the Great Hunt. You must be under cover by nightfall. There is a cabin a few miles from here. If we hurry, we should reach it well before dusk."

Working together, the two parties quickly broke camp and prepared to travel. Following Silver's suggestion, Hawk took the unicorns to a nearby glen bordering the forest and turned them loose to graze. The trails through the forest were narrow and treacherous. Only the main trade route was safe for riding. The mounts would wait for them here. If all went well, they would return and resume their interrupted journey. If not, the Wer would see that the steeds were returned to Aquilla.

Seeing Chauras readying his packs, Jasen walked over and laid a hand on the Centaur's shoulder. "I am sorry, my friend, but this is as far as you go. Our paths must part here for a while."

Chauras's cry of outrage was stilled as he saw the distant look in Jasen's eyes. The Centaur could not suppress a shudder as he recognized that look. Whatever the telepath saw, it was beyond the knowledge of this world.

"What would you have of me?" Chauras whispered.

"This world is changing my friend. There is a confrontation coming, one I can no longer ignore or avoid.

It seems this world has chosen to involve me in its affairs and, I cannot settle my own until I have fulfilled that destiny. The time has come for the inhabitants of Mystra to choose their fates. If your people wish to be free, then come to Malycon's holding. The final battle will be fought there. Send word to King Arcus. Tell him and the Elemental High Council all you have seen and know. They too must choose."

Suddenly, the faraway look left Jasen's eyes, and he gave the startled Centaur a dazzling smile. "Cheer up my friend. We will meet again. Your people will be free and Mystra will be whole again. Besides, I don't think you would enjoy traipsing through the brambles, would you?"

Chuckling, Chauras shook his head and embraced the telepath fondly. "You are a menace. You speak of upending the world one minute, and make jokes the next. I am dizzy with trying to follow you."

"That's our Jasen." Hawk and Tivonna joined them. "I take it our fearless leader has an unpleasant task for you? He loves sending others off to do his dirty work." He clasped Chauras's forearm in the Centaur fashion. "We will miss you big guy. Take care of yourself and remember to watch your back. Malycon bears you no love either."

"I too will miss you." Much to Chauras's amazement, Tivonna came forward and, standing on her tiptoes, kissed him on the cheek. "Thank you for all your help. We would never have made it this far without you."

The huge Centaur ducked his head and scuffed one hoof in the dirt, embarrassed but pleased at the show of affection. These were good friends and stout companions. He would not fail their trust. He longed to be with them, for he knew the dangers they would face, but Jasen had given him a task and nothing short of death would keep him from fulfilling it. If the telepath wanted an army, he would have one.

Lifting his head, Chauras found Jasen watching him, a

small smile tugging at the corner of his mouth. The Centaur sighed. Having anyone else know of his strong feelings would have embarrassed him, but this was Jasen. He did not mind being known by this one. His strong feelings for these three beings amazed him. He had never had companions so dear. Yet, he had known them for only a short time. In that time, they had changed his life. He had seen the world through their eyes, and could never again be content to spend his time in idle pursuits while others perished. He now had a dream, a goal for his life. His people would be free.

In a moment of exuberance, Chauras gathered his three friends in a huge bear hug, which threatened to break all their ribs. Releasing them, he gathered his packs and turned to address his new friends one last time.

"Well, I cannot say that it has always been easy, but knowing you three has definitely been educational. Be well my friends and guard each other well. The closer you get to Malycon, the greater will be your danger." He turned and watched the Wer scurrying around the campsite. "And be wary of your guides, they are an independent lot and hold no loyalties outside their packs. The temptation to gain honor at your expense will be high, no matter what their leader promises."

"We will be careful." Tivonna answered. "And tell my father and mother that I am well and that I love them."

Chauras gave a courtly bow. "It will be my pleasure, my lady."

Giving the others a salute, the Centaur shouldered his packs and turned to begin his journey back to his own people. His task would not be an easy one. Rallying and uniting the three forces of humans, elementals, and Centaurs would require careful handling, but unite them he would. Jasen wished it and that was that. Humming merrily to himself, Chauras headed homeward. The battle for Mystra had begun.

CHAPTER THIRTEEN

Far to the North, below the dungeons of Castle Cenchrea, Duke Malycon stood staring moodily at the ancient machines cluttering the room. Few knew of this secret chamber. Hidden deep in the earth, sheltered within a string of natural caverns far below the castle was his greatest treasure. He was the only one allowed to enter here.

Machines...the wonders of the ancients. Malycon reached out and ran a hand lovingly over the largest and most enigmatic of his collection. No one knew this device's purpose or how it functioned, but it radiated an aura of power. He had looted this beauty, along with a dozen or so other instruments from the ruins of an abandoned laboratory secluded far from the planet's more inhabited regions at Mystra's Northern pole. The lab had once been the haven for his scientist forefathers. Now, their secrets were his...all that is but one. This piece alone had defied his attempts to discover its workings. No being had yet been able to fathom the device's mysteries, but that was about to change. Soon he would have its secrets; and power, ultimate power, would be his as it once was his ancestors'. Soon, the technology and knowledge of the starfarer would be his.

So self-absorbed was the duke in his dreams of glory, that he failed to notice, as his roaming hand hit and depressed a button on the machine's face. In response, a momentary surge of energy flared from deep within the device and died as Malycon hastily jerked his hand from the mechanism. Holding his breath, the duke waited for disaster. When, after a few moments no cataclysm befell him, he relaxed. There was no danger after all. Perhaps, he had only imagined the spark of energy he had glimpsed within the machine. Well no matter, no harm was done.

Turning, Malycon left the secret chamber humming contentedly to himself. Soon, he would no longer need fear the power hidden in the ancient device. Soon, he would be master of machines as he would be master of Mystra, and then of the stars themselves. The strangers could not avoid his minions forever. They must surface eventually, and when they did he would have them. Malycon smiled to himself. He did not fear the travelers. They were powerful but he had power of his own, power enough to subjugate half a world. Then, there were his hidden resources. He had weapons even Tyr did not suspect. No, the dark haired stranger would surrender his secrets and then nothing would stand in his way.

While Malycon dreamed of glory, a strange transformation was taking place high above Mystra's skies. In response to the brief surge of power that had flashed momentarily within the depths of the derelict machine, patterns of unusual energy began to form within the energy curtain surrounding the planet. As the mysterious forces grew and pulsed within the shields, waves of dark energy were hurled outward away from the planet into the black void of space. Even after the pool of unnatural energies ebbed and died, the discharged currents of power continued to speed outward deeper and deeper into the neighboring space beyond Mystra.

Finally, the streams of energy entered the far corner of a neighboring star system. As the currents flowed harmlessly through the system, a subtle change began to take place in the wake of their passing. In the center of the fiery suns of this desolate sector of space, alien creatures began to stir. Responding to the siren song of the energy pulse passing through the system, the dormant sleepers began to awaken. Soon. The word rang deep in their sleep-dulled minds. Soon, it would be time to leave their nests deep in the hearts of the stars and feed. The time of birthing would be ended and the time of feeding begun. One by one, the huge creatures of fiery energy and their young began to drift toward awakening. When fully awake, they would swarm from their solar nests to feast on the unsuspecting worlds beyond, and nothing would be able to stop them.

Unaware of the titanic forces marshaling beyond Mystra's skies, Jasen, Hawk, and Tivonna followed their Wer guides through the dense growth of the forest. Forest was not exactly the best term to describe the riot of vegetation through which they traipsed, Jasen decided as he wearily tried to follow the twisting path before him. Jungle, would be more apt. The trees around them were huge, their dark green foliage masking sight of the sky above and casting the world below them into cool shadows. Life abounded beneath the dense canopy of their limbs. The landscape was a massive tangle of vines and other exotic plants, not all of which were benign. The thick carpet of plants completely obscured the ground from view and made walking hazardous.

Silver and his pack glided through this greenhouse-gone-mad as easily as a fish swam through the waters of its home pond. He, however, had to concentrate on each and every step or risk being ensnared by a vine or falling prey to some hidden gully. To make matters worse, he was unbearably tired. Now that the excitement had faded, a deep weariness had settled over him. Nor, did his fatigue stem solely from physical exertion. The tidal wave of energy he had channeled had changed something deep within him. His mental powers had grown stronger and it now took a conscious effort on his part to shield his mind from the thoughts around him. The mental effort required to hold his shielding was exhausting him more than the hike. Jasen shuddered as he recalled his actions in the clearing. He wasn't up to dealing with that just yet.

To distract himself and help block out the stray thoughts buzzing around inside his head, Jasen concentrated on locating the other members of his party. Tivonna was slightly ahead of him and appeared to be holding her own, although the look she gave an especially clingy vine left little doubt that she would just as soon be elsewhere. As for Hawk, Jasen smiled, well at least one of them was enjoying this romp. The Filidae glided through the thick undergrowth as easily as their Wer guides. It was obvious that he was having the time of his life. Jasen eyed his friend enviously. Leave it to Hawk, he could find a way to turn even the most miserable of circumstances into a game. On reflection, it wasn't especially surprising that Hawk was so at home in this setting. He was a creature of nature much like the Wer and this forest, which he and Tivonna were finding so hard to negotiate, was in fact very similar to Hawk's home world.

Having Hawk with him in the city so long had caused him to forget that the Filidae's natural habitat was anything but urban. Jasen frowned. It had been a long time since Hawk had experienced the freedom of the wilds. In truth, it had been well over a year since he had visited his home world. Every time Jasen had suggested that his friend might need a break from the city, he had changed the subject. Seeing him now with the wind ruffling his hair and eyes aglow with pleasure, Jasen realized how chained Hawk must feel in the confines of Terra.

The telepath sighed, at least he was having a good time now, which was more than Jasen could say about himself. He flinched and gritted his teeth as a wave of emotion-laden thought slammed through his weak shields and raced over his already tender mind. His whole brain felt bruised, torn, as if something had been ripped open during his struggle. He badly needed time to check himself for injury and to see exactly what transformations the wild energy had wrought within him. Unfortunately, there was no time for that now. Nor did he dare reveal his inner struggle to the others. Any sign of weakness on his part might bring them danger from the Wer. He just had to hold on for a little while longer. This trek couldn't last forever; it would be night soon. He would have a chance to assess the damage when they stopped to make camp for the night. Until then, he had to keep going.

Tightening his grasp on his failing shields, Jasen concentrated all of his energy into putting one foot in front of the other and his world narrowed to the trail before him. A few hours later, he was startled to awareness as Silver called a halt. Ahead of them, a small clearing had been hacked out of the dense brush. A ring of large stones encircled the clearing. The huge stone guardians glowed with a greenish luminescence, which bathed the clearing in a pale green light. Standing in the center of this ring of light was a small wooden cabin.

Walking to the edge of the stone circle, Silver beckoned for them to join him. "This is as far as we go today. Night is almost upon us. You three will stay here. The cabin is well stocked and there is a stream out back for water. You will find all you need within the clearing. But be warned, you must not leave the boundary of the stones before sunrise. There is danger in the night."

"What kind of danger?" Tivonna asked.

The warrior smiled. "None that need concern you, if

you follow my instructions. As long as you remain within the circle of stones, no harm will befall you. We will return for you in the morning."

Jasen studied the Wer closely. There was excitement on him, but the telepath could detect no sign of deceit or treachery. He was genuinely concerned for their safety. "Very well, we will do as you say."

"Till tomorrow then." Silver nodded his head slightly in acknowledgement. Then, with a signal to his pack, he turned and faded into the trees, leaving the bemused travelers alone beside the ring of glowing stones.

Shaking his head at the eccentricities of other races, Hawk turned his attention from the departed Wer to the cabin awaiting them. "Well, we might as well check out our quarters. It looks like this is home until morning." Suiting actions to words, he slipped between the two nearest boulders and headed toward the small cabin, with Tivonna close on his heels.

With a weary sigh, Jasen straightened his pack and proceeded to follow his comrades. As soon as he stepped between the two glowing stones before him, a strange sensation swept over him. Silence. No thoughts beat into his mind. The sudden cessation of the mental barrage he had been enduring left him dizzy. Amazed, Jasen stepped backwards. As soon as he exited the clearing, the thoughts of the distant Wer drifted into his mind. Intrigued, he stepped back between the stones. Sure enough, silence returned. Hesitantly, the telepath moved forward into the clearing. As he put distance between himself and the stone ring, he again began to pick up the thoughts of others. However, this time only those of Hawk and Tivonna reached him. Amazed, Jasen turned and looked at the glowing guardians. A psychic dampener, the energy in the stones acted as a psychic shield. With a grateful sigh, Jasen walked over and sat down at the base of the nearest stone. Leaning his head back against the rock, he tried to relax.

The silence was wonderful. He felt as if his entire mind was black and blue. He would just rest here a moment, and give his shields a chance to recover before joining the others.

Jasen did not intend to rest long, but the rock was warm and the faint throbbing pulsing through it felt good to his sore muscles. As the warmth, massage and quiet began to take effect, the tension drained from his body and a sleepy lethargy seized him. Unconscious of what he was doing, Jasen allowed himself to sink deeper into the relaxing tranquility gripping him. He was unaware when, moments later, he drifted into a deep trance.

Blinking in surprise, Jasen woke to find himself standing on a vast plain. Ribbons of glowing energy crisscrossed the skies above him. He instantly recognized the plain as a representation of his own mind. How had he gotten here? He didn't remember entering into trance, but obviously he had. Not a smart idea, considering where he was. With a shrug, Jasen gazed at the panorama before him. Well, as long as he was here, he might as well take a look. Everything seemed to be in order except for that gray blot on the far horizon.

As Jasen walked toward the hazy area, the blot resolved itself into a huge stone wall stretched across the plain. The wall ran for as far as he could see in both directions, there was no way around it. As he neared the obstruction, he could make out holes and cracks marring the wall's surface. Energy streamed through the openings, but the flow was erratic with no discernible pattern. Also, some of the bright energy ribbons, which represented his powers, had been trapped beneath the fallen stones, blocking the flow of energy.

Jasen stared at the barrier in shock. How long had this been here and, more importantly, why? It was obviously a mental block of some kind. Someone had deliberately placed it here and then hidden it from detection. The wild energy had stripped away its camouflage and broken through the block, but the process was unfinished. In order to balance his mental energies, he must remove the block completely. Gathering his strength, Jasen pressed his mind against the barrier, willing it to crumble. At first, the wall resisted him. Whoever had constructed it was a master. If not for the damage already done, he would have had no chance of breaking it. Finally, the wall began to yield. Cracks formed and spread outward in all directions. Then, with a loud rumble, the wall crashed and vanished as if it had never existed. Stunned, Jasen gazed at the panorama before him. Channels of energy flared and met. Existing pathways glowed and brightened and others, unknown and unrecognized, blazed to life.

Jasen stood motionless amid the radiant power of his mind. As energy forces surged and balanced, he stared at the vast expanse that was now his mind. Knowledge surfaced; memories, teachings, instructions, lessons learned long ago but forgotten, returned. It was too much to absorb all at once. His subconscious automatically filed the flow of information away for future use. The knowledge would all be there when he needed it. For now, it was enough to be whole again. His mind was balanced. His powers, those known and those yet to be remembered, were under control. And most of all, he finally remembered who and what he was. He was Jasen, last of the Manashtai.

Exhausted, but triumphant, Jasen slumped against the glowing stone, passing from trance to sleep. Hawk found him there a few minutes later curled contentedly at the foot of the giant guardian, sound asleep.

The Filidae studied the peacefully sleeping figure before him and shook his fair head. When he and Tivonna had discovered that Jasen had failed to follow them into the cabin, Hawk had returned to search for him. He had found the telepath sitting beneath the glowing monolith deeply entranced. Aware of the inherent danger in breaking a trance prematurely, he had chosen instead to watch and wait, hoping that in time Jasen would recover on his own.

That had been over three hours ago, three very long hours. Slowly, the tension began to ease from Hawk's rigid muscles. He had not been entirely sure that this latest unexpected twist of fate would resolve itself in their favor. Jasen never entered a trance without proper safeguards. To have him do so now, in the presence of this strange obelisk and surrounded by potential enemies, had boded ill. But seeing him now curled up and sleeping like a contented child, brought a smile to Hawk's lips.

With a weary sigh, he retrieved Jasen's pack and quickly located his blanket. Gently, he covered the sleeping figure.

"Sleep well my friend. You deserve one untroubled night. Tomorrow is time enough for questions."

Jasen muttered a few unintelligible words and snuggled deep into the warm blanket. Chuckling, Hawk left him to sleep in peace. Tivonna would rest better knowing that Jasen was well.

Hawk knelt and placed another log on the small fire sputtering in the cabin's lone fireplace. He watched silently as the wood caught and blazed to life. Carefully, he continued to stoke the now cheerfully burning blaze until assured that it would last throughout the rest of the chilly night. When all was going to his satisfaction, he rose and stretched his stiff muscles, trying to ease the persistent ache across his shoulders. Restless, he began to pace around the cabin's narrow confines. Movement seemed to help relieve his growing tension, but still sleep eluded him. What was wrong with him? A few moments ago, he had been as tired as Jasen and Tivonna, both of whom were presently enjoying a trouble-free sleep. Now, however, he was wide awake and filled with a nervous, restless energy. He needed to do something, but what? The tiny cabin was becoming oppressive. Its walls seemed to press in on him from all sides. Maybe some fresh air would help.

Silently, Hawk crept across the room and quietly slipped out the door. Outside in the crisp, cool night air, he felt better. He stood still a moment and savored the feel of the night. Mystra's sky was a thing of beauty and mystery, jewels on velvet with the pale white orb of the planet's moon peeking through to cast a silvery glow on the surrounding forest. Hawk stared at the huge dark trees tipped in moonlight and felt a deep longing within him. It was a night of magic, a night to race the wind and explore the cool darkness of the woods. Such nights were rare on his home world, but they sparked the same restless desire that he felt now here in this strange, distant land. He knew he shouldn't give in to these feelings; but, in the same moment, he knew he had little choice. These feelings were not to be denied, they were a basic part of the Filidae makeup. It was time to dance with the moon, and he was powerless to stop it. With a blur of white, the huge white wolf raced into the shelter of the beckoning trees.

The smells and sounds of the forest washed over his senses and calmed the aching in his soul. With wild abandon, he joined the other creatures of the night and excitedly began to explore this new and unfamiliar world. Time held no meaning as he gave himself fully to his wolf form. Suddenly, the wolf tensed and tested the air with sharp senses. Something was different; the forest had changed. The familiar sounds of the night had stilled, replaced by chanting coming from just beyond the trees ahead. With every sense alert, Hawk crept forward to investigate. As he moved toward the unfamiliar sounds, the landscape around him began to change. The trees thinned, then ended abruptly at the lip of a bowl shaped clearing of bare earth. Nestled in the center of the depression was a huge flat topped boulder on which stood a large silver wolf. Nor was the wolf alone. Lining the clearing, were hundreds of wolves of every size and color. They covered the crater, a sea of fur-covered bodies.

Silently, this horde of beasts stood staring at the boulder. No movement or sound escaped them. They might have been carved from stone. Fascinated, Hawk looked from the wolves to the boulder. The silver wolf was as still and silent as his brothers. His eyes, like those of the others, were fixed on the small figure standing at the base of the stone platform. A lone human figure dressed in the pelt of a black wolf stood, arms upraised at the base of the boulder. It was from him the strange chant issued. There was something compelling about the eerie melody. The strange words wrapped themselves around his mind calling, urging him forward.

Mesmerized, the white wolf left his place of concealment and started down the side of the earthen bowl. As if in response to a silent signal, the ocean of wolves parted, leaving a clear aisle to the boulder. As the wolf neared the boulder, a smile creased the human's face, but his chant never faltered. Caught up in the words of power, Hawk ignored the human and leapt onto the stone platform to face the silver wolf waiting there. The two huge wolves faced each other, low growls coming from both. Slowly, they circled each other, each taking the measure of the other. As his eyes locked with the wolf before him, Hawk found it impossible to look away. The Filidae part of him was screaming a warning; but, the spell laid upon him was too strong, he was too deeply ensnared in the human's magic. The two wolves remained locked in silent combat, each seeking mastery over the other. As the battle of wills raged, Hawk had the distinct feeling of being judged, weighed by the creatures surrounding him. His instincts told him to stop this foolishness and get out while he could, but another part of him refused to give way to his silver furred opponent. Filidae did not surrender. He would not be the one to yield.

As if reading Hawk's thoughts, the silver wolf suddenly broke the deadlock. Lifting its head, it let out a bone-chilling howl. The salute was quickly picked up and echoed by the watching wolves. Soon, the clearing rang with their cries. A warm glow filled Hawk. Accepted. In some strange way, the wolves had tested him and now adopted him as one of their own. Joyfully, he threw back his head and joined his voice to theirs. As one, the wolves ended their salutation and turned to race into the shelter of the forest. It was time to hunt. Side by side Hawk and the silver wolf led the pack from the clearing.

Watching the departing pack, the lone human smiled and fingered the medallion he held…a white wolf with silvery-blue eyes. "It has begun. At long last, it has begun. Count your days Malycon. The three have come, as was foretold, and your fall is near." Tucking the pendant safely within his tunic, the old medicine man began his journey back to camp. This night was for the young.

CHAPTER FOURTEEN

Jasen woke to the smell of coffee and a pair of emerald eyes watching him anxiously. Seeing her worried expression, Jasen was overcome by his feelings for the beautiful elemental. He could love her now. There were no doubts or fears to keep them apart any longer. Impulsively, he reached up and drew her to him. He kissed her passionately then, showing her the full measure of his love. When the kiss ended, Tivonna stared at him with stunned surprise. Sitting up, Jasen reached out and ran his fingertip down her cheek. "I love you, you know. I don't think I've told you that enough."

Tivonna shook her head in amazement and stared at the stranger before her. His expression was open, joyous and just a little boyish. It was strangely appealing. What had happened? Gone was the guarded, suspicious man she had known. This creature was one of light and laughter. He radiated joyous energy.

"Jasen, are you all right? What...?"

Seeing her confusion, Jasen gently pressed his fingertips to her lips to stem the flow of words. "Yes, I'm all right. In fact, I can't remember when I've felt better. Tivonna, I finally know who I am. It's fantastic. All the memories and teachings of my past are mine again. I know who and what I am and I now know that there is no danger of my becoming the monster people fear. I don't have to be afraid to love you."

"Jasen, there is no way that you could ever become the creature you fear. It is not in you. You heal, there is no way you could destroy." Tivonna's voice was filled with compassion and love. She had no idea that he still held such fears.

"I know. Consciously, I knew that telepaths, at least this telepath, were not evil. But subconsciously," he shrugged, "if you hear something long enough you begin to believe it. Especially when you have no memories with which to refute them. Oh, I had the written accounts of my people's history, but I had no actual first-hand memories of my own. I'm afraid cold facts are little use against irrational fears. But, all that has changed. My people were called the Manashtai and they were pledged to preserving life and helping others. There is nothing in my past to shame me. I know that now."

"Manashtai!" Tivonna gasped.

"Yes, do you know of them?"

"Of course, everyone knows of the Manashtai. There is not a race in existence that has not been aided at one time or another by them. It is said that they come in time of trouble and leave when danger is passed. It's strange though, in all the accounts I have read there is no mention of them being telepaths."

"Well, that's not exactly the kind of thing you want to advertise, the universe being what it is. I'm sure they were careful not to reveal too much to those they helped."

Tivonna was thoughtful a moment, "That is why you are here. There is danger and you were sent to stop it."

Jasen shook his head. "I'm not sure. I know that I must stop the Firehawks, but to aid Mystra? Who knows?

I just do what I must...but what about you? How do you feel about being bound to a man who is the pawn of fate? It is not an easy life I offer you. I can't change what I am."

With a bright smile, Tivonna leaned forward and showed him in no uncertain terms exactly how she felt about such a prospect. Sometime later, the two were startled apart by the sound of voices coming from the direction of the forest. The Wer were returning. Jumping quickly to their feet, the pair prepared to greet the new arrivals.

Jasen smiled at the sight that met his eyes. There, at the head of the pack, one arm draped companionably across Silver's shoulders and his other gesturing wildly to emphasize some obscure point, was Hawk. The animated conversation was broken off as the Filidae caught sight of Jasen. Leaving the Wer, he headed forward to greet his friends, smiling slightly as he noticed Tivonna's and Jasen's somewhat flustered appearance. Was that a blush he noticed on the elemental's cheeks?

Watching the approaching Filidae, Jasen tried to hide his own embarrassment by studying the Wer. Something had definitely changed while he slept. There was no hostility in the group now and Hawk acted like someone who was among close friends. His thoughts on the subject were interrupted as his friend reached his side.

"Good morning, and what have you two been up to?" Hawk asked, noticing as Tivonna's blush deepen at his words.

"It's not what we've been up to, but what you've been up to that interests me." Put in Jasen before his friend could continue his line of questioning. "I see you have some new friends."

Before Hawk could answer, Silver reached them. Stopping before Jasen, the Wer bowed respectfully. "Good morning, Lord. I trust your night passed well. Please forgive me for my earlier rudeness. I did not recognize you.

It was only after the messenger had revealed his true form that we knew of your arrival." Turning from a baffled Jasen, Silver greeted Tivonna. "My lady, I trust all was to your satisfaction?"

Tivonna, used to court protocol, answered smoothly, "Everything was fine. Please call us Jasen and Tivonna, there is no need for formality among friends."

Receiving Jasen's nod of agreement, Silver smiled. "As you wish, now we must eat and then prepare to move on. Our city is still two days' journey from here, and I wish to present you to the council as soon as possible. They have long awaited your coming."

"Then, we must not keep them waiting any longer." Tivonna declared. "I was just bringing Jasen his morning coffee when you appeared. I have plenty of food prepared, will you join us?"

At the Wer's acceptance, Tivonna turned and led the way to the cabin and the promised meal. Jasen stood silently for a moment watching the departing pack then turned to face Hawk.

"All right, let's have it. What happened last night?"

"Last night?" Hawk asked feigning surprise and trying his best to look innocent. "Did something happen last night?"

Jasen was not put off by the pose, he knew his friend too well. "I'm not buying it, so cut the innocent act. Something happened last night, and I'm betting that you were in the middle of it, so talk."

Meeting Jasen's stern gaze, Hawk sighed. When Jasen got that stubborn look, nothing would deter him. He was quite prepared to stand out here all day if necessary to get his answers. Unfortunately, Hawk wasn't at all sure that he had any answers to give. "OK." He began. "But I'm not exactly sure what happened myself. Everything's a bit vague."

"Try. From Silver's comments, I gather our meeting the

clan elders has gone past looking for permission to travel in the Forest. They expect something from us, and I need to know what. Preferably, before I have to face them. Anything you know might help."

With a nod, Hawk related his experiences of the previous night. As he told his story, Jasen lightly scanned his mind, studying the mental pictures that made up the Filidae's memories of the past night. One image in particular caught his attention. The Wer medicine man wore an ornate pendant in the form of a white wolf with silvery-blue eyes. Coincidence? Jasen no longer believed in chance, at least not where Mystra and her inhabitants were concerned.

As Hawk finished his story, Jasen stood silently, deep in thought. What was the connection? First, the Centaurs and now the Wer, it was obvious that they should be here now at this time but how did Malycon and Mystra fit in with the Firehawks? They were all connected somehow, of that he was certain, but how?

With a sigh, Jasen abandoned that line of thought. Now was not the time to try and solve the puzzle. Looking up, he found Hawk watching him patiently. "Sorry, I was thinking."

"That was obvious. Come up with anything good?"

"Just more questions." Jasen shook his head in exasperation. "This whole thing is one mystery after another. Fate has decreed that we be here, why I'm not sure. But both the Centaurs and the Wer seem to have prophesies detailing our coming. That shaman was wearing a pendant of you in wolf form. The details were exact. Undoubtedly, you are the Wer messenger who is to act as liaison between the Wer and someone else."

"That someone being you." Hawk guessed.

"So it would seem. Hawk, this is the damnedest thing I've ever seen. One man is holding four races hostage, and they are all sitting around waiting for me to come along and make it all better. As for me, I haven't the slightest idea of what I'm supposed to be doing. It's crazy. If this is what it means to be a Manashtai, I'm not so sure I want the honor."

"Manashtai?" Hawk queried ignoring Jasen's outburst, knowing that it was only a reaction to the stress and frustration he was feeling and nothing serious.

Seeing Hawk's interest, Jasen told him of his own night's adventure. When he had finished, he noticed that his friend showed little surprise at the revelation of his heritage.

"I'm glad you finally know," Hawk stated when Jasen had completed his tale. "I've a feeling we're going to need every advantage we can get to come out on top of this mess. So what do we do now?"

"What can we do?" Jasen answered. "We push ahead. Everything is tied together somehow. Of that, I'm certain. We just take it one step at a time and play it as it comes." He chuckled, his earlier mood forgotten as the humor of their present situation struck him. "This is turning out to be one strange planet. One minute I'm the boogieman and the next I'm royalty. My head is spinning trying to keep up. I wonder what I'll be tomorrow."

"Don't ask." Hawk answered in mock horror. "I've got a feeling things are just going to get weirder from here. Say, let's go get some breakfast. You wouldn't want me to have to face this crazy planet on an empty stomach, now would you?"

"Heaven forbid." Jasen chuckled, joining his friend as he headed toward the cabin where Tivonna was busily passing out rations to the Wer. "I know what you're like when you haven't been fed. I wouldn't wish that on anyone. Besides, if we keep Tivonna waiting, she just might come up with an interesting and unusual use for a lightning bolt. I, for one, do not want an elemental mad at me." That was a feeling to which Hawk gave a hearty, "Amen".

Hurrying to the cabin, they were soon enjoying a hearty

breakfast. An hour later, packed and fed, the party began its march toward the Wer village. The day passed pleasantly for Jasen. The Wer were friendly and talk and laughter accompanied the group on its journey. When night fell, they made camp by a sparking stream. Tired from the day's exertions, they ate and turned in early. Tomorrow would be another strenuous day.

To the South of the sleeping travelers, a large messenger bird took flight from the Centaur hideout and flew across the Great Plains toward Aquilla, a scroll clutched tightly in its talons. High overhead, a Cenchrean dragonrider turned his small red dragon northward toward the Wer forest. He was tired and cold. With night fast approaching, he decided to break off his searching and return to his camp. The dragon's new heading took it away from the path of the swiftly flying messenger. So its rider never knew the part he played in his master's downfall. Unhindered, the bird continued its desperate race for Aquilla. This was one message Malycon would not have.

The next day's journey was as pleasant for Jasen and his party as the previous day's had been. They made better time on this leg of the trip and, just after mid-afternoon of the second day, they arrived at the Wer city. City was a good word to describe the Wer encampment, Jasen decided, studying the panorama before him, a city in the trees. Perched high in the branches of the huge trees, interconnected by rope bridges, the city stretched for miles in all directions. There seemed to be three distinct sections to the complex, Jasen noticed as he followed Silver toward the largest group of dwellings. The houses within a certain section were all interlinked, but there were no passages joining the major sectors together. The three sections of the city formed a loose circle, with a large clearing at its center.

MYSTRA

"Well, what do you think of our little village?" Jasen broke off his study of his surroundings and turned to Silver who was walking next to him. There was a hint of pride in the Wer's voice. It was obvious he was proud of his people's home.

"Impressive." Jasen answered. "But I'm a little confused about the arrangement. Why aren't all the buildings linked?"

"Ah," Silver smiled, "It's obvious you know little about Wer." Seeing Jasen's puzzled look, he continued, "A Wer owes allegiance only to his clan and has little contact with those outside of his own tribe. There are three Wer clans - Wolf, Cat, and Hawk. Each clan maintains its own separate community. The clearing is neutral ground. It is there the elders from the three tribes meet to discuss and judge on issues which affect all the Wer."

While they had talked, the party had reached the grouping of houses that belonged to the Wolf clan. Stopping beside a particularly large and imposing tree, Silver pointed to the rope ladder fixed to its side. "Since you were found by the Wolf clan, you will be our guest. This dwelling belongs to my pack; please make yourselves at home. I must report to the elders. I will return as soon as possible. Until then eat and rest." With that, he turned and disappeared into the trees. The rest of Silver's pack were already swarming up the rope ladders attached to other nearby trees.

Tivonna eyed the rope ladder uncertainly, and then craned her neck to look up into the tall tree, which was to be their temporary home. Seeing her dubious expression, Hawk laughed. "Don't glower so, Red. After traipsing through the jungle, this ought to be a piece of cake." Then, suiting actions to words, he stepped past her, grasped the makeshift ladder, and began to climb.

Jasen shook his head, a smile tugging at his lips, as he watched Hawk's assent. The rope ladder posed little trouble for someone as agile as the Filidae. "Well, my lady, shall we less agile mortals give it a try?"

With a sigh of resignation, Tivonna reached for the rope. "I suppose we must. But I'll go first, that way if I fall you can catch me."

Smothering a chuckle, Jasen followed Tivonna up the ladder. A few minutes later, they joined Hawk in the treehouse above. One of Silver's pack brought supplies, and the three friends settled down to rest and refresh themselves while they had the chance. Their position among the Wer was chancy at best and anything could happen at this point.

Toward dusk, Silver returned, accompanied by a much older Wer. Hawk studied the new arrival closely. There was something familiar about him. The older man, obviously an Elder, judging from the deference Silver showed him, bowed graciously and seated himself on the cushion across from Jasen.

Turning toward Hawk, he smiled at the puzzled expression on the Filidae's face. "Yes," he answered the unasked question. "I am known to you. We met in the clearing a night ago."

"Then, I take it you are an Elder of the Wolf Clan." Jasen stated.

"I am Taymar." The old Wer replied with a smile. "And I have many offices - elder, shaman...seer."

"And in which capacity are you functioning tonight?" Jasen asked, his smile matching that of the Wer. He was beginning to like this strange little man.

"Ah, now that is a little difficult to say. As an elder, I am of course interested in all strangers found in the Forest; but as shaman and seer my interest is much greater." Taymar's bantering tone changed suddenly as he fixed Jasen with an intense stare. "Are you the one?" he asked softly. "Yes...yes, I can see that you are, but this is new to you. You did not know of your destiny before now. I am sorry, this must be very confusing for you."

"To say the least." Jasen sighed. "To tell you the truth Taymar, I could use some answers, all I seem to have at the moment is questions."

"What I can do, I will. You have but to ask."

"Well, let's start with you. You say you have been expecting me. Tell me about the prophecy."

"There is little enough to tell. When Malycon first enslaved my people, the seers began to dream. In these dreams, a leader would come to lead the tribes out of bondage. The form of this savior was unknown, but he would be identified by a messenger. A being akin to the Wer, but not Wer, whose form would mirror that of the clan." He lifted a pendant from the folds of his cloak. "This is the form by which I would know him." He turned to face Hawk. "This is the form in which you came to us."

Jasen nodded thoughtfully. "I agree that we were destined to meet. My question is, why? The Centaurs had the same type of prophecy, but I still can't understand why you need me. Malycon is only one man. I admit that he is powerful and ruthless, but he is no match for the combined strength of the Centaurs, the Wer, the Elemental High Council, and the forces of Aquilla."

"Aye, if they would agree to help us, but they have refused." The Wer glanced angrily at Tivonna. "Aquilla and the elementals care not what befalls us."

"That's a lie!" Tivonna declared, anger glinting in her emerald eyes. "My father would never turn down a call for aid, much less the council. Their oaths demand that they render help to those who need elemental assistance."

"Nevertheless," Taymar stated. "All our messages have either been ignored or have been met with refusal."

"What messages?" Tivonna ask, confusion replacing her former anger. "We have received no petitions from your people. In fact, we have had no word from you at all in months."

Jasen sat stunned by what he had just heard. Mental gears began to turn and the pieces of the puzzle fell into place. It was all so obvious now. Suddenly, the silence penetrated his thoughts. Looking up, he found all eyes fixed on him.

"OK, let me see if I have this straight." He turned to Taymar. "Your people sent messages to Aquilla and the Elemental High Council when Malycon began his games, and was either ignored or refused. Correct?" At the old Wer's nod, he turned to Tivonna and continued, "Your father and the Elemental High Council, on the other hand, have never heard a bad word from the North."

"Until we met the Centaurs, I had no idea that there was anything wrong in the North and no one knows of Malycon's actions or that there are elementals missing. Of that I am sure."

"Whew." Hawk gave a whistle of admiration. "That takes some network to blockade a whole continent."

"I agree, but it seems that Malycon has done it." Jasen paused in thought, then continued. "The question is what do we do now? I am convinced that somehow Malycon holds the key to our own problem, but in order to obtain that key, we're going to have to take him down. I doubt that he would help us otherwise."

"I am afraid you are quite correct in that." Taymar agreed. "Ever since the accident, Malycon has been a changed man. He cares only for his research and his quest to master the mysteries of machines. He was not always so."

Jasen froze, a tingling racing down his spine. "When did this accident happen?" he asked quietly.

Taymar shrugged. "About fifteen years ago I guess. I was visiting the castle at the time. It seemed that Malycon had uncovered the laboratory of the Ancients. He had all the equipment removed from the site and placed in a special room in the catacombs below the castle's dungeon.

There was no way to remove the devices from the planet, so he agreed to keep the machines buried deep below the earth. As long as no attempt was made to start them, it was deemed the best solution. Most of the pieces were easily identified from books. They were typical machines common to most laboratories, all that is but one. It was a huge machine and its function remained a mystery. Malycon became obsessed with discovering its use. Finally, in desperation he activated it. What exactly occurred, no one knows, but Malycon emerged from his secret room a changed man. He seemed to go a little crazy and his experiments turned cruel. He became obsessed with controlling Mystra and all who dwell upon her. He has come very near to succeeding."

An icy hand suddenly seized Jasen numbing him to the bone. His heart seemed to stop, and it was difficult to breathe. Fifteen years! Could it really be so simple? He was stunned by the implications in Taymar's words. Could this be the key? A sudden soft touch on his shoulder jarred Jasen from his introspection.

"It is not always easy to see more than others." Taymar drew a blanket around the younger man's chilled body. "Can you tell us what you see?"

Jasen sighed and snuggled into the blanket's welcome warmth. "I'm afraid not just yet. It's more of a hunch actually, one more piece of the puzzle. We had better stick with the present for now. What can we expect from the Wer? Will they accept us?"

Taymar was thoughtful a moment, then met Jasen's gaze squarely. "I am not sure. The Wolf clan accepts you, but convincing the others may be difficult. There are many hot heads among the tribes. There will be many who will wish to turn you over to Malycon or at least use you as a weapon against him. More, I cannot say."

Jasen smiled at the old seer's sincerity. "It is enough. We are all on the path of destiny, whatever happens tomorrow, we appreciate your trust." Jasen turned to look at Hawk, mischief twinkling in his golden eyes. "Now, I suggest we all relax and find some food. Hawk's beginning to get that look. We can't have a berserk Filidae swinging through the trees." He turned back to Taymar. "We would be honored if you would join us, sir."

Taymar studied the smiling man before him in bafflement. There was now no sign of uncertainty in him. The seer watched Tivonna and Hawk. They too were relaxed. Hawk was vehemently denying that he was prone to rampages when not fed, much to Tivonna's and Jasen's amusement. Watching the three young people, Taymar felt strangely calm. Looking up, he met Jasen's laughing eyes and smiled. He felt years younger, as if a great weight had been lifted from his shoulders. Whatever happened tomorrow, he had no doubt but that these young ones would rise to the challenge. Falling in with their jovial mood, he surveyed the group and shook his head in mock disapproval. "Young people are all crazy." He looked up as Silver, who had tactfully withdrawn from the room when the conversation had grown serious, entered bearing trays of food. "I just hope you didn't let Silver cook." The old Wer continued. "He even burns water."

"I have you know burned water is a delicacy." The younger Wer answered, unruffled by this slur. "I have been perfecting it for years."

The room exploded in laughter. Silver handed around the food, then sat down to join them. Soon, they were swapping stories of past glories and adventures. Good food and good companions, for now that was enough.

The next morning, Silver escorted the party to the clearing. Jasen surreptitiously studied their escort as they walked. Silver was tense but not really afraid. He was confident that they would sway the Wer to their cause. Jasen just hoped his confidence was not misplaced. As they neared the clearing, Jasen scrutinized the area intently.

At one edge of the clearing, sat three men dressed in flowing white tunics with ornate cloaks draped across their shoulders. The cloaks were made from animal hides representing the clans. These were the head elders and shamans. Behind the seated Wer, was a small group of men also dressed in white but without the decorative cloaks; these would be the pack leaders. Filling the rest of the clearing, except for the few feet immediately surrounding the elders, were the Wer. All clans seemed to be present. For once, they mingled freely, excited about the coming events. A formidable looking Wer standing near the elders suddenly caught Jasen's attention. He was huge and heavily muscled. Both his hair and eyes were black and a scowl marred his tanned face, dark emotions swirled around him. This Wer was definitely not at all happy; he would bear watching. Further observations were curtailed as Silver led them into the clearing to stand before the council.

"Bow to the elders, then sit. Taymar will plead your case. Do not speak unless addressed. Good Luck," the Wer whispered. Then he was gone, fading into the ranks of the gathered Wer.

Jasen, Tivonna, and Hawk bowed respectfully to the council members, then settled themselves cross-legged on the ground before them to await judgment. With fluid grace, Taymar stood and addressed the council. He related first Silver's and then his own experiences with the strangers. From the events in the clearing, when they had first been taken, to the night of the hunt, all was revealed. A murmur of excitement ran through the crowd. All knew the legend, could this be true? Suddenly, an angry voice cut through the excited whispers.

"It is all a lie!" The dark Wer whom Jasen had noted earlier stepped forward. "They are impostors sent here to trick us into betraying Malycon. They wish us to suffer his wrath. They will destroy us all!"

"You have no proof of your claim, while witnesses will verify the events that I have stated." Taymar's calm voice answered.

"Then, I will give you proof!" The angry warrior turned and pointed to Hawk. "I challenge this one to the Duel of Truth! Let us see who lies!"

Gasps of surprise and outrage greeted the Wer's words. Jasen quickly scanned the crowd, then linked with Hawk.

"This doesn't look good, my friend. That Wer, Balcar he's called, wants your blood and he's considered an expert with a knife."

"What happens if I win?" Hawk's thoughts were calm. He seemed unconcerned that he soon might be fighting for his life.

"You can't mean to fight him?" Jasen's surprise flowed through the link.

"Why not?" Hawk studied his opponent with a knowing eye. *"He's big, but I doubt he's ever fought my kind before. He won't expect me to be able to stand up to him."*

"Can you take him?" Jasen's mental tone was thoughtful now. He knew Hawk's abilities.

"Piece of cake."

"OK. Just be careful. We may be able to turn this to our advantage."

"I'm always careful," Hawk answered smugly.

"That's what worries me." Jasen muttered, as Hawk rose to face Balcar.

"I accept your challenge, Balcar." The Filidae's voice rang through the now silent clearing. "I believe it is with knives?"

Taymar opened his mouth to object, but caught the slight shake of Jasen's head. Rising to his feet, the telepath helped Tivonna up, then addressed the council.

"Sirs, with your permission, we would like to answer this challenge. It may answer many of your questions."

Taymar and the other seers and elders consulted briefly among themselves, then he turned and addressed Balcar and Hawk.

"Very well, the duel will be allowed. You both know the rules?"

"Yes!" Balcar growled.

"Yes sir." Hawk answered respectfully much to the Wer's amazement. Jasen had passed along the information as soon as they had agreed that Hawk would fight. It never hurt to impress an opponent.

"Prepare the circle." At Taymar's words, a large circle was etched into the ground in the center of the clearing. Knives in hand, Balcar and Hawk entered the circle and faced each other.

Hawk stood relaxed, his borrowed obsidian knife held confidently in his hand. No sign of worry or stress marred his pale face. Balcar clenched his own knife and began to slowly circle the off-worlder. Suddenly, with savage fury, he leapt forward to slash at his opponent, expecting to gut him with one blow. Only, the Filidae was no longer there! Just as the knife neared its target, the white haired stranger seemed to flow sideways, letting the knife slip harmlessly past him. Then, as if by magic, his dagger leapt forward to nick Balcar's out-stretched arm. The speed and grace of the attack stunned Balcar. No one could move that fast. He quickly reevaluated his earlier opinion of his opponent's skill. This would not be the easy task he had first thought. Calming his anger, the Wer began the duel in earnest. He dared not fail in this; Malycon did not tolerate failure.

From the sidelines, Jasen and Tivonna watched helplessly as Hawk battled for his life. Jasen knew that Hawk was a skilled knife fighter; most Filidae had a love of blades and practiced with them as soon as they could walk, but the Wer fought with all the unbridled savagery of his race. Hypnotized, they watched the ballet of death. The tension in the clearing was becoming unbearable. Balcar and Hawk were a blur of flashing blades; something had to give soon. At that moment, as if in answer to Jasen's thoughts, Balcar stumbled and fell heavily to the ground, his knife dashed from his hand. Immediately, Hawk backed off to give the Wer room.

Balcar knelt in the clearing fighting to regain his breath, anger coursing through every fiber of his being. Who was this freak of nature to humiliate him so? All thoughts of Malycon vanished from his enraged mind. He wanted only to destroy this creature that dared to stand against him. No one defeated Balcar, no one! In an eye-blink, thoughts were transformed into action. The huge, black panther leapt straight for the Filidae's exposed throat. The crowd's roar of outrage at such an underhanded act quickly turned to a gasp of surprise and disbelief as the black cat was struck in mid leap and sent crashing to the ground to lay stunned. The large, white panther slowly circled its downed prey, then raised its head to scan the crowd with blazing silvery-blue eyes.

While Hawk watched the hushed Wer, Jasen watched the elders. At Hawk's transformation, one of the seers had paled and clutched the medallion hanging from his neck. It was like Taymar's except that instead of a wolf, this one depicted a white cat with the same silvery-blue eyes. Of course, quickly he contacted Hawk, there may yet be a way to salvage this situation.

In response to Jasen's telepathic instructions, Hawk circled the clearing then came to a stop before the seer clutching the cat pendant. He nodded his head once in greeting then turned to face the third seer. If Jasen was right... As the elders watched in stunned silence, the cat blurred and a white hawk shot upward into the sky, its wild cry echoing throughout the clearing.

As Jasen suspected, the third seer jerked forward and pulled forth a medallion from beneath his robe. It was a hawk to match the wolf and cat. This was it. Calmly, the telepath strode forward to stand in the center of the clearing and faced the elders. Slowly, he raised his left arm and, as if on cue, the hawk spiraled down to gently perch on the gloved fist. In hushed awe, all eyes were fixed upon the pair.

"I believe gentlemen, that you have your proof." Jasen's quiet words shattered the silence. Soon the clearing was buzzing with talk as the Wer tried to come to terms with what they had seen.

Taymar and the elders whispered frantically among themselves, then seemed to come to an agreement. They turned to face the visitors who had so disrupted their lives. Jasen, Tivonna and Hawk, who had resumed his Filidae form, waited uncertainly to learn of their fate. Taymar studied the three young people for a moment then smiled. "I think it is time we talked. We have much to discuss."

CHAPTER FIFTEEN

King Arcus paced restlessly around the confines of his study. He hated waiting! Finally, exhausted by his fruitless exertions, he dropped into the chair at his desk. The parchment glared accusingly up at him from the cluttered desk top. Hesitantly, he reached out and picked up the offending document whose arrival had started this nightmare. He turned the scroll over in his hands. To think something so small and innocuous could so disrupt his orderly world. The arrival of the Centaur's missive had thrown the whole kingdom into turmoil. Even now, the Elemental High Council was in debate trying to decide if the information contained in the document was true and, if so, what course of action they should follow.

But, what was taking them so long? It was obvious to Arcus what needed to be done. The accusations in the scroll were too dangerous to overlook. If they were true, then the whole kingdom was in danger. Malycon had broken Aquillan law. The charges had to be investigated. If only these stodgy matrons of the council would get on with it!

Arcus calmed his temper. Malycon's worst crimes were

against elementals. He needed their sanction before he could investigate. Arcus sighed. How could Malycon have become so warped? He had always been independent, but Arcus had never thought him capable of treason.

The Northern Kingdom had been won by Arcus' great-great-great-grandfather centuries ago. The ruling of those Northern realms, however, had been left to their hereditary nobility. Arcus had never had to exert his right of rule on Cenchrea, until now. If Malycon was waging war on the Northern races and murdering elementals, Arcus shuddered at the thought, then it was his responsibility as sovereign to stop him.

Just when Arcus felt his patience could stand no more, the door opened and a weary Sivena entered. She smiled at her husband's obvious frustration.

"Relax, my husband. It is decided. When you go north, elementals will accompany you. Malycon must give an account of himself. If the charges are true," she paused and her next words sent a chill through Arcus' spine. "Then, he will pay."

Jasen pushed through the final vestige of forest and stood at last on the banks of Mer Lake. The sheer size of it stunned him. He could barely make out the distant shore. He did not look forward to crossing that. The small four man boat they had seemed inadequate for such a voyage, but cross they must. Mer Lake was actually a bay. Huge rock monoliths that sheltered the cove from the open sea, bordered one side, while rugged mountain peaks blocked the opposite shore. They had two choices: they either backtrack to the Great Plains, where their journey had been interrupted, and continued toward the eastern gap; or they crossed the vast lake.

Beside him, Hawk shook his head and muttered. "What is it with this world and mountains?" He gestured to the majestic peaks rising to their right.

Tivonna chuckled, "Mystra's terrain is not naturally occurring. When the Cataclysm hit, the whole planet destabilized, including the core. The elementals of that time were able to contain the meltdown, but it took changing the shape of the land to do it. The mountains were created at the stress points to relieve tectonic stress. Caverns and tunnels honeycomb the peaks and were used to siphon off lava, heat, steam and pressure. The central tunnels are large enough to ride a horse through. They make mining easier and many traders prefer traveling the tunnels rather than traipsing across the open plains. Earth elementals are employed to ensure the routes stay open and stable. There is a large area of rich farmland in the south and a smaller section in the north; but no, Mystra does not lack for mountains."

Jasen smiled. Mystra was an interesting world but that didn't get them to their destination any faster. Backtracking would take too long. Hawk had fashioned a mast and sail for their small vessel. With Tivonna controlling the wind, the lake crossing should take less than a day. Jasen sighed. By water, it was.

Two days after the fateful duel between Hawk and Balcar, Centaurs and Wer had met for a council of war. Messages had been prepared and sent to Aquilla using Wer from the Hawk clan as messengers to assure their safe arrival. A day later they had received a reply. Aquilla was on the move. Arcus was sailing North with three hundred of his crack soldiers and six elementals. The small fleet should not draw undue attention, as fishing boats plied those waters on a regular basis. The longer Malycon was unaware of their movements, the better. They would dock at the northern port and take the mountain tunnels to the eastern gap. There, they would be joined by another nine hundred or so soldiers from Aquilla's Northern holdings. The Wer and Centaurs would take the underground passages from the Centaur encampment and meet him there. Everything was going as planned. Then, it was discovered that Balcar was missing. Jasen, Hawk and Tivonna had volunteered to take the sea route in order to intercept the Wer. He could not be allowed to reach Malycon with news of their plans, or the knowledge that the Wer had sheltered those he sought. The duke's retribution against those who had betrayed him would be swift. The Wer were linked to the life of their forest. They would not survive its destruction.

"We're almost ready," Tivonna's voice brought Jasen back to the present. "Are you sure that you will be able to guide us through the fog?"

Jasen smiled. "If you can give us fog cover and a steady wind, I think I can find the shore for us."

Tivonna laughed, "Oh, I'll keep us covered. I have no desire to be dragon bait."

"Agreed." Jasen looked toward where Hawk was securing the make-shift sail to their vessel.

"Looks like Hawk is about done. I'll help him load our supplies, the rest is up to you."

"Just see that that thing stays afloat. I'll handle my end."

Chuckling, Jasen left the elemental to her work.

Focusing her thoughts on the job at hand, Tivonna reached outward with her senses, feeling the life of the world around her. Slowly, she gathered the forces she needed, molding them into the desired pattern. Minutes later, a thick fog began to roll in, obscuring the lake from view. Quickly, she hurried to join the others. Soon, the fog would be so thick nothing would be able to penetrate its depth. If they became separated, they would never be able to find each other. With a surge of relief, she spotted the vague outline of the boat. As Jasen helped her aboard, a gentle breeze sprang up and pushed them out onto the lake.

Sailing in the thick mist was unnerving and monotonous. For the hundredth time, Jasen probed the swirling grey shadows with his mind, checking their course and progress. They were making good time. Off to their right was a rocky projection that must be Mer Island. According to Tivonna, the island was located at the lake's center and was the meeting place between the Mer and other races. They were half-way there. A small sigh of relief escaped the telepath. He would be glad when this trip was over. He couldn't shake the sense of danger, of disaster waiting to happen, that had plagued him since they had ventured onto the lake.

Suddenly, Jasen's danger sense flared brightly. There were shapes moving in the water near the boat. He barely had time to cry out a warning to the others when the boat was struck by an unseen force, and they were pitched from their shattered craft into the dark waters of Mer Lake. As he fell, Jasen instinctively conjured a force shield around himself. He struck the water shaken, but unharmed. Frantically, he searched the murky waters for signs of Tivonna and Hawk. He soon spotted the elemental drifting unconscious nearby, but there was no trace of the Filidae.

Moving quickly to Tivonna's side, Jasen carefully extended his shield to include the injured elemental. He prayed that she was only stunned and not badly hurt. Calming his fear, he began to lift the force bubble toward the surface only to halt moments later as he found himself surrounded by a host of hostile, armed beings.

Under other circumstances, Jasen would have been struck by the beauty of these underwater dwellers. Their skin was white, with a faint tinge of green giving them a ghostly quality. Their hair was a deep green. From the waist up, they were humanoid in appearance but instead of legs their lower bodies consisted of a powerful tail covered with pearly green scales that seemed to glow with an inner luminescence. However, given his present predicament, Jasen cared little for his captors' appearance. What concerned him were the waves of anger radiating from the host. The force of the Mermen's anger threatened to overwhelm his shields. There would be little chance of reasoning with them in their present mood. He and Tivonna were in deep trouble. The air that had been trapped inside the force bubble was almost gone. Soon, he would pass out for lack of oxygen and they would be at the mercy of the Mer. Jasen broke off his contemplation of the Mermen as he felt movement beside him. Tivonna was stirring.

Tivonna opened her eyes and tried to make sense of her surroundings. She noticed the glowing shield with confusion, then gasped as she caught sight of the Mermen.

"Easy." Jasen tried to sound calm. "We're safe for the moment, at least until our air runs out. They can't penetrate the shield. Unfortunately, we can't get through them to the surface."

"Can we not reason with them? We are no threat."

"Afraid not. There's too much anger. Only the shield is keeping them back. When it goes, we'll be fair game. It's only a matter of time before we pass out from lack of oxygen."

"Maybe I can help." Tivonna murmured, deep in thought. "How quickly can you drop and reform the shield?"

"Instantly," Jasen answered, puzzled by her words.

"Good. Be ready to move the shield when I tell you."

Ignoring the thoroughly puzzled telepath, Tivonna turned her attention to the surrounding sea. Reaching out, she melded her senses with the energy of the water. There was no way she could control the vast expanse of the lake. However, she might be able to bend a small portion of it to her will, at least for a time. In response to her commands, the water around them began to shrink back from the trapped couple as if repelled by its contact with them. In moments, the golden bubble of Jasen's force shield was surrounded on all sides by a five-foot space devoid of all water. Quickly, Tivonna called to the air trapped in the seawater, pulling it forth to fill the open area with life giving oxygen. When the clearing was richly saturated with air, she turned to Jasen. "Now!"

Instantly, the golden field of energy winked out and reformed itself along the contours of the air pocket Tivonna had created. Breathing deeply of the rich air, Jasen smiled at his bondmate. "You're a wonder. How long can you hold this?"

"A few hours. But what are we going to do? We are still trapped here."

"True, but at least we have a few more hours, thanks to you. We'll think of something." Jasen pointed to the assembled Mer. "Our friends are intrigued. They don't know quite what to make of us." A movement among the Mermen gathered on their left caught his attention. "Now what?"

The Mer were stirring. Suddenly, their line parted and a lone Merman accompanied by a ... white dolphin, no it couldn't be.... came forward. By his bearing and the deference of the other Mer, Jasen guessed him to be a leader of sorts. Jasen's attention shifted back to the dolphin at the Merman's side. Did dolphins have blue eyes? Hesitantly, he reached out with his mind.

"Hawk?"

"You expecting someone else?" Hawk's calm thoughts, tinged with humor, filled Jasen with an unmeasurable joy.

"I thought you were dead! I couldn't reach you!" Jasen's thoughts conveyed all that he had felt at his friend's presumed death, and his joy now that he was with them again.

"Sorry. That explosion knocked me for a loop. Fortunately, I had just enough presence of mind to change. After that, things became pretty muddled for a while. When I finally regained my bearings, I found myself surrounded by Mermen. I've been trying to explain things to Cronus, he's their king, ever since."

"You can communicate with them?"

"Sure, dolphin is the universal language of all intelligent water breathers. Unfortunately, he's not quite convinced that we are benevolent. It seems that Malycon has been attacking their hatcheries. They view all surface dwellers as enemies."

Great, just what they needed! Jasen tried to control his mounting frustration. How could he convince these beings that he and his party were not a threat?

"If only I could know your thoughts as I do those of my brothers, then I could be sure!"

Jasen stiffened in surprise as the foreign thoughts drifted into his awareness. He had kept his receptors open to monitor any change in the sea people's attitudes. Now, he actively searched for the source of the strange mind-touch. There! It was the sea king. Jasen studied the Mer carefully, trying to hold down his rising hopes. If these beings were latent telepaths... Quickly, Jasen linked with Tivonna and Hawk and apprised them of his discovery.

"A telepathic race! No wonder they had to flee to Mystra. Who would have guessed?" Hawk's excitement suddenly turned to suspicion. *"Just what have you got in mind? Not what I think you have in mind, I hope?"*

Jasen's thoughts were tinged with amusement as he tried to decipher Hawk's question. *"Well, I was hoping to have a little chat with Cronus."*

"No! It is too dangerous!" Tivonna replied instantly, her fear carrying through the link.

"Dangerous! It's crazy"! Hawk was adamant. There was no way he was going to let Jasen get away with this.

"Calm down, you two. There's no other way. If I can convince Cronus to speak to me mind to mind, then I can convince him that we speak the truth. Otherwise, we are stuck here until Tivonna and I can no longer protect us. Then, we're dead."

Reluctantly, Tivonna and Hawk agreed. *"But I still don't like it,"* Hawk muttered.

"Nor I." Tivonna tried to control her fear as Jasen

needed their support, not useless hysterics. *"What can we do?"*

"I'm not really sure. I'm playing this one by ear. It all depends on Cronus and his abilities. Just sit tight and be ready for anything. Oh, and keep an eye on our friends."

Breaking the link, Jasen turned his mind outward toward the sea king. Tentatively, Jasen's mind brushed Cronus's in the telepathic equivalent of a knock. Instantly, the Mer stiffened and strong shields slammed into place. Jasen waited, making no attempt to force contact.

Finally, Cronus cracked his shields. *"Who?"*

The thought was strong and clear. Though the Merman was making no effort to broadcast, Jasen had no trouble picking the thought from the other's mind. He projected his own thoughts to the Mer. *"My name is Jasen. I am one of the surface dwellers. You can hear me?"*

"Yes. But how can this be. Mer can only touch the thoughts of their own kind, and then we need physical contact. How is it that you are different?"

Jasen hesitated. It was still hard for him to admit what he was. How would Cronus react to knowing that his every thought was open to reading? *"I am a telepath. I am picking up your thoughts and projecting my own to you."*

Cronus's shields tightened as he weighed this revelation, but Jasen felt no fear or revulsion from the Mer. After a moment, the Merman's shields loosened. *"You do not feel to be an evil being. But how can I be sure? Your mind is powerful and I cannot know if my thoughts are my own or your projections."*

"Cronus, I would not manipulate you. I find the idea abhorrent; besides, your own mental defenses would alert you to such an attack."

"I would like to believe this, but I have only your word that this is true. I cannot risk my people on so little."

"I understand." Jasen's thoughts raced. There must be a way to convince Cronus of the truth. The Mer was an honorable being he did not wish to destroy without reason. Jasen sighed inwardly. They had one chance, but it was not

one he looked forward to; nevertheless, he had to try it.

"Cronus?"

"I am here."

"I have an idea. If I let you touch me and lower all my shields, I believe that you will be able to probe my thoughts directly. With such intimate contact, there is no way to lie."

"You risk much. I am unskilled at such probing. I could harm you."

"I am willing to chance it. We can't very well stay like this forever. Besides, I trust you."

"Very well. I accept your terms."

After a quick, but heated, discussion with Hawk and Tivonna, Jasen walked to the edge of the force field directly opposite Cronus. Closing his eyes, Jasen tried to calm his racing pulse. This would not be pleasant. It would take all of his will power to allow this probing of his innermost mind. With all of his shields down, he would be completely at Cronus's mercy. Yet, he was not the only one taking a risk. If he failed to control his instinctive response to the mental invasion, he could hurt both of them.

When he was ready, he pulled the force shield back from the edge of Tivonna's clearing, leaving an air filled space between the water's edge and the shield. Taking a deep breath, he parted the shield and stepped into the clearing, sealing the shield behind him. Pausing, Jasen studied the shield, making sure that it was secure. Cronus would have to destroy his mind to lower the shield. Jasen just hoped that his instincts about the sea king were right.

For a moment, Jasen starred at the smooth wall of water in front of him. It was hard to imagine that this was the sea held in check by a woman's will. Tentatively, he reached out and pressed his hand against the seemingly solid barrier. The water had lost none of its malleability and parted before the pressure of Jasen's hand. Reassured, he thrust both arms forward, submerging them both up to the elbow.

It was now up to Cronus.

Almost immediately, he felt a cool touch on both arms, as webbed fingers reached to encircle his wrists. Taking a deep breath, Jasen began to lower his shields. It was not an easy task. A telepath had many levels of defense and, as each level was stripped away, he felt more and more exposed. Fortunately, the Mer seemed to be able to shield their thoughts, or else the barrage of their combined thoughts might well have slain him. Ignoring the leakage from the minds around him, Jasen continued to strip his mind of all defenses. Finally, only one barrier remained, the shields that guarded his most private self. Everything within him rebelled at abandoning this last refuge, but then it too came down and Jasen stood defenseless and open to the sea king's mind. He tried not to flinch as the Mer's mind invaded his.

Cronus joined his mind to the human's warily, expecting a trap. Instead, he found the other's mind open to him. Hesitantly, he began to probe the mind bared to him. He was not skilled at such probing. He could feel Jasen's muscles tense at his heavy handed touch, but the other made no move to pull away. Cronus's fear was soon replaced by fascination, as he wandered through the stranger's mind. Memories were uncovered and relived by them both. The beauty of Jasen's home world, his experiences since coming to Mystra, his love for Tivonna and Hawk, Cronus saw and experienced it all. There were older memories too. The loneliness and fear of a telepath growing up among strangers in a world that despised him, the death of a beloved father, and finally the horror of the Firehawks. Cronus pulled back at the pain of that awful memory. He had the information he sought. There was no need to prolong the contact any longer. Carefully, Cronus disengaged his mental probe and withdrew from Jasen's mind.

For a few moments, Jasen made no move to reestablish

his shields. He was concentrating so hard on overriding his natural defenses that at first he did not realize that Cronus had gone. Finally, his mind registered the Mer's absence and his shields slammed into place. Jasen huddled behind his mental barriers and tried to bring order to his scattered thoughts. He was more than a bit shaken from such intimate contact with another mind, as well as the emotions of old wounds reopened.

Finally, the storm of emotions calmed and Jasen was again in control of himself. He became aware that Cronus still held his wrists, but the Mer made no effort to establish contact. Shaking off the last of his disorientation, Jasen sent a tentative thought to the Mer. He could feel the sea king's concern and fear for him.

"Are you Ok? I didn't harm you did I?"

"I believe that is a question I should ask?" The Mer's thoughts reflected his relief. *"I feared I had injured you."*

"I'm fine, but I wouldn't want to repeat the experience anytime soon, no offense."

Cronus chuckled. *"None taken."* Then, in a more serious vein, *"I could not do what you have done. I have not the courage."*

"We do what we must. Well, what is your verdict? Your kingdom is lovely, but I have no wish to stay here permanently."

Cronus smiled. *"Of course, you are free to go. But I shall miss you my friend. You have opened new worlds for me. I am sorry your visit has been so unpleasant for you."*

"Not all of it was bad. You have given me a gift as well. I had thought I was the only telepath left. It's nice to know that there are others. I feel less alone.... less a freak. It may not make any sense, but thanks anyway."

"I understand. My people came to this world to escape such persecution. It is not an easy thing to bear. Know that you are always welcome here, you are one of us."

Jasen felt the warmth of the Mer's thoughts and smiled. "Thank you, Cronus. Maybe we will meet again under better circumstances."

"I look forward to that day. There is one other thing I must tell you. I read in your mind that you came seeking a Wer. You need not fear him any longer. He tried to cross the lake.... he failed."

Jasen made no attempt to hide his relief. He hated that Balcar had died, but he was relieved that he had not made it to Malycon with his information. Their plans were safe.

"Thank you, you may have just saved all our lives."

"If we can aid you in your struggle, we will gladly do so. Now, go in peace, and may victory be yours."

With that, the Mer released Jasen's wrists and, with a final wave, turned and disappeared into the dark waters. Backing away from the wall of water, Jasen turned and dismissed the force shield. Instantly, Tivonna was at his side.

"Jase! Are you all right? What happened? Are we free to go?"

"Whoa!" Jasen chuckled, "One question at a time. I'm fine, and yes, the Mer have released us. Just let me inform Hawk, and we can be on our way."

Linking with the Filidae, Jasen quickly informed him of all that had transpired. *"...so Cronus has promised us his help and we are free to go.* He concluded his tale. *Tivonna and I will meet you on Mer Isle."*

"Great, I've had about all of the wet life I can stand for now." Hawk agreed. *"I'll try to locate our packs and meet you both on dry land. And Jase, try to stay out of trouble for a little while, huh. I'm not sure my nerves can stand another episode like this."*

Chuckling, Jasen broke the link and turned to Tivonna. "Time to go. Hawk will meet us up top."

Tivonna smiled. "I'm more than ready to leave this domain, my lord." Reaching out, she gently released her hold on the surrounding water, allowing the sea to return to its natural state. Then, side by side the two land dwellers swam for the surface. Moments later they climbed wearily onto the rocky shore of Mer Isle.

A few hours later, weary but triumphant, a much bedraggled Hawk waded ashore onto Mer Isle. In his arms, he clutched the much sought after packs. Nearly every Merman for miles around had offered to help in the search, but still it had taken some time to locate the missing pouches. But, they had finally succeeded and Hawk looked forward to donning clean, dry clothes. That alone made his efforts worthwhile, that plus the medi-comp, of course; they didn't want to lose that!

Hawk searched the deserted beach. There was no sign of Jasen or Tivonna. A narrow trail ran from the beach back into the interior of the island. Cronus had mentioned a guest cabin. They had probably gone there. Shifting the packs to a more comfortable position in his arms, Hawk began the trek inland. The cabin proved to be closer than he had supposed, and within a few minutes, he reached his destination.

The cabin sat nestled in a clearing amid the trees. A pebbled walkway led to a small courtyard enclosed by a low wall and floored with smooth tiles. Beyond the courtyard, the cabin looked warm and inviting. Tivonna sat on a stone bench before the cabin combing her long hair. Seeing the waterlogged Filidae, she jumped to her feet and ran to greet him.

"You found them!" She cried, taking a pack from his laden arms. "Hawk, you are a wonder, I never thought I would have clean clothes again."

"What! Condemn you to wear the same thing twice?" Hawk answered in mock horror. "Madam, I am shocked."

"Oh, Hawk." Tivonna shook her head and tried to suppress a laugh. Taking in his rather pathetic state, she turned her mind to more practical matters. "Come on, let us get you dried out and fed."

"Fed? As in food?" Hawk asked hopefully.

Tivonna shook her head ruefully. The Filidae was incorrigible. Laughing, she led her weary, slightly soggy, friend into the courtyard and relieved him of the heavy packs. Then, with a wave of her hand, she drew the water from his clothes and hair. Finally, she led him to a small table and soon he was working his way through a delicious stew. Two helpings later, his hunger assuaged, Hawk pushed back his bowl and sighed. "That was wonderful."

"Why, thank you. The cabin is remarkably well stocked. It seems the Mer take good care of their guests." Tivonna smiled. "I am glad you are back. We were beginning to worry."

"It took a while to locate those." Hawk indicated the packs stacked on the floor. "But it was worth it. Say, where is Jase anyway?" He was suddenly struck by a disturbing thought. "He's OK, isn't he?"

Tivonna was quiet for a moment then nodded. "Yes, he seems to be. He just needed some time alone. He went to check the dock on the far side of the island. Unless we can find a sea worthy craft, we may be stuck here."

Hawk shrugged, not overly concerned with the prospect of being marooned. "I can always fly back and get another boat from the Wer. It's Balcar I'm worried about.

"You need not be concerned about him," Tivonna answered quietly. "Cronus told Jasen that he is dead. The Mer killed him."

"Well, I can't say I'm sorry he's gone." Hawk shivered. They could just as easily have suffered a similar fate. "He caused a lot of people a whole lot of grief." With an effort, he put Balcar from his mind; that was in the past. Feeling restless, he rose to his feet. "I think I'll go see how Jase is making out. Coming?"

"No thanks," Tivonna gave him an impish smile. "I found a perfectly delightful pool for bathing and, now that I have clean clothes, I am going to take a nice leisurely bath. So you two just take your time examining the boats. This is one instance in which I have no need of company."

"I'm crushed." Hawk mocked, giving a credible

performance of wounded innocence. "Do I look like the kind of fiend that would spy on a lady's bath? No, no don't answer that. I don't think my ego could handle the answer." He turned and picked up his and Jasen's packs. "Jase and I will just have to find our own cold, unheated pool and," he sighed dramatically, "make the best of it."

At the Filidae's put upon expression, Tivonna could no longer contain her amusement. "You faker." She laughed. "This is a tropical island. Now get out of here and leave me in peace."

Hawk suddenly broke into a beaming smile. "Well, if that's the way you feel about it." He headed for the path that led to the docks. "I'll just have to go pester Jasen. See you later, Red. Enjoy your bath."

Tivonna watched his tall form disappear into the trees and smiled. What an unusual creature he was. There was no doubt that she felt better. Hawk had a way of lifting her spirits no matter what the situation. Gathering her things, Tivonna headed for the secluded pool. Maybe the Filidae could work his customary magic on Jasen. He had been quiet and withdrawn since their arrival on the island. Tivonna's thoughts brightened. If anyone could convince Jasen to talk, it was Hawk. She would leave him in his capable hands.

Hawk's lighthearted mood dropped from him as soon as Tivonna was out of sight. If Jasen was seeking solitude, it meant that something was bothering him. He sighed. Jasen was his dearest friend, but sometimes he drove him right up the proverbial wall. "Too introspective." Jake had once said after Jasen had been especially trying. "He thinks too much; tries to carry the world on his shoulders. Thinks he's responsible for the lives of everyone he meets and blames himself whenever things don't go just right." Hawk gave a wry smile. Well, he wouldn't be Jasen if he wasn't compassionate, caring, and a royal pain in the butt. He would just have to go and shake him out of whatever introspective miasma he was in this time.

Sure enough, a few moments later he found the telepath, standing beside the dock looking out across the waters of the lake, lost in thought. Hawk studied his friend silently. He didn't look depressed, or especially worried. What he did look was profoundly weary. Hawk walked over to stand quietly beside him. The two stood together in companionable silence watching the water lapping against the dock. He made no move to speak or to draw Jasen's attention to his presence. If Jasen wanted to talk, he would; otherwise Hawk would wait.

"Have you ever been afraid, Hawk?" Jasen's soft voiced question broke the silence and jarred him to alertness. This did not sound promising. Carefully, he sought an answer.

"Of course," he answered matter-of-factly. "Only a fool is never afraid. Why do you ask?" Alarms were going off in Hawk's mind. Something was definitely wrong. "Jase, what's wrong? What's happened?" Then, with sudden insight, he continued in a softer tone. "What have you seen?"

Ignoring his friend's question, Jasen continued speaking in the same calm, flat voice. "If something happens to me, I want you to take the Ourora and leave Mystra. Go home. There is a slim chance that your people may be able to develop the telekinetic shield that my people didn't have time to complete. It's your only chance against the Firehawks."

"Damn it, Jase!" Hawk grabbed his friend's arm and pulled him around to face him. "I don't want to go anywhere, I want to know what's bothering you and I want to know now!"

Jasen sighed. His golden eyes, shadowed with worry and pain, searched Hawk's face. Seeing the Filidae's stubbornness, he shook his head wearily. "I'm not really sure I can explain. It's just a feeling I have, a particularly strong and unsettling feeling, as if something bad were about to happen and there's nothing I can do about it. I just...." Suddenly, Jasen reached out and grasped Hawk's shoulder tightly. "It's just...Hawk whatever happens.... well, you know how much you mean to me...." Golden eyes locked with silvery-blue and, in them, Hawk saw reflected all that Jasen could not say. There was no need for words between them. They had always been closer than brothers. Jasen was saying goodbye. The thought sent a chill through Hawk's soul. No, he would not believe it. There must be some other explanation. "Jase, it might not happen. You're new at this premonition thing. Don't give up yet. It could mean anything."

A ghost of a smile tugged at Jasen's lips, and some of the tension eased from his body. Dropping his hand from Hawk's shoulder, he turned to face the water once more. "OK, so I'm jumping at shadows. You're probably right. It's nothing, I'm just tired." He chuckled. "Having a stranger rummaging around in my head must have made me paranoid."

Instantly, Hawk grasped at the chance to lighten Jasen's mood. "Poor Cronus, he will probably never be the same again. You're a lot to take all at once."

Jasen's answering laugh was music to Hawk's ears. "Actually, I think he was rather fascinated. He's something of an adventurer you know."

"Yes, well he can afford to be. After all, he had shields."

"Good point. I'm just glad everything worked out." Jasen turned to face his heart brother and, this time, there was no mistaking the smile he wore. "And yes, you have succeeded in pulling me out of another blue mood. It seems to be your specialty."

"Lots of practice." Hawk answered blandly. "Come on let's find us a nice quiet pool and relax. Whatever's going to happen, worrying won't change it."

"Agreed. There's a nice spot near the cabin that should be ideal for a bath."

"No way!" Hawk answered in mock horror. "Tivonna promised to fry me on the spot if I even thought of going near her bathing hole."

Chuckling, Jasen retrieved his pack from where Hawk had dropped them and headed back toward the cabin. "Then, by all means let's look elsewhere. I'd hate to have my best friend turned into a lightning rod. I know of another spot that will serve us just as well. The lady can enjoy her bath in peace. Coming?"

Lifting his own pack, Hawk followed his friend's retreating form into the trees. Jasen's light manner did not fool him. He was hiding something. Jasen had obviously "seen" some danger...danger to himself...maybe even death...and he was trying to keep the knowledge to himself. He intended to face the threat alone. "No way brother." Hawk muttered too low to be heard. "Whatever happens we'll face it together, no way you go this alone." Determined not to let Jasen out of his sight, he hurried to catch up with his companion. Minutes later, they were relaxing in the cool water of the stream.

It was a much cleaner and refreshed group that sat around the cook fire that night. Jasen said nothing more of his premonition and, to all outward appearances, was once again calm and carefree. Only Hawk knew that underneath this façade, Jasen was anything but relaxed. They retired early that night having decided to leave the island at sunup. Luckily for them, the Mer were gracious host and kept a small boat on the island for their visitors' use. Jasen and Tivonna quickly dropped off to sleep but Hawk lay awake for hours turning events over in his mind. What had Jasen seen? Finally, fatigue overtook him and troubled thoughts finally gave way to restful sleep.

Hawk groaned as the warm morning sunlight streamed through the open window near his bed and struck him full in the face. For one brief moment, he considered pulling the covers over his head and ignoring the sounds coming from outside the cabin. With a heartfelt sigh, he stretched languidly and crawled out of bed. From the noises outside, it appeared that Jasen and Tivonna were already up and preparing for departure. Soon, they would be coming to drag him away. He might as well save them the trouble. Dressing quickly, he packed his things and headed for the door.

To Hawk's surprise, only Tivonna was present in the court yard. She smiled when she saw him and beckoned him over to the fire.

"Good morning. We had almost given up on you." She teased, handing him a plate of food that she had been keeping warm. "I saved you some breakfast."

"Thanks." Hawk took the plate, savoring the delicious aromas a moment before digging into his meal. As the first pangs of hunger vanished, he paused and gave Tivonna a questioning glance. "By the way, where's Jase?"

"He went to check the boat. He said something about making sure that this one did not crumble out from under us in the middle of the lake." She gave a mischievous smile. "I believe Jasen is not overly fond of underwater expeditions just now."

The Filidae laughed. "For once, I agree with him."

Finishing his breakfast, Hawk joined Tivonna in straightening the cabin and court yard. They had just finished up when Jasen returned. Glancing around the ordered campsite, Jasen nodded in approval. "Good timing, the boat's ready. If you two are done here, we can load up and be on our way."

Lifting a pack from the pile at his feet, Hawk held it out to Jasen. "Suit up and let's get going. I for one am ready to get back to civilization."

Handing Tivonna her pack, Hawk reached down to retrieve his own and froze as a dark shadow fell over the clearing. Jerking his head up, he scanned the sky and gasped. His cry of warning died unuttered as a large sphere struck the ground nearby and shattered on the hard stones of the courtyard. Instantly, a huge cloud of noxious, green smoke spewed forth from the shattered globe, engulfing the hapless trio and searing deep into their unprotected lungs. Fighting the burning pain in his lungs, Hawk struggled to crawl out of the deadly cloud, but already his body was growing numb. His last conscious thought before the blackness took him was of huge golden orbs boring into him; then he was incapable of thought for a long, long time.

He was first aware of fiery pain where his lungs should be, followed quickly by a throbbing in his temples. Alive then. Nothing dead could feel this rotten. With a groan, Hawk opened his eyes and struggled into a sitting position. The sudden movement brought a wave of nausea and the throbbing in his head began pounding in earnest. He sat still, hands pressed to his temples, waiting for the pain and dizziness to pass. The cool morning air quenched the fire in his chest and, with each breath, he felt better. Finally, the pain faded to only a dull annoyance and he carefully raised his head and glanced around the clearing. Tivonna lay nearby, of Jasen there was no sign. Carefully, he crawled over to the prostrate elemental and pulled her into a sitting position.

"Come on Red," he shook her gently, "fight it. Come on back."

With a groan, Tivonna opened her eyes and immediately clutched her head. Hawk held her close as her body shook off the effects of the gas. At last, she raised her head and gave him a small smile.

"I'll live, but I'm not overly sure that is good news. What happened?"

"Gassed. A particularly nasty version of knock out gas I'd guess. A present from our friend Malycon no doubt."

"I don't think much of his taste in gifts." Tivonna answered, as Hawk helped her to her feet. "Where's Jasen?"

The Filidae's expression darkened. "I don't know, but I fear Malycon may have him."

"No! Then he's dead!"

"You don't know that!" Hawk snapped. Tivonna's fear echoed his own, but he was not ready to give up hope. "Malycon has gone to a lot of trouble to snatch Jasen. I don't believe he has chased us all this time just to kill him out of hand. No, he wants something and until he gets it, he'll keep Jasen alive."

"All right. So we have a little time." Tivonna tried to still the trembling in her voice. She was willing to believe that Jasen was alive, but that did not mean he was safe. Malycon had ways of getting what he wanted. "Still, we must find a way off this island and then find where they took Jasen." Before Malycon killed him or worse. Hawk could read the unspoken thought in her eyes, it echoed his own.

"Let's check the boat." The two made the trip to the dock in silence, each fearing what they would find. Minutes later, the smoldering ruins of what had once been a boat confirmed their fears. Malycon was taking no chances of pursuit.

"What are we to do now? It will take us days to get another boat." Defeat was evident in Tivonna's voice. Hawk fought his own despair and tried to order his errant thoughts. It was true that they could escape the island but it would take time, time Jasen did not have. No they needed swift transport to follow the dragon's trail. Suddenly, a picture of glittering golden eyes and scaled hide flashed through his mind and Hawk smiled. Turning to the elemental his smile grew. "Tell me, my lady, have you ever ridden a dragon?"

Tivonna stared at the grinning Filidae in stunned

disbelief, then slowly understanding dawned. "No, good sir," she answered, her own smile echoing that of her companion, "but there is always a first time."

King Arcus stared at the waves crashing against the bow of the ship as it plowed through the dark waters. They had made phenomenal time. With the elementals controlling the wind and weather, the small fleet had sped northward far faster than any thought possible. Arcus's eyes were drawn to the land in the distance. Tomorrow, they would be on the border of Cenchrea and a day later he would finally be able to confront Malycon. He still could not believe that the tales he had heard were true or that he had been so blind. How could one man so terrify a land? Outside the borders of Aquilla, the people were locked in a strangle-hold of fear. Even those who plied the trade routes had been silenced, their loved ones held as hostages for their obedience. But to murder elementals, it was unthinkable. A deep weariness dragged him down, in just a few hours, the piece of a lifetime would be shattered by war.

Malycon gazed through the cell bars at the unconscious figure lying motionless on the narrow cot. This was the duke's third visit and still he could not shake the hint of worry that had taken root in his mind. It had been nearly two days since the dragonrider had returned with his prize, and still the man remained unconscious. There was no sign of fever, but he was very pale. Shock, the herb woman had said, keep him warm and quiet. Malycon sighed. He had forgotten in his excitement that the being he sought was in truth an alien. What if he had caused him permanent harm? Turning away from the cell, he walked over to the nearby table. There, neatly arranged were the items he had found in the stranger's pack. His eyes were drawn to the golden box which lay gleaming mysteriously among the other more mundane articles. What wonders did it hold? Frustrated, he turned again to face the cell and its silent occupant. He must be patient; the stranger would recover in time. Then, Malycon vowed, he would learn the secrets of the golden box and other things. The star traveler's knowledge would be his. His dream was almost within his grasp. He could afford to be patient.

The white dragon flew steadily through the cool mountain air. On its back, Tivonna shifted her weight to a more comfortable position and savored the feel of the air rushing by. Hawk's dragon senses had quickly picked up the other dragon's scent and they had been trailing it steadily northeast. It had not taken Tivonna long to deduce that their destination was Castle Cenchrea. They would soon be at the duke's stronghold. Tivonna struggled to control her rising fear. They had to reach Jasen in time. Beneath her, Tivonna felt the dragon slow. Wondering why, she raised her head and gasped. Before them, the air was filled with dragons. These were not the small kind that had taken Jasen, but full grown adults. She glanced behind her and sure enough she and Hawk were completely surrounded. The dragons to their left parted, leaving a narrow corridor of space. Taking the hint, Hawk obediently banked and headed in the direction indicated. Their escort promptly fell into a guard formation around them. There was nothing to do but go where the dragons took them. With a heavy heart, Tivonna watched the mountains of Cenchrea fade in the distance, taking her ever further from Jasen. She glanced ahead where the foreboding peaks of the Dragon Mountains were just becoming visible and shivered. She could not help Jasen now. It would be a miracle if she and Hawk could help themselves. It was rumored that no human entered the dragon's lair and lived to tell the tale. Now, she would see if the rumors were true.

CHAPTER SIXTEEN

Slowly, Jasen opened his eyes and blinked in the dim light of his cell. Where was he? With careful movements, he worked himself into a sitting position and studied his surroundings. A cell, probably a dungeon. How had he gotten here? It was difficult to think, his head felt heavy, his thoughts were sluggish and disjointed. God, he hated being drugged. His system never acted as expected, and he was always left with a headache. This time was worse than usual. His whole body ached, not just his head. How long had he been here? Were Tivonna and Hawk also here? It was time for some answers. A discreet probe should provide him with the information he needed.

Cautiously, he extended a mental feeler to explore his prison. Immediately, pain stabbed deep into his mind and nausea rose to choke him. With a cry, he fell back onto the cot and curled into a tight ball, clutching his head. For agonizing minutes, he lay there before the pain began to fade and something like rational thought returned. When he was certain that he had recovered as much as he was going to, he stretched out on the cot and tried to calm his thoughts. The drugs he had been given had affected him in some way. He needed to discover the extent of the damage.

Focusing his thoughts inward, he began a careful scan of his bio-functions. When no pain met his tentative probe, he relaxed and scanned deeper. His physical condition was about what he expected. Exhaustion and the physical aftereffects of shock and illness were present, but thankfully, there were no signs of brain damage. There were, however, signs of stresses due to an intense allergic reaction. If his present difficulty was due to an intolerance for the drugs he had been given, the effects should wear off in time; meanwhile, he needed to determine just how much of his mental abilities were affected.

Remembering the intense pain when he had attempted a mental probe, he was not looking forward to the experiment. OK, active probing brought pain but internal probing did not. His shields seemed unaffected. Cautiously, Jasen lowered his shields and let the surrounding thoughts drift to him. He sent out no active probes, just listened to the noise that was always around him. No pain. He listened to the sounds of the castle long enough to ascertain the basic information he needed; then raised his shields blocking the outside transmissions. A nasty suspicion was beginning to form in Jasen's mind, not very comforting to one in his current position. There was one way to test his new hypothesis.

Steeling himself, he tried to summon his telekinetic shield. The resulting stab of pain caused him to black out momentarily. When consciousness returned, he lay quietly on the cot and let his abused nerves recover. It was as he suspected, all active offensive abilities were effectively blocked. Only passive abilities and those that worked within his own body were untouched. He could shield and regulate his body metabolism. He could lower his shields and eavesdrop on the ongoing chatter around him; but, outside of those limited abilities, he was totally helpless. He was unarmed in the camp of the enemy.

Tivonna glanced around the huge cavern and edged closer to Hawk. They had been taken far within the depths of the mountain and abandoned here to await the Dragon King. A huge boulder blocked the only way out of the chamber. She could not suppress a shudder at the thought of facing the ancient dragon. The tales of her childhood came back to haunt her, and she imagined all the horrible fates that could befall them. So deep was she in her thoughts, that she was startled when strong, warm arms came around her trembling body. She had been so engrossed in her fears, that she had not noticed when Hawk had shifted form.

"It's all right. Relax." His calm words and comforting embrace finally penetrated her numbed mind. She clung to him and tried to pull herself together. Hysteria would do them little good.

Hawk held her till he felt the trembling cease, then gently released her. Tivonna raised her head and gave him a tentative smile. "I'm fine now. Thank you."

"Good, then let's see about getting out of here, shall we?"

"But how? In case you haven't noticed, we are locked behind several tons of stone in a place crawling with dragons. I can remove the stone, but we would never make it to the surface undetected."

"My, aren't we the pessimist?" Hawk teased as he studied their prison. "This is a natural cavern. There must be another entrance, I feel air moving."

Now that he had called her attention to it, she too felt the slight draft in the cave. Extending her senses, Tivonna traced the moving air to its source.

"There!" She called excitedly, pointing to the ceiling at the rear of the cave. "There's an opening near the top."

"Great, I'll check it out." Shifting to hawk form, the

Filidae flew upwards to scan the cavern top. Sure enough Tivonna was right, he could make out the entrance to a side shaft in the back wall near the ceiling. It would be too small for a large man, but he and Tivonna should have little trouble. He quickly returned to tell his companion of his findings.

"Hawk, I'm frightened. We have no way of knowing where that shaft leads or even if it remains that large throughout. What if we become stuck?"

"We won't." Hawk assured her confidently. "Look, I'll go first. If I get stuck I can always shift to a smaller form. The worst that can happen is that we have to back our way out. It's the tunnel, or we wait here for the dragons."

"Well, if you put it that way," Tivonna smiled, "then lead on, good sir. I have no desire to be the guest of dragons. I assume you have a way for us to reach yon shaft, I do not fly, you know?"

With a chuckle, Hawk placed his arms around her waist and she was suddenly whisked from the floor. The being holding her so carefully was unlike any Tivonna had ever seen. The closest comparison she could make was that it looked like a giant bat. Its leathery wings lifted her quickly to the mouth of the air shaft. A narrow ledge circled the top of the cavern and she sighed with relief as she felt solid rock once again beneath her feet. Seconds later, Hawk was beside her, leading the way into the small dark tunnel. Quelling her misgivings, she followed close behind him.

The shaft seemed to have no end. They had been crawling for what seemed like hours and still there was no sign of an ending. Tivonna smothered a groan as she forced her cramped muscles forward. Her whole body ached from the unnatural crouching position they were forced to endure. She glanced ahead at her companion, at least she was not the only one in discomfort. They had been extremely lucky so far. The tunnel was relatively straight and showed no signs of shrinking as she had feared.

Still, she prayed that it would come to an end soon. Just then, as if in answer to her unspoken plea, Hawk dropped from sight.

"Hawk!" Tivonna, hurrying as much as her cramped position allowed, made her way to the sight of the Filidae's disappearance. In the darkness, she almost missed the large opening that suddenly appeared in the floor of the shaft. Halting beside the hole, she carefully peered over the edge. There was brightness below. Lowering herself into the new shaft, she slowly crawled toward the light. She emerged moments later in a second cavern, larger than the one in which they had been imprisoned. In the center of the chamber, perched on a huge mound of jewels and coins painted a gleaming gold, gazing around in stunned awe, was Hawk. The glittering mound ended only a few feet from the tunnel's mouth and had broken his fall. Relieved, she called to him.

Hearing his name, Hawk broke off his scrutiny of the treasure room. Glancing upwards, he smiled as he saw the elemental peering at him from the ventilation shaft. "Hi, look what I found. Come on down." Rising, he scrambled down the side of the mound, leaving room at the top for Tivonna to drop down.

Tivonna lowered herself over the side of the shaft until she hung by her hands, the mound of treasure directly below her. It was not really that far, all she had to do was let go. Just as she was readying herself for the fall, a scratching sound caused her to glance at the far side of the chamber. A large opening in the wall marked the main entrance and coming through the doorway was...

"Hawk!" Tivonna's cry caused the Filidae to turn just as a large scaled hand crashed into him, smashing him with bone jarring force into the cave wall.

The large red dragon circled the piles of treasure as it advanced on his helpless victim. All its anger was directed toward the invader crumpled on the floor before it. Intent on its kill, it was oblivious to the second intruder dangling precariously from the ceiling above.

Hawk, stunned by the impact with the wall, could only blink dazedly as fiery death descended on him. Dragon flame raced forward, only to stop inches from him. The flames bent backward as if swatted by a massive invisible hand. The dragon yelped as its own fire was deflected backwards into its face. Extinguishing the flame, the dragon backed away, eyeing the intruder suspiciously. However, it was not given time to evaluate this unexplained phenomenon as a gust of wind tore through the cavern. Gold coins and other treasures rose in clouds and hurled themselves against the dragon.

Hawk pulled himself slowly to his feet. Fighting dizziness, he searched for his attacker. He was momentarily nonplussed by the sight of a red behemoth being attacked by a cloud of swirling coins and gems. Then, he remembered his companion and quickly scanned the cavern for Tivonna. The elemental had quietly lowered herself into the cave and now stood on top of the mound of plunder, hands raised, eyes locked on the struggling dragon. Assured that she was safe for the moment, Hawk began scouring the chamber for some type of weapon. Tivonna had the dragon momentarily distracted, but dragons as a rule were tricky opponents.

While an elemental had the necessary power to destroy even a dragon, the use of such power in this enclosed space was dangerous. A battle with a dragon was never a sure thing. They were too unpredictable to take chances with it. He would feel better if he had some kind of weapon, just in case. A glint of light caught the Filidae's eye, and he reached out and pulled a finely crafted golden sword from a nearby pile. The crystal affixed to the blade's pommel shimmered with a silvery light. The glow from the crystal had been what had attracted his attention. A matching line of crystal decorated the blade. The sword felt natural in his hands and he instantly recognized the golden pseudo-metal of Jasen's race. This sword was a long way from home. There was something familiar about the blade; but for now, it eluded him. A tingling ran up his arm as he drew the weapon, then swiftly faded. Turning his attention to the battle between elemental and dragon, Hawk saw that his discovery had come none too soon.

With a roar of anger, the red dragon lashed out blindly, its long serpentine tail colliding with the mound of treasure and jarring Tivonna to her knees. Freed from the elemental's attack, the dragon advanced on its victim. Racing forward, Hawk sought for anyway to distract the dragon from the downed woman. The tingling in the blade returned, and with it came knowledge. There, on the back of the beast's left leg, was a spot where the scales did not quite join, making it vulnerable. With one swift lunge, Hawk drove the blade into the dragon's leg. With a roar of outrage, the dragon turned and knocked the Filidae across the room. Totally enraged, it charged the downed warrior. However, it never reached its attacker. Hawk's last conscious sight was of the huge red dragon being slammed against the opposite wall by a hurricane wind. Tivonna had reentered the fray.

A few minutes later, Hawk opened his eyes to see the concerned elemental staring down at him. "Welcome back." Her concern changed to anger. "Just what did you think you were doing? You should know better that to attack a dragon with a sword. It could have killed you."

"Sorry." He put on his best sheepish expression. "I got carried away. Say, where is our friend anyway?"

Now, it was Tivonna's turn to look uncomfortable. "Well...Ah....I kind of..."

"Yes?"

"Well, I kind of dropped part of the ceiling on it."

"You dropped the ceiling on it?" Hawk burst into laughter. "I must admit that is a new one on me. You are a very dangerous lady. I don't believe I've ever heard of anyone slaying a dragon using the ceiling."

"Oh, it's not dead," Tivonna answered helping the Filidae to his feet, "just stunned. So if you are able, I suggest we leave here before it awakens or something else discovers us. I wasn't very subtle."

In answer, Hawk started making his way toward the door of the cavern. "I'm with you."

Picking their way through the scattered debris, they had almost gained the exit, when Hawk jerked to a sudden halt. "Oh, damn, it's just not our day."

In the doorway, blocking their only means of escape was the biggest, blackest dragon Tivonna had ever seen. It exuded an aura of controlled power and majesty. There was no doubt that here was the Dragon King. The black dragon glided into the room and surveyed the battle scene, its keen eyes missing nothing. Then, it turned its intense gaze on the two intruders who had so disrupted its orderly world.

Tivonna shivered as the cold black eyes seemed to dissect her, and moved closer to Hawk. It was a relief when the being turned its attention to Hawk. The Filidae stood calmly before the dragon's scrutiny, the stolen sword still in his hand. Tilting his head back, he met the dragon's gaze. A sound of what may have been surprise escaped the dragon lord.

"Who are you?" The dragon's deep voice held no anger, only curiosity.

"I am Hawk. My companion is the Lady Tivonna."

"You are Filidae, are you not?"

"Yes."

"It has been long since I last saw one of your race." The monarch glanced over to where the red dragon was beginning to show signs of recovery. "Your work?"

"No." Hawk chuckled. "I know my limits. That is the Lady Tivonna's doing."

"Most impressive. So what brings a Filidae and an elemental to these mountains? Have the humans finally decided to make an end of us after all? Are you their new method of attack?"

"Whoa, my lord, I have no idea what you're talking about. The only ones being attacked around here are us. We are here because your minions took us prisoner and brought us here. Before that, we were searching for our companion who has been kidnapped by one of your people." Hawk met the dragon's stare without flinching. "I have always known dragons to be a noble and honorable race. Why do you now serve evil?"

For a moment Tivonna feared the great beast would attack, but it only shook its massive head sadly. "There is much you do not understand Filidae." It studied Hawk thoughtfully, then seemed to come to a decision. "Come with me."

Tivonna stayed close by Hawk's side as they followed the Dragon Lord from the chamber. Outside, more dragons waited, but they made no move to interfere with the king's party. In silence, they followed the great dragon down twisting corridors into the very depths of the mountain.

Finally, they halted before the opening to a large chamber. Inside, nestled in the hot sands of the cavern floor, were row upon row of eggs.

"This is why we serve Malycon." There was no apology in the statement, only a deep resignation. "This chamber holds the life of our race. It lies upon an unstable fault line and has become subject to severe quakes in the last few years. When the humans and other races declared war upon my kind, the Elemental High Council refused us their help. We had no recourse, but to submit to Malycon's demands."

Hawk nodded in understanding and sympathy. Dragons had one major weakness. They were bound to the sight of their birth. They could mate or bear young nowhere else. Destroy the dragon's nesting ground, and you destroyed them as a race. Nor could the eggs themselves be moved to establish a new nesting site. Dragon eggs were susceptible to environmental changes. They could only be moved within the nullifying effects of a stasis field. On Mystra, such technology no longer existed. This was the dragons' only breeding site. Destroy it and the dragons would no longer be able to reproduce.

While Hawk understood the dragon's plight, Tivonna did not. She glanced from the nesting chamber to the black dragon in confusion. "I don't understand. There are no fault lines here. This is the most stable site in the kingdom. You are in no danger."

So preoccupied had the dragon been with finding a Filidae on Mystra, it had ignored the woman. Now, it turned its attention to her. "You are mistaken human."

Fear forgotten in her outrage, no one called her a liar. Tivonna matched the dragon lord stare for stare, "I am Tivonna, daughter of Arcus, King of Aquilla. I am a level four elemental. I do not lie, there is no fault line. There are signs of a few minor quakes, but they were created not natural. Your hatchery is in no danger. And, how dare you accuse us of trying to destroy you? It is your kind who hunt and prey upon us. Furthermore, the Elemental High Council refuses help to no one."

Dark eyes widened in surprise at the outburst; but behind those eyes, the dragon's mind was calculating swiftly. Bits of information were clicking into place. He had always suspected Malycon of treachery, but until now there had been no proof. So, the duke had been spreading rumors to keep dragons and humans apart, keeping each side convinced that the other was out to destroy them. Meanwhile, he offers the services of his pet elemental to save the dragon race, thus making them dependent on him and knowing that no other elemental would be around to contradict his lies. Malycon was clever, but this time, he had underestimated the workings of fate. For here stood an elemental with the power to know truth from lie, and her words had set the dragons free.

"I am sorry, my lady. It seems that we both have been deceived by Malycon's lies. Your words bring great gladness to my heart and mean freedom for my people. I thank you." The dragon then turned to Hawk. "This companion of yours, why does Malycon want him so badly?"

"Malycon thinks to get technology which will work on this planet. Jasen is his ticket to power."

"Then you must rescue him. The duke must not be allowed such knowledge. Come, I will lead you to the surface."

The journey out of the mountain was a pleasant experience for Tivonna and Hawk, as they admired the dragon's underground world and asked endless questions. The dragon lord had just finished explaining to Tivonna how the caves were lighted by a phosphorescence lichen, when a thought struck him and he turned to regard Hawk. "Tell me Lord Hawk, since when can Filidae become dragons? I did not know such a thing was possible. I assume that our missing white dragon was you?"

Hawk chuckled. "Yes, unlike my fellow Filidae, I can assume many forms. I decided that the best way to catch a dragon was to be a dragon. Only, it seems that I'm the one that was caught."

Minutes later, they entered the main assembly hall of the dragons. Hawk surveyed the room with interest. This was the center of all social activity among the clan. He remembered hearing stories of his ancestors spending nights spinning tales and toasting past feats of daring in a similar room with dragons from another time. However, the fevered activity in this room had nothing to do with celebration. All around the chamber dragons were preparing themselves for battle.

"My Lord." A small brown dragon hurriedly approached the Dragon King. "Malycon has sent word for all dragons to report to his castle. The humans have gone to war."

"Hold." The king's voice echoed through the chamber. "All warriors are to return at once. Our pact with the human Malycon is over."

"My Lord," Hawk interrupted. "We must reach the castle. If Aquilla attacks, Malycon may kill Jasen just to keep him out of Arcus's hands. What about those dragons already fighting for the duke, how will you stop them?"

"Mount up. I will take you to the castle myself. Dragons will not fight for Malycon this day."

As Hawk moved to climb onto the dragon's back, he noticed the sword he still carried. Unclipping it from his belt, he held it out to the dragon. "I believe this is yours."

"Take it with you, a Filidae blade belongs with a Filidae. It has been nothing but trouble since it was stolen from your people long ago. Its name is Faultfinder; you may have need of it. Now mount."

Soaring through the air on the dragon's back, Hawk studied the sword in his hands. Faultfinder. He thought of the battle in the treasure cave, and remembered his sure knowledge of where to strike his foe. The sword was old and reputed to convey the knowledge of an opponent's weakness to its wielder. It had been a gift to his ancestor from a Magus, probably one of Jasen's people, during the Kryllidar war. The only catch was that it could only be used by a Filidae. Its magic was unpredictable and dangerous to those not of his race. No wonder the dragons were willing to part with it. He marveled again at the hand of fate that brought him an enchanted weapon on the eve of battle. Thinking of Jasen and the possible war to come, he had no doubt that he would find a good use for this unexpected gift from the gods.

"Come." Malycon looked up from the papers he was reading, as a guardsman entered his study. Coming to a stiff brace before the duke's desk, the soldier reported.

"My Lord, our scouts have detected a large army amassing on our Southern border near the mountain pass. Also, there are three fishing vessels anchored at the port that were not there this morning. There is no sign of their crew. Rumor has it that a large company disembarked and headed immediately for the mountain tunnels. They have not been seen since."

"So my old friend has finally awoken to what has been happening in his land." Malycon chuckled. "Oh, Arcus it is far, far too late for your meddling." He addressed the guardsman. "Rouse the army, I want them ready to leave at once. Also, alert the dragon master. I want all dragons and riders stationed at the pass. When the Aquillan army comes through, we will be waiting. ...Waiting to greet our loving monarch with drawn sword and flaming dragon's breath. See to it. Dismissed."

Saluting crisply, the soldier turned and hurried from the room to carry out his Lord's decrees. Malycon watched the guardsman depart with a feeling of barely contained triumph. Arcus would never know what hit him. The old fool was making things too easy. With Arcus gone, there would be no one left to stand in his way.

A soft knock on the door roused him from his thoughts. At his answer, a page entered with a note. The prisoner was at last awake.

Jasen sighed and placed his cup on the table. Since awakening, he had been allowed a small table and chair and food. He still had no appreciable appetite, but the drugs had left him with a powerful thirst. The cool water, at least, was welcomed. He was just about to return to his cot for more much needed rest when he became aware of a presence. He was no longer alone. Turning toward the door of his cell, he faced his captor. For there was no doubt in his mind that this was the duke. Power and authority rested on him like a mantle. Power and madness. Jasen tightened his shields and waited.

Malycon studied his prize. He noted the signs of suffering still evident in the strong face. Somehow such marks of frailty did not make the man look weak. On the contrary, the figure radiated quiet strength. The golden eyes watched him calmly, no hint of what he thought was betrayed by his impassive gaze. Malycon's eyes strayed to the table and the water pitcher on it. He would have to be careful with this one, he would not submit easily. Fortunately, Malycon had more than one way to ensure obedience; and even this elusive, enigmatic stranger would not be impervious to them all.

"Greetings stranger. I hope you find your accommodations comfortable."

A small smile tugged at the corner of Jasen's lips. "I've slept in worse places. I take it that you are the Lord of wherever it is I am."

Malycon chuckled. The stranger had style. "I am Malycon, Duke of Cenchrea and you are in my castle, or to be more precise in my castle's dungeon. Now that you know who I am, I would like to know who you are and where you come from."

"Are you in the habit of kidnapping people you don't know?"

"Sometimes. Will you answer my questions?"

"Maybe. My name is Jasen and where I come from no longer exists."

"But, you are not from Mystra, are you?"

"No."

"How did you come here?"

"I don't remember. I was unconscious at the time. I assume you brought me here."

"Not here to the castle, here to Mystra." Malycon was beginning to lose his patience.

Jasen shook his head and fixed the duke with a golden stare. "Look, let's cut the act and get to the point. If your spy net is as good as I've heard, then you know how I arrived and I can make a good guess at what it is you want from me. I'm afraid the answer is no. I can't give you what you want."

"Oh, but you can, and you will." There was no longer any pretense of benevolence in Malycon's voice or manner. "You have a technology that works on Mystra and a ship that can land here. You will give both to me."

"What you ask is impossible. It's true that my technology works on this planet. However, my technology is such that it only works for me. You couldn't use it even if I let you have the knowledge, which I won't."

"You lie." To come so far and to be denied now. No, Malycon would not believe that. The stranger was lying. He seized the golden box from the display stand and waved it in front of the prisoner. "This device is of your making and it was used by others besides you. You will not deceive me so easily."

Jasen shook his head wearily. The duke was obsessed; he would never believe the truth. "That is a medical device. It's been rigged so that others can activate it, but they can't program it or change its settings. I'm the only one who can do that."

Malycon calmed his rage. Jasen was too valuable to risk injuring, but there were other ways to get the information he needed. In a day or two the golden eyed alien would only be too glad to give over the information Malycon requested. Patience. "I do not believe you, but there is time to talk of this later. You are still ill. Eat and rest, we will talk again later."

Turning his back on his captive, Malycon replaced the golden box on the display stand and left the dungeon.

Jasen watched his departure in confusion. He was sure that Malycon had been close to ordering the information beaten out of him, when the duke had done a complete about face. He was up to something, but at the moment Jasen had no idea what. He was too tired for riddles. There was nothing he could do but wait and see. Walking to his small table, he poured himself a cup of water. The cool liquid eased the burning in his throat. He tore off a small chunk of bread and forced himself to eat. He would need all his strength to face Malycon's tricks. With the need for food assuaged, the need for sleep made itself felt with renewed vengeance. He barely lay down on his small cot, before exhaustion plunged him into a deep slumber.

Bryon sat his huge red dragon and studied the pass below. Hidden out of sight, the army of Cenchrea awaited the arrival of their enemies. Enemies. That thought did not sit well with the warrior. He had sworn fealty to Malycon and would obey his orders, but to attack the king, and from ambush like some unscrupulous bandit, left a bad taste in his mouth. Malycon's soldiers would hit the king's forces from three sides, supported by dragons from above as they cleared the pass. They would be trapped with nowhere to flee, except toward castle Cenchrea, where archers and others would be waiting. They didn't stand a chance.

A few hours after daybreak, Bryon heard the sounds of animals and the unmistakable clang of weapons. The Aquillan army had arrived. Quickly, he sent the warning to prepare. With mixed feelings, he watched the king's troops file from the pass and into danger.

King Arcus led his men into Cenchrea. The Northern holdings had more than exceeded his expectations, and his small force of three hundred had swelled to over four times that number. There was no sign of the Wer or Centaurs, as yet; but Arcus was not overly concerned. He still could not convince himself that Malycon would make war on his king. When faced with the sight of an army at his door, the duke would be reasonable. A cry of pain drew the king's attention and he watched stunned as his standard bearer fell from his saddle, the shaft of an arrow protruding from his throat. From all sides, armed men charged the bunched army, while horses reared and bucked at the unfamiliar smell of dragons. In moments, the quiet plain was a swirling mass of men and animals locked in deadly combat.

Chauras led his band from the cave and paused to get his bearings. They had come out near the eastern pass. Arcus's army should not be too far away.

"Chauras, I hear sounds of battle." Silver had followed the Centaur from the tunnel and now stood with ears straining to catch the faint sounds. The Wer had arrived at the Centaur camp shortly after Jasen and his party had left in search of Balcar. The two factions had joined forces and hurried through the underground network of passages to reach Cenchrea in time to aid the Aquillan king. It appeared that they may be too late. Quickly, they raced toward the sounds of battle.

Outnumbered and at the mercy of the dragon's flame, Arcus's army was being cut to shreds. Burned and bloodied bodies littered the plain. With one accord, the Wer and Centaurs rushed to the king's aid.

Arcus felled his attacker with one powerful swipe of his sword; then looked up as a dark shadow covered him. Nearby, an archer loosed his shaft, but it fell far short of the huge behemoth. As he waited for fiery death, Arcus thanked the Creator that he had suggested that the elementals follow the army at a distance. Sivena at least would be safe. The dragon swooped in for the kill, only to rear back with a scream of pain. A wave of arrows struck its body. The missiles could not penetrate its tough hide but, where the arrows touched, burning pain followed. With a cry, the dragon broke off its attack and flew out of range of the burning arrows.

Arcus watched in amazement as one of the Centaurs galloped to his side, fitting another arrow into his powerful bow. "Dragonsbane." Chauras smiled at the human's astonished look. "One should never fight dragons without it."

With the Centaurs holding the dragons at bay, Arcus rallied his men. Backed by the savage Wer, the army of Aquilla began to gain ground.

"Fall back to the castle." Bryon sent out the order to retreat. With the appearance of the Centaur and Wer, the Cenchrean army had lost its advantage. Bryon would not risk his men needlessly. Malycon had more effective weapons. Sending a runner to inform Malycon, Bryon began the task of luring the attackers within range of the castle walls.

Malycon stood on the battlement above the central gate and watched the battle below. His army had retreated almost to the gates of the castle, before turning to press the attack. His men fought well, but the combined efforts of Aquilla and its inhuman allies were proving a match for them. Already, the Centaurs had rendered his archers useless. He would have to do something to tip the odds in his favor.

"My Lord." Malycon turned and smiled as Tyr approached; behind her stood a dozen vacant eyed women. "My Lord, is this really necessary?"

"Obey your orders, my dear." Malycon's tone belied the smile still on his face. "You know the consequences if you fail."

Nodding, Tyr led her charges away from Malycon and toward the rampart running below the South tower. From there, they would have an unobstructed view of the battlefield, but would be safe from flying arrows. Tyr's throat tightened as she saw Bryon. He had abandoned his dragon in order to fight hand to hand and led his troops with skill and cunning. What would he think of what she was about to do?

Arcus and Tychicus fought valiantly; holding back the circle of warriors pressing down on them. Suddenly, an ominous rumbling ran through the ground and a large crater erupted beneath their feet. The Captain grabbed frantically and hauled his king away from the crumbling earth. Nearby, men screamed as lightning struck and fierce winds battered friend and foe alike.

Tyr watched the elemental forces tear into the struggling armies, and something inside her snapped. The twelve women beside her never blinked. They just stared vacantly at the battlefield, and continued to unleash the destructive forces of nature as they had been ordered. Tyr shuddered. They were mindless tools burning themselves out with the raw power they were channeling. Unknowing and uncaring, they would continue until they died. Suddenly, everything became crystal clear. She knew what she must do. Silent as a shadow, Tyr slipped away from the tower.

Sliding from the Centaur's back, Sivena surveyed the battleground with growing horror. Someone was using elemental powers to attack the soldiers. Even as she watched, a Cenchrean warrior fell to the ground consumed by fire.

"There." Firice pointed to the South tower. Sivena gasped as she caught sight of the twelve women standing on the rampart below the tower. No, it wasn't possible, they were all dead. "The Centaur was right." The older woman continued. "Malycon has done worse than kill. He has killed their minds, but left their bodies to do his bidding. We must intervene."

"Agreed." Sivena replied. "But are we strong enough to stop them? We are outnumbered two to one, and they fight without regard to what such use of power does to them."

Even as they watched, one of the women collapsed; burned out by the unstable forces she was channeling. "We can only try." Firice replied. Nodding in agreement, the six elementals prepared to use their power in battle.

On the battlefield, Arcus gasped as the crushing weight of the wind disappeared as mysteriously as it had come. A strong hand hauled him to his feet and he recognized the Centaur who had led the attack on the dragons. "Your lady wife has things well in hand for the moment, but we must reach Malycon quickly. They cannot hold for long."

Arcus looked to where the six elementals, guarded by Centaur warriors, were locked in a war of wills and nodded. Slowly, soldiers were gaining their feet. Almost half of his army were dead or injured, and the Cenchreans were not in much better shape. They had to finish this quickly, before any more brave men died.

Malycon stalked across the battlement fuming. How dare they mock his power? His own army was useless. They had failed him once too often; now they would all die. "Unleash the berserkers," he ordered. His berserkers never failed.

"Oh, my God." Tivonna stared at the scene of carnage below. Dead or injured Dragons, Wer, Centaurs, and humans were strewn across the ground. Even the earth itself looked ravaged. Then, she caught sight of the silent battle raging between her mother's forces and those on the tower wall. "Hawk, Malycon is using elementals to attack the army. I must help mother and the others. Find Jasen; if he loses, Malycon is sure to kill him."

The Filidae's answer was drowned out by a loud roar from the Dragon King. Discharging his passengers, the large black dragon hovered in the air bellowing forth his summons. Across the glade, dragons turned on riders, emptying their saddles of the hated humans. As one, they rose to follow their king home.

Oblivious to the cries of jubilation greeting the dragon's departure, Sivena struggled to hold out against the increasingly violent attacks from the rogue elementals. Three more women had fallen, consumed by their own power; but, still the attacks did not lessen. She felt the shifting of the forces of the air as a lightning strike was unleashed from the tower. She and the others struggled to turn the strike before it hit the vulnerable troops, but they were exhausted. They could only watch helplessly as the streaks of energy crashed earthward.

Soldiers watched as death reigned down from the sky. At the last possible moment, the streaks of death seemed to pause in midair, before turning to race back to the tower. Ignoring the cheers coming from the grateful warriors, Tivonna focused her thoughts inward. Using the channels Jasen had given her, she pulled power from the air and funneled it into the earth, shaking the castle to its foundations and tumbling the elementals off their feet. While her opponents were stunned, she reversed the currents of power and pulled energy from the earth to shape the elements of air. From her outstretched palms, twin bolts of lightning hurled outward to strike the tower, collapsing the already weakened structure, and trapping her foes under the fallen stones. Assured that there was no fight left in the fallen women, Tivonna turned to help her mother to her feet.

Sivena stared at her daughter with awe, and not a little fear. The ease with which Tivonna had used her powers to dispatch her enemies was staggering. Something of her emotions must have shown on her face, for the young elemental smiled reassuringly. "Don't look so surprised mother. You are not accustomed to using your powers in war. Unfortunately, I have had all too much experience with defending myself from attack. Also, Jasen has taught me many things. He........" Suddenly Tivonna stiffened, a look of horror on her face. "Jasen! No............"

Bryon stood surveying the damage to his forces and shook his head in disgust. Malycon must be mad. So much loss and for what? Nearby, a stunned Arcus struggled to regain his feet. Almost before he realized what he was doing, the Captain reached down and assisted his king to his feet.

"My Lord." Bryon knelt and offered his sword to the king. "I swore an oath to Malycon, but I can no longer in conscience honor it. I surrender my forces to you."

Arcus was impressed with the young officer's bearing. Here was a good soldier, a man of honor. He opened his mouth to accept the surrender, when a grating sound echoed across the clearing. As one, all eyes turned to the barred portal beneath the North tower. The gate was being raised and from the black depths emerged...

"Berserkers." Bryon rose swiftly to his feet. "My Lord, he has loosed the berserkers. We must flee."

Like a swarm of locust, the armored brutes tore into the exhausted armies. With mindless savagery and fury, they struck out at Cenchrean and Aquillan alike. Swords and arrows bounced harmlessly off the ceramic armor protecting their bodies, while the wicked blades embedded into their gauntlets ripped and tore at their prey. Unstoppable, they cut a swath of destruction through the assembled warriors. On the battlement, Malycon watched and laughed.

Ignoring the chaos around him, Hawk raced for the castle. Jasen was in trouble. He felt the danger in every cell of his being. He had to reach him in time. Suddenly, a massive armored shape loomed up in front him. In his hand, Faultfinder flashed and the berserker fell to the ground, decapitated by the golden blade. Oblivious to the pandemonium his action caused, Hawk sped onward.

Jasen snapped awake as pain lanced through his body. White fire ran through his veins, searing every nerve. Muscle spasms and contractions racked his frame as he convulsed uncontrollably. He had never felt such pain. His whole body was alternately trying to turn itself inside out and tie itself into a knot. Poisoned. Jasen glanced at the water pitcher still standing on his small table. He had been poisoned. Then, all thoughts were wiped out of his mind as the convulsions increased and pain became his world.

Silver watched as the white haired Filidae dispatched the berserker blocking his path, and excitement stirred in his heart. The berserkers were mortal. They could die. Quickly, the Wer tried to understand what he had seen. The golden blade had struck the throat where helmet and mailed shoulders met. That was it. The helmet was not fastened to the armor. Human swords and arrows were too thick to penetrate the thin crack where the two pieces joined. Only the Filidae's sword was so keen. But if the helmet could be removed.... It would be dangerous. Only the Wer possessed the necessary agility. It was up to them. Rallying his people, Silver quickly outlined his plan. Feral smiles greeted his words and, shifting forms, the Wer moved to the attack. In packs they hit the berserkers, Wolf and Cat clans harried and distracted the brutes, always keeping just out of reach of the deadly blades. Then, when their foe was off balanced, hawks swooped down and grasped the helmets in sharp talons and lifted, exposing the bare throats to the teeth and claws of their cousins. One by one, the monsters fell prey to the Wer's savage attacks.

From his perch, Malycon cursed in anger, all his plans ruined. His army had turned against him. His prize berserkers were gone, slain by that Wer scum. Madness gleamed in the duke's eyes. He would show them. His dreams for Mystra were broken, but they would not have the technology. He turned and left the rampart. If he could not have the stranger's secrets, then no one would.

After what could have been minutes or eons, Jasen snapped to awareness. Somewhere far off in the distance, he heard what sounded like a woman's scream. He felt light and the pain was gone. Slowly, he opened his eyes and blinked in surprise. Below him, his body writhed as a new convulsion hit. He was floating above the cot. A thin golden thread was the only thing connecting him to the body below. Even as he watched, the thread thinned and the golden glow dimmed. He was dying. Knowledge surfaced in his mind. Lessons in astral projection and working the higher planes came back to him, and he understood what had happened. Instinctively, he had fled his body to escape the pain. He could reenter the body by following the thread, but to do so would be to reenter the pain.

As he watched, the dungeon door was suddenly flung open, and Malycon stormed into the cell with a dagger clasped in his right hand. Dispassionately, he watched as the duke raised the weapon to plunge it into his writhing body. Already, Jasen could feel himself drifting away. It was hard to care that he was about to die. Suddenly, a shadow detached itself from the wall near the cell door and rushed at the duke. With a cry, Malycon stiffened and fell to the floor, a dagger protruding from between his shoulder blades. Without a word, Tyr turned and left the cell.

Moments later, Hawk burst into the room. Stepping around the duke's still warm body, he raced to the bed. Jasen lay limp and pale on the cot. Hawk's heart tightened in fear. He didn't appear to be breathing. Quickly, he felt for a pulse. No. No, he couldn't die. Not now, not after all they'd been through. Gently, he cradled the still body in his arms, tears streaming down his face. "Oh, Jase...."

Jasen was jolted from his state of blissful lethargy by the sound of someone calling his name. He tried to ignore the anguish in that summons. It was peaceful here. There was no pain, no hatred, and no more fighting the prejudices of others in this quiet realm. Yet, somehow he couldn't refuse that cry of help. Something stirred deep in his mind, and memories began to play across his consciousness. Tivonna and Hawk laughing. Hawk.... Hawk was calling him. His friend, his brother, needed him. He had to return. With an effort, Jasen forced his way back into his battered body and awoke cradled in the Filidae's arms. He had a moment to realize that his friend was crying as tears splashed against his cheek. Then, a convulsion seized him.

"Jase!" Hawk gasped as he felt the body in his arms jerk to life.

"Poison." Jasen managed to force out the one word before he was dragged down again into a world of fiery pain. It was up to Hawk now.

Frantically, Hawk searched the dungeon. Jasen's things must be here somewhere. There. Grabbing the medicomp, he hurried back to Jasen. Pinning the writhing body to the bunk, he strapped the device to his friend's arm and activated it. The next few minutes were a nightmare for Hawk as he tried to restrain Jasen's convulsing body, while the medi-comp flashed and chirped. Finally, the body beneath him gave a final twitch and went limp. Desperately, he searched for a pulse and almost cried out when he felt a faint throb. Jasen still lived. Dark eyelashes fluttered and opened. The golden eyes were clear, and a slight smile tugged at the lips.

"Thanks." Jasen croaked. "Too close."

With Hawk's help, Jasen carefully eased his trembling body into a sitting position. He winced as pulled and strained muscles made themselves known, but he was alive.

Hawk held Jasen close, the fear and trauma of the past few minutes making it impossible for him to speak. For his part, Jasen was content to rest against his friend's strength while the energy flowed slowly back into his abused system. He had been very close to death. In a way, he had died, but love and duty had brought him back. For now, he let himself rest in that love, while his mind struggled to throw off the last vestiges of that other world.

Suddenly, a loud explosion hit the castle, knocking them to the floor. The castle rocked as blow after blow hammered at its walls. "Tivonna." Using the wall for support, Jasen climbed stiffly to his feet. "It's Tivonna. She thinks I'm dead. We have to reach her."

Without a word, Hawk supported a still weak Jasen as they made their way out of the cell. As they walked, the telepath began to recover. Soon, he was able to walk without aid, but still Hawk hovered close. Jasen smiled to himself. He had scared the Filidae badly, and it would be sometime before Hawk trusted him out of his sight. Another blow rocked the castle and they hurried their pace. Jasen remembered the faint scream he had imagined and knew now that it had been no dream. Tivonna had felt him leave his body. She must think him dead. What happened to an elemental when her kiosan died?

Jasen and Hawk left the castle and entered a world gone mad. A pinnacle of earth rose from the center of the field. Molten lava and rings of fire circled the spire. Lightning flashed across the black sky and winds hurled across the clearing. Standing in the center of the pinnacle, eyes blazing and her auburn hair tossed by the winds, was Tivonna. Electricity crackled around her hands and as they watched she raised one hand and sent a bolt of energy crashing against the castle wall.

"Hawk, I've got to stop her. She's totally out of control."

"How? You can barely stand. She'll fry you where you stand."

How indeed? Hawk was right. He was in no shape to fight. His powers were gone, and even if he still possessed all his abilities, he didn't have the strength to use them. There had to be a way. Jasen watched the soldiers hug the ground trying to withstand the battering of the winds. Tivonna was losing herself to the power. There had to be a way to stop her before she lost herself forever. Wait. What had she told him? He was her kiosan, her safety valve. An elemental could not harm her kiosan. Unbidden, a word drifted into his mind; he had the key.

"Hawk stay here. I can stop her. She won't hurt me." Jasen raised his hand to quell the objections he knew were coming. "Trust me, I know what I'm doing but I can't afford any distractions."

Reluctantly, Hawk nodded. "Be careful. I don't want to lose you again. What do you want me to do?"

"Just keep everyone back."

Jasen had done a lot of risky things in his life, but none as daring as what he planned now. Calming his mind, he cleared out all thoughts except one. He was Tivonna's kiosan, she could not harm him. Slowly, he began to walk toward her. The winds seemed to part before him, opening a path to his goal. Keeping his eyes glued to her face and ignoring all else, he made his way steadily forward.

Tivonna barely registered the approaching figure. Her anger consumed her and the power sang in her veins. They had killed her love. Now, they would pay. She turned glittering eyes on the encroaching figure. She would start with this one. The onlookers gasped as the lightning streaked toward the defenseless Jasen, but the calm, serene figure kept walking. At the last second, the bolt of energy veered away from him and struck the ground nearby. Tivonna screamed in fury. As Jasen approached the lake of fire and lava, murmurs arose from the transfixed watchers, but Jasen ignored them. Confidently, he stepped into the burning pool. Unbidden, a stretch of rock emerged from the boiling liquid, forming a bridge to the rocky pinnacle.

Tivonna watched in fear as the lone man climbed her rocky perch to stand before her. Emotions warred within her as she stared at the golden eyes trying to remember. She should know those eyes. As her bewilderment grew, the dark haired man smiled and reached out to briefly touch her cheek. He spoke a single word, and Tivonna's world turned dark. Jasen caught the unconscious form of his lady love and slowly sank to his knees. For a moment, silence gripped the area as the survivors struggled to understand what had happened. Then pandemonium reigned. The war was over.

CHAPTER SEVENTEEN

The little girl ran through a sea of wild flowers, chasing the brightly colored butterflies. It was a beautiful day. In the distance, her father and brothers were preparing for another day of work on their small farm. Suddenly, a bright light streaked across the blue sky. Transfixed in horror, the little girl watched as birds of fire glided over the glen. Streams of energy radiated from their bodies to touch the earth below. Wherever those beams of light touched, matter became energy, which was quickly absorbed by the blazing bodies of the creatures. As she watched, plants, animals and even the rocks themselves disappeared before her eyes. Her body shook with fear. There was nowhere to run, nowhere to hide. Soon, they would come for her.

With a gasp, Jasen jerked awake. His body was drenched with sweat and his heart beat rapidly with fear. A dream, it had just been a dream. He wiped the sweat from his face with shaky hands and tossed back the rumpled covers of the bed. Unsteadily, he rose and walked to the bedroom window. The cool night air helped revive him and his pulse began to slow to normal. The same dream had been haunting him for the last three nights. His memories were now fully restored and he knew that this was no ordinary nightmare. The dreams were prophetic. The little girl's world was the next target of the Firehawks. If they did not find a way to stop them, the creatures would kill again.

It had been a week since the fighting ended. The first day following the battle was still a little hazy to Jasen. When he had finally regained his faculties, he and Hawk had decided to fetch the Ourora to Cenchrea. The total of dead and injured was staggering. Jasen possessed medical technology which might save many of the severely injured. With the speed of dragon flight, they soon had the starship docked near the castle. The Ourora's extensive medical facilities had worked around the clock treating the injured.

While the Ourora's medi-drones tended the wounded, Jasen had locked himself into the ship's lab and hunted for a cure to Malycon's drugs. It soon become evident that everyone in the castle and the surrounding villages was addicted to the duke's poisons. It had taken him almost forty-eight hours to work up an antidote for the withdrawal symptoms, and a counter agent to break down the drug remaining in the food and water. The surviving soldiers, armed with medi-comps and hypos, had canvassed the kingdom, treating everyone and everything they could find.

Jasen listened to the quiet of the night. They had been remarkably lucky. They had lost almost one third of the combined Aquillan, Cenchrean, Wer and Centaur forces. The dragons had far fewer casualties. They had also lost ten villagers to withdrawal symptoms. The numbers were high, but far below what they would have been without the Ourora's aid. Only those killed outright or who had sustained extensive brain damage had been beyond saving.

Then there were the elementals. Malycon's combination of drugs and crude surgery had broken their minds. Those not killed outright, died of shock. In their damaged state, they had been unable to protect themselves when their own power had been deflected back against them. Their kiosans had been found, lost in a trance, copying the medical and scientific information Malycon had demanded. Most died shortly after the loss of their bondmates, never awakening to the real world. Of all the northern elementals and kiosans, only Tyr and Byron remained. Malycon had needed only one undamaged elemental to handle contact between Cenchrea and the outside world. He had chosen Tyr for her strength. Her love for her bondmate had ensured her obedience. Byron possessed vast knowledge of military history and strategy. Malycon had been loath to lose his expertise and had left the kiosan healthy and undamaged.

Once the castle dungeons had been emptied and the hostages returned to their grateful families, it looked as if the kingdom might finally be able to return to normal. Then, his dreams had started. It was time he began to give serious thought to his own mission. He had ordered the castle searched, but there was no sign of mechanical devices anywhere. They had to be here somewhere. Malycon would never destroy a machine, of that he was certain. Turning, he made his way back to bed. Tomorrow, they would search again.

"Jase, we found it." Hawk raced up the stairs, Silver close behind him. Most of the Aquillan, Wer, and Centaur forces had returned home. Silver, along with Chauras and a few others, had chosen to remain and help with the search.

Jasen and Tivonna were on their way to breakfast when they heard his friend's excited words. They halted as the jubilant duo reached them. "We found it, Malycon's treasure room." The Filidae's eyes shone with excitement.

"What treasure room? Where?"

"We were searching around in the dungeons. Silver had noticed that there was one area where only Malycon seemed to go, at least that was what the scent traces said. So, we went over it board by board and discovered a secret room.

It was well hidden; we almost didn't see it. Well, this room is full of machines, all kinds of machines."

Jasen felt as if a weight had been lifted from his shoulders. This had to be it. "Show me."

Breakfast forgotten, Jasen and Tivonna followed the two explorers into the depths of the castle. Minutes later, Jasen stepped into Malycon's sanctuary. As the others watched, he slowly circled the room, trailing his fingers lightly over the assembled instruments. Most were ordinary machines; but far in the back, dominating one corner of the room was a large instrument like nothing he had ever seen. Jasen's pulse quickened. Even as he reached out to touch the device, he knew. This was it. As his fingers made contact with the cool surface of the machine, images flashed through his mind.

Malycon bumping the knobs on the machine's face and sending a pulse through its circuits. Malycon pacing around the room vocalizing his plans to the oblivious mechanisms. Then, further back, fifteen years ago, a land of ice and snow where it sat idle, its power dormant, waiting for its vanished makers. Then, figures digging it from the frozen ground. A younger Malycon laughing with triumph upon unearthing it and taking it back to his fortress. The duke, contemptuous of the legends forbidding machines reaching out to unleash its sleeping forces. Jasen's mind reeled as reality warped. Otherworldly energies flooded the room, changing the arrogant duke forever. A doorway suddenly appeared in the center of the chamber and Jasen looked through the portal into another dimension. A universe where blazing red planets circled white hot stars and graceful winged creatures of flame glided among the planets, feeding on the rich energy of the glowing bodies before returning to nest in the hearts of the white infernos. Then, the image was wrenched away as the duke finally halted the machine. The portal closed as the deadly emissions faded and the device fell dormant once more.

Jasen wrenched himself away from the machine and

struggled to assimilate all that he had seen and felt. It had been Malycon. In his arrogance, the duke had caused three star systems to die.

"Jase?" Hawk and the others stood nearby, watching him with worried expressions.

"I'm all right. It's just...." Jasen indicated the now silent machine. "It all started here. The Firehawks are extra-dimensional beings trapped here when Malycon activated this device fifteen years ago."

"Fifteen years?" Hawk asked. "Then..."

"Yes," Jasen nodded. "This is what killed my world."

Hawk punched his order into the food dispenser and plopped himself down at the mess table to wait. "Any word yet?" he asked.

On the other side of the table, Tivonna watched with fascination as the tabletop opened to place a plate of steaming food before the Filidae. "No. Nothing. Hawk, I am beginning to get worried. He has been locked in there for days. He doesn't eat, he doesn't sleep. I fear for him."

"Hey, easy. It'll be all right." Hawk lay a reassuring hand on her arm. "It's just Jase's way. When he gets his teeth into a problem, he won't quit until he solves it. Besides," he smiled, "the worse that can happen is that he exhausts himself and falls asleep at his computer. Look, if it'll make you feel better, I'll go check on him. OK? Now eat your dinner."

"Yes sir," Tivonna smiled. "And Hawk, thank you."

Tivonna lay in her bunk and studied the golden tattoo on her left forearm. The delicate lines of gold and crystal mimicked the elemental tattoo adorning her right arm. Beautiful and functional, a trait shared by all the technology of Jasen's race. She had been on the Ourora three days and still everything felt strange. Straining her senses, she felt the fire burning in the hearts of the passing stars. She was the first of her kind to ever leave Mystra's surface. The liftoff itself had gone smoothly. Using the sensor data collected during their landing, Jasen confirmed that the ancient scientists had succeeded in their attempt to open a dimensional doorway. They had succeeded too well, instead of opening one doorway, they had opened dozens. The clash of opposing dimensional energies, coupled with Mystra's unique energy fields, had caused a chain reaction that resulted in destruction. As the elementals had stabilized the planet, the ring of dimensional rips had settled into a unique equilibrium where rifts with opposing frequencies were on opposite sides of the planet. With this information, Jasen was able to plot a safer, less mind twisting path through the dimensional barrier. He had placed her and Hawk into stasis sleep as a precaution. It was easier to shield one mind than three. Her first sensation on awakening had been one of loss. She had felt blind and deaf, cut off from the familiar energies she had known since childhood. Then, as the first wave of panic had subsided, she had felt the brush of alien forces against her senses. She soon discovered that space was not the barren and empty place that she had thought it to be. Fire burst from the hearts of the nearby stars, while solar winds and magnetic storms raged through the void and chunks of earth drifted through an endless sea. With a little adjustment, she had soon been able to sense the energies of space as easily as she did those of her native planet. She was glad that she had come. An elemental's powers were not limited to Mystra, and now there was nothing to keep her from Jasen's side. Nothing, except Jasen himself that is. She remembered all too well the scene on Mystra when he had announced his plans to take the newly discovered machine off planet to study.

"Not alone." Hawk had interjected. "Don't even think it. We have had this conversation before. You'll need help.

I'm coming."

"And I." Both men had turned to face the elemental, surprise and disagreement written on their faces. "No." She had held up her hand to stop their outburst. "I'll go mad if I stay here. I have to be with you. I have to know."

Jasen had studied her intently for a moment, then relented. "All right. You have a right to be there, both of you. But Tivonna, we will have to go off world. I don't know what that will do to you."

"Then, now is the time to find out." She had answered calmly. "Jasen, where you go, I go. I need to know if I can leave this world. I may as well learn now as later."

"OK. You win. I'll explain things to Arcus tonight. In the morning we leave."

Tivonna sighed. She was not sorry that she had come, but this waiting was driving her crazy. She felt so useless. She hated it when Jasen shut her out. No, that was not really fair. Jasen was working feverishly to save lives. There was nothing she could do except distract him. If she wanted to help, she would have to learn to be patient. When he knew something, he would tell her. In the meantime, she would try to sleep and acclimate herself to her new environment. When Jasen needed her, she would be ready.

After seeing Tivonna off to bed, Hawk headed toward the Ourora's lab section. He hadn't wanted to alarm Tivonna, but he was a little worried himself. Jasen was quite capable of working himself into exhaustive collapse. After what he had been through the last few months, it wouldn't take much. The Ourora had repaired the physical damage, but emotional and mental stresses were something else.

The light in one of the labs was still on. Quietly, he slipped into the room and stopped short. He could not suppress the smile that came to his lips at the sight which greeted him. It seemed he had guessed right. Oblivious to the worry he was causing, Jasen sat slumped over his computer console sound asleep. Shaking his head, Hawk walked over to the work station. Laying a hand on the chair, he spoke a single command. Obediently, the chair transformed itself into a recliner complete with blankets. Carefully, he lifted the sleeping figure off the terminal and eased him back onto the lounger. Hawk tenderly wrapped his friend in one of the blankets, then gave the command to extinguish the lights. Turning, he left the lab as silently as he had come.

The next morning Hawk and Tivonna looked up as a ravenous Jasen entered the mess room. Hawk watched as a heaping plate appeared before the telepath, and he began to eat with relish. Well, his appetite had definitely improved. He also looked rested. No, it was more than that. He looked like a man who had had a heavy load lifted from his back.

"You've figured it out." It was a statement not a question.

"Yes." Jasen put down his fork and looked from Tivonna to Hawk. "It's not without risks but I believe there is a way to stop them."

"Jasen, that's wonderful. But what kind of risks?" Tivonna was happy that he had solved his puzzle, but she had a bad feeling that the only person Jasen would be risking was himself.

"Finish your breakfast, and I'll take you down to the lab and explain everything."

"Have you lost your mind?" Hawk paced agitatedly around Jasen's office. "There is no way you're going to play bait for a bunch of planet killers."

"Hawk is right," Tivonna agreed. "It's far too dangerous."

Jasen sighed wearily. "There is no other way. I'll try to explain this to you again. I have repaired the portal device. I've studied the notes left behind by its creators, and have done extensive testing here on the Ourora. I opened a small doorway to the Firehawks' universe, and studied the energy emissions from their dimension. The Firehawks are totally alien to our universe. Their energy patterns lie in a range outside of the normal human reality. What we see is only a part of the creatures that they have extended into this plane of existence. Their true forms are on another plane. I can open a doorway to send them home, but first I have to find them and make them understand what's happening. To do that, I have to be able to communicate with them. Presently, they are inhabiting one of the more obscure levels of the astral plane. I can exist briefly in that realm, long enough to show them the location of the portal, and explain that it's the way home. They are totally oblivious to what is happening on the physical plane. The only way to get them through the portal is to put it in terms they can understand. I have to manipulate their current spiritual plane in order to get them to respond in the physical."

"Astral projection." Hawk remembered what had happened the last time Jasen had left his body. "I still say it's too dangerous."

"The alternative is to let more worlds die. I can't live with that. Can you?"

"No, no I can't. OK, you win but I still don't like it."

"Tivonna?"

"I don't like it either, but I see no alternative."

"Good. I'll need your help to operate the machine and to make sure my body is not moved. Once I go into trance, open the gateway. If all goes well, the Firehawks should show up nearby and enter. Once they have all gone through, close the portal. I should come out of trance shortly afterward. Any questions?"

It only took a few minutes to prepare. Hawk eyed the

machine standing in one corner of the lab with distaste. A cot had been placed nearby, and Tivonna was helping Jasen loosen his clothing and make himself comfortable. She leaned down and kissed him on the forehead. "Please be careful and come back to me."

"Don't worry. You won't get rid of me so easily." Taking a deep breath, he let it out slowly, willing his body to relax. As his body grew more relaxed, Jasen turned his thoughts inward. Using techniques learned long ago on a now dead world, he left his earthly body and traveled into the hidden realms of the mind.

Hawk watched as Jasen's breathing grew shallow and his pulse slowed. Once assured that the telepath was deeply entranced, he reached out and activated the hated machine. Outside the ship, a section of space warped and wavered. The blackness seemed to grow blacker until it obliterated the stars. The gate was open. Now it was up to Jasen. Pulling their chairs closer to the cot, Hawk and Tivonna watched and waited.

Homing in on the Firehawks' unique mental transmissions, Jasen made his way through the myriad planes of reality. He concentrated on his goal, blocking out all else. It was easy to get lost in these outer realms. He would have to keep a tight rein on his thoughts. In this place, thoughts were reality. At last, he entered a plane he had never seen before. It was far from the levels his race usually frequented. The world was completely alien. Quickly, Jasen surrounded his astral form with a shield of golden energy. Concentrating, he created an oasis of normalcy in the chaotic landscape. He now stood on a rocky plateau; behind him gaped the entrance to a cave. As he concentrated, the cave mouth became a vortex of swirling black energy. Good, the portal was open. Its dimensional energy reached even into this obscure domain. He could not stay in this realm long. Already, he could feel the energies of the plane tearing at his fragile illusion. If his shielding failed, he would lose himself to the madness of this level.

Shadowy forms glided around him, drawn by the energies of the gate, but none braved the spinning portal. Gathering his strength, Jasen sent out a probe.

"?" The brush of alien thoughts was a shock. True communication was not possible, but at least he was registering on their awareness. He adjusted his thoughts to match those of the foreign mind as closely as possible. The strain was immense. Humans were never meant to cope with such imagery. Desperately, he sent an image of red planets circling white suns and the feelings of home, security, and belonging.

"Where?" The thought was clear and tinged with excitement and longing. Using the last of his rapidly failing energy, Jasen sent the image of the swirling portal and of shadowy forms entering it to emerge in a universe of red worlds and white stars.

There was a surge of energy in the plane, and all around him the air was filled with shadowy shapes. Singly and in groups, the shadows flew into the depths of the black vortex. Suddenly, Jasen felt himself being drawn to the portal. His shielding was failing and his illusion had collapsed. He was being sucked into the madness of this reality. Desperately, he wrenched himself from the plane's grip and fled to another level. Unconcerned, the dark forms continued to file into the doorway home.

On the earthly plane, Hawk and Tivonna jumped to their feet as all around the wavering opening of the portal, fiery winged beings blinked into existence. Tivonna gasped as she caught her first look at the infamous Firehawks. It was hard to believe something so beautiful could be so deadly. As they watched, the horde flew unerringly into the inky blackness of the gate and winked out of existence. In moments, they were gone and the Ourora was once again alone in space. With a sigh of relief, Hawk reached out and shut off the machine. He watched with satisfaction as the large dark portal faded away and the stars shone once more.

"Hawk." Something in the elemental's voice caused him to hurry to her side. Tivonna was kneeling besides Jasen's cot. The telepath lay unmoving on the bed. He was pale and showed no signs of rousing from his trance.

Kneeling on the opposite side of the cot, Hawk grasped one of Jasen's cold hands. "Call him. Give him a point of reference. Will, him back to us." He had willed Jasen back from the edge of death once before; maybe they could do it again. Together, Filidae and elemental poured their love into the silent form between them. With all their strength, they willed him back to them.

Jasen surveyed the barren landscape around him in confusion. He was so tired and his mind hurt. He had fled the Firehawks' level without any conscious destination in mind. Now, he was lost. There were literally infinite planes to explore and the longer he stayed in a disembodied state, the harder it would be to discern what was real and what was not.

Suddenly, Jasen felt a tugging sensation. With a surge of hope, he relaxed and let himself be drawn in its direction. In the distance, two columns of light rose out of the barren ground. One was a bright green, and the other a vibrant silver. Jasen let himself be drawn closer to the two beams of light. The green was soothing, calm, and serene as an ancient forest. Jasen sighed as the green energy wrapped itself around him, easing his overstrained synapses. Energy radiated from the silver column, sweet life giving energy, flooding him and strengthening his depleted reserves.

As he recovered, Jasen noticed a third point of light. Between the two towers, nestled a faint spark of gold. Leaving the embrace of the green and silver radiance, Jasen felt himself drawn to the golden spark. Cautiously, he reached for the ember. As his fingers brushed the tiny flame, it burst into life. Suddenly, Jasen felt the thin thread connecting him to his physical form. With a sense of relief, he followed the golden thread down and awoke once again in his body.

Opening his eyes, he smiled at the two worried faces above him. Once again, love had brought him home. That night for the first time in years Jasen, last of the Manashtai, slept without fear.

EPILOGUE

Jasen, Duke of Cenchrea and Crown Prince of Aquilla, left the castle and walked toward the sea. In his hands, he carried a golden box. He smiled as he passed a group of revelers and shook his ebony head. He had thought the celebration following his and Tivonna's wedding had been wild, but this going away party was turning out to be even wilder. The thought of his beautiful wife, like always, brought a smile to his face. He could feel the link between them humming with contentment and joy.

The partiers smiled and bowed as he passed. He still could not get use to his new rank. Marrying Tivonna had automatically made him a prince, but duke and ruler of Cenchrea had come as a surprise. Well, the kingdom was in good hands. Bryon and Tyr would be good stewards, and the land was prospering. The last two months had been the best of his life. He and Tivonna had spent the time following their honeymoon visiting with their newfound friends, humans and nonhumans alike, while Hawk had roamed the forest with the Wer. They had all needed the rest.

He chuckled as a group of humans flinched at the sight of dragons overhead. His and Tivonna's wedding had been unlike anything the kingdom had ever seen. Dragons, Centaurs, Wer and Mer had all attended. Relations between the races had improved, and he had been appointed chief judicator for any inner-species disputes. He was sorry to be leaving; but he owed it to Matt and the others at Blackthorn Industries. They deserved to know that Jake and the Empress's crew had not died in vain. There was just one more thing he had to do before leaving.

Cronus was waiting at the water's edge when Jasen arrived. "Greetings, Lord Jasen."

"Please, you can drop the Lord. I'm just Jasen to friends. Thank you for coming." He sat down on a nearby boulder.

"Your message said that it was important. How may I serve you?"

Jasen held up the golden box. "In here is the cause of much death and destruction. It almost destroyed your world and it did destroy three other star systems."

Cronus eyed the box nervously. "And why do you bring such a thing to me?"

Jasen smiled. "Relax, by itself, it's safe. I destroyed the machine your ancestors used to create the cataclysm. It was powered by a unique crystal, one capable of interacting with dimensional energies. I didn't dare try to destroy the crystal. I'm not sure what would happen if its energies were released. So, I've sealed it in this box. I'm the only one who can open it and it is lined with energy dampening crystals to assure no energy can get in or out. I want you to take it and put it where it will never be found. Will you do this?"

Cronus studied the box, then held out his hand. "You are wise. Such a stone would be a temptation to those who might try to unlock its mysteries. I will see that it is lost, forever. The sea does not readily give up its secrets."

"Thank you."

"May your seas always be calm, my friend, and know that you are always welcome in our waters."

Jasen watched as the sea king disappeared beneath the blue waters then turned and headed back to the castle. He still had a lot of friends to say goodbye to.

The next morning, Jasen, Hawk, and Tivonna stood beside the Ourora's boarding ramp and made their final farewells to the royal family.

"Don't stay away too long, son. This is your home now, and we expect to see all of you often."

Jasen smiled at the King. "Don't worry, sire. Your daughter will see to that."

Laughter followed them as they headed up the access ramp and Jasen's heart lightened. Arcus was right, this was home. He had never felt he belonged anywhere, but now looking out over the myriad faces gathered to see them off, Jasen knew that he belonged here. And that wherever he roamed in the vast universe, he would always return to Mystra.

Mystra. He had come here seeking answers to a riddle; instead, he had found his heart's desire. He had found not only a home, but family and friends as well. He had also found a woman who was his equal in every way, one who would stand beside him through whatever may come. When Jake had found him all those years ago, the last of his kind, he feared he would never again find a place to call his own. Instead, he had found two people who loved him unconditionally and a planet whose diverse people accepted him for who he was. Out of the ashes of death and destruction, new life is born.

"Stop daydreaming, hot shot, and let's get this show on the road. We have a universe to show the lady."

Shaking his head, he followed the mercurial Filidae up the ramp. Sealing the starship, he secured Hawk and Tivonna in stasis sleep and made his way to the bridge. Moments later, the golden vessel climbed into the bright sky heading for the distant stars and new adventures.

ABOUT THE AUTHOR

Crystalphoenix is a research chemist at the Centers for Disease Control and Prevention in Atlanta, Georgia, with a penchant for the metaphysical. She lives in Kennesaw with two great roommates who encourage her to pursue a creative outlet (as in nags her to write), one spoiled dog and a tiger that masquerades as a Bengal cat who oversees her work.

Made in the USA
Charleston, SC
27 August 2016